I0788171

THE BRIDES OF PURPLE HEART RANCH

ILLUSTRATED SPECIAL EDITION

SHANAE JOHNSON

THOSE JOHNSON GIRLS

Copyright

ON HIS BENDED KNEE

THE BRIDES OF PURPLE HEART RANCH
BOOK 1

CHAPTER ONE

The sound of the hooves impacting the earth brought to mind the sound of artillery fire. It was a sound Dylan Banks knew all too well. He'd spent the last five years in a war zone. Any day during that time he might look up and see skies of azure blue, rolling hills of sand, or fields of pastel blooms. It was a cruel joke. War wasn't supposed to be pretty.

The sky was blue in this place. Farmland stretched out. The sound of the horses trotting and galloping wasn't the only thing reminding him of war. His men were there too. The ones that had made it out alive, anyway.

Those who escaped with their lives had lost many things. Family, friends, a part of their body, a part of their soul. But this place, the Bellflower Ranch, was healing them.

He looked over and caught the sigil of the ranch. It was a purple flower with rounded petals. The flower clearly resembled a heart. The veterans who now inhabited the sanctuary had taken to calling the ranch the Purple Heart Ranch, in honor of the scars and wounds they'd each brought home with them.

Dylan pushed his horse and himself to go faster. The sweet spring air hit his face. He pushed his body past what the doctors told him he was capable of doing. His hips had to work to absorb and control the movement of the horse. He felt the horse's powerful muscles stimulating his own, giving him the strength he needed to heal.

He hadn't believed healing was possible when he'd awakened in a military hospital and found himself no longer a whole man. But he was getting a part of himself back now on the Purple Heart Ranch. They all were.

This place had become a sanctuary for the wounded. A place where they wouldn't need to hide from their sleeping or waking nightmares. He hadn't been on good terms with God after his discharge. But when he had set foot on the ranch and climbed atop his first horse, he realized that God had given him a new purpose.

The military doctors had saved his life, but hippotherapy gave him his life back. The practice of using horseback riding as therapy for impaired movement had been what truly brought Dylan back to life after the war and his injuries.

He loved riding horses. He loved being on this ranch. He loved that he no longer had to take cover under a beautiful sky. After the hell that he and the other men had seen, the Purple Heart Ranch was the closest to heaven he'd ever get.

With a pull of the reins, Dylan urged the horse to a slow trot. They made their way back into the training area where Dylan dismounted. If he'd felt a pang of pain before, he felt a definite pounding as he lifted his thigh up and over the horse's back. The prosthetic stuck out like a sore thumb as he did so, and the muscles of his hips and thighs screamed.

The trainer, Mark, held back. He knew better than to offer a hand to the proud warriors. But he also knew when to ignore their pride and step in to give them extra care.

Although Dylan was sore, he didn't need the extra care today. He carefully lowered himself to the ground using mostly his upper body strength. He stood awkwardly for a moment until he had his bearings, and then he nodded to Mark.

The trainer only shook his head. He hadn't bothered arguing or offering commentary. But another man did.

"You went a little longer than you were supposed to, soldier."

Dylan stared Dr. Patel down. But even though Dylan had a good foot and a half on the older man, Dr. Patel still had a commanding presence. He smiled, but his eyes were stern and sharp, missing nothing. His voice was chiding, but at the same time paternal with the lilting accent of his homeland of India.

"I can take it," Dylan said as he moved toward the man. He tried to hide his grimace as his prosthetic leg tried to buckle.

Dylan knew he hadn't fooled the psychologist who watched him with a raised brow. "Just because you can take it doesn't mean you should."

The older man moved closer, but like Mark, Dr. Patel knew better than to offer assistance unless absolutely necessary. Dylan made sure it was never necessary. The problem didn't require a hand, just a readjustment of his load.

The socket of his prosthetic had likely loosened. He stood still and bared down, pushing his stump until he heard the telltale clicks of the socket reconnecting with the liner.

"The old ball and chain and I are getting along fine," said Dylan as he straightened to his natural height. The prosthetic leg gave him an extra inch. That was a benefit, at least.

"Your body is healing," said Dr. Patel. "All of the men here are doing well in body. But you also have to heal your hearts. Love heals the internal wounds."

Dylan had heard this speech from the man before. He'd agreed to the therapy for his mind. After all he'd been through, he recognized that he needed someone to talk to about the horrors of combat. But he didn't like it when the good doctor aimed for the heart.

"Maybe you should get your family up here?" Dr. Patel suggested.

Dylan shook his head. He had no desire to see his family. And they'd made it clear that, now that he was half a man, they were just fine without him.

"Or maybe leave the ranch for a date?" offered Dr. Patel.

None of the veterans staying at the ranch left for dates. Well, except for Xavier Ramos. Ramos still had all his limbs and his looks.

The women he went out with never saw his wound unless he took off his clothes.

"Although, I'm still skeptical about dating with phone apps and computer programs," said Dr. Patel. "In my country, we trusted our elders to find us life-partners."

Dylan had met Mrs. Patel a number of times. It warmed his heart whenever he saw the couple together. They each took such care with one another, offering secret smiles, and fussing over tiny things.

Dylan had always imagined himself so fortunate. But the woman he'd given his ring to had handed it back before he'd even left the hospital. His injury hadn't allowed him to go after her. His pride would not have let him. His heart hadn't made it a priority.

"I'm not looking for love right now," Dylan said. He conveniently left off the words *at all*.

He wouldn't be looking for love ever again. If his own family couldn't love him, if his fiancée left him after she'd seen what he'd become, how could a stranger ever love the man he would be for the rest of his days.

"That's the thing about arranged marriage," said Dr. Patel. "You get the partner first. Love comes in time."

"Are you ready to start our session?" Dylan asked, pointing the way to Dr. Patel's office to get him on a different track. "I've been having some nightmares."

Unlike some of the other vets on the ranch, Dylan never had nightmares. His sleep was dreamless and dark.

Once again, Dr. Patel wasn't fooled, but he let Dylan lead him to his office. Dylan knew the old man meant well, but this wasn't a road he wanted to go down. He'd been hurt enough in this life.

CHAPTER TWO

Maggie looked down at the sleeping animal on the surgery table. The bright lights of the surgical theater illuminated the room, casting no shadows on her performance. The blade in her hand wasn't working its normal magic, and she had no more tricks up her sleeve. The dog would lose both its hind legs.

Though the dog was asleep, his lower lip trembled as though he knew what was about to happen to him. It looked as though he was trying to keep a stiff upper lip in the face of adversity. She, of all people, understood that. Life had beaten the little guy up and spit him back out to deal with it on his own.

He had no tags. No collar. He'd been left on the doorstep of the veterinary clinic sometime in the early morning. Maggie had arrived to see the animal bleeding on the pristine steps. He'd eyed her warily, too tired to snarl. His eyes had simply closed in resignation while he waited for her to try and do worse to him. What she did was scoop him up and set down to work.

The dog could tell Maggie's own life story. Though she'd never been physically beaten, she'd taken more than her share of emotional hits. She'd been abandoned by her parents while in elementary school. Literally, while she was in elementary school. They had simply left her there and never picked her up.

She'd gone into the foster system to wait them out. They never came back.

At first, she took it as her due. She knew that many animals abandoned their children at young ages. But that reasoning hadn't stuck long as she continued to see parents picking up their kids from school, loading them in their car, and taking them home. She watched as siblings and kids from the same neighborhood or kids with the same interest formed packs and stuck together, preying on anyone who was a lone kid.

Maggie was alone. The other kids in the foster system either hadn't accepted her into their group or they got adopted and never came back. Maggie had never had a pack; not a human one at least.

No adult had ever advocated for her. She'd been left to rot in the system, never finding a family to adopt her as their own. She'd been fostered, another word for used for a paycheck or cheap labor, until she came of age and picked herself up and out of the vicious cycle.

But this poor dog could no longer stand on its own four feet due to its injury. It would never run again. No one would want a disabled dog. It had no one to stick up for him and now it would be put down permanently.

Maggie put down the blade and picked up the needle filled with blue juice. The pentobarbital would be a mercy to the poor creature. She knew that. She'd seen countless cases that began with a different wound or illness and ended up right back here on this table, under these lights, in the middle of a surgical theater with no one watching or caring about the show.

"Maggie, let's hurry this up. I have a 2 pm tee time on the golf course."

Dr. Art Cooper was the owner of the theater Maggie was currently performing in. He had a script for times like these, and the story always ended the same way.

"Just prick the mutt already so I can close shop." He said the words without glancing up at her or the animal at the end of his life.

A sound on the other side of the door had Dr. Cooper glancing up. He slipped on his interested face as one of the new vet nurses walked by. Of course, he smiled at her. He had to keep up the facade that he was a decent human being.

A second later, his interested face turned over to his excited face as a client presented her ancient, smelly, arthritic cat to him. She was a very good client; coming for every screening he suggested, buying the most expensive brand of pet food that he was pushing that month, and always ready to take a look at the newest pet insurance offerings. The moment the cat lady and her cat were gone, the animated expression melted off his face and was replaced with disgust.

Maggie hated the man. How could anyone work with animals and have no care for them? They were all nothing but a paycheck to him. As a vet tech, she had the luxury of not making enough to be so callous.

She really had no luxuries at all. Definitely not enough to care for another wounded animal. Maggie looked down on the table at the sleeping dog. A single tear slid down his cheek, and the floodgates opened.

Maggie looked up at Dr. Cooper and painted on a smile to rival his performance. "Why don't you go ahead and head out. I can take care of this and close up shop for you."

Dr. Cooper eyed her suspiciously. Then he looked down at the dog. "We're not going to have another problem, are we? You've already had one strike, another and I'll let you go."

That was one thing about being a doctor, they were some of the smartest people. The last time Maggie had been asked to put a dog down, she'd snuck him out the back door of the clinic. He was now resting comfortably in her home. Probably in her closet on a pile of her shoes.

"This animal won't have any quality of life," Dr. Cooper was saying. "It would take hundreds of dollars a month to maintain him."

Wasn't a single life worth that, she wanted to say. But she hadn't. Instead, she told the truth. "I understand. I've learned my lesson. I need this job to take care of the animals I do have."

She had four dogs, all of whom had severe injuries and illnesses that cost her more than her rent to care for. If she lost this job, she wouldn't have the money to care for them or keep a roof over her head.

Maggie picked up the needle and gave it a few flicks with her index finger.

Dr. Cooper looked at the time. Then he looked back at her. His tee time won out like she knew it would. He turned in his expensive gator boots and walked out the door.

Maggie breathed a sigh of relief and put the needle down. She bandaged the dog. The damage had been done long before she'd gotten to him and healing had already begun. Now she just needed to heal his spirit alongside his body.

Maggie wrapped the dog up in a blanket, and she made her way to the back. She was nearly out of the door when she rounded a corner. Dr. Cooper looked up from his watch at her. And of course, that's when the dog decided to wake up from his meds and bark.

It was a low, groggy bark that she might have been able to play off as her own stomach grumbling. She had missed lunch again. But the trickle of liquid that streamed out of the blanket and onto Dr. Cooper's expensive boots, she had no excuse for. In fact, she was quite pleased by it.

The little dog was a good boy. She wasn't sure how she'd feed and care for him now that she was out of a job, but she was keeping him.

CHAPTER THREE

Dylan headed back to the stables after his session with Dr. Patel. The good doctor hadn't pushed him on the fake nightmares. He hadn't exactly pursued the discussion of dating either. What he'd done was far worse. He'd engaged Dylan in a chat about his broken engagement.

Hilary Weston had been the girl next door. But next door had been one floor down from the penthouse of one of the most exclusive residential buildings in New York City. Living his life on top of her, watching her preen beneath him, it was inevitable that one day she'd end up on his arm.

Hilary had been Dylan's first everything. His first crush. His first girlfriend. His first … everything.

She hadn't been happy when he announced he wanted to go into the military. With his family money and his trust fund, Dylan could've sat on his laurels for a few lifetimes over. But he'd felt called.

He'd left with promises to do only one tour and then come back for a wedding as grand as she wanted to make it. They'd joked that it would take her the duration of his tour to plan the social event of the decade. But when Dylan returned covered in bruises and missing a limb, Hilary made other plans.

It hadn't mattered to her that he could've taken care of her financially, she was an heiress in her own right. It hadn't mattered to her that he was a war hero. She was a society darling, constantly in the gossip pages. Appearances mattered to Hilary Weston, and having a wounded warrior covered in bruises and missing a limb was not a good look.

She'd let the door slam behind her as she walked out of the military hospital room. She'd gotten engaged to another man and married him all within the last six months. Dylan heard the guy was some type of reality star, and now Hilary was too.

He'd liked to think he'd dodged a bullet. But he'd dodged them in real life. Her rejection stung.

But that life was over. This was his new reality now. And it was one he thrived in.

Dylan turned from his sour memories and looked around the ranch. He'd given up high society living for mucking out stalls and tilling the earth. It was the best decision of his life.

The ranch had been fledgling before he infused it with what amounted to a small portion of his inheritance. His parents had balked at the idea until they realized their deformed son would be safely tucked away out of society's and their eyes. Like Hilary, the Banks were all about keeping up appearances. A decorated soldier serving his country looked good. An amputee hobbling about did not.

For the second time today, the sound of hooves reminded him of artillery fire. But Dylan didn't suffer from PTSD in the normal sense. It was just the trauma of his family that affected him. So, when he saw Sean Jeffries riding at a trot, he could only smile up at the man.

Jeffries had come home from war with all his limbs. But like all the men on the ranch, Jeffries had left a piece of himself behind in the war zone. Jeffries dipped his head in greeting, pulling his cowboy hat low over his brown forehead. Dark shades covered his face. The sunglasses cast the dark man on the steed in a full shadow. Jeffries didn't like people looking at the scars on his face.

Still, Jeffries held his posture erect and his head high. Life looked differently from on top of a horse. Not only did the therapy help improve physical injuries, it also helped improve balance, control, and coordination of the mind. Having control of a great beast and regaining control of one's self increased self-esteem and gave a sense of freedom.

The ranch didn't just offer horse therapy. Gardening helped with sensory and tactile functions. Chores like pushing a wheelbarrow, raking, hoeing, weeding, planting and even arranging flowers all built or rebuilt motor skills.

Reed Cannon was on his knees in the gardens. Cannon moved aside the dirt and planted flowers, evenly spacing them out. The fingers of one hand worked in the fertile soil, while the others remained stiff against the dirt. The stiff hand was a prosthetic. He'd lost the real one in the same explosion that took Dylan's leg.

Dylan walked on through the haven, passing by the purple bell-flowers for which the ranch was named. There weren't just the flower and vegetable gardens in this sanctuary. There was also a butterfly garden that offered the vets peace and tranquility. This place was not just for healing mentally and physically, but also emotionally. Dylan and the others had lain down wheelchair paths to make it accessible for all.

Older veterans came to the ranch for help as well, getting care for wars long past but whose scars were still fresh. Someday Dylan hoped they would be able to open up the ranch to troubled youth and give them the care they needed to have a chance at a bright future. So no, he didn't bemoan leaving high society behind. This was the society he wanted to create.

As Dylan came away from the gardens, the smell of livestock hit his nose. Francisco DeMonti moved amongst the sheep. The care of small animals helped the men to learn to once more form relation-ships with others. Animals were the perfect specimens. Many offered unconditional love, especially if there was food in your outstretched hand.

Fran had no visible scars. His wounds were all internal, and they still had a good chance of killing him.

"Good ride this morning?" asked Fran as he came out of the enclo-sure and joined Dylan on the path toward the main buildings.

Dylan nodded.

"Got a call from an old buddy at the vet center," said Fran. "They're wondering if we could house a couple more soldiers?"

"We've got the space."

There were living quarters on the ranch. Though most soldiers didn't stay after their therapy or rehab was complete. Many had fami-lies to return to, or they found that long-term ranch life didn't agree with them. The five vets who made the ranch their home didn't have that luxury or didn't want to go back to it. For them, this was home now.

"We'll take anyone that needs the help," said Dylan.

And they could at little to no cost. Between their pensions, which Dylan refused to let anyone spend, the government aide, which Dylan put to giving all the workers a pay increase, and Dylan's trust fund, which took on the bulk of the expenses, they would never need to turn anyone away. Unlike how his family treated him.

"Have a good evening boys," called Dr. Patel. The man headed to his car with his briefcase in one hand and a Bible in the other. In addition to being a licensed psychologist, he was also a man of the cloth.

"Headed to church?" asked Fran.

"That I am." Dr. Patel smiled. "There's room in the passenger seat if you'd like to accompany me."

"Another time," said Fran.

Dylan remained mute. He still hadn't healed his relationship with the man upstairs, and he wasn't quite ready to start now. But Dr. Patel simply smiled that knowing smile at both of them. If Dylan didn't respect the man as much as he did, he'd be annoyed at his universal upbeat attitude, perpetual patience in the face of adversity, and consistent certainty in all things.

As Dr. Patel pulled his car door open, another car pulled up. It was an expensive luxury model. For a moment, Dylan wondered if it was his father. But he knew his father would never leave Manhattan to come out into the middle of nowhere America.

The man who stepped out of the car wore an expensive suit. The ensemble was off the rack and not tailor-made. His father would never be caught dead in something that wasn't crafted especially for him. Dylan recognized the man as Michael Haskell, the land agent for the ranch.

Haskell was no-nonsense and to the point. He didn't fuss around with niceties and unimportant details. Dylan had been leasing the land for nearly a year waiting for the sale to go through. There were only a few minor details left before the deed was in Dylan's hand.

"We got a problem," said Haskell. "The land was originally designated for family use. The sale won't go through unless there are families here."

"This unit of soldiers is a family," said Dylan.

"This unit is a group of men," said Haskell. "None of whom are married."

Dylan couldn't understand how this was a problem? He was buying land not an amusement park. What did it matter who lived on the land?

"How do we fix this?" asked Fran, ever the practical one. "Can we get the zoning changed?"

"It'll take months to get the zoning changed, and you'll need to vacate while you do," said Haskell. "I don't suppose any of you are getting married anytime soon?"

CHAPTER FOUR

"I let you get away with two dogs when the rules clearly state one small dog. Over the past two years, you've accumulated four dogs and only two of them are small."

Maggie cradled one of the small dogs in her arms as her landlord spoke. Soldier had lost her front paw after being hit by a car. She'd been brought into the vet clinic during Maggie's first month there. She'd been able to heal Soldier, amputating her mangled leg and teaching her to walk on three legs. The little dog thrived, but no one came to claim her nor welcome her into a new home. She was slated for being put down, but somehow she'd magically disappeared before her date with death.

Maggie put Soldier down on the hardwood floor of the entryway. Her nails clinked as she sauntered across the floor, clearly not enjoying Mr. Hurley's company any more than he was enjoying hers.

The three other dogs Mr. Hurley referred to kept their distance. They were typically a very loving bunch, eager to greet new people and make a new human friend when anyone came to the door or they were out in public. But they instinctively knew that Mr. Hurley was not the buddy type.

"And now you're adding a fifth?" demanded Mr. Hurley.

The fifth dog cowered beneath her coffee table. He'd recovered nicely from his surgery and had been up and curious the next day. Maggie had fitted him with a doggie wheelchair that she'd fashioned herself. It took the dog just one day to master the apparatus and now he was flying around her small apartment. Maggie had named him Spin.

Maggie went over and picked up Spin. Then she turned and faced her landlord with her most winningest smile. It was all she could afford since she no longer had a job to pay rent. She hoped the little Irish Terrier's sweet face would win over Mr. Hurley.

"They've never caused you any trouble," she said as she nuzzled the side of Spin's face. The dog gave her an appreciative lick, then hid his head beneath her chin. "You barely know they're here."

Her dogs didn't bark much. Maggie guessed that they'd learned that raising their voices could lead to a strike from a human. So, they were mostly quiet.

She didn't mention that Stevie, her partially blind Rottweiler, had scratched up the cabinets in the bathroom. Or that Sugar, her diabetic Golden Retriever, had thrown up in the bedroom so many times that Maggie had lost her ability to be nose-blind to it.

But it wasn't necessary. Mr. Hurley was unmoved by any of their puppy dog eyes. "That's beside the point. You're breaking the rules. I would've let it go with two dogs, but not five. Unless you can follow the rules and have only one small dog, you'll need to find a new place to live."

"You can't be serious? I can't choose between my dogs."

"Find them a good home with other families."

That hadn't worked the first time. That's why they were all there. Most single professionals and families with children weren't interested in taking in an older or wounded animal. They all wanted puppies just out of the womb who would run around on all four feet and have enough energy to catch a ball.

And she knew from experience that she couldn't put the dogs in a shelter while she found a new home. They'd be put down before the end of the week. That is, if she could even get a new job to put a roof over their heads, food in their bowls, and medicine in their bodies.

What was she going to do?

Mr. Hurley walked away without another word, deaf to her protests.

That was a blow. One she had known was possible. She had been breaking the rules for quite some time. But she hadn't thought he'd actually throw her out. Now she saw that her time was up. She had no job and now would have no place to live.

But she wasn't giving up. She never gave up. No matter how bleak the situation. There was always a way.

One by one, Maggie piled the dogs into the back of her truck. She had to put the dogs in crates while she drove so that they wouldn't injure themselves any further. Soldier, the Chihuahua, Star, the Pug, and Spin went into the back. Spin was not at all happy about being confined and immediately began to cry. Maggie took a moment to soothe him with a chew toy, then she piled Sugar, the retriever, into the back front seat and guided Stevie, her partially blind Rottweiler, into the back.

With the gang all loaded up, she started the car and headed to the only place she could think of. Church. She needed a miracle to get herself out of this one.

The church was tucked in the back corner of the city, as though it were a secret. But the congregation was a healthy size, had always been since Maggie had started going there as a teenager. Next to the church sat the cold, gray group home that Maggie had spent most of her youth in. It was a drabby, unattractive sister next to the red brick and white trim of the church.

The church was the place Maggie had found solace on her bleak nights. She'd prayed to God to bring her parents back to her. When those prayers went unanswered, she'd prayed for a new mom and dad to love her. Even when those prayers hadn't been answered as she'd hoped, Maggie never gave up because at some point while she was on her knees in the pews, she looked around to realize that the people of the church had become her family.

Maggie pulled into the parking lot near the back of the church. One by one, she took her dogs out and walked them to the grassy yard where many a summer picnic had been held. Pastor David was a dog lover. He and Maggie had bonded over their love of animals when she was young. She'd hoped that Pastor David would adopt her, but he was unmarried and had remained so all his life. Still, he always left the door open for her. And that policy of open doors continued even after his death.

"There's my favorite veterinarian."

Maggie turned at the sound of the familiar voice. Her smile was big and her arms opened wide before she saw Pastor Patel.

"There's my favorite shrink."

The two embraced. As the embrace ended, Maggie gave the man an extra squeeze. It had been too long since she'd been held, and she needed the care today.

Pastor Patel pulled away but kept a hold of her. He didn't ask any questions. Just cocked his head, looking down at her with those light brown eyes and waited.

"I'm fine." She waved his concern away, but the tears had already formed in her eyes.

Maggie never cried. As a foster child living in the group home, she knew it was pointless. She wouldn't get any extra care. When she was placed in a foster home, she knew it was pointless. Her foster parents had no care for her, only that she was another paycheck for them and that she was old enough to care for the rest of their fostered brood.

But, like Pastor David, Pastor Patel had always cared for her. And he was always able to get her to divulge her feelings.

"I've just had the worst week," she said. As though he heard her talking about him, Spin came up to her leg, wheel coming to a halt as he looked up at her apologetically.

"I see you have a new pack member." Pastor Patel bent down and offered the back of his hand to Spin. Spin gave the hand a sniff. Then a lick. Then a bob of his head, as if recognizing that Pastor Patel was good people.

Maggie gave a sniff of her own and then it all came out in a rush.

"They wanted me to put him down because he was injured. When I said no, they let me go. And now my landlord says I have to get rid of four of them if I want to keep my place. How can people be so cruel? They're my family. Just because they're wounded doesn't mean they don't deserve love."

Pastor Patel looked down at her. His eyes always made her think of a serene Buddha statue. She knew he'd seen all of that before she'd said a single word. "Quite right, my dear. A wounded animal is best healed by love."

"I didn't know where else to turn," said Maggie. "I was hoping for a miracle."

Dr. Patel nodded, eyes sparkling with some revelation. "I think I might be able to help."

CHAPTER FIVE

"Wives? As in married? To women?"

"Unless there's something about you that we should know, Ramos."

Xavier Ramos reached over and tried to smack Reed Cannon in the head, but the other man raised his prosthetic arm to ward off the attack. There was nothing wrong with his reflexes. Ramos's flesh hit Cannon's metal and Ramos winced.

"Can't we get the zoning changed?" asked Sean Jeffries. He had his sunglasses off now that they were all inside one of the ranch's barns.

The men had converted the old barn into a gaming room complete with large flat screens, an old-fashioned record player and tape deck, and every gaming console including an antique Atari which Reed had brought back to life with his techno-genius.

"It would be a long process," said Dylan. "And in the meantime, we'd all have to leave the ranch while the powers that be waded through all the red tape."

The men were lounging in recliners or sitting on bar stools, but an anxious hum went around the room. The ranch was their haven, their home. Even for those who had somewhere that they could go, leaving was not an option.

Unlike with Dylan, Jeffries's family hadn't rejected him. They called the ranch on a regular basis. It was Jeffries who didn't want them to see him. It wasn't just the scar on his face that shamed him. He suffered from PTSD and was prone to flashbacks. He could be taken back to the war-torn deserts of the Middle East when he slept, or with loud noises he could readily identify. The men surrounding him knew how to manage his episodes. But Jeffries was terrified of hurting someone he cared about. And so he stayed away from his family and wouldn't receive their calls.

"Aren't you all missing the obvious?" They all turned to Reed and waited for his revelation. Reed took his time. The man had a bit of the flare for the dramatic at times. "We just need to get married."

Eyes and heads rolled as everyone turned away from the proclamation. Except Fran.

"It's not a bad idea," Fran said. "People do it all the time. For green cards, for financial stability, some fools even do it for something called love."

Dylan had been such a fool who wanted to get married for love. Or what he thought was love. He had no idea where the plan came from as his own parents hadn't been in love.

Catherine and Charles Banks had married for social standing. The irony was that they couldn't stand each other. Though the rest of society would never know it. At parties, they put on a show of devotion and compatibility. They used to put on the show at home for Dylan when he was a kid. But they soon stopped caring about what he saw behind the closed doors of their many homes, which they often occupied separately.

"Who would want to marry a bunch of broken soldiers?" asked Sean.

"Hey, we're not broken." Dylan almost believed the words coming out of his own mouth. "We served our country. We are highly skilled. We are loyal, dedicated men."

Though the speech was impassioned, the faces around him looked doubtful.

"Frances might have a point," said Xavier, using the feminization of the name to get under Fran's skin like they all did from time to time. "There are a lot of hard-up women out there. Some probably need a place to stay, money in their pocket, or just a good lay."

Now it was Dylan who rolled his eyes and neck at the preposterous direction the discussion was taking. He needed his men to focus on viable solutions to this very real problem. But the other men were listening to Xavier's nonsense.

"Dr. Patel is always saying we need a good woman to heal our hearts." Reed picked up the gauntlet of the insanity. He was a romantic at heart and still believed love was waiting to come into his arms. "Maybe now's the time."

"Patel had an arranged marriage," said Fran. "And it worked for him."

"This is the Wild West," said Reed. "This kind of stuff happened here all the time. Remember the Gold Rush Brides?"

"That was California," Sean said. The man was a walking encyclopedia. "You mean mail order brides."

"It would be email now," said Fran. "No one uses the postal system."

"We are not finding women on Craig's List," said Dylan, pinching the bridge of his nose and squeezing his eyes shut in exasperation.

"Then how are we gonna stay here?"

Dylan wasn't sure which man said it, but he knew they all were thinking it. He opened his eyes and faced the room full of men. They'd looked to him for leadership when they were in combat, and they looked at him the same way now. How would they win this particular war on the home front?

"We'll petition the court," said Dylan. "I have a few contacts in the government."

"We have more recruits coming in a couple of month. What are we gonna do with them?"

Dylan didn't have an answer for that. He didn't know how he would take in another wounded soldier only to potentially turn the man away. As he prepared to turn around, a flash of fur ran through the room.

No, ran wasn't exactly the right word. Two front paws ran. The two back paws were not there. Instead, two wheels acted as legs that the little dog used to propel himself onward.

Dylan wasn't the only one who spotted the animal. The other soldiers turned and stared at the creature. The dog stared back. It also slowed down as it looked up at all the big humans eying it.

The dog had had a grin on his face, but under the close scrutiny, his muzzle closed. He pulled his lolling tongue back into his mouth and let out a low whimper.

Dylan bent down to be on the dog's level. He rested on his good knee, which was a difficult feat for him after a long day. But he had to get a closer look at this dog and his apparatus.

The dog made a slow beeline for Dylan. Dylan put his hand out to the dog. The dog gave the back of his hand a tentative sniff and then a lick.

Who would do such a thing as to take a dog's hind legs? But more importantly, who would take the time to make a contraption that gave the animal back a semblance of the life he once knew?

"I'm so sorry," said a feminine voice. "That's my dog."

Dylan looked up into the face of the woman. She was dressed in a T-shirt and jeans. Her hair was pulled back in a messy ponytail. She wasn't wearing a lick of makeup. She looked fresh, clean, capable.

She marched into the room, not like she was on a catwalk, but like she was on a mission. She reached for the dog and he saw her hands were un-manicured. When one of her rough fingers brushed the skin of his forearm, Dylan felt a spark. His breath caught and so did hers.

CHAPTER SIX

*D*azzling.

That was the only word Maggie could use to describe the blue of his eyes. They weren't crystal clear because there was a hint of navy. But the color was a little too light to be categorized as exactly navy. So, dazzling it was.

And he was staring at her. No, not staring. Gazing.

Maggie knew the difference. She'd had plenty of people stare at her in elementary school when they discovered that Santa had never come to her house. Or when she wore outdated hand-me-downs in middle school. Or when she temporarily went vegan in high school. Or when she insisted she could save an animal that was clearly bound for pet heaven.

Those were all stares that said, "What is with this girl?," or "Would you look at this poor thing," or "What an annoying woman."

None of those was the look coming from the dazzling blue eyes gazing down at her. That look was one of curiosity. It was a look of surprise. Was it a look of … interest?

No. That couldn't be right. A man that beautiful, with dazzling eyes like those, and a strong square chin, and blond hair that settled in perfect waves, wouldn't be interested in a girl like her.

Maggie was plain, where he was perfect. She was slight, where he was fit and toned. She was not unattractive per say, where he was drop-dead gorgeous.

Then she realized, that gaze wasn't meant for her. He'd lifted his gaze from Spin to her. That curiosity, that surprise, that interest, it had to be for Spin and his apparatus. She was just receiving the residual effects of him looking at her dog.

Still, that was a huge mark in the man's favor. He'd shown compassion and kindness to a dog, a wounded one at that. The man had scooped Spin, apparatus and all, up into his strong embrace.

Spin was happily wagging his tail in the man's arms. The dog's tongue lolled as he panted happily and gave the man pure puppy dog eyes. Spin whimpered when Maggie tried to take him back. And that's when she felt it.

Though Maggie had little to no experience with men, she was a red-blooded woman. She knew what the spark was. That's what she felt when her fingertips touched the big, gazing, dazzling man.

The spark wasn't hot like a fire. It was like Fourth of July sparklers being set off all over her skin. She wanted to shiver, but she felt too warm.

"This is your dog?" he asked.

If his skin was like sparklers, his voice was like honey; golden and smooth with just the right amount of sweetness. It took Maggie a moment to find her voice. Even after a moment of searching, her voice still wouldn't come out of hiding. So, she simply nodded.

The man stretched out his muscled arms to hand Spin over, but the dog again whimpered. Spin was cradled back in the man's arms looking doubtfully at Maggie.

"We're new to each other," she said. "We only just met a few days ago when I rescued him."

"Rescued him?" The man took one hand and rubbed Spin's head. The dog preened at the attention.

"I rescued Spin here from my boss. He wanted me to kill him."

Low growls went up through the room. Maggie turned to see that she was in a room full of equally big and beautiful men. But she didn't feel an ounce of fear. She was a good judge of character when it came to danger. She got the sense that any of these men would stand up to defend the weak.

"I'm a vet tech," she said. "Or at least I was. My boss, the veterinarian, wanted me to put him down because he felt it was a kindness with his injury."

The mood changed in the room. She could tell she was in a room of people who strongly disagreed with Dr. Cooper's prognosis.

"Instead, I patched him up and dognapped him."

"Atta girl," someone called.

"Yeah, well, I lost my job because of it," she said. "That's why I'm here. I'm looking for Pastor—I mean, Dr. Patel. He said there might be a place for me here?"

"A place for you here?" The man who held her dog repeated her words.

Maggie nodded. "Yeah, he said it would include room and board and a place for my animals, as well. I just got kicked out of my apartment for having too many dogs. So, I'm hoping this job pans out because it's all I've got."

Heads turned to and fro. The men all looked at each other as though they shared an inside joke. Only, no one was laughing.

CHAPTER SEVEN

ylan learned that the woman's name was Maggie. The name suited her somehow. It was a strong sound with just the right amount of femininity.

They all filed into Dr. Patel's office. And by *they* he meant himself, Spin the dog who'd burst into the barn, Maggie, and her dog Soldier, whom she said didn't do well with new people. Her other three dogs were outside checking out their new surroundings under the watchful eyes of the other soldiers.

The Rottweiler with a gash over his eye had given one sniff to Sean's leg and began trailing blindly after him. Sean gave the dog a scratch behind the ears and walked slowly so the partially blind dog could keep up.

The Pug, with star-like patches missing from his back, and the overweight Retriever began a sorry looking game of catch with two of the other soldiers. Reed tossed a ball with his good arm. The dogs sauntered after it. Then stared down at it instead of picking it up. Finally, Fran picked up the ball and tried again. With the same effect.

Xavier held back. He'd introduced himself to Maggie with a cocky grin and a wink. But when Maggie took the rest of her dogs out of her truck, Dylan wasn't surprised when Xavier took a few steps back.

He'd once been a dog person, but that was before he'd lost not one, but two war dogs.

Dylan held the door for Maggie and then waited for her to sit down with the Chihuahua in her lap before he settled with Spin who still refused to be parted from him. He couldn't help but notice that the little dog was missing a front paw. Like Spin, the little dog had an enhancement to help it get around. It seemed all of Maggie's animals were wounded in some light.

Dylan looked up at Dr. Patel, suspicion etched in the grooves on his forehead. But as always, the man smiled a patient, wise smile. The Chihuahua jumped down from Maggie's arms and wagged his tail until Dr. Patel picked her up and settled her onto his lap.

"So, Maggie, I see you've met Dylan."

Maggie turned and smiled at Dylan. Once again, Dylan felt a spark of something in his chest, something he thought long snuffed. He had the urge to lean across his chair and sniff her like Spin was doing to him. He held back from the insane urge, cradling the dog in his arms as a barrier.

"I have," Maggie said as she faced him. "Are you the one in charge here? I'm sorry, I didn't dress formally or bring in my resume. I didn't realize the job interview would be today."

"Job interview?" Dylan turned to Dr. Patel.

"Like I told you in the barn, I'm a vet tech," Maggie said. "Pastor Patel led me to believe you needed help here on the ranch? I was coming by to check it out."

"Oh, Dylan needs help," said Dr. Patel. "But it's a different type of job."

Dylan could feel his face growing hot. He felt a phantom ache in his knee that was no longer there.

"What kind of job?" asked Maggie, still oblivious to Dr. Patel's machinations.

"A permanent one," said Dr. Patel. "The two of you have a lot in common. Commonalities make for strong relationship bonds."

"If you're suggesting what I think you're suggesting, then just stop," said Dylan. But he knew better. Dr. Patel always pushed the issue in that gentle, unassuming way of his.

"Maggie is a good girl; a kind soul that only looks to help others. You're the same. She just lost her home, and so have all of these animals. You're about to lose your home, and so will all of the soldiers here. If the two of you joined forces, each of you could come away with what you want, and perhaps more than you were expecting."

"I don't understand?" said Maggie.

Dylan couldn't stand for Dr. Patel to say it in that patient, rational way of his. The idea was certifiably insane, and the tone and the word choice needed to emphasize that. "He has the crazy idea that we should get married."

He waited for a breath before he turned to face her. Maggie's face was screwed in confusion. She turned in her chair and looked Dylan up and down. Dylan held still, feeling as though he were caught in the crosshairs of a sniper rifle as Maggie beheld him. Her verdict had to be that she found him wanting because she leaned back.

Dylan didn't listen as Dr. Patel further explained the predicament they found themselves in and the benefits of his solution. Dylan turned his focus on the dog.

Spin looked up at him with sad eyes. His front paws scratched at Dylan's heart. Spin's mouth split into a hopeful grin, like a divorced kid who wanted a new daddy.

Dylan gave the dog a scratch behind the ears, and the dog sighed, grateful for the attention. It was all he could do. He wouldn't become this dog's daddy.

"You can't be serious," Maggie was saying.

She was pretty, with a good heart, and smart. She might take in wounded dogs, but wounded men were a different story. Dylan had always imagined being married and having children. But that door was closed to him now. He couldn't be a father to a child in his condition. He couldn't be a husband to a wife either.

He had to admit that he found Maggie attractive. She was unassumingly pretty. Not like the society girls he was used to. She was the girl next door, but from a different neighborhood. It probably took her a few minutes to get ready in the morning, and the little effort is what made her stunning.

Her face was fresh and clean. Her scent earthy and not expensive and cloying. She didn't cross her legs at the ankle as she sat. Both of her hiking boots were planted firmly on the ground. There had been an animal resting in her lap. Now that her lap was vacant, she rested her elbows on her knees as she leaned forward listening intently to Dr. Patel.

No, she was not Dylan's type. The only reason he felt any attraction to her had to be because it had been so long since he'd been with a woman. So long since he'd even been around an available woman. But none of those old dreams were available to him.

"Maggie," Dr. Patel was saying, "you told me yourself, you have nowhere to go. And you have little money. No place you could afford would allow you to take all your dogs. You'll have to take them to the pound, and you, of all people, know what would happen to them."

Maggie chewed at her lower lip, at the same time twisting the corner between her thumb and forefinger. Dylan couldn't take his eyes off the movement of her fingers and tooth. He felt himself panting like the dog in his arms.

"I know you haven't had any luck at love," Dr. Patel said. "Dylan's a good man, an honorable man. And like I said, the two of you are a match. My gut tells me so. The two of you would suit if you give it a chance."

Maggie's cheeks had flamed as Dr. Patel talked about her love life or lack thereof. Want dropped in Dylan's belly, so heavy his gut grumbled.

"He does have a point," said Dylan.

Maggie lifted her gaze to him. The color slowly drained from her cheeks as she did so. Her gaze was uncertain, wary, as though she was expecting to hear the punchline of a bad joke at any second. But Dylan wasn't joking. A strategic plan was forming in his mind.

"We could give it a trial period," he said. "You can stay here, with your dogs, of course. We could use a hand with the farm animals. You can earn some extra money, have a roof over your head. And if it doesn't work out in thirty days, if we find we don't click, you'll have some extra cash and the time to look for someplace where all of you will be accepted."

Maggie's lips parted. Dylan had to swallow down the desire that rose. This was a business arrangement, just like the guys had outlined in the barn. He could do this.

"You'd do that?" she asked.

"Sure," said Dylan. "It's the only way I think this little guy will let me put him down."

Maggie grinned at Spin with so much love and care in her eyes. She'd said she'd only had the dog for a few days. She'd rescued him, healed him, and given him a new lease on life. Dylan wondered if feelings that deep could develop so quickly and last longer than a dog's lifetime?

CHAPTER EIGHT

Maggie rolled over in her bed. Her legs tangled in the top sheet. She'd been dreaming of a strong, warm, male body with corded muscles, a serious facade, kind eyes and a scent that reminded her of a fall day.

She'd tossed and turned all night. Now that her eyes were open, everything was bleary. She couldn't help feeling that yesterday had been some sort of dream. But she knew it had been real.

She'd been proposed to.

Sort of.

Dylan had offered more of a business proposal than a potential love match.

The very idea was crazy. But the idea wouldn't leave her alone. It kept buzzing around her brain, sneaking into her dreams, and nagging her now that she was awake.

She flung her arms out across her bed and met fur. Sugar rested on the right side of the bed, snoring softly. Stevie sat awake at the foot of her bed, waiting patiently for her to rise. The two smaller dogs rested comfortably in their doggie beds on the floor. Spin sulked in the closet where Maggie saw his eyes flash at her.

Maggie was certain she knew what the dog was thinking. *Why are we here alone in this drafty apartment when we could be on a ranch with space to roam and run free? We could be working alongside animals who were trained in the noble cause of helping wounded soldiers. And we could be spending time getting closer to one of said soldiers who'd offered his home, his support, and his hand in marriage.*

Maggie flung herself back on the other side of the bed, turning away from Spin's accusing glare. When she did, Stevie woke up with a confused bark, which woke up the smaller dogs. By the time she sat up, her entire household was awake and looking to her for their sustenance, healing, and direction in life.

Her dogs had been immediately taken by Dylan. Dogs were good judges of character, after all. It was clear that Dylan was doing an honorable thing in trying to save the ranch for the wounded soldiers in his care. And he had kind eyes. Beautiful eyes, set in a face so hand-some that Maggie shuddered under the warm covers.

The idea was preposterous; marrying a stranger. Sure, she knew people did it all the time. Pastor Patel and his wife had been matched by their families. The two had married only after a few weeks of meeting for the first time. She knew that the Patels were very happy, with a large family of adult children—some of whom were matched in the same light.

The thought of that sounded nice; having parents who knew her so well that they succeeded in finding her the love of her life. Having parents she trusted enough to ask for their assistance in matters of the heart.

Maggie had never known that kind of parental inquisitiveness. Her parents had barely known her at all before they abandoned her. Her foster parents only cared that she did as she was told. They didn't take a singular interest in her outside of her duties as their free child-care and maid service.

Pastor Patel was the one person in the world who knew her best. And he said that Dylan was a match for her. It bared a moment's thought. It had deserved that night of tossing and turning. Maybe even a full day of pondering.

Maggie threw off the covers, upsetting the lounging dogs all around her. She got up and went to the bathroom. She handled her morning business and then went to her closet. But the thoughts followed her around.

Dylan had made his offer so calmly, so logically so that it all made sense. Marry him, live and work on the ranch, and everyone gets what they want. And then there was Pastor Patel with his compatibility argument. But they both missed one thing; love.

Maggie wanted to be in love when she got married. If she ever got married. The way things had gone in her love life, she had already begun to doubt she ever would. So her lack of love life would be a better statement.

But if she said yes, she could have a love life. Not only that, she could have a home. She could have a man who would stand up for her, a built-in family with the other men of the ranch, and a place for her animals.

Why was she hesitating again? Oh, yeah. She didn't love him.

But she didn't doubt that she could if given the opportunity. The question was, would he give her the opportunity? Would he offer up his love in return?

But did she really need his love? She'd been in the system and enough foster homes to know that most people only wanted her because she could fill a need. There was a need for her at the ranch. Just like she had in the foster system, she could sit quietly and make herself useful so that Dylan and the other soldiers would keep her.

This would be no different. She didn't need love, just a place to belong for as long as she could.

A sound at the front door, had her tossing on her robe. It didn't sound like a knock, but there was definitely someone out there. The dogs trailed her out of the bedroom. Maggie looked through the peephole and only saw someone retreating. It was her landlord. She opened the door when the coast was clear. But the storm had landed on her door and left its destruction.

An eviction notice hung from her door knocker. Well, that was that. She really had no choice. But she did have options.

She pulled out a suitcase and began to pack. She'd take Dylan up on his offer of thirty days. She'd try and see if she could fit into his life. She'd make herself useful, make herself scarce, and maybe he'd let her stay forever.

CHAPTER NINE

*D*ylan tossed and turned in his bed. His leg tangled in the sheets. He'd been dreaming of soft curves, hair like falling, brown leaves in autumn, intelligent eyes that shied away from a direct gaze, and the subtle scent of roses mixed with a hint of something that reminded him of the bear-skinned rug in his father's hunting cabin.

He couldn't get the thought of Maggie Shaw out of his mind.

He'd asked her to marry him. He thought he'd never utter those words to another woman in his life. But the words had come unbidden from his lips, and he'd meant them.

Oh, he didn't imagine himself in love or anything foolish like that. To him, Maggie and her dogs were another set of beings he could rescue. There was a sadness, an apartness about her that was familiar to him. He knew, without a doubt, that the Purple Heart Ranch would heal her internal wounds just like they were healing his external ones.

That was the only reason he'd offered to help her. And if she said yes, he'd be certain to make that clear. Unlike what Dr. Patel thought, Dylan's heart was not a part of the equation.

Dylan pushed himself up to a sitting position. With the covers turned around his good leg, his stump was on clear display. He looked down at the hunk of meat that was all that was left of his leg. He'd been having a fevered dream about a brown-eyed girl, but looking down at his reality was better than a cold shower.

He went through his morning ritual of cleaning the stump. Infection was always a concern for an amputee. He rolled on the liner over his stump. His first prosthetic had been a newer model with a silicone liner, but it never felt quite right to him. A bad fitting prosthetic did more harm than good. So, Dylan kept it old school.

Over the liner, he slid a prosthetic sock to hold the limb in place. And finally, he slipped his stump into the prosthetic limb. Standing, he pressed his body weight down until he heard the telltale audible signal of the pin clicking and locking into place.

Over his leg, he pulled on long cargo pants that hid both his legs. Though his natural leg was whole, it had not escaped unscathed. He had many scars on his shins and thighs from the explosion that had hit his entire unit.

Dylan never showed his leg to anyone but his physical therapist, Mark. Not since his family and his ex-fiancée had seen his stump and turned their backs on him. He would never go through that again.

So, what made him think he was marriage material now? Maggie had left shortly after his botched business proposal. Women wanted love and romance, not facts and logic. He doubted he'd ever see her again.

So imagine his surprise when he walked out of his cottage to see her beat up truck pulling up to his drive.

"So," she said out of the window. "Would I get my own room?"

"Of course." Dylan kept his hands behind his back, certain that if they were loose he'd reach out to her and pull her into a hug of gratitude.

"The dogs sleep inside," she stated in a tone that was non-negotiable.

"Absolutely."

"You expect me to cook and clean up I suppose." The wince that appeared on her rounded face could only be described as adorable.

"I expect us both to cook and do household chores," he said. "You're not a domestic worker, Maggie. We'll be partners."

That got a surprise rise of her eyebrows. She was looking at Dylan head on. No more shy side gaze. In that unguarded moment, Dylan saw her clearly. And he liked what he saw.

"Thirty days?" she asked.

"Thirty days," he confirmed. "And then we decide."

Maggie bit her lip. Dylan had to look away. He was dying to know what her bottom lip tasted like. With this arrangement, it wasn't like he'd ever get a sample of that delicacy.

Maggie opened the door. Before she could step down, Dylan was at her side, offering his hand. She took it and climbed down.

He didn't immediately let go of her hand once she was securely on the ground. He wasn't sure why? The pads of her fingers were rough, not soft. She was a hard-worker. He knew that by her profession. He also knew that she'd seen death. Likely not of a human being, but watching helpless animals die had to take a toll.

Dylan rubbed his thumb over her finger pads. She looked at him uncertainly. The sound of barking broke their study of each other. One by one, they unloaded the animals. Spin bounced excitedly on his front paws when Dylan handed him down from his crate and Maggie attached his apparatus.

"Come on," he said. "Let me show you all around the ranch."

The dogs nipped at their heels as they began their tour. He'd had to let Maggie's hand go as they took the dogs down. Maggie led the partially blind Rottweiler around on a leash with one hand. She carried the Chihuahua with the missing paw around in her other arm.

He wasn't sure what to say to her. They kept looking over at each other and then immediately looking away. It was worse than the first day of middle school.

But the silence wasn't uncomfortable. And the dogs occupied most of their attention. The pack of animals was excited to be in new surroundings and sniffed at every leaf and bush they came into contact with.

"There you are, Dylan."

Dylan looked up to see his trainer, Mark. Mark was a good ten years older than Dylan, but the man didn't look it. He was tall and well built. When the few women that came by the ranch stopped by, their gazes always found and lingered on Mark.

Dylan turned to Maggie. Her gaze wasn't on Mark. It was on the horse he led.

Dylan couldn't blame Maggie for that. Bailey was a beautiful specimen of horseflesh. She was a gentle creature and well trained. So, she didn't spook when the small animals came near.

"Hey, Bailey," said Dylan as he reached out to the horse. "You're looking good today."

The horse bowed her head and gave a soft whinny.

"And who do we have here?" Mark prompted, eyes on Maggie.

"This is Maggie. She's …" Dylan looked at Maggie. Should he call her his fiancée? She hadn't exactly accepted his proposal. They were just trying things out for a while. So what did that make her? She's my girlfriend."

Maggie's eyes did that wide thing again that allowed Dylan to see into the depths of her being. It was surprise and something else. Dylan decided he liked it. He'd have to find other ways to get that rise out of her.

He realized he also liked that title on her. Girlfriend. Soon fiancée. Maybe one day, wife.

CHAPTER TEN

Maggie shook the hand of the trainer—what was his name again? Oh, yeah; Martin? No, Mark. Something that began with M. She had no idea. No other words registered after Dylan said that single word.

Girlfriend.

Dylan had called her his girlfriend. She'd never been anyone's girlfriend before. She'd only been on a handful of dates in her entire life. But now she was someone's girlfriend.

Logically, she understood why he'd decided on that title. She'd seen the decision making in his blue eyes. He couldn't call her his fiancée. She hadn't entirely agreed to that.

But they were dating in a sense. They were taking time to get to know each other. Time to see if they would suit as a couple. That qualified her as his girlfriend.

Maggie's chest puffed up at the new title she now carried. Her head swam high enough to reach a cloud with this new role. She had a boyfriend. And one that was not too shabby if she did say so herself.

Dylan hadn't balked when she insisted her dogs stay inside. He'd even divvied up the domestic chores. What man does that?

What man, indeed? Maybe he was gay? Maybe he was using her as his beard to hide that fact.

But no. Pastor Patel was his psychologist, surely he'd know if Dylan wasn't truly interested in Maggie. There was also the way he'd looked at her when she'd pulled up in his drive that morning.

There had been relief in his raised brow. But there had been something else at the corner of his eyes. Just a flash, but she'd seen it. It looked to her like interest. It was possible that he had more than a business interest in her.

Maggie was definitely interested. Dylan was handsome, thoughtful, and kind. Where was a pen? She was ready to sign on the dotted line to make this man hers for a lifetime.

But right now she was his girlfriend. She let the word wash over her again. She remembered the feel of his fingers rubbing her thumb as though he could take off the rough calluses and smooth things over. She had a feeling he could.

Those fingers now rubbed Spin's head. The mutt looked at her smugly. That was fine. Spin might be in the running for this particular man's best friend. But Maggie was currently his girlfriend.

A girlfriend got handholding. She got long walks. She got taken to dinner.

Hmmm? These were all benefits a pet enjoyed from their humans. But, so what. Maggie would take it.

Maggie chanced a glance up at her new boyfriend. He worried his lip, as though he were insecure about the title he'd just given her. Maggie smiled brightly at him, trying to communicate her acceptance of the role. Then she decided to use her words.

"Hi." She stuck out her hand to the trainer. Mark—that was his name. "I'm Maggie, Dylan's girlfriend."

"So I've heard." Mark smiled and gave Maggie's hand a polite shake.

As Mark released her hand the horse scooted over to the fence and rubbed itself against the wooden planks. Maggie's eyes zeroed in on the horse's rear. She noted that there was a patch of inflamed skin there.

"Is she suffering from Sweet Itch?" Maggie asked.

"Yeah," said Mark. "I just sprayed her down with repellent but those midges seem to like the way she tastes."

"Have you put a fan in her stables in the evening? Midges and gnats like to come out in the evening and find damp places or areas where there's stagnant water."

"You know," Mark scratched at his chin, "that's a good idea. I didn't know you were dating a vet, Banks."

Maggie opened her mouth to correct the trainer, but Dylan beat her to it.

"She's a vet tech," he said. "She's very dedicated to animals."

Dylan smiled down at her. His brow raised again, lifting with what looked like relief, stretching wide with what looked like interest. Maggie needed a fan under his gaze. She felt suddenly hot and damp all over.

"She's going to help out around here," Dylan continued.

"There are also some foods I can recommend," Maggie said. "Sweet Itch is often a sign of a compromised immune system. I could write up a list."

"Why don't we chat about it on the way to the stables?" said Mark. "It's time for Dylan's training session."

"That would be great," Maggie beamed.

"No."

Both Maggie and Mark turned to stare at Dylan. His single word had been forcefully said. His eyes, wide and open only a moment ago, were now narrowed and hooded.

Dylan cleared his throat, but the tension was still there in his clenched jaw. "I mean, you should go and get settled in, Maggie."

He didn't look directly at her. Instead, his gaze was on her ear. Maggie resisted the urge to tug at her ear. Just as she knew what interest looked like, she was more familiar with what disinterest looked like. Dylan was not interested in her coming along to his training sessions.

As further proof of her assumption, he handed Spin to her. When his forearms and hands brushed hers, there was no spark. Instead, a shiver went through her body.

Dylan's gaze flicked to hers for just a brief second, and then he looked away again. "I'll see you when I get home this evening."

And with that, he turned to Mark and walked away. Mark gave her an apologetic shrug, then he and the horse turned to follow Dylan.

Dylan walked away stiffly. He took with him all the closeness they'd built. Once again Maggie was left standing alone and shut out.

CHAPTER ELEVEN

Dylan was sore after his session, but not just physically. Something ached inside him. Something he couldn't yet work out. The whole ride he couldn't get the look on Maggie's face out of his mind.

They had had a great time in the span of walking from his house to the training grounds. When he'd called her his girlfriend, he'd initially tripped over the word. But it hadn't felt like a lie. It felt like a newly discovered truth.

Until he'd went and ruined it.

But he couldn't let her see him train. His leg was awkward and stiff as he mounted the horse. He couldn't cast it over the horse's back. He needed a hand. He used his own hand, refusing to allow Mark or the others to assist him.

Beyond that, his sessions were often brutal, mainly because he pushed himself. Dylan was a true believer in the adage No Pain, No Gain. If it didn't hurt him a little, he was certain he wasn't working hard enough.

He wouldn't have minded her watching him ride. Even when he pushed himself, he felt powerful in the mount, riding high on the horse. But then there was the dismounting, which was even trickier than the mounting after he'd pushed his muscles so hard.

No. He didn't want Maggie to see that; weak and vulnerable. The last time he'd allowed anyone to see his weakness it had crushed his spirit.

Dylan had liked the way Maggie had looked at him today. She'd looked up to him like he was capable, like he was her savior. Better that she look disappointed for a short time, rather than look down with pity on him for the rest of their lives.

He had to remind himself, and her, that this wouldn't be some great love affair. This was a practical arrangement. They could be friendly. They might even become friends. But love wasn't in the cards for someone like him. Someone who didn't have their whole selves to offer.

He knew a woman like Maggie deserved more. But as much as he was doing this for the soldiers in need of this ranch, he was also doing it for himself. It felt good to have a woman near. To have a woman on his arm. To have a woman gaze upon him like he was a full and complete man.

So, even though he was more sore than he'd been in months after a training session, Dylan set a quick pace back to his house. When he came upon the small cottage, the lights were on in the kitchen. He saw movement through the window. He heard the excited barking of dogs, more like begging whimpers.

Dylan opened the back door to the smell of ... something burning.

His training immediately set in. He took a quick glance around the room to assess the danger. There was one pan on fire. A pot of boiling water spilled over onto the stovetop. And smoke plumed out of the oven.

Maggie looked up at him. Her hair was frazzled. There was a smear of something—grease? food?—on her cheek. A mix of panic, defeat, and shame dimmed her usually expressive eyes. "I'm sorry."

Dylan rushed into action, stepping over and around barking, yipping dogs as he did so. He put the burning pan into the sink. He shut off all the burners. Then he opened the oven door to allow the smoke to make a full escape.

"I'm sorry," Maggie repeated again. "I was trying to make grown-up food."

Dylan pulled out a charred steak from the oven. The dogs all took steps back and moaned at the travesty. Dylan recognized potatoes in the pot of water, but they knocked audibly against the bottom of the pan as though the boiling water hadn't affected the spuds at all. He wasn't sure what had been in the pan? Maybe greens? But they were now brown.

"I've only ever cooked for kids and animals," Maggie said. "I'm great with hot dogs and chicken nuggets and fries."

"I like hot dogs, nuggets, and fries." He offered her a smile, but she was too busy scrubbing at the mess on his stove to notice.

"Really?" she asked as she mopped up the spilled water. "I took you for a fine dining kind of guy."

"What gave you that impression?" Dylan pulled out the frozen fare from the freezer.

"Pictures of your family." She turned and faced him, eyes wide with guilt. "I wasn't snooping. They were on the mantel. You were all at some fancy place."

Dylan nodded. "My father won't eat out unless a place has a Michelin star, and my mother won't eat food portions bigger than her thumb."

"But not you?"

"Not me."

Maggie chuckled at his words, the tension visibly seeping from her shoulders.

Dylan's palms felt warm even though he held frozen foods in his hands. He pulled out a pan from the cupboard, sprayed, and laid out the food. "What about you?"

"Me?" The tension crept back into her shoulders, and she looked away from him. She sat down in one of the chairs and lifted Soldier into her arms. The Chihuahua licked at whatever was on her chin. Dylan felt a hint of jealousy towards the little dog.

"I don't have family," Maggie said. "My parents abandoned me at a young age. I was in an orphanage until I was a teenager. I assumed I'd be there until I turned eighteen. I got fostered. But that family just wanted me as an unpaid nanny to their younger kids."

She said all of this while caressing and cuddling Soldier in one hand. With the other, she reached down and scratched Stevie behind the ear. Dylan had the strongest urge to take her into his arms and hug her. Instead, he poured her a glass of juice and placed it in front of her.

Maggie accepted his offering. She was starting to make sense to him. A woman who'd been abandoned as a child, who'd dedicated her life to saving wounded animals. A woman who hadn't known parental love now trying to find a way to fit in and make herself useful.

Maggie had been discarded and misused, just like her animals. Dylan needed to let her know that he wouldn't do that to her. He wanted to tell her that she had a place here for as long as she wanted. He wanted to guarantee her forever.

A place. Not his heart. He could guarantee her a place forever so that she finally felt at home.

"Maggie," he said softly, then waited until she lifted her gaze to him. "I know our relationship is essentially a business relationship. But I was thinking, maybe we could be friends? What do you say we get to know each other?"

CHAPTER TWELVE

Her new boyfriend, and possible fiancé, and potential husband wanted to be her friend. Was this ranch some kind of alternate universe where plain girls got the prince?

And he could cook.

Maggie opened the door to the oven and took the fries out. This time there was no smoke accompanying the meal. The spuds were golden brown and cooked through.

When Dylan had appeared at the door, she'd expected him to blow a fuse at the sight of his once pristine kitchen. She'd noticed that about him. Not that he was prone to anger. That he was very … orderly was putting it nicely.

The furniture was high quality. The knickknacks dispersed around the small home would be better labeled as accouterments.

Dylan had said he wasn't into fine dining. He may not hunger for expensive things, but he certainly had expensive tastes.

Maggie still wore many of the hand-me-downs and Goodwill items from her senior year in high school. What few furnishings she had were all second-hand. She wasn't certain that she could measure up to this guy.

"Ketchup or mustard?" he asked, holding up both condiments.

"Both."

"Me too," he grinned. "Relish?"

Maggie wrinkled her nose at the offensive suggestion. "Pickles belong on burgers. Or in tartar sauce for fish nuggets."

"So it shall be decreed," Dylan said with a grin. He put the relish back in the fridge.

Turning toward the plates of bunned hot dogs, Dylan maneuvered around the excited dogs nipping at his feet. Maggie noticed he stepped carefully over and around them, but he did so stiffly. He hadn't told her what his injury was from the war, but she'd had an inkling since the first day they'd met. Though he made a concerted effort to maintain an even gait, Dylan favored his left leg.

Having dressed the hot dogs, he reached into the cupboard where she'd placed the dog food. His pant leg hitched, and she saw the barest glint of metal instead of a fleshy ankle.

Self-consciously, he reached back and yanked his pant leg down. Quickly, Maggie averted her gaze. It hadn't taken her long to realize the reason for his curt dismissal of her at the training fields had been because he didn't want her to see him struggle with his injury.

Dylan turned, but by then Maggie was already looking down. She placed the fries on the plate next to the wieners. Still, she caught him giving his right pant leg another tug to hide his wound before bending down on his good knee.

He poured out a measured cup and placed it in the bowls, giving each dog a scratch behind the ear or pat on the back.

He straightened a bit awkwardly, using the counter to help him back to his feet. Maggie continued arranging the fries until he'd resumed his full height.

She understood wounded animals and their need to hide their injuries. She'd have to back off until he came to her and saw that she meant him no harm, she was no threat. She wanted to care for him. She'd simply have to wait him out until he trusted her and allowed it.

Feeding a wounded animal was usually a good ploy. But she'd failed spectacularly at that. Now that she had his help in the kitchen, things were smoothing out a bit.

Dylan washed his hands and then they sat at the table with their food. He reached out his hand to hers. Maggie stared at his open palm.

"I bless my food before eating it," he said.

"Me too. I just—I mean—" She shut up and handed him her hands. There was that spark of awareness again. She lifted her gaze to his and knew, the rise of his brow and the flare of his nostril, that he'd felt it too.

Dylan said a blessing over the food. Then he released his hold on her, but Maggie still felt a connection between them.

They took a few bites in silence appreciating the simple fare. A smidge of ketchup dotted his jaw and she giggled. He grinned, wiped at the smudge. Then he pointed his red fingertip at her.

Maggie wiped at her cheek. She felt a dollop of moisture there. When she pulled her thumb away, she came away with a glob of mustard. She grinned, popping her thumb into her mouth and getting rid of the evidence.

When her gaze lifted to Dylan's, his smile had slipped, his gaze still locked on hers. There was heat in his blue eyes. It made her shiver.

Dylan sat his half-eaten hot dog down and rose. He went to the freezer and grabbed a few ice cubes. They plopped with a splash into his glass of water before he sat down again.

"So, Dylan." Maggie struggled for a topic of conversation that didn't have to do with animals or her lack of kitchen skills. "What branch of the military were you in?"

"Army. I was a Sergeant E-5."

"I don't know what that means? I don't know much about the military and rank."

"It's a fancy sounding title that let me boss other men around."

He was grinning again. Maggie felt she was on safe ground with him once more. "Where were you … stationed in the war?"

"I was deployed," he corrected her. "We're not technically at war. I spent three years in the armed forces. Mostly as a part of Operation Inherent Resolve in Syria and then in Operation Resolute Support in Afghanistan."

"It's most dangerous in Afghanistan, isn't it?"

Dylan shrugged. "There are operations stationed all around the world in areas where civilians vacation."

"Do you not want to talk about it?"

Dylan flexed his arms behind his head and leaned back. Maggie tried not to stare, but even his biceps were attractive. She wondered what it would be like to be inside his embrace.

"You'll find that most soldiers don't want to talk about it." His words were blunt, but he couched them with a small smile. "It's hard to talk about it with someone who wasn't there."

"Okay." Maggie finished off her hot dog and wiped her mouth. She looked down at the full-bellied dogs who were all laid out on the floor at their feet.

Dylan chewed at his lower lip. He rubbed his forefinger around the lip of the glass. All the while, Maggie held her breath and hoped.

"I lost my leg in the last mission I was on." He said it so quietly she thought she'd imagined it. "We were helping the local forces to build a school in Afghanistan. The locals were thankful. They were so full of hope."

He took a deep breath. Maggie thought he might not continue. But she knew there was nothing for her to do but stay quiet and still and let him come to her.

"We were all so full of hope. We were all a part of that mission. The entire squad didn't make it. Those of us that did ... we all lost something that day. That's why we're here. We're trying to rebuild ... our lives."

Spin made his way over to Dylan. He gave a whimper, and Dylan picked up the dog. Placing the terrier in his lap, Dylan stroked behind his ears.

"You made this apparatus yourself?" asked Dylan.

"I tinkered with the design. An original could cost a couple hundred bucks. Most families looking to adopt a dog aren't willing to fork out the expense or the time. That's why wounded animals get put down so often."

Dylan gazed at her as he continued to stroke Spin's coat. "The Purple Heart Ranch is dedicated to rehabilitating the wounded."

"I know. I'd like to help." Before she could think better of it she added, "The animals as well as the soldiers."

Dylan's throat worked before he answered. "It's different with humans, Maggie. Men especially. Nothing on this earth has more pride than a wounded man."

"I don't agree. I've found healing has one constant ingredient; patience."

He didn't argue. He didn't meet her gaze again. "It's been a long day. We're all tired. I'll walk you to your room."

Dylan sat Spin back on the floor as he stood. Together, and in silence, they cleared their plates and loaded them into the dishwasher. With the kitchen clean, Dylan reached out his hand to her. She didn't hesitate. She took hold of his hand and walked with him down the hall. The dogs trailed in their wake.

It was a short walk to the door of her bedroom. Once outside the door, he paused. She turned to him. There were only a few inches between them. He'd loosened his hold on her hand, but he still held onto a few of her fingertips. Slowly, his gaze lifted to hers.

Maggie's heart raced. Was he going to kiss her? They'd just had dinner and conversation. Before that, it had been a stroll around a ranch. This was practically a second date, at least by her measure.

She watched him gulp, watched his chest work. Slowly, he pulled his fingers away from hers, one by one.

"I'm really glad you're here," he said. "I think we can make this work. I can't give you everything a true husband can. But if you agree to be my wife, we can save this place, and I can offer you this home, and a sense of security, and my protection."

As proposals went, that was practically perfect.

"I'm not rushing you," he continued. "We have time. I just want you to know that you would always have a place. Even if we lose the ranch. You and your dogs would have a place to stay with me."

Maggie's heart was doing flips. She was certain he could hear it.

"Anyway," he took a step back. "Good night, Maggie."

He took another step back and bumped into Spin. Maggie clenched her hands into fists and glued them to her sides so she wouldn't reach out to help Dylan as he wobbled. She knew it would not be appreciated, though she ached to do it.

Dylan righted himself, then he reached down to pet Spin. The dog looked up at him with pure adoration. Maggie knew her eyes were doing the same. To hide her burgeoning feelings, she turned and opened her bedroom door. Four dogs rushed in to claim their spots. One remained on the other side of the threshold.

Spin looked between Maggie and Dylan. Then he wheeled himself closer to Dylan.

"It's fine," Dylan said scooping up the dog. "He can hang with me tonight."

The two of them disappeared into the room at the end of the hall. Maggie shut the other dogs and herself inside her room. It was going to take a lot of patience, but she was determined to get closer to her wounded soldier.

CHAPTER THIRTEEN

There was a warm body lying next to Dylan in his bed. He reached for it instinctively bringing it inside his embrace like he'd wanted to do all through dinner. Like he'd wanted to do when he'd walked her to her bedroom door. He'd entwined his fingers with hers without thinking about what he was doing. That was how strong his attraction was to Maggie. He sought her out whenever she was near, like a magnet finding its charge. But when he reached out this time, seeking her positivity, instead of warm, womanly curves he felt fur.

Dylan opened his eyes just in time to see a wet tongue lap him up from his chin to his cheek. The smell of doggie breath had him turning away. But Spin simply pawed at Dylan until he had his attention again.

The dog's tail wagged and thumped his front paws so animatedly that Dylan couldn't be upset. He gave the dog a scratch, trying not to think about the woman who had rescued him. The woman who was making Dylan feel things he hadn't in a long time, things he never thought he'd feel again.

Dylan lifted himself and swung his leg over the bed. Spin pulled himself over to the edge of the bed and looked down at the floor.

Dylan bent over and brought the dog's apparatus up on the bed. He'd taken both his apparatus and the dog's off last night before they both curled up on the mattress and fell into a deep sleep. Now he hooked the dog into the contraption and set Spin on the floor. Then Dylan turned to his own leg.

Spin eyed the rump that was left of Dylan's leg. He ventured closer and sniffed it. Spin gave a nod of his head, as though he accepted Dylan's state. Then he took off to explore the rest of Dylan's room, wheeling around his bed and into his closet.

Dylan smiled after the dog. The dog's easy acceptance thawed something in Dylan's heart. If only every living soul could be so accepting of his wound. A knock at the bedroom door sent Dylan reaching for the covers to hide his mangled leg.

"Dylan?" called Maggie from the other side of the door. "Are you up?"

Panic settled over Dylan. It would take him a few moments to get his prosthetic on, but not before cleaning the area first. And then he'd have to get to his closet to find a long pair of pants to cover the apparatus.

"Don't come in," he shouted.

"I won't."

There had been the sound of morning sun in her voice when she'd knocked on his door. Dylan clearly heard a cloud in her tone now. He hung his head in his hands. Just last night he'd promised to be her protector. And yet at every turn, he kept hurting her.

"I wouldn't do that," she said from the other side of the door, her voice still small but filled with a compassion that brushed the rough edges of his heart. "I told Mark I'd help him this morning with the Sweet Itch problem. I just wanted to let you know where I was going."

Dylan removed the blanket from his leg and rubbed at the ache there. It wasn't soothed. The pain was lower, in his shin—a shin that was no longer there. He was a constant sufferer of phantom pains, but more so these past couple of days.

He watched Spin go to the door. The terrier wagged his tail at the sound of his owner's voice. A part of Dylan wanted to do the same.

He wanted to open up to Maggie, but he couldn't even open the door. He didn't want her to see him like this.

"I'm putting the dogs in the backyard so they'll stay out of trouble," she continued through the wooden barrier. "You can put Spin there, too. Or take him with you. It's up to you."

Dylan looked down at the dog. The dog looked between Dylan and the door as though he didn't understand why there was a barrier between the three of them. The phantom cramp returned to Dylan's absent leg. No matter how much he massaged it, it never left him. It was always there.

"Do you need anything … from me?" she asked.

There was so much he wanted from her. But he could never ask it. "Thanks, Maggie. I'll catch up with you later, okay?"

"Sure … sure."

He waited until he heard the sound of her steps, followed by many feet padding across the wood floor. He waited until he heard the heavy back door shut. Only then did he go through the motions of putting himself together.

Maggie had tried to sound positive, but he'd heard it. He'd turned her brightness to something dim. Maybe this was a mistake. He kept taking two steps forward with her, only to remember he couldn't stand on his own two feet and fall back.

Dylan showered, taking special care to clean his stump. When he was finished, he dried himself, taking special care around his missing limb before he put on the prosthetic.

After getting dressed, he led Spin to the back door. The dog took one look outside, then looked back up at him. Seemed the dog had no intentions of leaving Dylan's side, but he'd have to. Dylan wouldn't be able to keep an eye on the dog and do his chores.

With a firm command, he urged the dog out the door. Spin made a grumbling sound, and he did as he was told, but not before casting one more forlorn look over his shoulder. Dylan almost laughed, but he was feeling too low to muster up the sound.

"How's wedded bliss?" asked Fran when he met Dylan on the path to the training fields.

Dylan grimaced, his facial features scrunching up into confused angles. When he let his face relax, he sighed.

"That bad?"

"She's amazing. I just … It's only …" Dylan sighed again.

"Because if you don't want to marry her, I'm sure X would have no problem manning up." Fran pointed off in the distance.

Dylan had to shade his eyes, but then he saw it. Xavier was leaning against the fencing. He had his cowboy hat pulled low. He leaned in and said something to Maggie. She startled. And then she laughed, brushing her hair over her shoulders. Dylan knew that when a woman brushed her hair away it was a sign that she was interested.

His feet were in motion before he realized. His prosthetic struck the ground with purpose as he moved toward the two.

Maggie looked up as though sensing his presence. She'd been smiling at Xavier, but when she spied Dylan her face lit up like it was the sun dawning.

Dylan nearly tripped at the brightness of her smile. He reached out to the railing to steady himself. She was within his reach. He felt the pull to her again. It was too strong to resist.

And so he reached out to her. At the first contact of his fingertips on her forearm, he felt a humming sensation tremble through his finger pads. That's what made his hand close her in a grasp and tug her into his side.

Maggie gasped, her eyes going wide in the open vulnerable way that did something to his insides. Dylan circled his arm around her back. When he did, his palm crossed over capable shoulders able to handle a heavy load. His instinct was to take all the weight away and heft it onto his own back.

Maggie came willingly into his embrace, fitting perfectly into the space between his arm and chest. Warmth spread through Dylan. But that's not what made him know he was in trouble.

When he looked up, he saw both Xavier and Fran smirking at him.

CHAPTER FOURTEEN

Maggie hated simpering women. Women who shrank like violets and didn't speak when men came around. Women who let men speak for them and no longer said anything intelligent when their significant other came into the room.

She was standing in the open air. She'd been having an interesting conversation with a man. A very handsome man at that. Xavier Ramos could only be called beautiful.

He'd been flirting with her, in that way where men didn't really mean it. Where their entire vocabulary consisted of come-ons because they didn't know how to engage a woman's brain. Xavier's interest in her wasn't true. He was flirting because it was in his nature.

Maggie hadn't been bothered by it. They both knew he wasn't serious. It felt more like he was feeling her out than actually checking her out.

Maggie appreciated that. It meant he was looking out for Dylan. This was a preformed squad she was walking into. A cohesive unit. A battle-hardened, well-suited family. And it seemed like she was being accepted. First by Fran, who'd greeted her and walked her to the stables to find Mark. Then by Mark, who'd listened to her suggestions and ideas to heal the ailing horses.

She was sure she'd won over Xavier by not taking his bait. She was certain they all saw her as an intelligent, capable woman.

Then the moment Dylan showed up, the words slowly seeped out of her brain. When his arm made its way around her shoulder, she forgot how to breathe. She didn't shrink into herself out of shyness. She didn't recoil from his touch. She melted into his welcome heat with an aim to become a part of him.

"Don't you have somewhere to be, X?" Dylan growled. But Maggie didn't mind. The reverb sent a tingle down to her toes.

"Just making nice with the prettiest lady on the ranch." Xavier winked at her.

That snapped Maggie out of it. She laughed at Xavier's fake flirting. "I'm pretty sure I'm the only woman on the ranch, outside of the four-legged variety."

"Well, your legs are—"

"That's enough." Dylan cut Xavier off with another low growl.

Dylan's voice made Maggie jump, but Xavier only smirked. He tilted his hat to Maggie. Then he smirked again at Dylan before taking off.

Fran gave her a friendly smile and then gave Dylan the same smirk.

Maggie turned to face Dylan but found that she couldn't. His grip on her shoulder was vise-like.

Was he jealous?

That was absurd. No one had ever had any cause to get jealous over her. But Dylan's grip was really tight, as though she were something he had no plans to let go of or share.

"Dylan? Are you … I mean … This might sound silly but …"

His grip loosened now that his friends had disappeared into the stables. Maggie turned to face him, feeling less brave now that she was looking up into his blue eyes. He looked uncomfortable and shifted his weight from one leg to the other.

"Ramos is a good guy," said Dylan. "I trust him with my life. But he's bad news with women."

"Why is that information necessary for me to know?"

Dylan looked even more uncomfortable.

He *was* jealous. She might not know men well. But she knew animal behavior. He was exhibiting the telltale markers of having his territory threatened. She was his territory. She didn't mind him prowling around her perimeter. But she needed him to know that she had no plans to stay.

"I gave you my word," Maggie said. "I'm not the kind of girl to play around on a guy. I wouldn't know how. I've never had a boyfriend."

Dylan eased up his hold. Maggie regretted the loosening embrace, but she wanted any show of affection to be genuine and not some alpha male reaction.

"I didn't take Xavier seriously. He was kinda funny. Not as funny as he thinks though."

Dylan looked slightly less uncomfortable. He chewed at his lower lip as he'd done last night at dinner. It was like he was chewing over the words he wanted to say, seeing if they were bitter or sweet before he offered them up.

"I was wondering if you'd like to have lunch with me? In the Big House this time. We have a cook."

"Oh." Maggie felt her grin spread stupidly-wide. "I'd like that."

Dylan nodded, meeting her gaze now. Neither of them moved. A gentle breeze ruffled the ends of their hair. The sound of a bird's cry and the answering call filled the air.

"Sergeant Banks, there you are."

The spell broke. Maggie and Dylan turned to face a man in a suit. The man reminded Maggie of Dr. Cooper. She did shrink away now, moving slightly behind Dylan. The Cooper doppelgänger looked entirely out of place on the ranch.

"I'm glad I caught you in person," said the man. "I wanted to deliver this notice to you."

Dylan took the proffered papers. Maggie's heart sank with recognition as she spied the bold letters on the document. For the second time this week, she saw the word EVICTION in bright, red letters.

"You said we had until the end of the month to file," said Dylan.

"I'm sorry." The man didn't sound sorry in the least. "They want their hands on this land. If there was something I could do, I would. This goes through at the end of the week. Unless you're getting married in a couple of days, I don't see how this could be turned around."

"We are getting married tomorrow."

Both men looked over. Maggie nearly turned around herself. But she knew the sound of her own voice. She had said those words. She had made that proclamation.

"Who are you?" asked the man.

"I'm his fiancée." Maggie reached down and entwined her fingers with Dylan's. "And like I said, we're getting married tomorrow."

She looked to Dylan for confirmation. His gaze had widened as if to ask if she was sure. Maggie knew it could be thirty days, it could be three days. Her mind wouldn't change. She wanted to be with Dylan for the rest of her life.

As though he could read her mind, Dylan squeezed her fingers. The paper crumpled from his hand.

CHAPTER FIFTEEN

Dylan straightened his tie. The knot was perfect. The ends hung even.

The color brought out his eyes. He knew this because his mother had told him so when she'd bought it for him before he'd left for the army. She was always conscious of details regarding his outer appearance. But she had never once looked into his eyes and saw anything but the hue.

He yanked the knot and began the process over again.

He gave a gruff response to the knock at the door. Reed poked his head in the door. His grin preceding him as his prosthetic arm spread the door wide. Behind Reed, Sean slid into the door. He was sure to present the right side of his face, hiding the scars on the left.

"Man, you really cheated us not having a bachelor's party," said Reed. "We could've made a quick trip to Vegas."

Reed crossed his prosthetic arm over his chest. Unlike Dylan, he was not one to shy away from showing it.

Sean gave Dylan a full smile. With the injury on his face creasing into deep grooves, the smile spread deep into his skin.

"Being the good friends we are," Reed continued, " we do come bearing gifts."

"We'll take over your chores for the next couple of days," said Sean. "So you can enjoy your wedding night."

Both men waggled their eyebrows and made juvenile lewd gestures unbecoming of men their age and rank. Or so Dylan thought. The good humor fell from Dylan's face.

"It's not that type of marriage," he said.

The eyebrow waggling ceased. Both of the men's mouths dropped open in confusion. Their loss reminded Dylan of Sugar, Maggie's diabetic dog that didn't understand why he was constantly denied treats.

Sean and Reed looked at one another, then back at Dylan.

"It's a marriage of convenience," said Dylan.

"Maggie looks really convenient to me," said Reed.

Dylan narrowed his gaze at the man.

In response, Reed held up a plastic hand, metal glinting from his forearm. "For someone that's looking for convenience, you sure have a lot of feelings when it comes to this girl."

"I hardly know her." Dylan turned back to his tie, doing a quick and efficient knot and leaving it at that.

Sean turned to Reed and addressed the other man as though Dylan wasn't in the room. "Ramos told me he nearly bit his head off yesterday when he caught her talking to him," said Sean.

"Yeah, and I've seen the way he carries around her dog like it's their kid," said Reed.

Dylan knew if he denied it any further, the men would just keep ribbing him. So instead, he pulled on his jacket and headed for the door. The sounds of snickers followed him out of the room.

The ceremony was to be held in a gazebo near the pond. The three of them rode in a golf cart across the ranch to reach the area. Fran and Xavier had already set up chairs and a few Christmas decorations. It wouldn't be the wedding of the season that his mother and ex would've planned for him, but they had done their best. Dylan was touched. He just hoped Maggie wouldn't be too disappointed.

There was already a small gathering. Dr. Patel stood inside the gazebo. As an ordained minister, he had the power to officiate, which was good since the wedding was on such quick notice. But the man had been the one to suggest the match. For the past year, Dylan had put his mental health in the doctor's hands, and he hadn't disappointed him. Now he'd put his future, and maybe even his heart in Dr. Patel's hands.

He'd committed to seeing this through. He wanted to take care of Maggie. He wanted to be the one person she could always depend on. He wanted to be the cause of her comfort and her smiles and her eyes widening in joyous surprise. He wanted to take a closer look into her gaze and see what was past her brown eyes.

Dylan gave his head a shake. He had to remind himself; this wasn't some great romance. It was an arrangement, a convenience to them both.

They could be friends. It was fine for friends to look into one another's eyes to check on their health and well-being. That settled, Dylan walked down the aisle.

He saw the faces of his men, his friends. He saw the faces of his trainers and the ranch staff. No one looked doubtful about what he was doing. They all knew why this marriage was happening. It was saving their jobs, their livelihoods. But still, they were all smiling as Dylan took his place.

They'd all only known Maggie for a couple of days. But it seemed she had made quite an impression on everyone. Maggie's five dogs sat obediently at the front of the archway. Spin had been looking beyond the gazebo at the pond water, but he got up and wheeled his way to Dylan when he sensed the man's presence. Dylan bent down to give the dog a pat before he took his place before Dr. Patel.

The older man gave him a knowing smile. "How are you feeling?"

"This is the logical thing to do. I think we've both thought it through, and I'll take care of her."

A chuckle tickled out of Dr. Patel's mouth. Before the man could say more, his gaze lifted and his eyes lit.

Dylan turned to the way he'd just come and ceased being able to form a coherent thought.

Maggie stepped out of a golf cart with the help of Fran. She wore a simple white dress. No frills, no embellishments. Just like her.

Dylan's palms felt moist, so he rubbed them against his pants. His neck felt hot, so he reached to loosen his tie. A thumping sound filled his ears, and he wondered if the horses had gotten loose. But no. It was his own heartbeat pounding.

Maggie looked nervous. She fidgeted. Dylan fought the need to go to her. He wanted to soothe her. He wanted to assure her that he would take care of her, that he would take care of it all. He wanted her to trust him, to believe in him.

Her gaze locked on him. She let out a breath that he would've sworn he felt tickle his nose. And then she began to move.

Faintly, Dylan heard music playing. But his gaze stayed trained on Maggie. With steady, sure steps, she came toward him. There was no sway in her hips. Just even strides toward him. Before he knew it, she stood before him.

Dylan heard Dr. Patel saying words. Lots of words in his calm, even tone. But Dylan paid the man no heed.

Instead, he watched Maggie's lips move. Her words made no sense to his head, but his heart pounded at the utterance.

He felt someone nudge him at his side. Dylan turned to glare at Fran who stood up beside him as his Best Man. Fran cocked his head toward Dr. Patel. The good doctor smiled at him and then repeated the words.

Dylan turned back to Maggie and said his vows. As each promise left his lips he was not surprised to realize that he meant every word. He intended to keep each vow; the vow he would make to Maggie, his bride.

"I pronounce you man and wife."

It was done. He was married. Maggie was his wife now, his responsibility. He wouldn't let her down. He wouldn't let any of them down.

"You may now kiss the bride."

Dylan stiffened. How had he forgotten that part? Maggie looked up at him with those wide eyes. Suddenly, the only thing in the world that he wanted to do was kiss this woman, his woman, his wife.

Dylan bent his head slowly, giving her every chance to back away. She didn't.

His lips met hers on the softest of brushes. She inhaled sharply but did not pull away. And so he pressed forward.

Maggie was everything soft and sweet. She was willing and pliant. She was innocence and eagerness.

Dylan found his hand coming to the small of her back. She exhaled, and he drank in her essence, wanting more, needing more, taking more. He gave her torso a tug, and she came to him, fitting snuggly against his chest as he continued to press into her. She clicked into place.

There were cheers coming from a distance. And then he remembered where he was, where they were. He broke the kiss abruptly.

"I'm sorry," he said.

What had come over him?

Maggie's wide eyes narrowed, coming slowly back into focus. She averted her gaze and said nothing. So much for taking care of her. His first act of holy matrimony was to paw at his wife.

CHAPTER SIXTEEN

Maggie had to concentrate hard not to press her fingertips to her lips. They still tingled, even an hour after Dylan had kissed her. Her first kiss.

It had been everything she'd dreamed and more. With a man who she never could have imagined would be hers. And he was hers now.

She was Mrs. Dylan Banks.

The problem was that being Mrs. Dylan Banks felt very much like being Ms. Maggie Shaw. She and Dylan sat at their reception, which was dinner laid out in the ranch's equivalent of a mess hall. There was a store bought cake beside a heap of barbecue fare and grilled meat. The soldiers were having a grand time, laughing and clapping each other on the back, as well as clapping Dylan on the back.

Just about every one of the guys had come up to her and congratulated her and shared some funny story about Dylan. Even Sean, the most secluded soldier came over. Sean only gave her his good side when he spoke to her, but it was something. The only person that hadn't come up to her was her new husband.

Dylan stood at the grill turning hamburger patties until Reed shooed him away. Then he checked for more plates until Fran showed up with a stack. Dylan was the first to rise when someone asked for something else, anything else. And each time, everyone would shoo him down or away from the chore.

Finally, Maggie decided that she needed something that only her new husband could give her. She got up and went over to Dylan. When he saw her coming she detected a sense of wariness in his eyes.

Her steps faltered. He rose and took the last few toward her. He reached out his hand as though to bring her close. At the last second, he snatched it back.

"Did you need something?" Dylan asked. His voice wasn't gruff, but there was a note of hesitancy.

Was he regretting this? Their marriage? It hadn't even been twenty-four hours. She'd been passed over so many times in her life. Left abandoned and disappointed. He'd promised her that was over. Now it was time for him to make good on that promise.

"I was hoping we could have our first dance as husband and wife?" she said.

She watched him swallow. His throat working over words. His eyes darted here and there, likely searching for an escape.

"I know this isn't a traditional marriage, but—"

"I can't." He swallowed again even harder this time. "Dance, I mean."

Maggie looked down at his covered leg. She felt her face redden. "Oh. I'm sorry. I should've realized ..."

"I'll do it."

Maggie turned to face Xavier. The dark-haired man held out his hand to her. She turned back to Dylan. Her husband's jaw was clenched, but he nodded his permission.

Trying not to appear defeated, Maggie took Xavier's hand and allowed him to twirl her onto the makeshift dance floor which was just a patch of dirt in the picnic area. Xavier whirled and twirled her for one song.

Xavier was replaced by Reed who whirled and twirled her with his steel arm. Fran and Sean lined up beside her to do a coordinated dance. Before she knew it, she was laughing, breathless, and having the best time of her life.

The men surrounded her, accepting her like she was one of them. The dogs nipped at their heels getting in on the fun. It was what Maggie had always dreamed of; she was being welcomed into a group, a clique, a unit as one of them.

Still, every few beats Maggie snuck a peek at Dylan. His eyes never left her. He also never moved closer. Until the moment he was standing in front of her.

The music slowed and the others moved away. Maggie was about to beg off the next dance as well to catch her breath. But with Dylan standing before her, his hand outstretched, her heart sped and her breath quickened.

"We're supposed to have the first dance as husband and wife. I don't want to buck tradition," he said. "We'll take it slow, okay?"

Maggie took his hand and slipped into the circle of his embrace. For the first time in her lonely life, she understood the meaning of the word home. They barely moved, only swayed to the beat.

It didn't matter if they took it slow or not. She had already arrived. She was already in love with this man. And she had a lifetime to wait for him to catch up with her.

CHAPTER SEVENTEEN

She felt good in his arms. She felt right. So good, so right that after the song ended, he didn't let her go.

When the music stopped, Dylan's hand slid up Maggie's back, tracing her spine. He followed the path of her shoulder blades and on down the span of her forearms until he found the back of her hands. One by one, each of his fingers entwined with hers until their digits were wrapped around each other.

Dylan felt warmth course through his body. The heat shot up his arm, it pooled in his chest and then spread down to his legs. Both of his legs.

A fever replaced the phantom ache in the leg he'd lost. It was a spark that insisted he could run again. It was a flare that swore he could fly.

Dylan looked down at Maggie. Somehow, they'd moved from the dance floor and were seated at the head of the main picnic table in front of the half-eaten wedding cake. Their clasped hands rested on the bench between them.

Maggie wasn't looking at him. She was feeding a bone to one of her dogs; Stevie, the overweight Rottweiler. He knew the Rottweiler couldn't see him. Still, Stevie's panting mouth split wide, as though he were smiling. His eyes sparkled as though to say, *welcome to my family*.

Dylan's gaze returned to Maggie. She still held his hand, but she leaned her chin on the other and looked across the table, smiling and laughing. His friends gathered around them at the table, regaling Maggie with embarrassing stories about him, asking her about her life.

That raging fire that had grown in Dylan now banked into a steady burn. The men who'd trusted him with their lives and their future had welcomed the woman he'd chosen for his life and future.

They'd accepted her and her dogs. They were all a unit now. Dylan knew that just as the men had each other's backs, they now had Maggie's.

"So you got any girlfriends you could hook me up with?" asked Reed.

Reed was one of the only men excited by the venture of holy matrimony. Dylan knew that Reed wanted a family and a wife to care for. Unlike himself and the other men, Reed was one to not let his very visible wound get in the way.

"I really don't have many girlfriends," said Maggie.

Somehow, Dylan knew that translated to she didn't have *any* girlfriends. Maggie had moved through life alone. At the worst times, she'd been used and abused by the system. That life was over.

"I spend most of my time with animals," she said.

"Then you'll fit in perfectly here," said Fran.

Maggie blushed, but her smile said everything. She was overwhelmed by their acceptance, and he could tell that she was grateful for it. Dylan didn't know where he'd be without these guys. They'd saved his life. That's why he was fighting for theirs. And now that Maggie had taken his hand, they'd all be safe. They could keep this haven they'd found and make it their permanent home.

The sun was setting on this momentous day. Maggie turned to him, and it was as though she were gasoline pulling the flames of the fire inside him high enough to touch the sun. But when she stifled a yawn, the blaze once again cooled. Dylan leaped into protector mode.

"All right guys," he said. "I'm going to take my wife home."

The men made simpering sounds and kissing noises like grade schoolers. Dylan rolled his eyes. He almost opened his mouth to deny what the men were thinking, but then he looked down at Maggie.

Her blush was near crimson now. She knew this wasn't to be a physical marriage. Still, Dylan was certain he caught a spark of desire in her eyes. That's what killed the words on his lips.

Would he never have a physical relationship again in his life? Well, he was married now. So his only option would be with Maggie. He would never dream, never think to go outside of his marriage. But could he possibly perform his duty inside his marriage?

He stood awkwardly. His leg aching from all the activity of the day. He had his answer.

Maggie saw it. He knew she did by the sudden tension in her hand, which he still held. By the quick averting of her gaze.

She said nothing. Instead, she turned and thanked everyone for all they'd done for her special day. Her sincerity rang loud and clear in her words and tone. She bid them all a good night. Then, with a signal to her dogs, she and Dylan headed back to their home.

They walked side by side, slowly. Their fingers were still entwined. Dylan couldn't think of a single thing to say to her, his wife. All he could concentrate on was the feel of her fingers, the brush of her forearm against his.

He thought back to the desire he'd seen in her eyes. And then that kiss that went on longer than he'd planned. That kiss that she hadn't pulled away from. That kiss that which, if he looked at the way her fingertips touched her lips, he had to assume she wanted to continue.

Maggie had wanted to dance with him. She hadn't let go of his hand. She leaned against him now. Maybe this marriage could be more than convenient? Maybe it could be something real?

But then her leg brushed against his, and he froze. He couldn't feel the flesh of her thigh as he felt her fingers and her arm. His prosthetic could feel nothing. Dylan looked down to make sure his pants leg covered the evidence. Seeing that it did, he disentangled his fingers from hers.

They were at the front door of their home. The door was unlocked as always. They had nothing and no one to fear on the ranch.

He opened the door for her. She hesitated, looking down at the threshold. Then she gave herself a chiding shake before stepping over the threshold and into the house.

The dogs marched in behind them. Four of them rushed to Maggie's bedroom door. One rushed to his. Only the two humans stood in the hall unsure which door to approach.

"It's been a long day," he said.

Maggie nodded, looking up at him. Her lips parted. Her tongue darted out and moistened her lower lip.

Dylan's gaze tracked the movement. His stomach grumbled. His mouth watered. His palms itched. He need only bend his head and he could take another taste of her. He straightened.

"I want to thank you for everything you've done for me and my men," he said. Even to him, his voice sounded formal.

"Of course," she said, just as stiffly. She closed her mouth and crossed her arms over her body.

"Sleep well, Maggie. I'll see you in the morning."

Before she could say anything else, or he could change his mind, Dylan opened his door. Spin rushed in before he shut it firmly closed. Dylan sagged against the frame. One thing he knew for sure was that he wanted Maggie. He wanted her in the way a man wanted a woman.

If he were honest with himself, he'd admit that it went beyond the physical. Maggie Shaw -now Maggie Banks- found a way into his system. The assault was mounting for an attack on his heart. If she got that far, all would be lost.

CHAPTER EIGHTEEN

Maggie hadn't slept well. She'd tossed and turned all night, moving from the right side of the bed to the left. She awoke sore, irritated, and confused.

On the one hand, Dylan had made it clear that this was a marriage of convenience for them both. Then he'd made pretty speeches about taking care of her every need and becoming her family.

On the other hand, he insisted there would be nothing physical between them. Then he kissed her senseless, got jealous anytime another man showed interest. He held her hand and held her close only to leave her at her bedroom door on their wedding night.

Maggie no longer knew which way was up and which way was down. She did know the way to Dylan's door. She got out of the bed and dressed for the day. Then she opened her door and, preceded by her furry army, she headed for his.

She knocked lightly at first. Then she knocked more firmly with insistence. Maggie had always been a good judge of character, of both animals and dogs. She didn't worry that he'd be upset with her. What she wanted from him was emotion.

She was safe here with Dylan, with these men. More importantly, she had a shot at a real relationship, a real marriage. And she wasn't giving that up.

Dylan was a wounded animal. He'd agreed to some healing here on this ranch, but he needed more. His leg was under control, but there was a deeper, internal wound.

Maggie hadn't had a lot of experience with love for a man, but she was willing to try. God, she wanted to try. She just needed Dylan to get down from his high horse first.

She'd seen the way he'd looked at her last night before turning away at her bedroom door. He'd held her hand, rubbing at the webbing between her fingers as though he wanted to join with her at the root. And then there had been that kiss …

It had been her first kiss. It had been her only kiss. As first and only kisses went, it had been the stuff of dreams, the stuff of story-books. She wanted this story to come off the page. She wanted a shot at the reality.

Maggie knocked again on Dylan's door. The silence coming from the other end let her know he wasn't there. He'd run away from her again.

She trudged down the stairs, dogs following in her wake. Her empty stomach grumbled, demanded attention as her heart continued to ache. She went into the kitchen. On the stove was a stack of pancakes in a sea of fresh cut strawberries.

It was the sweetest, most thoughtful thing anyone had ever done for her. She shoved the pancakes in a Tupperware container and then stormed out of the house.

Indifference, she could handle. Ignoring, she understood. Being used, she was used to.

But this hot and cold, this sweet and then absent, she couldn't do that.

Maggie shut the dogs in the backyard, leaving their food outside and making sure they had plenty of water. Then she went in search of Dylan. She found him in the training arena.

She stopped in her tracks when she saw him struggling to get on his mount. He hefted himself up with this good leg. Then he had to reach over and bend his prosthetic leg to swing over the horse. The balancing act looked treacherous and her every instinct told her to go to him.

She spied Mark on the other side of the horse. Arms crossed, gaze diverted. But Maggie could tell that the man watched Dylan like a hawk ready to swoop in at any sign of danger.

Dylan made a miscalculation. He readjusted his leg. To do so, he had to lift his pants leg, and that's when he saw her.

His face turned horror-stricken. He yanked the material back over his exposed prosthetic. He swung that leg back over the horse and down to the ground. He landed with a nasty sounding thud and winced.

"What are you doing here?" he demanded when he rounded on her.

Maggie jerked back. Her lips parted in surprise at the vehemence in his voice. Her breath caught at the glare in his beautiful blue eyes.

Dylan's upper body caved in on itself. He shut his eyes in a wince and clenched his fist. When his gaze found hers again, he looked ashamed. But it wasn't enough.

Maggie steeled her spine and marched up to him. "I'm your wife. My place is wherever you are."

Dylan turned away from her, likely looking for his escape. Now she was the one who rounded on him.

"In sickness and in health, Dylan. That's what I promised you. I'm not going to shy away because you have an injury."

"I'm not one of your pets to fix, Maggie."

"No, we're partners. That was the deal. But you keep shutting me out. Let me help—"

She reached out her hand, but he yanked his arm away from her. He took an awkward step back with his prosthetic leg.

Maggie cradled her rejected palm in her hand. "Was this all you needed from me then? Just the marriage? You don't want me even as a helpmate?"

He sighed. His blue eyes finally found hers. They implored her to understand. But how could she when he didn't contradict her.

Maggie took a deep breath. The air was filled with the stench of horses and sweat. She nodded at Dylan. Then she turned and walked away.

Indifference, ignoring, and using she was used to. And it seemed it had come back to her again. What else could she conclude when she walked away? Dylan didn't call after her.

CHAPTER NINETEEN

ylan watched as Maggie walked away from him. Her retreat began as a slow march, that turned into a brisk walk, and finally a run. He couldn't catch up with her if he'd tried, not with his prosthetic. He'd only wind up hobbling after her, embarrassing himself even further. And so he stood still on stiff legs, watching his wife put distance between them because he'd hurt her.

Again.

Spin nosed at his pants leg. The dog looked between Dylan and Maggie's retreating form, then turned back to Dylan. Spin nosed at Dylan's leg again, pushing the fabric into the cold steel of his metal leg.

Spin cocked his head to the side in confusion. Then the dog let out a sigh, his little head shook left and right from the impact of the harsh air.

Over on the other side of the horse, Mark looked at Dylan with the same look of disappointment. "If you don't run after that woman, you're a complete idiot."

"I can't run after her." Dylan banged his thigh with a closed fist.

"If you truly believe that, then you don't deserve her, and you need to let her go." Mark turned and walked in the other direction.

Spin howled low, as though he were in pain. He looked again between Dylan and the door. When Dylan still didn't budge, the terrier turned and made his way after Maggie, hobbling along at a steady and awkward clip.

The dog had more bravery and gumption than the man. Spin had been trailing after Dylan since he first got here. But he showed his true allegiance now when he turned his back on Dylan.

When Dylan's parents and ex-fiancée had rejected him, they had turned their backs on him with a look of disgust. Maggie had just turned her back on him now. But the expression on her face hadn't been one of disgust. It hadn't even been one of pity. She'd been hurt and disappointed, but mostly hurt.

It had been a long time since Dylan had been in a position to hurt anyone. This last year that he'd been in recovery and rehabilitation, he'd been so busy supporting those around him. The moment someone had tried to care for him, to offer him support, and maybe even love, he'd pushed her away.

The thing was, Maggie hadn't left him because of his leg. She'd insisted it didn't bother her. She'd accepted him in spite of his injury. The reason she'd run from him wasn't because she was disgusted by his external wound. No, she'd become disgusted with him because of his internal wound, the wound he kept inflicting on her.

Dylan was so afraid of her rejection of him, that the moment she got close enough to hurt him, he pushed her away. No, he shoved her away. Hard.

But even worse, her absence only made him crave her more. So the second she was apart from him, he'd do something to bring her back close. Like, make her a stack of peace pancakes. God, he was a bastard.

"I just saw Maggie running out of here," Fran said as he came into the training area. "What the hell did you do?"

"Stay out of it. It's none of your business."

"Actually, it is my business. It's all of our business."

"We're not getting divorced, so the ranch is safe. I'll fix it."

"You can't think this is about that? You're not that dense."

Dylan didn't answer. He couldn't. He could see it wasn't just a business transaction for her. It was clear she wanted more. It was becoming evident that he did too. But it couldn't be.

"I've seen the way you are around her," Fran continued.

"But she hasn't seen me. Not the real me."

"Is this about your leg? Because you do realize you married a woman who heals animals that would be helpless without her."

Maggie hadn't balked once at the knowledge of his wound. But knowing it and seeing it were two different things.

"The reason this is my business," said Fran, "the reason this is all of our business, is because that woman is now our family. You don't fix this, you keep hurting her, and you'll have this entire unit to contend with."

There was a part of Dylan that wanted to high-five Fran for coming to Maggie's defense. But the shamed part of him kept his hands clenched in fists at his side.

"You have a woman who's opened her heart to you, who accepts you for who you are, but somehow that's not good enough?"

"That's not what it is."

"Then what?"

"*I'm* not good enough. I can't be the man she needs."

"But it looks to me like you're the man she wants."

Dylan closed his eyes. There was no argument he could forge against Fran's words. Still, he couldn't believe them.

Maggie had no angle. She had no agenda. She made no demands, except on his time and attention. Did he wish she'd come after his inheritance?

Money he could spare. Time he had. Attention he could give.

Maggie wanted a piece of his heart. The erratic beating he felt in his chest told him his heart wanted her back. It skipped a beat, making him think that he'd lost the organ, just as he'd lost his leg. He knew the only thing that would fill it.

It was only the phantom pain in his leg that held him back. His stump itched. Both of his legs itched. He itched to move toward her, to run to find her, to bring her to stand next to him.

Dylan began to move toward the exit before he was conscious.

Behind him, he heard Fran cheer, "Hoorah."

Dylan moved faster than he had in months, but it wasn't fast enough to reach her. He turned back into the training area. Fran was standing by holding the reins of the horse.

Dylan took the reins. He hefted himself up and onto the horse. Then he took Fran's hand to steady himself as he swung his straight leg over the horse.

"Don't screw it up this time," Fran called after Dylan as he took off at a gallop.

Dylan couldn't promise that. He'd seen the answers, but he'd been too afraid of the question. Now the only question that remained was was it too late?

CHAPTER TWENTY

There was so much land. Land as far as the eye could see. Maggie could run in any direction that she wanted. The problem was that she desperately wanted to go back in the direction she'd come.

She heard something behind her. Her heart pounded faster as her legs slowed. Had he come after her after all?

Looking over her shoulder she didn't see a big man. She saw nothing on the horizon. But the sound persisted. Looking down, she saw it, Spin wheeling furiously after her.

Maggie stopped. She went to the little dog so that he didn't have to run any farther.

The poor thing. He was panting. His wheelchair was about to come loose. It wasn't meant for running. But the terrier had come after her.

Maggie scooped him in her arms and squeezed him tight. He gave her cheek a number of licks, as though he were trying to soothe her. It was something. But it wasn't enough.

The only one who could soothe this ache was her husband. But he couldn't bring himself to reach out to her.

Maggie came to the gazebo where she'd been married just the day before. Many of the decorations were still hanging. She steered clear of those memories and headed to the pier. It was a short pier over-looking the small pond.

The water wasn't blue. It looked as though there was a lot of refuse in the waters. Maybe it was run off from somewhere? It was no matter, she wasn't going in. No matter how much she wanted to sink down into the abyss.

What had she gotten herself into?

Dylan's reaction to her just now had been worse than indifference. She knew he cared, but he had let his fear and his shame get in the way of what they could have. He was hurting, wounded, and she knew that she had what it took to heal him if only he'd let her.

But he wouldn't.

Maggie looked up at the sky. That was a mistake. The azure of the sky was the same blue of Dylan's eyes. Now, each time she looked up, she'd be reminded of him.

Everything she'd ever wanted in her life was here on this ranch. A group of people ready to accept her as one of their own. A place for her animals. A job helping other animals. And a man who was kind and considerate and strong. He just had this one flaw. He bolted and lashed out when she got too close to his injury.

Could she spend the rest of her life in the face of his flaw?

She had said for better or worse in her vows. The better was good. It was really good. Could she manage the worse?

She had to. She'd promised. She'd simply have to find more patience until he trusted her.

He wasn't like the other animals she'd worked with. He was a man. Those beasts were notoriously hard to train and control.

She wouldn't put this relationship down. She'd find a way to foster and make this marriage thrive. She wasn't a quitter. But, man, was she tired. She'd rest here a bit and then go back for the next round.

Maggie closed her eyes and let the healing rays of the sun seep into her skin. When she caught her breath and felt a bit more rejuve-nated, she gathered herself together and prepared herself to jump back into the fight. That's when she heard the splash.

She looked beside her to see that Spin was nowhere in sight. The waters of the pond rippled. Oh no. He'd fallen in.

But then he surfaced. His little nose spewing water, his paws swiping at the surface. Maggie leaned over the edge of the pier to grab him. He was too far.

Maggie had never learned to swim. But that didn't matter, not when a life was on the line. Spin's head dipped back below the water's surface. His legs paddled, but the wheelchair weighed him down. His head sunk below the surface again and resurfaced a second later.

Maggie scooted further out. She almost had him. Just one more inch … and she was in the water.

She was submerged before she'd even taken a breath. The water came at her from all sides. But in front of her was the dog. She reached her arms out and pulled Spin to her.

She kicked and punched, but the water still held her. They were going to die out here, on a ranch full of heroes, with no one coming to their rescue.

CHAPTER TWENTY-ONE

Dylan pushed the horse harder than he ever had in training. In pushing the horse, he pushed his wounded leg. The ache was very real this time. But he pulled on his training and sucked it up. The pain would be tenfold if he didn't get to Maggie in time before she left him for good.

He pulled the horse to a stop. Pausing to look around. The vastness of the ranch spread out before him. Which direction had she gone?

In the distance, he spied the gazebo where they had been married just the other day. She'd looked up at him with such trust, with such hope, and he'd dashed all of her dreams. He'd give anything to have her look up at him again like that.

The sound of splashing tore him from his reverie. Dylan turned to the pond beyond the gazebo. Those waters weren't the cleanest, definitely not safe for swimming. It was on their long list of repairs for the ranch, but because most of the men didn't like to show off parts of their body, a swimming hole wasn't a high priority.

There was another splash. Then a pitiful bark, followed by a strangled cry. Had one of Maggie's dogs fallen in the water? With their injuries, they might not be able to swim. Dylan took off toward the lake.

He arrived to see Spin's head coming up out of the water. The dog coughed and spurted, paddling his front legs but moving nowhere. It looked odd that the dog was raising up so high. Then he realized, it was Maggie raising the dog. She must have dived in to save the dog not concerning herself with her own safety and livelihood.

He knew the dog couldn't swim with the apparatus on its leg. How the dog came to be in the water, he had no idea. But Dylan knew the added weight would only let the dog sink. And sink he did when the hands holding him up slipped down in the water.

But why wasn't Maggie surfacing? Was she caught on something in the water? Couldn't she swim?

Dylan didn't wait to find out. He dismounted. Crashing to the ground, he felt the impact of his hard landing all the way up his stump, but it didn't compare to the pounding in his heart.

He moved faster than he knew he could down the short pier. Neither dog nor woman had surfaced again in over a minute. Was he too late? Too late to save her life? Too late to win her back?

Diving in that water, he knew the moisture would wreck his prosthetic. He also knew the waters could get into his stump and cause an infection. He didn't hesitate at the pier's edge. He leaped in.

Opening his eyes under the water, he saw nothing but bleakness and blackness. He kicked with his good leg, the prosthetic weighing him down.

He reached out his hands and felt nothing but more murky water. But he didn't give up. He couldn't give up. Not on Maggie.

She'd kept coming back to him, even after every time he'd pushed her away. When he'd tried to put distance between them, she'd step just a bit closer. She'd never felt she belonged anywhere or to anyone. He'd offered her a home and a family, but he'd put a door between them, he'd crossed his arms over his heart, he'd walked away from her.

No more. Not ever again.

Dylan reached out to her, determined to find her and pull her into the safety of his heart.

His hands met with fur. Then flesh. He grabbed them both to him and gave a powerful kick with his good leg. When he did, the prosthetic came off, freeing him to make his way up.

He felt lighter as he kicked them all to the surface. They broke the surface with a mighty gasp.

"Hold onto me," Dylan said when he'd taken air into his lungs.

"I can't let Spin go," said Maggie.

"One hand on Spin, one hand on me. I'll get us to the pier."

Maggie did as he instructed. He wrapped one arm around her and kicked with all his might to get them to safety.

Once they reached the pier, Maggie handed Spin onto the pier. The wheelchair had fallen from his small body. Only his two stumps remained. Spin collapsed in a sodden heap on the wood of the pier.

Dylan made sure Maggie's hands were braced on the pier. Then he boosted her up. The water weighed her down, and she made it clumsily onto the pier.

When it was Dylan's turn, he was dead tired. His limbs cried from exertion. But, with great effort, he hefted himself out of the water as well.

He collapsed on the pier, soaked and exposed. Not just his body, but his heart, his soul.

Dylan's and Maggie's gazes connected. Maggie looked him up and down. It took everything in him to hold still while she looked at his missing leg.

But he did it. He held still for her. No more hiding.

Her gaze slid over him, and then her hands followed. Her movements quick and efficient, not a caress or affectionate.

"Are you hurt?" she asked.

A laugh escaped Dylan. At first, it sounded like a cough as he freed a bit of pond water from his chest. Then the laughter rolled out of him like fresh waves. Of course, that would be her first concern.

"Yes," he said after he sobered. "I'm hurt."

Maggie's brows went up in alarm. Before she could move into

action, he caught her hands. He brought himself up to a sitting position so that he could look her in her eyes.

"I am a hurt and wounded creature," he said. "Not the kind to lash out, the kind to hide away so others won't see and pity him."

"I don't pity you," she said.

"No, you don't." He ran the backs of his fingers down the side of her face. He'd just come so close to losing her. If he hadn't have followed after her she might be dead. He brought her into his arms, holding her so close he felt her heart beating.

"I don't pity you," she said again. "I love you."

Dylan pulled back to peer into her face. What he saw sent a rush of emotion through him that was so powerful it nearly knocked him on his back.

"I know that wasn't part of the deal," she said, averting her gaze. "But I couldn't help it. Despite your stubbornness, and your infuriating need for independence and self-reliance, you have the biggest heart of any person I've ever met. You are so selfless in how you take care of others. I want to be the one to take care of you."

"Okay." It was the only word that he could get past his constricted throat. Just those two syllables.

"Okay?"

"I want that," he nodded. "I want all of that. I want you. I want all of you. Not just on paper. I've felt like half a man for so long, but you make me feel whole. I'm a whole man when I'm with you."

Maggie looked up at him and beamed. Her face was full of trust and hope. Dylan's heart lurched for her. And then he was pulling her close.

Their lips met under the sun's gentle rays. The water had chilled him, but the press of her lips to his warmed him through. He pulled her tighter into his embrace to offer her everything that he had to give.

"I love you, too," he said when they broke apart.

"You do?"

"I do."

She swallowed, choking back tears, but one escaped her right eye. "No one's ever said that to me before."

"I'll say it every day from now on." Dylan wiped the solitary tear away. When he did, another fell. "I'll say it so much you'll grow tired of hearing it."

"I don't think that's possible."

"Let's see."

He pulled her in for another kiss, but before their lips could meet they were both showered with a spray of water as Spin shook the excess water from his coat.

Maggie and Dylan laughed at the little dog's antics. Spin stood tall on his two front legs, entirely unconcerned and unfazed about his appearance. Maggie's hand fell away from Dylan's shoulder and landed on his stump.

He waited for instinct to kick in and cause him to jerk from her touch. That instinct never showed up. Instead, he covered her hand with his. Their fingers entwined as both their palms rested on the wound that no longer ached.

"We need to get you both back to the ranch and clean those wounds," Maggie said. "You both are at risk for infection."

Dylan scooped the dog into his arms. "This is one brave dog."

"He's the reason we're together. If I hadn't have saved his life, I wouldn't have lost my job and found my way here."

"Seems like this rescued dog, rescued us."

"Yeah," Maggie agreed, giving the terrier a little scratch behind the ears.

Then she looked up at Dylan. They both did. Spin with trust in his gaze. Maggie with love in hers. Maggie ran her hand down Dylan's face, and he melted into her touch. Spin settled between them as their lips met again.

EPILOGUE

Four little dogs nipped around Fran's heels as they all made their way from Dylan and Maggie's backyard to the front of the house. Fran walked slowly and carefully so as not to step on any tails or feet or prosthetics.

The dogs were all excited to see their masters returned from the hospital where Dylan had spent a few days to treat an infection he'd acquired after jumping into the pond to save Maggie and her little terrier, or the Little Terror as Fran had christened him. The little dog followed Fran everywhere in Dylan's absence.

The dog was clearly in need of a leader to suck up to. That could never be Fran. Fran didn't have time to lead anyone. He meant that as a literal statement. His days were numbered and everyone knew it.

Fran looked back in the yard, noting that the fifth dog had yet to make his way over. Sugar, the Golden Retriever, sat under the shade of a tree. The sleeping dog opened one eye and then gave a sigh as he slowly got to his feet and trudged over. The poor dog had diabetes, a manageable disease, but the dog needed insulin treatments, and he was constantly thirsty and sleepy. Fran made sure to give the dog an extra pat. He and the dog had formed a bit of a friendship since Sugar couldn't always keep up with his doggy siblings.

Fran understood not being able to keep up with the pack. When he was up on a horse, he wanted to push the great beast to gallop, but knew it wasn't the best thing for his own health condition. So he kept to a light canter at most on his rides, which never left him satisfied. Fran waited for Sugar to join him, then the two made their way out the back gate.

At the front of the house, Reed and Sean sat rocking in porch chairs. The dogs wound about their legs. Reed pulled the tiny Chihuahua, Soldier, who'd lost his front left arm, onto his lap. Sean gave Stevie, the partially blind dog, a scratch behind the ear. In the distance, they could see Maggie's truck make the turn into the ranch and begin down the long road toward the living quarters.

"You really gonna give up living on the ranch?" Reed asked Sean.

"Don't really have much choice," said Sean. "No woman will want to marry me with a mug like this."

"If you're fishing for a compliment, Jeffries, you won't find one here," said Reed.

"I'm serious," Sean rolled his eyes. He wasn't wearing his sunshades today as they were the only ones around him. The deep gashes on his face added to the frown he gave Reed. "I look like a monster."

"So, you're headed home?" asked Fran. He knew the answer to the question though.

Sean shook his head. "I'll figure something out. We still got two months before the new paperwork gets filed."

Fran had options. They just weren't any that he liked. He'd rather stay here with his friends and be surrounded by those that cared about him for his last days. However long they were. But he knew the shrapnel that lay dangerously close to his heart could move at any minute. How could he offer his heart to any woman under that threat?

The truck pulled to a stop in front of the home. Dylan stepped out of the truck, leaning on Maggie. He wore shorts, exposing his prosthetic leg.

"Aw man, Mags," moaned Reed. "You brought him back alive?"

"Sorry," she grinned. "It was unavoidable. The hospital was very eager to release him."

"What did he do?" asked Fran. He knew his friend wasn't the best patient.

"Let's just say, nurses don't respond well to commands," Maggie said.

"You will note that no one said I was wrong," Dylan grumbled as they came up the steps.

Dylan leaned down to Maggie's upturned face and planted a soft kiss at the corner of her mouth. The two gazed at each other as though no one was there. Until the dogs began to bark for attention.

Maggie and Dylan broke apart with a grin and looked down at their brood. Ears were scratched, heads were patted as they all made their way into the house.

"You guys coming in for dinner?" asked Maggie.

"Depends on who's cooking," said Reed.

"Hey!" She reached back and gave him a punch on his shoulder.

The punch elicited a chuckle from Reed. Dylan pointed to his chest to indicate that he'd be the one doing the cooking. They all loved Maggie. She was great as a healer and a friend, but cooking was not her strong suit.

Dogs and humans filed into the front door, full of energy and life. Fran kept step with Sugar who made slow progress up the stairs. Once on the porch, the dog needed to rest a moment before heading inside with the rest of his family.

So, Fran waited a few moments with the dog until they both caught their breath. Their illnesses might slow them down, but it wouldn't keep them from their goals. Sugar's goal was to get to the offering in his doggie dish and then pal around with his pack. Fran's goals were somewhat similar.

He wanted to break bread with his fellow soldiers. But more importantly, Fran wanted to make sure his pals were all situated on the ranch for as long as they wanted to remain. And that would mean Fran would have to find each of them a bride in two months.

If he was still on this earth after that, he could visit the ranch on weekends and holidays. He'd watch his friends flourish in this place that had given them all back their lives after combat had scarred them. But the ranch could only heal Fran so much.

With a sigh, Sugar got back to his feet and took the steps to cross the threshold into the house. Fran understood; being sick sucked. It kept you from the things you wanted most in life, the things you once dreamed of and now insisted you didn't want because they were out of your reach.

～

A good man like Fran,
who puts those he cares about before himself,
is destined to find a woman to heal his ravaged heart.
Watch him fall hopefully in love in
"Hand Over His Heart"
the second book in The Brides of Purple Heart Ranch!

HAND OVER HIS HEART

THE BRIDES OF PURPLE HEART RANCH
BOOK 2

CHAPTER ONE

Fran watched the blip on the monitor. It spiked high as though traversing the tallest peak and instantly fell low like a man with a failed parachute. Only to rise and do it again.

If that wasn't a metaphor for his life, he wouldn't know what was.

He watched the EKG monitor as his heart beat a few more times. The pulsing was strong, consistent. For now. But just as the doctor monitoring his heart knew, Fran knew that the beating could stop at any moment.

"Looks like there's no change, Corporal DeMonti." Dr. Nelson's voice was steady, monochromatic like the blipping on the screen he watched. He scribbled notes on a pad with a pencil, looking from one machine, to another, to his watch. Not once at Fran.

Fran was used to being overlooked by those who thought they were superior to him. As a Corporal in the U.S. Army, he'd striven to a higher rank. He'd been a heartbeat away from advancing to Sergeant. Until one mission went terribly wrong.

So, no, the doctor's lack of attentiveness didn't bother him. What did was the fact that the man wrote with a pencil instead of a pen. The graphite touching down on the page was impermanent to Fran. It could be wiped out with the pink eraser on the other end. Just as Fran's life could be wiped out with the wrong move. If the shrapnel that had lodged itself in his chest moved a few millimeters to the left and punctured his heart he would be erased from existence. Gone from the page of life.

"Unfortunately, it's still too dangerous to go in and remove it," said the doctor. He looked up and faced Fran finally. "All we can do is keep up with your therapy and pray."

It always shocked Fran when he heard a doctor prescribe prayer. He would think that most of the scientifically minded men and women would prefer the tangible instead of the spiritual. But he was often wrong. At least he was in the veteran's hospital. Many of the men and women here had been in and gotten out of situations that could only be attributed to a higher power. So, they didn't shy away from calling on the Lord when their minds couldn't solve a physical problem.

Fran knew full well that his best bet at life was the Lord. So, he had no problem taking the medicine prescribed. He just wished he knew the Lord's plan more clearly. Did He want Fran to come home to him soon? Or was his will to let Fran stay out and play for a while?

Fran preferred having a solid plan. But he also knew the old adage; Man plans and God laughs.

He didn't think God was laughing at him. He wouldn't allow himself to believe that the Creator would make such a cruel joke.

As Fran left the exam room, a few of the women in the halls smiled at him, trying to catch his eye. To the naked eye, Fran looked entirely healthy. He hadn't lost a limb or gained any visible scars, except on his chest. No, his wound was deep. Past the metal in his chest. This wound went down into his soul.

It was all his fault.

Fran and his squad had been doing work to improve the lives of women and children when it happened. The blast that put shrapnel in Fran's chest hadn't taken any lives. But it had taken away six livelihoods, plus the human bomber who'd sacrificed his life for a misguided calling.

For the survivors, their lives were forever changed. And just when they were all getting their lives back on track at the Bellflower Ranch, another bomb had exploded in their lives. No, this couldn't possibly be a joke. It was all too cruel.

Fran pulled out of the vet hospital and headed across town to the ranch. His heart swelled as he looked out at the scenery before him. Montana was simply beautiful.

Fran had grown up in New York City. His mountains had been skyscrapers. His fields had been asphalt. But there was nothing like seeing the beauty and majesty of nature rise up into the sky.

Afghanistan had had the same effect on him. In a place described as a desert, there had been rugged mountains and deep valleys. Snow topped the jagged peaks. The valleys were fertile for crops and livestock.

He'd been shocked to find beauty and bounty in a place portrayed as vile. But that portrait did not include everyone in its frame. The good people of the country tried to keep out of the picture. Very often, they were unsuccessful and the brush stroke of violence colored their lives.

Fran pulled up to the ranch. When his squad leader had purchased the ranch, the soldiers quickly renamed it The Purple Heart Ranch. The lush, violet leaves of a bellflower looked like the emblem of the same name. The Purple Heart was awarded to those who served in combat and were wounded by enemy hands. Each man in his squad had been wounded, and now that they'd come here to heal, they'd been dealt another blow.

Fran and the men of his squad had to get married in a matter of weeks if they all wanted to stay on the ranch that had begun to heal their wounds and had given them back their purposes. The problem was there weren't many women who would want to be shackled for life to a group of wounded warriors. Definitely not one who couldn't give his heart because it could stop beating at any moment.

So, Fran would need to leave the ranch soon. But not before he saw that the rest of the men were settled. Since he'd been responsible for them all losing a part of themselves, he owed them that much.

He'd make sure they'd all have the security they deserved. And who knew, maybe they'd even find love.

It was a nice dream. One he'd once had for himself. But it was one he knew he'd never have since his chest was a ticking time bomb.

CHAPTER TWO

Eva took a deep, steadying breath. Still, her fingers shook. She lifted the pen off the slip of paper, shook out her fingers, and tried again.

She did the math mentally in her head. She couldn't make a mistake writing the numerals and their corresponding amount in words. This was a big check. The biggest she'd ever written in her life.

After triple checking, and then triple checking again, she put the pen down. It rolled away from her, but she let it. She didn't need the ink any longer. The money was spent, and her account was now empty. But it was worth it.

She carefully tore the check from the book. It was check number one. She had never written one before. She'd always paid in cash. This was her first checking account that was used to write and not cash checks. And this was her first check.

She handed it over to the woman behind the counter. Her eyes were kind, and her smile patient. She looked over the check.

Eva held her breath. She couldn't have made a mistake. She couldn't afford another dime to be squeezed into that check.

"Everything looks good, my dear," said the woman.

Eva's shoulders visibly dropped at the confirmation.

"Here's your schedule." The admissions representative handed Eva a half sheet of paper with room numbers, class names, and professors printed in neat lines. "We'll see you on Monday, Ms. Lopez."

"Yes," Eva breathed "Yes, you will."

"Enjoy your classes, sweetheart."

"You, too. I mean, thank you. Enjoy your day."

Eva turned from the admissions window clutching the schedule to her chest. Behind her, the line of students aiming to register was long. They looked bored and tired. None had the excitement in their veins that she had. Likely because most of them had scholarships, or financial aid, or parents to pay for their education.

Not Eva. She'd earned every penny she'd just signed over to the school. It had taken her three years, but she'd done it. She'd saved enough for her first semester of college. Not online. She was going to an actual campus. And not a few community college classes. This was a state university.

She wasn't being a snob. Well, actually she was. For the first time in her life, she was part of the elite class. She just wished her parents could see her now. Somehow, she knew they were looking down on her and beaming with pride.

She'd done it. She'd made her dream come true. Her parents had told her from the first day of kindergarten; education was the key to her dreams. With schooling, anything was possible.

Eva didn't know exactly what she wanted to do with her education. She only knew that she wanted one. She loved being in school, sitting behind a desk while the teacher worked magic on a whiteboard.

These last three years since graduating from high school had been dreary. But soon, she'd be back behind a desk where she belonged. Then, anything was possible.

Eva hopped on the city bus and began the trek home. Home was beyond the nice neighborhoods surrounding the college. Home was beyond the trendy apartment complexes in the business district. Home was a rundown complex in the less than trendy part of town where people worked hourly wages that were often below the state minimum.

The bus didn't get close to her complex. It let Eva off at the church. She'd come to this church a few times in the past few months since she'd been living here. Wherever Eva moved, she always made sure to find a church. Even if she didn't know anyone, church was always home.

"Good afternoon, Ms. Lopez."

Eva turned at the sound of the older man's voice. A smile broke across her face. "Hello, Pastor Patel."

Eva went over and shook the man's hand. He brushed that away and gave her a hearty hug. Eva accepted it gratefully. Pastor Patel gave the kind of hugs her father used to give.

"I haven't seen you for a couple of weeks," Pastor Patel admonished her.

"I picked up a few extra shifts to earn money. But you'll see me now. I'll have more time on the weekends. I've done it. I've enrolled in college."

"Oh, my dear, I'm thrilled for you." He rubbed her shoulder affectionately like her mother always did. "Still, I wish you had taken the church funds."

Eva shook her head. In addition to the need for a good education, Eva's father had also impressed on her that they didn't take charity. They worked for everything that came to them. Give to the church and the less fortunate. For the rest, they relied on family. That was the Lopez way of life.

"Well, now that you're a college woman," said Pastor Patel, "you'll come and give a talk to the youth group tomorrow?"

Eva hesitated. She wasn't sure she had anything to teach anyone yet. She had trouble getting her own siblings to listen to her advice for life. She knew Pastor Patel wouldn't take no for an answer. So, she agreed. With one final hug, he let her go on her way.

Eva walked briskly down the street. It was evident why the bus didn't go into her neighborhood. There was glass on the street. Stench came from some alleys. Men lounged on the street corners in the afternoon before the end of the workday. One of those men was a little too short to be considered a man.

"Carlos," Eva called.

The boy didn't turn, but she knew he heard her.

Eva marched up to her brother. She stopped short of yanking up the pants sagging around his bottom. Where was the belt she'd bought him last month? He turned to her with wary eyes. The guys around him began to snicker.

"I was just hanging with my friends," he said.

"Well, it's time to come and do your homework."

The boys snickered some more.

"Go with your fine sister, little man. When you're done with that school work, I got some real work for you."

Eva cut the thug with her eyes. But the Evil Eye only worked on blood relations.

Carlos came with his sister. She knew she'd embarrassed him. But better those boys think he's a mama's boy or sister's boy. She'd ruin his reputation if it meant he'd be saved from the streets.

"Hanging on the streets won't get you anywhere," she said once they'd crossed the street.

"And school will? Look where it's got you." Carlos raised his hands to indicate the neighborhood. All she could see was various shades of brown, from the buildings to the dirt on the streets to the dirt on the kids' faces.

"This is going to change soon," said Eva. "A college degree is a way out of here. You'll see."

The problem was it would take at least two years to show him the truth of her logic. She just hoped she had that much time to prove her point. In the meantime, she would not let the streets claim her baby brother.

CHAPTER THREE

Fran parked his truck in front of his place. It was a four-bedroom bungalow nestled in the corner of the land. He'd set up shop here when he'd arrived. He'd been the first to arrive a year ago after they were all discharged. He'd assumed they'd all stay in there, but as the men came to the ranch still suffering from their pains, they each sought out their own space.

Dylan took the two-bedroom cottage next to Fran's. Reed, Sean, and Xavier each settled into the small row houses at the end of the road.

Fran looked up at the place he'd called home for a year. It was a comfortable home, but too big for him. He supposed one of the other guys would move in once they found their brides. Hell, maybe they'd even start families and fill the rooms.

That was yet another dream that Fran wouldn't see come to light. He couldn't fathom bringing a child into this world. Not when he wouldn't be around to care for him, to see her grow, or to leave his wife alone with all of his responsibilities. He wasn't built that way.

He'd have to start packing up soon. But not today. Today, he just needed to check on the other guys and make sure they were on track to matrimony which would secure their stays on the ranch.

The door to Dylan's house opened. Barks and yips spilled over the threshold before any humans did. The first over the threshold was Star, a pug with patches of skin missing from her back. The dog had a tendency to walk sideways, as though she didn't want others to see her imperfections.

On her tail was Stevie, a partially blind Rottweiler with a beautiful grayish-blue coat. The dog kept his nose close to Star to guide his way.

Sugar, the Golden Retriever, made slow work out of the door. His head perked up when he sensed Fran. Fran's spirit lightened at the sight of the dog. Dog and man made their way to each other. From all outer appearances, Sugar looked like a healthy dog. But the retriever had diabetes which slowed him down from time to time.

Fran bent down and gave the dog's head a good rub. The two had taken to each other the past few weeks the dogs had been there. Diabetes in dogs was rough, but not the end of the line. Maggie, Dylan's wife, took care of all her wounded dogs. Watching her had shown the soldiers that their wounds weren't impediments to love.

"You're back."

Fran looked up to find Dylan coming down the porch steps of his home. He held a dog in his arms. Spin, an Irish Terrier, had lost his hind legs a few weeks ago. Dylan put the dog down and attached a wheelchair apparatus to his hindquarters.

As Dylan straightened, Fran caught sight of the man's own prosthetic leg. It was an unusual sight. Dylan usually kept his legs covered with long pants to hide his injury. But since getting married and finding acceptance for who he was, he'd begun wearing shorts and cargo pants, letting his prosthetic shine.

"How'd it go?" Dylan asked. "What did the doctor say?"

Before Fran could answer, Maggie poked her head out of the door. All of the dogs turned to her, tails wagging and tongues lagging. Dylan turned to her as well. His tongue didn't fall out of his mouth, but his grin spread wide.

"Hon, don't forget Sugar's medicine when you go into town."

Dylan scooped his wife into his arms. He planted a kiss at the space between her cheek and her nose. Maggie smiled into the embrace. Her head turned and her gaze landed on Fran.

Fran had meant to look away, but his eyes soaked up the affection that he would likely never have for himself.

"Fran, you're back," said Maggie. "What did the doctor say? Is there any change?"

This was the other reason why Fran couldn't be in a relationship. Maggie wasn't even his partner, yet she had hope in her eyes. Hope that he'd miraculously be cured. It was an unlikely chance that would ever happen. He was lucky just to be alive.

Fran shook his head and braced himself for their compassion and goodwill efforts.

"I've got a lead on some specialists," said Dylan. "We'll go take a visit."

"I'll keep praying for you," said Maggie. "We're not giving up."

Sugar rubbed up against Fran's side. He leaned down and gave the dog his attention as his friends continued to try in vain to save his life.

"In the meantime," Dylan said, "you need to get looking for a bride. We're running out of time if we all want to stay on the ranch."

Fran hadn't bothered arguing. Dylan outranked him and would have no problem giving orders. Though this was an order Fran would not feel compelled to follow. So, instead, he nodded and changed the direction of the conversation.

"Reed said he was having success finding women through a dating app," he said.

"It's a crazy idea," said Dylan. "But desperate times, desperate measures. Right?"

"I'll catch you guys later." Fran turned to leave. Sugar trailed in his wake. Fran turned back to Maggie. "Is it okay if he tags along?"

"Of course," Maggie smiled. "Just don't let him get too excited. And watch that he doesn't eat anything he's not supposed to."

"I know the drill," Fran assured the dog's owner.

He and the dog took off down the path. The ranch sprawled out around them. He saw Xavier riding one of the therapy horses. The horses helped strengthen limbs lost, but just the feel of being atop a horse gave a man back his sense of power. Fran's day to ride was tomorrow. He wished he could go faster than a trot. But with his condition, he had to be careful.

Instead of riding hard, Fran spent a lot of his time in the gardens. Working the soil was good exercise for the body, but also the mind. Watching things grow under his care soothed his soul.

"Fran, wait up," Reed called out to him.

Reed came from the mess hall of the big house where they ate many of their meals together, even though each bungalow had its own kitchen. Reed waved a phone in his good hand. The sleeve of his shirt was rolled up and pinned to the shoulder of his shirt where the forearm had gone missing, left behind on a blast back in Afghanistan.

"Look at this." Reed shoved a cell phone in front of Fran's nose. "Fifty responses so far."

On the screen was a carousel of images of women. Doctor Patel had told them about the app. It was designed by one of the psychologist's relatives. Patel had a hand in the compatibility algorithm.

"Are these all women who want to meet you?" Fran asked.

"Not just meet me. They want to marry me. And we thought this would be hard." Reed cradled his phone in his palm, swiping left and right with his thumb. Not much slowed the man down or got the man down much less a missing limb.

"Marry you? Complete strangers want to marry you? Do they know about ... you know?"

Reed clicked over to his profile picture. It showed him clearly. He was in uniform with a missing arm. "Only thing a woman loves more than a man in a uniform? A wounded soul she thinks she can heal."

Fran sighed. Not because Reed was being a jerk. Fran knew the man expected to find his true love out of this ordeal. Reed was optimistic to a fault.

"This app matches compatibility to ninety-nine percent. If I can't find my life partner here, then she doesn't exist. I've narrowed it down to these five. This one has a ninety-eight percent match."

Reed held up a picture of a pretty woman. The photo was staged, like she was a model. She was blonde with light green eyes but a touch too much make-up for Fran's liking.

"She's practically perfect," he said. "I've invited her out for drinks this weekend. But she's out of town until the end of the month."

Fran wasn't sure what to say. He wasn't sure if Reed was off his list of soldiers to watch, or if he'd need to keep an even closer eye on the guy to ensure his future was truly set. Fran was determined that all of the men would be settled and able to stay on the ranch after he was gone. Maybe this arranged marriage thing was something, especially if everyone knew what they were getting into beforehand.

Reed continued on, telling Fran more of the woman's attributes. But Fran's attention was elsewhere. Sean Jeffries came down the steps of the medical offices. It was a converted barn they used for Dr. Patel and the nurses and other personnel who attended them and the therapy animals. Sean held the door open, making sure to turn his head so that only his good side was presented to those who came out.

Out came Ruhi Patel, Dr. Patel's daughter. Ruhi was a nurse and often came to help her father with the soldiers that lived on and visited the ranch for their care.

Ruhi and Patel chattered as they came down the steps. Sean looked down at the ground. But Fran saw him sneaking glances at Nurse Ruhi.

Fran sighed. He'd long suspected Sean had a thing for Ruhi. If he did, Sean wouldn't consent to finding a bride on a dating app. That would mean Sean would be leaving the ranch too.

Dr. Patel looked up, spotting the other men. He waved them over.

"I see you're using the app," Patel said to Reed.

"I have a date next week with a seventy-two percent match," said Reed, holding up his phone to showcase a brunette with a round face. Looked like he'd forgotten all about the ninety-eight percent model.

"I think it's criminal what they're forcing you all to do," said Ruhi. "Forcing you to marry to keep your home."

"I thought you believed in arranged marriage," said Reed.

"This is forced marriage. That's illegal."

"No one's forcing us," said Reed. "We don't have to if we don't want to. We can live somewhere else and come here for our treatment."

Sean looked away. Fran knew the man didn't have anywhere else to go which meant there was force in his situation. Fran didn't want to go either. He loved waking up on the ranch. But he didn't have a choice. His heart wouldn't let him stay.

"My father's been trying to match me since I was a teenager," said Ruhi. "I have no interest in arranged marriages. I don't think I ever want to get married. There's no need in this day and age."

The way Sean's throat worked told Fran that the guy was beyond liking Ruhi and was likely full blown in love. This would be a problem.

"What about you, Francisco?" asked Dr. Patel. "Are you in the market for a bride?"

"I can't give my heart away. It's broken."

He'd said it with a smile, hoping to get a laugh. No one did. They all knew his condition.

"It's a cliché, but they say love heals wounds," said Dr. Patel.

Fran wanted to say love couldn't move metal, but he held his tongue and nodded.

"If you're not ready for love, perhaps you can spend some time inspiring the next generation? It's Youth Day tomorrow at the church. I have a feeling your insights, especially your belief in a good education, could enlighten some young souls."

CHAPTER FOUR

$\mathcal{E}$va and Carlos climbed the steps to their apartment. It was a three flight walk up. On the ground floor, one of the neighbors had aluminum covering the holes of her screen doors. There were more patches of dirt than grass in what barely passed for a yard.

The heavy glass security door required a key to enter. But as always, it was propped open so that anyone could gain access. Eva didn't bother moving the box from propping up the doorway. She knew that as soon as the door closed shut, someone else would prop something else in the entry.

She climbed the steps with her brother in tow. Bugs skittered out of their way. Off in the corner, a rodent looked up at them as though annoyed that their footfalls had disturbed its peace.

They reached their door and Eva produced a set of keys. She set about unlocking the three sets of bolts before the door gave way, but only a little. The chain link was on.

"Rosalee," Eva called between the chain.

There was a rustling inside. Then the pad of socked feet on the worn wooden floors. Without socks, splinters were an issue.

Brown eyes appeared in the slit of the door. Then it closed. There was a rustle of chain and the door came open, but only wide enough to let the two bodies in. Then a slam and the clanking of all the locks being put back into place.

"You have a good day at school, Rosalee?"

Rosalee shrugged. Her skin was pale. She was lanky instead of plump from her inactivity. Eva knew her sister needed to get out more, or she wouldn't develop better social skills. But inside was safe, so she didn't argue much.

"Got an A on my science paper," said Rosalee, "but a B on my English paper. I'm revising it now to resubmit next week."

Eva nodded. Her sister believed in schoolwork to exclusion of going out and being sociable. Her brother preferred to spend his time outside rather than in the classroom. If she could just merge them together, she'd have the perfect kid.

Carlos went to the fridge. From here, Eva could see it was pretty bare. Things would be hard for a few weeks while she got settled in class. She should be hearing back from the student worker program soon. In the meantime, it would be Ramen every night for a while.

"Aunt Val is in her room with her boyfriend." Rosalee headed back to the room Eva shared with both her younger siblings in the cramped two-bedroom apartment.

Aunt Val had taken them in last year after Uncle Ricardo had his son come back to live with them. Before that, they'd stayed with some distant cousins, but that neighborhood was worse than this one, and Eva had quickly moved them out. Aunt Val's daughter had left the state with her boyfriend, and Eva had jumped on getting her room. Val had lived there for years, which meant there would be some stability.

Giggles and heavy breathing came from her aunt's closed door. Stability was a relative term. Her aunt had a revolving door of men coming and going, but she'd stayed put in that apartment for ten years. Eva just needed her to stay for two more years, and then she would be able to afford her own place with a college degree and job prospects.

All Eva needed was two years—three tops—before she had her

degree secured, a job in the career she chose and moved her family into their own three-bedroom home.

Eva went to the kitchen to prepare the Ramen just as her aunt's bedroom door opened. The burly boyfriend of the week spilled out. He gave Eva a once over that lingered a little too long. Eva kept her gaze averted. She didn't need any trouble with this man.

"Oh, Eva, you're back. I have great news."

Val was in her early forties, but she looked a bit older. She'd had a hard life, raising three kids and losing two of them to the streets.

"You'll never guess." Aunt Val held out her finger. There was a worn, faded-silver band on her fourth finger with a speck of a diamond. One gem was missing. "I'm getting married. Mike proposed. Can you believe it? At my age. I'm getting married."

Eva's hand stilled on the pot she'd just filled with water. "Wow. That's great." Though you couldn't tell from her tone. "So, Mike will be moving in here?"

Mike grimaced. "No. I'm taking my bride and moving her in with me."

Eva gulped. She turned a mutinous glare on her once stable aunt. "You're leaving?"

"Yes, but you can have the apartment all to yourself."

"I can't afford this apartment on my own."

Aunt Val frowned. "Sure you can. Your job pays enough for it."

"I quit, remember. I enrolled in college today. I put all my savings into tuition."

"So? You can do both. You'll figure it out. Oh, Eva. My dreams are coming true."

Her aunt's dreams might be coming true. But Eva's were now dashed. How was she going to pay for this apartment, put food on the table, and go to school? And with the semester starting next week, she couldn't get a refund. She was screwed.

Fran walked into the room inside the church. It was a Sunday school classroom but the boys and girls inside weren't toddlers. Though they sure were acting like infants.

Boys with sagging pants, even though they wore belts, sat on desks making overtures to young girls who wore more makeup than grown women and small shirts that were meant for five-year-olds.

They were out of their seats or half in their seats. The seats were not in lined up rows. One kid had his shoes unlaced as he swaggered amongst the crowd. The disorder gave Fran a headache.

Even worse, they were all talking over one another. One kid was blaring loud music from his earbuds. That couldn't be safe. This had to stop.

Fran took a deep breath and in his most commanding voice, called the madness to a halt. "Ah-ten-tion!"

All action ceased. All eyes went to him.

"Kindly take your seats."

All of the girls did as they were told, finding seats for their barely covered rumps. About half of the boys followed suit. A few hesitated. One defiantly stood his ground. It was the unlaced kid.

"Who are you to tell us what to do?" The kid swaggered up to

Fran. His pants sagged enough to show off his dingy underwear. He stopped short of coming within grasping distance.

Fran closed that distance with two long strides. "Corporal Francisco DeMonti. Are you in the right place, son?"

Though there was no verbal threat in his words, Fran made sure the menace in his voice was loud and clear. He knew he shouldn't get himself this worked up. But his heart rate hadn't increased for fear of this kid. It increased because he saw himself in this kid.

A little punk wanting to prove his manhood, but unsure how. Wanting to puff up his chest, but not having any hairs on his chest yet. Having an increasing ego that could be popped with the wrong prick.

Fran didn't want to deflate the kid. Just bring him down to the size he still needed to be. Not a little kid. Not a grown man. Just a young man.

"Because if you are in the right place," Fran said, "then you might be able to help me out."

The kid chewed at the side of his lip. Fran caught the flicker of relief in the kid's eyes that he wouldn't have to go toe to toe with this bigger man against whom he was obviously outmatched. But still, the kid held his ground, not backing down in the light of authority.

That was unlike Fran in his youth. When a recruiter had come to his high school, Fran recognized the command and took the direction. Not this kid.

"What do you need help with, sir?"

Fran peered over the unlaced kids head to another kid. That kid was notably smaller than the others. Fran couldn't tell if he was younger. There was a mature fire about the kid like those brown eyes had seen more of life than a kid should. But unlike the bigger kids, there was still a light in that kid's gaze.

"I'm supposed to give a speech in this room, but the chairs are out of order. I was hoping to make a circle so I could see everyone's faces and they could see mine. Do you think you could get everyone to make a circle for me?"

"Sure. I can do that."

Fran stood back while the kid got everyone up and out of their seats to form the circle. It wasn't a perfect circle, but it accomplished what he'd set out to do. With the attention off him, the unlaced kid slunk into a seat between other sagging butts. Once the brown-eyed kid was finished and everyone seated, he turned back to Fran.

"This good?"

"Yeah, this is great. Thanks for that …?" Fran held out his hand while he waited for the kid to offer up his name.

"Carlos."

"Thanks, Carlos. You've got some leadership skills. That's what I'm here to talk with you all about. Leadership."

Carlos took his seat and gave Fran his attention. The other kids followed suit. Most of them. Unlaced kept his gaze on his shoes.

"Life will eat you up alive if you don't have a plan," Fran began. "Even with a plan, you have to be alert. Don't do anything without honor. Honor brings you loyalty. Loyal people will follow you. I've heard there's been some gang activity in this neighborhood?"

Fran looked around. A few of the boys averted their gazes.

"Isn't a gang like the army?" said Unlaced. "They have a plan. You have to be loyal to get in."

Fran didn't immediately cut the boy off. He nodded, while he thought over the logic. "You make some good points. But dig deeper. What is the plan of the gang?"

"To get money," said another kid. "To protect the neighborhood."

Again, Fran nodded. "But who are the gang members getting money from? Usually, someone who is weaker."

The group of boys, who Fran now noted were wearing the same colors, had no come back for that.

"A real man, or woman, doesn't prey on the weak. In the military, we protect this whole country from those that would try to do us harm. We reach out and help our friends when they are being bullied. That brings honor. To ourselves, to our families, to our community, to our country."

"Are you here to get us to join the military?" asked Carlos.

Fran shrugged. "It's an option. I'm here to make sure you know the difference between someone having your back because of loyalty and someone standing behind you because they're using you."

Carlos's gaze went thoughtful. It was clear he was taking in Fran's words, mulling over their meaning. Meanwhile, the saggy gang huddled in on themselves, closing off anyone on the outside.

That was pretty much the end of Fran's big speech. After a brief silence, he took questions. All anyone wanted to know about was his time in duty, if he'd killed anyone, if he'd fired a gun.

Fran kept the conversation tame. He noted a few of the boys leaning in with keen interest. Carlos was one of those few.

When Fran's time was up, Carlos lingered behind as the others filed out to hear another presentation, or in the case of the gang of boys, leave. Fran's chest swelled with pride that he was able to get through to at least one kid.

"You know what you said in there was nice and all ..." Carlos began.

Fran frowned as he heard the telltale pause of an oncoming *but*.

"But what if the neighborhood you live in is bad?" said Carlos. "And you don't have the money to get out? The only way to keep your family safe just might be by being in a gang."

"There's always another way. Like education."

"You sound like my sister."

"Your sister sounds smart."

"Yeah, she is. But she's still stuck in that neighborhood, too. Her education hasn't gotten us anywhere good so far."

The struggle on the kid's face was clear to see. He wanted to believe, but reality was too harsh. A kid like him would be a prime candidate for the youth program that Fran and Dylan wanted to start on the ranch. Plans on that program had stalled after the edict that everyone get hitched in order to stay. No time like the present to get it moving again.

"Look," Fran fished in his pocket for a card, "I want you to come out to this ranch. We're starting a program that I think you might be interested in."

The kid shook his head and stepped back from the card. "My family doesn't believe in charity. We work for what we get."

"It's not charity. It's work."

He perked up at that. "Paid work?"

Fran considered that for two seconds. They had the funds between Dylan's inheritance, government grants, and their own monthly pensions. Why not? If Carlos was old enough for a work permit. "Yeah, but there's training you have to go through first. You'll be working with animals. Interested?"

The kid shrugged and lowered his head, but not before Fran saw a light of interest in his eyes. Carlos pocketed the card and headed down the hall in the same direction the little gang had headed.

But Fran was undaunted. Minds didn't change in a matter of minutes. It took time. He'd gotten some of the kids interested in the military. One he was sure he'd corralled. He wanted to get more. He even considered going after the motley crew. He wanted to see the light burn in their eyes as well.

As soon as the thought took root, he dug it up. His leadership days were done. He wouldn't want to have anyone else's life in his hands for the rest of his life.

"It's a great deal of responsibility to have someone else's life in your hands. That's why you have to have a plan."

The voice came as though from an angel over his shoulder. It was soft, but strong and resonant at the same time. It stirred the hairs at the nape of his neck, urging him to turn and find it.

Fran turned, and there she was …

CHAPTER SIX

"It's a great deal of responsibility to have someone else's life in your hands. That's why you have to have a plan. Education is one of the best paths to a good life."

The words tasted bitter as they came out of Eva's mouth. It wasn't the first time she'd given that speech. It was part of her valedictorian speech back in high school, just three years ago.

And here she was giving it again. In the same slacks and blouse, no less. Nothing had changed about her life. Except for her living situation. That was the only thing that kept changing in her life. Since she was fourteen, there had been no stability in her home life. The only thing she clung to, the only thing that ever gave her anything in return, were her grades.

"Excelling in school, getting a good education, will open doors for you."

A's had opened doors. They got her sent on trips. They got her special privileges. They got her scholarships and awards. They got her recognition. But they couldn't get her family the stability they all required.

An A could get her invited to a fancy dinner, but it wouldn't put food on the table every night. An A could get her a fancy, all-expenses-paid trip, that she couldn't go on without her brother and sister.

"Education can lessen the challenges you'll face in life."

When Eva was a high school senior on the stage, the speech hadn't included qualifying words like *can* and *might*. She'd gone into her speech making full, declarative statements. Not any longer.

"Knowledge can lead to more opportunities that might enhance your personal life and could enhance your career."

She looked out at the book-smart girls, wondering how many would end up in dead-end jobs. How many would have to take out loans for their education, and then work to pay it back for the rest of their lives? Because that's the life she was looking at now. And that was only if she could get a loan.

She had no collateral. She didn't have bad credit. It was worse. She had no credit. It was unlikely anyone would loan her some advice. And she could only get half her money back from the college with classes starting in a couple of days.

She was screwed. But she didn't know what else to tell these kids. Go into a life of crime? No, that would end their lives sooner. Get married and depend on your spouse? And take a big step back in the women's movement.

She took a step back from the lectern in the small classroom. When she did, she spied someone in the doorway who wasn't a kid. He was definitely all man. And he was staring at her, gazing at her. Could he see she was a fraud?

Despite everything, she'd been through, and all of her setbacks, Eva knew that what she was telling these kids was the only solution, the only chance these kids had. And so she went on.

"Life doesn't always work out the way you plan," she said. "But what does? You can't give up because you will get knocked down. That's just one more check off the list of the wrong way to go. You'll get there eventually. If you just don't give up."

She'd told herself right then and there that she wouldn't give up. No matter how long it took, she'd get her degree. She'd get her family into a good financial and living situation. It was just going to take even longer than she'd planned. But it was her plan.

The end of her speech was met with polite applause. The kids got up and filed out of the room in haste. Eva preferred to think it was due to the snacks being served in the hall and not her lackluster speech. She pinched the bridge between her nose and forehead, then gathered her belongings, and made for the door. A broad chest blocked her path.

Eva looked up into the eyes of the man who'd been standing at the door. He gazed down at her with a smile. She felt that he saw right through her.

"I'm sorry," she said.

"What for?"

"What I said. I must've sounded like an idiot."

"I loved what you said."

"You loved it?"

"Yeah, your words. I agree with you. Education, having a plan, those are the keys to success."

"It didn't work for me," she admitted. "I got all A's. I got a full scholarship. But I wasn't able to go to school."

She had no idea why she was spilling her soul to this guy. Something about his face made her trust him, let her know that she was safe. Her gaze slid back down to his chest. She wondered what kind of hugs he gave. She bet they were strong and secure.

"What's holding you back?"

"Pardon?" She felt her cheeks flaming. Had he heard her thoughts?

"Why haven't you gone to college?"

"My parents died. My dad died in an accident. My mom died of cancer."

"I'm sorry."

"I have two younger siblings. I've had to take care of them. Couldn't do that while going to college at the same time. I know some people do it. But I had to work to pay the bills and put food on the table."

"There was no one else in your family to help?"

She took a deep breath, trying to determine how to keep this story short. She didn't want to go into it. He seemed to sense that. Something in his eyes, in his wry smile, told her that she didn't have to tell him anything. Which made her want to tell him everything.

"I didn't give up," she said. "I made a new plan. It was going to work. I was so close. But it fell apart."

"What's happened?"

"I have to drop out. Again. I had to give up my scholarship the first time because the relative I trusted to take care of my siblings didn't. I came home to work and care for them. I saved every penny I could over the last three years. I was ready to go back. But now the new relative we're staying with has let us down again. I already paid for the semester, and I can't get all of my money back. It's a mess."

The words all came out in a blubbering mush. Tears streamed down Eva's cheeks.

And then she was enveloped in a hug. A strong heartbeat next to her ear. It was the best hug of the century. Warm, fluffy in the center. Firm at the edges. And did she mention warm? She wanted to stay forever.

But she couldn't. This guy was a stranger, and she was blubbering all over him. Eva pulled herself together and away from him.

"It's okay." She was soothing him, more than she was soothing herself. "I have a new plan. Or at least I will. I just have to get my family straight first."

"You mean, Carlos."

"You know my brother."

He nodded, gazing directly into her eyes. Her breath caught as he held her there with only his eyes. He wasn't touching her any longer. Just looking at her without pity, only compassion and certainty.

"I want to help," he said. "There's a ranch for troubled kids—"

"My brother's not troubled."

"Not yet. He wants to do good, I see it in him. But he's eyeing the wrong path. This could help set him on the right path. I ..."

His words trailed away. His—she didn't even know his name. Whoever he was, his gaze was beyond her. Out the window.

Eva turned and saw a group of boys. She recognized them as members of the neighborhood gang. And standing in the midst of them, being shoved around, was her brother.

CHAPTER SEVEN

The scene out the window came slowly into focus. The group of boys encircling one didn't hold Fran's full attention at first. The woman encircled in his arms did.

She smelled of a gentle summer breeze mixed with a hint of soap and the spicy noodles he used to eat in college. He had the urge to put his nose just behind her ear and inhale. It had been so long since he'd held someone.

She was all soft curves and warm heat. She was small and vulnerable, but there was still a strength in the way her back didn't bend as she leaned into him.

When her head came to rest against his heart, it didn't skip a beat. It stopped. One second it thumped rhythmically. In the next, it stood still, as though sensing something big, something important. Not danger, but something life-altering just the same.

When it started up again, it went from zero to sixty. The pounding made Fran's breath catch, which in turn brought more of her scent into his nose.

Down her scent went, over his tongue, down his throat, past his heart, and into his gut. It rocked him back onto his heels. Her fingers clenched where they rested on his lower back. It brought her chest into his, which made his heart beat even faster.

This was not good for his wounded heart. He had to let this girl go. But how could he when she was in distress. If this hug helped her, it was the least he could do. Right?

He couldn't do anything about her unreliable family, or the tragic death of her parents. But he could do something about her brother. Which brought his attention back to the window where Carlos was being surrounded by the group of boys from the talk.

Fran went to tell Carlos's sister only to look down and find that she was no longer in his arms. She was already headed for the exit. Fran kicked himself into gear to go after her.

He caught up to her just as she pushed the church doors open and stepped outside.

"Oh, look, here comes your sister."

"Get away from him," she said.

The boys were all younger than her, but they all had at least a foot on her. Didn't appear to deter the little scholar. She marched right up to them with her head thrown back and her hands on her hips. It would've cowed Fran. Unfortunately, these boys weren't as smart as he was.

"Or what?" said the kid with the unlaced shoes. "This has nothing to do with you." The boy raised his hand and shoved the woman's shoulder.

But before the kid could make contact, or Fran could rip his arm off, Carlos was there, shoving the boy's hand aside. "Don't you dare put your hands on my sister."

"Or what? You ain't got nobody but women to protect you. You should've joined us when you had the chance."

Behind the boys, someone cleared their throat. They all looked over to Fran. Fran towered over everyone before him.

"What are you gonna do, soldier boy?" But there was a tremor in the kid's voice.

"I'm going to ask real nice and hope that you have the brains to listen."

The kid snorted, showing he had no brains. "There's four of us and one of you."

"Yeah, pretty unfair odds."

Fran reached out and grabbed the boy's hand, the one that had almost touched the woman. With a flick of his wrist, Fran tweaked the boy's joint. The kid dropped like a sack to his knees. His eyes teared up.

Fran caught movement out of the corner of his eye. He turned to face the other three boys. They'd been moving in. They hesitated now. With the glare Fran gave them, they each took a step back.

"Apologize to the lady." Fran's voice was a low growl. His heartbeat was steady now. These punks he could handle. He would not countenance any of them harming a woman, especially this woman who'd felt like a sunbeam caught in his arms.

"What? Fu-ahhhhhh!"

Fran tweaked the kid's arm more, sending his chest into the ground while his arm stuck out at an unnatural angle behind his back. His boys made to move. Fran lifted a brow at them. That was all it took for them to back down.

"Sorry, sorry, Eva. Sorry," the boy sang like a canary.

Fran loosened his grip, not gently so that the pain would ebb. No, he let the joints crack. The kid crab walked his way to his friends. His eyes glowed with fear, but his chest rose and fell with sore pride. His gaze jerked from Fran and found Carlos.

"Watch your back, you little punk," the kid said as he scrambled to his feet.

Eva stepped in front of her brother, a menacing look on her pretty face. Fran's heart skipped at the sight of her fierceness.

"Why did you step in?" said Carlos, turning on his sister once they were gone. "Now everyone will think I'm a mama's boy."

"Would you have rather I let them push you around and beat you up?" Eva demanded.

"At least that would prove that I'm a man."

"No," said Fran. "That wouldn't prove you're a man. Standing up for your sister when that punk came at her proved it. The fact that they came at you in numbers proved they're not men at all."

"But you have a unit," said Carlos.

Fran nodded. "My brothers would have my back. But they'd stay at my back and keep out of it if the fight was fair. That was not a fair fight. There was no honor in those boys. You did good."

"Come on, Carlos, let's get home," said Eva. "The bus will be here soon."

"I can take you," said Fran. "My truck is just out front."

Eva looked him up and down. Just a moment ago he'd held her in his arms while she let her guard down. Now her shields were up.

"Please," he said. "I'd like to make sure you two got home safe. Those kids might still be lying in wait."

"They'll be lying in wait tomorrow," said Carlos. "Or the next day."

Eva's face contorted. Fran wanted to wipe the look away and soothe her worries. For now, he could offer them a ride home and offer to take Carlos under his wing at the ranch.

Eva went inside to get her things. Then they all piled into his truck. Carlos in the passenger seat, Eva in the back seat. Fran didn't like her so far out of his reach. But it was for the best.

He drove them about two miles down the road into a part of the town he hadn't been before. There was trash on the sidewalks. It was run down with men hanging on the street corners. The way their eyes followed his car reminded him of the locals in the war zone, hungry and desperate for a way out.

Eva remained quiet in the back seat. He could see the wheels turning over in her head. He wondered what plan she was making. He wanted to hear it out loud so that he could be a part of it.

When Fran pulled up to the building, Carlos hesitated in unlocking the door to let them out. The building looked worse for wear. Yet it was the best looking place on the block, and that wasn't saying much.

Carlos hopped out first. Fran went to the back door to hand Eva out. When he opened the door, she seemed surprised to see him there. Even more surprised at the offer of his hand.

"Thank you for the ride," she said.

"Name's Fran."

"I'm Eva. Thank you again, Fran. For your help back there. It was really nice to meet you, even under the circumstances."

"This isn't it." They both blinked at the vehemence in his voice. "I mean, I'd still love to have Carlos come out to the ranch for the program I was telling you about."

"We'll have to discuss it and—"

"Eva!"

They both turned to the sound of the high-pitched voice. A young girl who was the spitting image of Eva ran out of the glass doors.

"I'm so glad your home," said the girl through her trembling cries. "Someone was at the door. They knocked and knocked and wouldn't go away. They said they wanted Carlos to come out. Eva, I don't want to stay here anymore."

Eva looked around, helpless. Fran could see the crack in her countenance. His resolve was firm. It had taken the car ride for her to put herself back together, but this seemed the final straw.

"Go get your things," he said. "You're coming home with me."

CHAPTER EIGHT

There were times in her life when Eva planned every detail to the last dotted I and crossed T. She'd study the situation, make notes about all the possible answers, and then come to the best conclusion.

This was the first time she'd made a split second decision.

Eva raced up the three flights of stairs to the apartment with her siblings. They pulled out bags—trash bags, because they never could afford suitcases—and packed all of their belongings in under thirty minutes. There wasn't much to pack.

Over the years, they'd grown so accustomed to being shuffled around by their relatives that they had resorted to living out of garbage and duffel bags. They grabbed those bags now and shoved the few things they had in the small room they shared into the bellies of the bags.

A creak on the floorboards had Eva looking up. She grabbed the first weapon she could, which unfortunately happened to be a hairbrush. A gush of relief left her chest when she saw that it was Fran.

The sight of him made her feel safe and protected. She'd known the man for less than an hour. But already, he'd given her more comfort and offered to do more for her than her entire family.

First, with his protection of her and her brother back at the church. Then the ride just a few miles that they could've walked or caught the bus. And now he was offering them a place to stay the night.

Eva was sure this whole thing with the street thugs would cool down. Maybe? In a couple of days? Hopefully?

God, who was she kidding? This had been brewing since they'd moved in. She knew there was no way the streets would let Carlos go unscathed. She knew her sister would continue to retreat deeper into herself beyond just staying inside four walls. And she was supposed to work her fingers to the bone to afford it all? They couldn't stay there a second longer.

"You all stayed here?" asked Fran. "In this one bedroom?"

His face was part disbelief, part disgust, shaded with a whole lot of anger.

Eva became self-conscious. Had she been selfish all these years? Should she have put all of her money into getting them a better place to live instead of trying to save for college to make her dreams come true? Maybe she was no better than her aunt?

"Take everything," said Fran. "You're not coming back here. I have plenty of room at my place."

"Just for a night or two," Eva insisted.

He didn't answer. He took her bag from her, and then Rosalee's. Eva noted that Rosalee hadn't shied away from Fran like she had most people. What was it about this guy?

Fran preceded her family down the three flights and into his truck. He loaded up the back with their things, hopped inside, and pulled away from the apartment. In the rearview mirror, Eva saw the little thugs watching their retreat.

No, they couldn't go back there. She'd figure out a new plan.

They drove for what seemed like hours, but she knew was more like thirty minutes. Buildings gave way to mountains. Concrete gave way to rolling fields. The smell of industry and fast food gave way to brisk wind and cut grass.

Peering into the back seat, she saw Carlos staring out in wonder.

Rosalee had rolled down the window and was leaning her head out. Eva looked at the man beside her.

Fran's face had relaxed somewhat. His shoulders were still tense. He pumped the brakes as they pulled into a gate with a purple flower on the front. The gate opened and gave them access to a world out of a western movie.

"I've never done anything like this before," Eva confessed.

Fran turned to her, taking his eyes off the road for a moment. The second his gaze hit hers Eva felt something spark in her chest. She wondered if he felt it too? Was that the reason he jerked his gaze back to the road?

"Anything like what?" he asked.

"Hopping in a car with a strange man and spending the night with him."

"I'm not a strange man. I was invited to your church by Dr. Patel."

"Pastor Patel?"

Fran nodded. "He's a psychologist."

"Hmmm." Eva hesitated to ask her next questions.

"Yes, I am his patient."

She noted the smile in Fran's voice. But the smile slipped away with his next words.

"My entire squad is. We were all wounded in the service. Dr. Patel works on the ranch to help us."

"You have PTSD?" She tried to make her voice nonchalant and was certain she failed.

"In a manner of speaking."

"I'm so sorry if I'm offending you."

"You're not. You're a smart woman, and you're asking smart questions of the man you just ran off with to spend the night."

Eva gasped.

Fran chuckled as he made a turn.

His laugh was nice. She liked how it crinkled his face. She waited for any sign that she should run. None came. She knew she was entirely safe with this man.

"I have my demons," he said. "But they only come after me. I have never lashed out at an innocent before in my life. You're safe with me, Eva. I won't let anything happen to you or your brother and sister. You have my word."

With those words, she relaxed back into the seat of his truck.

If Eva had thought the drive up was lovely, the ranch that sprawled out before her was something out of a dream. There was green as far as the eye could see. Beyond that were mountains. What pavement there was clean and clear.

Fran parked the truck in front of a small ranch house. Eva had never lived in a house, not even when her parents were alive. They'd always lived in apartments, up off the ground floor, sharing rooms. She'd never had a yard. Across the way, a couple of dogs yipped in a neighboring yard.

The kids hopped out and greeted the dogs. No one was more surprised than Eva when Rosalee bent down to scratch at a little Chihuahua's head.

"They're all friendly," Fran assured her.

Eva hadn't thought the dogs posed a threat, especially the one in a wheelchair. She hadn't even fretted as the Rottweiler, a breed notoriously deemed vicious, trotted over to Fran. Its head was down as it made its way over followed by another dog, a Golden Retriever.

"Hey, Sugar," Fran bent over and patted the Retriever's head.

Eva had learned that dogs were the best judges of character, and each of these dogs vied for Fran's attention alongside yipping for pats on the head from her siblings. Yes, hopping in this stranger's truck, this was a good decision.

"I'm sorry my horde of beasts got let loose. They're all harmless."

Eva looked up to see a pretty brunette closing the door of the home next to Fran's. She had a wide smile. Eva hadn't had many girlfriends because she moved around so much, and she rarely wanted to bring anyone over for sleepovers or study group or tea. She didn't even drink tea. But this woman looked like she had people over for tea.

"Maggie, this is Eva," said Fran. "She and her siblings are coming to stay with me for a while."

Maggie took Eva's hand in hers. Her palm was warm and welcoming. She covered Eva's hand with her second palm. It was like a hug for her hands.

"I'm so happy to meet you. You'll come over for dinner tonight with me and my husband. It's just hot dogs and chicken tenders—"

"Hot dogs?" said Carlos.

"Chicken tenders?" said Rosalee.

"Eva, please?" They chimed in together.

"I don't want to impose," said Eva.

"No imposition at all," said Maggie. "I'd love to get to know you better, and I could use some help feeding the dogs if your brother and sister don't mind."

"We don't mind," said Rosalee.

Eva stared at her sister. Rosalee never invited herself over to others' houses. But there she was volunteering.

"Okay," said Eva.

CHAPTER NINE

This was a bad decision. What had he been thinking? The sight of Eva in his living room, amongst his things, had his heart going double time. This was not good for his health. Not just because the effect it was having on his heart. It was because of his heart that she couldn't stay.

He'd offered her a place to stay when this place wouldn't be his for much longer. Fran was living on borrowed time. He had no business promising any of that time to anyone, let alone someone like this family who had been abandoned and disappointed by so many in their lives.

"There are four bedrooms," said Rosalee.

Fran looked up into her bright eyes. When he'd first met the little girl, her eyes had been filled with fear. But now they sparkled with excitement, gratitude, and hope.

"Would I be allowed to sleep in one on my own?" she asked.

"Of course," Fran heard himself saying.

"Fran, that's too much," said Eva. "We don't want to put any of your roommates out."

"I don't have any roommates. It's just me. You each can stay in your own room. For as long as you like."

His tongue darted away from his teeth inside his mouth, escaping from being bitten and hushed. Maybe he could get his foot in there instead. But his feet were planted firmly on the ground as he watched Carlos and Rosalee disappear into separate bedrooms. The smiles on their faces were so big they trailed behind them.

"We won't be a bother," said Eva. "It'll just be for a couple of days. While I figure out what to do next."

"You can stay as long as you like. I want you to be safe."

He wanted to pull her back into his arms and hold her again. But she wasn't crying. She wasn't distraught. He'd made it all better just by opening his door to her.

From the corner of his eye, he saw Xavier and Sean headed toward his front door. An idea started forming in Fran's head. Perhaps he could make this stay forever for Eva and her siblings.

"Why don't you go and get settled?" he told her.

Eva nodded. Her sigh of relief visibly shook weight from her petite frame. She took her bag from him and headed for one of the two remaining bedrooms.

"That's my bedroom," said Fran.

"Oh," she blushed. "I'm so sorry." She side-stepped and disappeared into the last bedroom. The one next to his.

Fran's heartbeat had settled, but there was still a fluttering in his chest. He felt light-headed and hungry. Instead of going to the kitchen, Fran turned to the door as Xavier and Sean came up the steps. He shut the door behind him and faced his friends.

"Heard you brought a woman home," said Xavier. He was the playboy of the bunch. X went out to the bars every weekend and spent the night with a different girl.

Fran put his back to the man and turned to Sean.

"So, you changed your mind about a wife?" asked Sean

"No, no," said Fran. "She's not for me."

Xavier and Sean looked at each other.

"You know I can't …" Fran waved his hand in front of his heart which was still beating the same rhythm as when he'd held Eva in his arms. "But one of you could."

Sean took a step down off the porch. His eyes went wide like a steed about to be neutered. Sean hadn't lost a limb, only skin from his face that had hardened into tough scars. Because there was nothing wrong with his legs, Sean could easily outrun Fran with his heart condition.

The moment the words were out of Fran's mouth his heart did a funny little flip. It was a bit painful and he winced. "Eva and her family need a place to stay, and those kids need strong male figures in their lives."

"I told you," said Xavier. "I'm not getting married. I'll take this to court. We need to challenge this."

Sean remained quiet. He turned his scarred face away from them both.

"Eva's amazing," said Fran. "She's beautiful and smart—"

"So why don't you marry her?" said Xavier.

"I already told you—"

"Yeah-yeah, you think you're gonna die. We're all gonna die some-day. If you really think marriage would help this girl and her family, you should do it. That way, if you really die, which I doubt you'll do anytime soon, she won't have to put up with you for long."

Fran's heart stopped that flipping and settled like it liked the idea.

The door to the house opened and Carlos poked his head out. He saw Rosalee hang back in the living room. Fran wanted her to know that she was safe there. He wanted to take the girl to see the baby chickens. He wanted to teach Carlos to ride and to shoot. To show Rosalee that the world wasn't dangerous everywhere. To show Carlos what it meant to be a real man.

And he could help Eva make her plan. He could help her imple-ment it and be there to help her correct course if something veered her off. Fran thought about the closed door of the bedroom next to his. Once again his heart did a flip.

CHAPTER TEN

Eva ran her hand over the comforter on the bed. It looked as though it had never been slept in. The whole room looked unused but somehow cozy. She could sense Fran's presence there even though he said his room was next door. She placed her hand on the wall and was positive she felt it hum with his easy smile.

Eva jerked her hand away. What was she doing? What was she thinking?

She was staying in a stranger's house. In the bedroom right next to his. She was thinking she could feel his presence in the room, in the walls. Was she developing feelings for this guy?

She could not be developing feelings for this guy. She had two kids to take care of. An education to get. And a living situation to figure out.

The living situation might just be figured out. Fran had said they could stay as long as they'd like, which would help both the education situation and the kid care situation.

But no. The only kindness she'd ever depended on was that of her family.

And look where that had gotten her.

They would stay here a couple of nights. Two weeks tops. That would give her time to figure things out. Or at least to get a new job. They couldn't take advantage of Fran beyond that.

Eva reached for the door to her bedroom—his bedroom. The borrowed, temporary room. She turned the knob, pulled open the door, and walked right into a wall of chest.

Fran caught her when she stumbled. His arms came around her, embracing her and holding her steady.

"I was coming to check on you," he said.

"I was coming to …" She didn't know what she was going to say. She just didn't want to move out of his strong hold. But it was not her place. Fran let her go.

"Can we talk for a moment?" he asked.

Something in his tone made the goosebumps on her arms stand up. Had he changed his mind? Had the kids gotten into trouble?

She spied her siblings out the window in the driveway. Carlos played basketball with two men. Rosalee sat watching the game as she petted two dogs.

Eva trailed Fran into the living room. His movements were jerky. His hand rubbed at the back of his neck, lifting the short tendrils of hair at his nape until they stood up. He took the seat opposite from her. He was nervous. She could tell.

"Eva, there's a slight problem with you staying here."

She knew it. She knew it was all too good to be true. Nausea sent basketballs around in her belly that constantly missed the hoop.

"It was impulsive of me to ask you to stay."

"It's okay. We can go."

"No," he said, raising his hands up in a stop motion. "That's not what I'm saying. I want you here."

Relief flooded her. The balls in her belly stopped bouncing. But they didn't hold still. Something told her the game wasn't over.

"I want you all here. There's just a condition that I should've told you about before bringing you here."

"What condition?"

He wouldn't meet her gaze. He also stumbled over his words.

She'd only known him a couple of hours, but she knew instinctively that this was uncharacteristic behavior for him.

"The ranch was purchased as a rehabilitation facility for wounded veterans."

"I see. And I'm not a vet."

"That's not it. You don't have to be a vet to stay here. You have to be ..."

He took a deep breath. He lifted his head and met her gaze. But his words stalled as he bit at his lip and scratched at the fabric covering his chest.

"We've been here for a year, but the paperwork was slow to go through. We found a hiccup with the zoning."

Eva nodded encouragingly as he hesitated to get to the point.

"The zoning is for families only. You have to be a family to live here."

"I have a family," she said, certain she was missing something.

"Technically, you're single. And so am I. So are most of the guys living here, except Dylan. He and Maggie just got married."

"So, I'd have to be a married woman to live here?"

Fran nodded. "So do I. Be a married man, I mean. Otherwise, I'll have to leave soon."

"So, you're getting married?"

"Getting married would solve the problem. It would solve both our problems."

"Marriage?"

Fran nodded.

She was still missing something ... Wait? "You're asking *me* to marry *you*."

"It would solve the problem," he repeated.

Eva checked her pulse. It wasn't racing. Just like it hadn't raced when she'd hopped in the truck with Fran and let him drive her away. He'd just asked her to marry him, and she was calm. A life with Fran didn't scare her in the least.

"So you want to get married now and get divorced later?" The thought of marriage hadn't kicked up her heartbeat. It sounded like the most natural thing in the world. The thought of divorcing Fran, however, made her stomach burn and left a bitter taste in her mouth.

"No, no need to get divorced."

So, he wanted to be with her forever? Now her heart did flip and flop. She had never been one for fairy tales or knights and castles. But Fran had just whisked her off in storybook fashion. Now he was throwing in a happily-ever-after.

"I won't be here long," he said.

"You're leaving?"

He hesitated. "Yes, in a manner of speaking. I'm dying."

He held his tongue, waiting for her to digest that pronouncement. She had to have heard him wrong. He couldn't have said what she thought he'd said.

"Dying?"

Fran slipped a button of his shirt open. Eva's emotions were already all over the place with his kindness in providing her family a safe haven, then with his proposal of marriage, and now he was showing her the goods so to speak. But the goods were a series of scars on his chest where his heart would rest.

"I have shrapnel in my chest," he said. "It's inoperable. The metal fragments could shift at any moment in the wrong direction and kill me."

Eva stared at him, at those eyes that hid nothing from her and made her feel safe. He was telling her that someday soon she wouldn't be able to look into those eyes. She'd rested her head on his chest. But someday soon she wouldn't be able to come into his arms and feel safe, because he'd be gone.

"The zoning of this land requires that only families live on the ranch. I have until next month, and then I'll need to leave. If we married, I could spend the rest of my days here with my squad, and you and your family could live here indefinitely."

Eva ran his words through her head again and then again.

"You could go to school and not worry about finding a place to stay. Your brother and sister would be safe and surrounded by people who would look out for them, especially Carlos. He'd have half a dozen male role models that would lead him down the straight path. Rosalee would feel safe coming outside. And you, you could finally have your dream of going to college and finishing that plan you started."

It was a dream. She was in a dream. This all had to be some cruel, wonderful, sick, delightful, twisted dream.

"But what about you?" she asked. "What if you live long, you'd be stuck with us."

Fran shrugged. "It's been a good day, so far."

But Eva didn't laugh, she couldn't.

"I could make it another year, maybe two. If I go on living any longer, I wouldn't contest a divorce … if you wanted one."

"I wouldn't … I mean, I wouldn't abandon you."

"So, is that a yes?"

CHAPTER ELEVEN

Fran stood at the railing as he watched Sean help Rosalee mount Bailey, a gentle mare. He hadn't missed Rosalee's smile or the fact that Sean gave her his scarred side. Stevie, the nearly blind Rottweiler sat quietly in the field. None of Maggie's dogs had any fear of the horses.

Star, the Pug with patches missing from her skin, trotted close to Carlos's heel as Carlos and Xavier led another horse out to pasture.

The kids had fallen in with ranch life like they'd been born to it. They'd spent all day Saturday running about like wild creatures amongst the farm animals. They hadn't hesitated to lend a hand with any chore asked of them. At dinner last night, they'd attacked Maggie's grade-school fare of chicken nuggets and hot dogs with a gusto and then surprised all the adults by offering to do the dishes and take out the dogs.

Eva had been mostly quiet through the whole affair. Fran had caught her sneaking glances at him every now and again. The moment his gaze met hers, she'd turn away.

She still hadn't given him an answer to his proposal. He told himself to be patient, it had been less than forty-eight hours that he'd asked. About the same amount of time since he'd met her.

She'd asked for time to think about it. And he'd given her her space. But he was aching for a bit of claustrophobia. She'd hung back with Maggie today. He itched to know what the two were talking about.

Fran knew the plan of marriage was the best plan for all involved. He would not let them go back to that neighborhood or that dismal apartment. He'd heard their family motto of no charity.

This wasn't charity. It was common sense. He just hoped she would put aside her pride and see it too.

"What's crawled up your butt?" said Reed.

"I asked Eva to marry me yesterday."

Reed hadn't seemed surprised, likely because he already knew. Fran had told Dylan, and he was sure Dylan had told Maggie, or Eva had told Maggie. But that was all it took on the ranch. Once one person knew your business, everyone knew it. So there was no sense in hiding it.

"She'll say yes," said Reed. "You think she'd pass up on all this." Reed spread his arms, his fleshy one as well as his prosthetic one, around the ranch.

"She's not some gold digger."

"This place isn't filled with gold, DeMonti. It was a joke."

But Fran was too grumpy for humor. He just wanted to know she'd be safe.

Reed stared at him. "You like this girl, don't you? Otherwise, I'd be able to make a comment about her without you jumping down my throat."

"I just … want to help."

Reed nodded. "Like you said the other day, she's a smart girl. She loves her family and will do what's best for them. So clearly, she'll pass you over and choose me. Kidding."

Reed held up his hand when Fran glared at him. Fran's heart pounded in his chest at the thought of Eva and Reed, or Eva and anyone else. Which was selfish of him. He wouldn't be around forever, and she'd need to move on after he was gone. Still, the thought made his shoulders cave in. Fran gripped his chest at the shock of pain.

"You good?" asked Reed coming over to him.

"Yeah," Fran said taking a deep breath. "It's over now."

Every once in a while, the shrapnel in his chest reminded him of its presence. Luckily, this time it was a reminder and not a last call. Fran wanted to make it official between him and Eva before his curtain came down. That way she'd be protected for the rest of her life.

"Uncle Fran, look! I'm riding."

Fran looked up at Rosalee on the horse. He plastered a smile on his face and waved at the girl. Both she and her brother had taken to calling all of the soldiers *uncle*. The sight of little Rosalee smiling made his heart ache a bit more. He wanted to teach her so many things, watch her grow in confidence. Even if Eva said no, he'd figure out a way to keep them all safe.

"Hey, Uncle Reed." Carlos came up to them. He extended his hand and gave Reed a complicated handshake that the two of them made up at some point yesterday.

Neither of the kids balked at the injuries each of the soldiers faced. They didn't know what Fran's injury was, just that he had one. But they hadn't asked, and Fran wasn't inclined to tell them. He didn't want to scare them.

"Uncle Fran, can I go with Uncle Xavier down to the pond? He said I needed to ask your permission."

Fran hesitated. He should consult Eva about this. Yeah, … he should consult Eva about this. He should go and find her and make sure it was fine with her.

"You go on," said Fran. "I'll let your sister know where you are. But mind everything Xavier tells you. Do I have your word?"

"You have my word." Carlos loved giving his word. His chest puffed out every time one of the soldiers asked him for it. Then the kid strove to do all he could to keep that word.

Fran knew he'd grow into a fine young man. He'd give the kid all the time he could to help him on that trajectory. But for now, he'd go and talk with his sister about their immediate future.

CHAPTER TWELVE

"*You* married him within a week of knowing him?"

Maggie nodded. Her eyes getting that glazed faraway look of someone deeply in love. The two women sat at Eva's kitchen table.

Well, no. It was Fran's kitchen table. Though serving Maggie a glass of lemonade made Eva feel like the mistress of the house.

She'd found things easily in the cupboards. She'd likely have to attribute that to Fran. His organization system made sense. Cups over the sink. Plates over the stove. Silverware in the drawer next to the stove.

When Maggie had asked to come over after dinner the other night, Eva had cut up fresh lemons and put them in filtered water with some sugar. She'd rarely had fresh lemonade. The fresh lemons themselves were usually more expensive than the cheap bottled, store-brand gallons. Fran even had some mint that she tossed in the mixture.

He'd given her free reign of the kitchen and the fridge. That morning before he and the kids left, she'd made a huge breakfast. Pancakes, eggs, sausage, and a fresh fruit salad. She hadn't eaten like that since her parents had still been with them.

She'd worried it had been too much. The look on Fran's face when he'd seen the fare told her it was perfect. He vocalized his appreciation around mouthfuls of food as he chatted with her siblings about their plans for the day. Eva had begged off, telling them she had some thinking to do.

Fran had given her a meaningful look when she'd said that. She still hadn't given him an answer to his marriage proposal. She wasn't sure what held her back? Nothing did. She only knew that something should.

"So, it was love at first sight?" she asked Maggie.

"It was something at first sight. I don't know if I'd call it love, but love came quickly. The first time I saw Dylan, I knew he was someone I could trust, someone who'd keep me and my dogs safe."

Eva had felt the same way about Fran. She'd felt safe in his arms. She'd known he would keep her and her siblings safe. The thought of a lifetime of safety sounded good to her.

"You know, he's ... not in the best of health?" said Maggie.

There was that. "Is it as dire as he says? There's no hope?"

Maggie shrugged. "After the month I've had, I believe in miracles. What I do know for sure is that Fran is one of the best of them. All these guys are. I saw the way he looks at you."

That piqued Eva's attention. Fran had been looking at her? She'd felt something between them, but she had such little experience with men she wasn't sure if she was reading it right.

"I haven't known him long, but I saw that same look in Dylan's eyes when he proposed to me."

"You don't think it's crazy that I'm even considering this? Well, of course, you don't. You married quickly. The funny thing is we met at the church while I was giving a talk about preparing for the future."

"Let me guess," said Maggie. "Pastor Patel asked you to speak?"

"Yes, he did. Do you know him?"

"I know him, all right." Maggie grinned, her gaze softening once more. But it was how Eva used to look at her father.

"Right, Fran said he works here with the soldiers."

"Hmmm." Maggie's eyes reflected the light of mischief. "You could call it that."

"I want to get married. I want my education too. But getting married for a place to live, I don't know?"

"It's more than a place to live. It's a family. This land belongs to Dylan now. It'll take him some time to get the zoning changed so anyone can live here. In the meantime, no matter what, or when, you'd have a place here. You and your family would have people who have your back here, whether you wanted us to or not."

The tone of Maggie's voice sounded as if she was trying to sound threatening but failed. Her words sounded like heaven to Eva. A knock sounded at the back door. When they turned, Fran poked his head in.

"You don't have to knock on your own door," said Eva.

"I didn't want to interrupt," he said coming inside. His gaze fastened on her, and she felt her cheeks heat.

"I was just about to head out," said Maggie. She gave Eva a squeeze. "See you at dinner in the hall tonight, okay?"

Eva let go of Maggie's friendly embrace and turned to Fran. They were alone. Though he stood apart from her, she felt the heat from him. Just being close to him made her body settle like feet sinking into the sand, or better yet, a seed settling into rich soil.

"I'm not here to pressure you about that question I asked you the other day," he said.

Was that disappointment she felt sinking in her chest?

"You can take your time on that," he said.

"I thought we didn't have much time."

"We'll make time. It's a big decision, and I want you to be sure. I just came to tell you that Carlos …"

Whatever Fran said afterward trailed off like the volume slowly being turned down on a television set. Eva watched his lips move. The hum of his deep voice felt good as it traveled through her eardrums and into her head. For someone so level-headed, Fran made her feel dizzy.

She snapped back to attention when silence filled the room. He was waiting for her response. Patient as always. Like a tree that had been there for centuries, strong and solid.

"Yes," she said.

"So, it's okay that Carlos goes fishing at the pond?"

"What?"

"Carlos. I told him it was okay, but I wanted to double check with you. If it's not okay, I'll go get him."

"It's fine. I trust you and all of the guys here. That's not what I was saying yes to."

She heard his breath catch. Fran's gaze locked on her. She felt like a target, and he was a heat-seeking missile.

He took a step toward her. "What were you saying yes to?"

Eva swallowed. She was certain, but that hadn't stopped her hands from shaking and her heart from going a mile a minute.

"Yes," she repeated. "Yes, I'll marry you."

They stood, gazing at each other from across the room. Eva wanted to run to him, to envelope herself in his arms and stay. But she held still, unsure of exactly what to do.

"I'll take care of everything," he said.

Eva was pretty sure that those were the sexiest words a man could ever say to a woman. "I trust you."

His grin spread as though those were the sexiest words a woman could ever say to a man.

"Of course, our marriage will be platonic."

Eva blinked. She cocked her head to the side to shake the words into a comprehensible order. No matter the arrangement, the meaning came out the same.

"I wouldn't ask that of you."

"Right," she said in a halfhearted, tepid tone. "Of course not."

The thought of sex hadn't entered her mind. But she doubted it was far from her mind. Hearing that it was off the table? Well, it hadn't exactly thrilled her.

She supposed it made sense. They'd just met. And he was dying. And this was a marriage of convenience. They weren't in love.

Still, her heart thumped an erratic rhythm at what she would not be offered on the plate.

CHAPTER THIRTEEN

"*W*as it love at first sight?" asked Rosalee.

Fran looked down at his bride's little sister. Rosalee stood at the gazebo with Fran in the late afternoon sun. She was dressed in a new dress that he'd bought for her.

Fran had seen the girl eyeing the dress that morning as they went to grab a few essentials for the ceremony. Eva had turned over the price tag and pinched her lips together. Fran hadn't even looked at the tag, but grabbed the dress from the rack and put it in the cart.

Before Eva could protest, he'd said the words that had shut her mouth when he'd purchased their rings and a small bouquet of flowers. "We're family now."

And just like that, the words stopped her protest. He realized he could get away with a lot with those three words. But they didn't suffice in answer to the kids' questions.

"Are you gonna be, like, my dad now?" asked Carlos. He hadn't asked for any new clothes, but Fran had still purchased him a white collared shirt to wear with his jeans. The kid fidgeted in the stiff clothes.

"Well, she's your sister," said Fran, choosing to answer the easier of the two questions launched at him. "So, that would make us brothers."

Carlos grinned at that idea. His head bobbed in a nod as his shoulders straightened.

"When did you realize you loved Eva?" Rosalee pressed.

"Obviously, in the last couple of days, Rosie," Carlos said. "Otherwise why would he be marrying her. That's why people get married, right? Because they're in love."

"Or because the girl got pregnant," said Rosalee.

Carlos turned shocked, mutinous eyes on Fran. Pride filled Fran's chest as he watched the young boy's hackles rise to think anyone would take advantage of his older sister.

"Eva's not pregnant," Fran assured him. Turning to Rosalee, he tried an academic argument. "Marriage isn't just about love. It's about protection, property, financial stability. It establishes rights and obligations that the government will recognize."

Both kids frowned at him as though they were sitting in the back of the class, and he was droning on at the lectern.

"I liked your sister from the first moment I saw her. Just like I liked you all when we first met. I wanted to be a part of your family, and I wanted you to be my family."

"You could've adopted us," said Rosalee. She was a smart kid.

"True," Fran said.

"You don't have to marry Eva for that."

"I want to marry Eva." That came out a bit more vehemently than Fran had planned.

She didn't say it, but he saw the question why in the sparkle of Rosalee's eyes. Eyes so like her sister's. Thankfully, he didn't have to answer that question as he saw movement in the distance.

Two golf carts pulled up. The first contained Reed, Sean, Xavier, and Dr. Patel who would be officiating the ceremony. In the second golf cart was Dylan, Maggie, and Eva.

Fran's eyes caught and held on the second golf cart. He couldn't see what Eva was wearing. She was sitting in the back seat. But he could see her face.

Her face was tilted up to the sun, as though drinking it in. Her nostrils flared, and her shoulders lifted as she took a deep breath. Was she nervous? Was she having second thoughts?

Fran felt his heart give a kick. He wanted to run to her, to grab hold of her and do what it took to convince her that this was the right decision. The thought of her going back to that apartment. The thought of not seeing her inside his home, having her close to protect. The thought of her not frowning up at him as he threw down his credit card to buy her and her siblings whatever their hearts demanded. Well, he did not like any of those thoughts.

As though she'd heard him, Eva's face tilted down. Her eyes opened, and her gaze found his.

A twinge went through Fran's heart. A twisting ache that rattled his teeth. He battled through the pain, not allowing it to show on his face. Even if the shrapnel chose that moment to take his life, he would make sure Eva saw him smiling at her.

Thankfully, the twinge died down by the time everyone was in place, and Eva walked toward him at the gazebo. He was sure there was music, as he saw Reed with speakers. He was sure words were said to him, as he was vaguely aware of Dr. Patel's lips moving. But Fran's eyes held rapt to Eva.

She wore a simple dress; one she insisted on buying with her own money. It was little more than a white sundress, made of cotton with a lace trim. It sat on her strong shoulders, the lace making those shoulders look delicate. The dress grabbed at her bodice making Fran's palms itch to do the same. And then it flowed down around her torso, touching the tops of her knees. Strappy sandals completed the look.

She was a vision. He knew that when the metal finally took him and his life was flashing before his eyes, that vision would hold for long moments before he turned into the light.

"You look beautiful." It was the first words he'd said to her. He realized those words weren't said at the proper time as Dr. Patel cleared his throat with a smile, and the audience gathered sent up a chuckle.

Fran shut his mouth, but he hadn't apologized for telling the truth.

Eva did look beautiful. He wanted to hand over his credit card to her to buy more dresses just like that one so that he could gaze at her loveliness every day, instead of seeing her in ill-fitting jeans and T-shirts. He wanted to look down and see her painted toenails instead of scuffed sneakers and well-worn, black flats.

He would do that, he silently promised her. He knew if he said it out loud, well, he'd interrupt the ceremony again. But he also knew that she would refuse. Anything he gave her would have to be done in stealth mode. At least until she realized that everything he had was all her due.

"Francisco?"

Fran pulled his attention away from Eva and turned to Dr. Patel. The doctor seemed to have been waiting for him to respond for a moment by the way his patient eyes looked at him. "Yes?"

"It's time for the vows. Will you repeat after me?"

"Yes, of course."

"I, Francisco DeMonti, take you, Eva Barry, to be no other than yourself."

Fran repeated the words. With each statement, he realized the truth of the statements.

"Loving what I know of you, trusting what I do not yet know, I will respect your integrity and have faith in your abiding love for me, through all our years, and in all that life may bring us."

Fran had first been taken by Eva's integrity and moral character. She strove to be the best she could be and to hold her head high in a world that was constantly pushing and shoving at her. There might not be love between them, but he would take the best care of this woman she'd ever known. He'd treat her with kindness and tenderness every day that he drew breath. He would provide for her and protect her and everyone she held dear.

"Eva, I take you as my wife, with your faults and your strengths, as I offer myself to you with my faults and strengths. I will help you when you need help and turn to you when I need help. I choose you as the person with whom I will spend my life."

Tears glistened in Eva's eyes at this final pronouncement. Fran's heart pounded in his chest, but there was no pain this time. Just the beating of truth. Though this marriage was one of convenience, she must have known he meant every word he'd said.

As she repeated the same words to him, he felt his own eyes burn with the light of her truth. Just as she'd spoken fiercely about her family and her dreams, she spoke her promise to him. Her tone resonating with sincerity and veracity. Though he'd stopped speaking, Fran's throat was raw as he took her words in.

He knew, without a doubt, that she meant each of them. He believed her when she said she took him with his faults. He knew she'd be a help at every turn. He was honored that she chose him, that he would spend the rest of his life, however long, with her.

"You may now kiss your bride."

Fran's lips parted before Dr. Patel finished speaking. The ache that had been in his heart migrated to his fingertips. His breath quickened causing his lips to dry out. He snaked his tongue out to moisten them.

How had he forgotten that part? His and Eva's was to be a platonic marriage, save this one kiss. But it was tradition, expected. He had to get on with it.

He moved in slowly, carefully. He placed one palm on her shoulder, to keep her steady or to hold himself steady, he wasn't sure. He placed the other hand at her cheek to tilt her head up to his.

He swallowed down his desire, telling it that it had no place in that moment. That it was just the culmination of a ritual, an end to the ceremony. But Fran couldn't get past the lump in his throat.

Eva let out a small sigh as he came closer. Her breath was the sweetest thing he'd ever tasted in his life. It soothed the dryness of his lips. So, he came closer.

He pressed his lower lip to her upper lip. The first brush of her soft lips felt like the strongest wind. He would not let it knock him down. He pressed forward. He'd only meant for the kiss to be a brief connection of lips. He was a fool to think he could stop there.

His thumb came under her chin, tilting her head back a bit more, to give him better access. When he felt no resistance, he captured both her lips in his, and knew he was lost.

CHAPTER FOURTEEN

*E*va had been kissed before. She'd had a couple of dates in high school. There'd been a handful of guys who'd piqued her interest in the years after.

Kissing the high school boys had been mostly a bumping of noses, gnashing of teeth, and a sloppy exchange of spit. The men afterward, had been only a bit better, with a nice warmth from the press of lips, and a few interesting licks of the tongue.

What was happening in her mouth with Fran, in a crowd of onlookers, was nothing like what she'd experienced in all of her dating life.

There was no bumping or gnashing as Fran's hand expertly tilted her head exactly where he wanted her to go. So dazed by his nearness, she'd given him complete control of her head, of her body, of herself.

Fran's lips were warm against hers. But the heat went beyond nice. He pressed into her mouth using only the firm softness of his lips. If he'd introduced his tongue, Eva was certain she'd have expired on the spot.

He captured both of her lips with his. But he'd taken hold of more than her lips. Her heart thumped an increasing beat, as though it were marching toward him. Her brain fogged and then cleared, like a cloud moving out of the sun's way.

Everything was so clear. She saw her entire life laid out for her, a life with this man, folded into the safety of his arms.

For so long she'd thought school had been her dream. She saw it clearly now. School was a goal. Fran had been her dream. A dream she hadn't known she'd had until that very moment.

The tip of his tongue darted out and tasted the fleshy part at the center of her upper lip. And just like in the storybooks, like in the teen angst movies, like in the soapy, romantic dramas on the small screen, Eva let out a swooning sigh.

Luckily, she hadn't fainted. She'd stayed on her feet. She'd had too. She wasn't about to miss a second of that kiss. And, man oh man, it did not disappoint.

Fran pulled away, leaving her bereft. But he did not let her go. He encased her in his arms, holding her close. His breath was heavy against her ear, his voice shaky as he spoke.

"I've got you," he said.

He did have her. All of her. Eva laid her head against his heart. It beat a rapid rhythm. She wondered if that was bad. It couldn't be. It had to mean he was feeling what she was feeling. She would keep his heart beating for as long as she could.

"I now pronounce you, husband and wife."

Eva opened her eyes to see Pastor Patel smiling at her, at them both. He had that sparkle in his eye, the same sparkle he'd had when he'd asked her to speak at the church event.

Had he known? Had he known that she and Fran would wind up in this very spot?

Pastor Patel hadn't balked when they'd asked him to perform their ceremony after only knowing each other for less than three days. In fact, he'd had that weekend free which was unusual for such a busy man of the church and a doctor with a booming practice.

Applause sounded from around the gazebo. Eva stepped back from Fran's embrace, remembering that they weren't alone. All of

Fran's friends filled the area. The only people to represent Eva were her brother and sister.

She'd called her aunt and a few other family members. But they all said they couldn't make it so far on such short notice. The drive was only thirty minutes, and she doubted they had much else to do.

But whatever.

She was very happy at the turn out of people who cared about her. Rosalee sat next to Maggie. Both girls grinning and whispering to each other while clapping their hands. Carlos sat between Reed and Sean. Her little brother looked all grown up in his new shirt and his hair combed back.

"I present to you, Mr. and Mrs. Fran and Eva DeMonti."

Eva's heart gave another lurch at the sound of her new name. The lurch wasn't of fear. It was the feeling of settling in, clicking into place.

Fran took her hand, wrapping his fingers around hers as they made their way down the steps of the gazebo.

The lunch reception was a blur of stories of Fran. Questions fired at her to get to know her better. Being twirled around by each of Fran's fellow soldiers. And then she was in Fran's arms again, swaying slowly to a sappy Top 40's song.

"No regrets?" he asked as he gazed down at her.

"Not a single one." She bit her lip at the forwardness of her response. She had to remember that this was still a marriage of convenience, not one of love. Not yet anyway. "What about you?"

"I meant those vows, Eva. I plan to take very good care of you and your family so long as I'm here."

That threw cold water on her warm emotions. Fran constantly reminded her of his failing heart. But all she could focus on was how generously it beat for all those around him.

She'd watch him give of himself to his brothers. And now he gave all he could to her and her siblings. She'd let him take care of them. That didn't mean she couldn't take care of him too.

"About that kiss," he began.

Eva felt her cheeks heating. Not from embarrassment. She hoped he was about to bless her with another kiss.

"I'm sorry about that," he said.

"You're … sorry?"

"I guess I just got caught up in … everything. It won't happen again."

"It … won't?"

"You have to know I don't expect any of … that from you."

"Right. No affection."

"That's not what I meant." Fran seemed to struggle. "I care about you. I care a lot. I don't mean I'll be cold to you. Or that I won't offer you my arm or my hand when we're out walking. Or that I won't hug you when I see you or hold you when you need a strong arm."

"That's good. I like hugs."

Fran pulled her closer as they continued to sway to the song. "You can have all the hugs you want."

But no more kisses? Still, being inside of Fran's arms was the best feeling in the world. She'd content herself with that.

For now.

CHAPTER FIFTEEN

"Are we gonna change our last names? Or will you?"

Fran glanced in the rearview mirror at Rosalee. The kid was filled with questions since the ceremony yesterday.

She was strapped into the back seat of his truck in another new shirt and matching skirt set. She hugged her backpack to her small chest. Brown, inquisitive eyes stared back at him in the glass reflection.

"Only Eva changes her name," Carlos answered his sister.

"When my friend Lisa got a new dad she changed her name, too. It was hyphenated."

Carlos considered that.

"Her stepdad adopted her," Rosalee continued to press.

"Rosie, Fran isn't adopting you," said Eva.

"That's something we can discuss," said Fran.

Eva's mouth gaped at the pronouncement. Her pupils flicked rapidly, left to right like she was trying to read between the lines. Like always, there was nothing hidden in his words. Fran said what he meant.

"I'd like to hyphenate," said Rosalee. "So we have a piece of mom and dad and a piece of Fran."

Eva turned back and faced forward. From her profile, Fran saw her throat work. She was holding back emotion.

"Yeah," said Carlos. "That sounds good to me. After the adoption, I'll hyphenate too."

"What will you do when you have kids of your own?" asked Rosalee. "I guess they'll be DeMonti."

Now Fran faced entirely forward, eyes on the road, hands gripping the steering wheel. They hadn't addressed much of the truth of their marriage with the kids. Rosalee and Carlos hadn't even realized that Fran and Eva hadn't slept in the same bedroom last night.

They'd waited until after the kids had gone to bed to slip inside their respective rooms. It hadn't been just a slip inside. Fran had walked Eva to her room. He'd tried not to stare at her. She was still dressed in the sundress from the ceremony but her feet were bare on the hardwood floors. He'd found himself staring at her pink toes.

When he'd lifted his gaze, he was met with the curves he'd been trying to ignore all day. A little higher and there was her beautiful face, still flushed from the day's excitement. They'd laughed until they were hoarse, danced until they were sore, and ate until they were glutted. It was the best day Fran had had all year, in many years.

As they stood at her bedroom door, Eva's hair was loosened from the do she'd worn earlier. Her hair was a halo around her face, making her look like a sleepy angel. Fran itched to push a strand back behind her ear.

He clenched his fist instead. Like he'd done when instinct drove his fingers to hold her hand while they sat side by side at the picnic table. Like he'd done when impulse put his lips next to her ear to whisper something funny while they danced. He'd pulled his hand away before taking hers in his. He'd turned his head to the side before confiding in her.

He had to constantly remind himself that this wasn't a real marriage, it wasn't a love relationship. It was a convenience, a means to an end to keep her and her family safe, and to allow him to spend the rest of his days near those who cared about him.

But that night, after his friends had left them to their home and after the kids had gone to sleep, as he stood with his new wife outside her bedroom door, Eva had slipped inside his arms. He'd told her she could. It was the only thing she'd asked of him.

Hugs.

Fran's arms came around her. His palms met her warm flesh. His nose came to rest atop that cloud of hair. And it was heaven.

She hadn't said anything. Just rested her head against his heart for a moment. Then she'd let him go and slipped inside her bedroom door. Fran had stood outside her door for long moments after, waiting for his heartbeat to settle and his desire to cool.

This was a convenience. It wasn't real. It couldn't be real, because it wouldn't last. There would be no tall children with long limbs and brown eyes. But there were these two children in his care, and he would do everything to make sure that Carlos and Rosalee were cared for.

"I'm so sorry we're taking you out of your way," Eva said as Fran pulled up to the kids' school.

The middle school was a twenty-minute drive from the ranch. There was no school bus service that far. Someone from the ranch would have to drive them every day.

"I'll figure out the city bus service soon—"

"Absolutely not," said Fran. "They're not taking a twenty-minute bus ride every day. And neither are you."

Eva did a double take. Fran shrugged. He would not budge on this.

"If I'm busy then one of the guys will take them," he said. "Or you can just take the truck and take them yourself."

"I can't take your truck from you."

"Then let me buy you your own car."

"I can't let you buy me a car."

"Why not?"

"Because it would take me forever to pay you back."

"I'm your husband," Fran said patiently. "What's mine is yours. And your siblings'."

"You can buy me a car," said Carlos.

"You can earn a car by doing work around the ranch," said Fran.

"Deal," Carlos agreed.

Fran looked to Rosalee. He knew that smart little girl was paying attention. He was right.

"I want a bike," she said.

"That's doable. Your sister and I will discuss how you can earn it."

Eva sat silently next to him. She didn't look upset. Just a bit shell-shocked.

Fran pulled up to the school drop-off point. He reached back and gave Carlos some dap. Rosalee leaned across her seat and gave her sister a hug. Then she turned to Fran and gave him a kiss on the cheek. Once the kids were inside the doors, Fran pulled back into traffic.

"Did I overstep my bounds back there?" he asked after a couple of miles of silence.

"No," Eva said quietly. "You just made our boundaries bigger."

"That's a good thing, right?"

"Yes." She turned to him. Her smile was more in her eyes than on her lips. "I'm not used to this, Fran. I'm not used to having a partner. I'm not used to having help with all of my responsibilities. I'm not used to giving them anything beyond the basics. They deserve more."

"You do, too."

"You're not buying me a car," she said firmly.

Fran didn't bother hiding his grin. "Not for a while."

She shook her head at him, but her smile had spread. Not just across her face. Her smile had spread to him. It crawled over his skin and then seeped inside, like rays of sunlight.

He pulled up to her campus. There was a drop-off spot called Kiss and Ride. The sign stared them in the face.

Eva released the seatbelt. She placed her hand on the door handle. Before opening the door, she turned to him. Releasing the handle, she put her hand on his chest. She leaned over, coming closer to him.

Her lips met the side of his face, but she might as well have kissed him on the lips. Her soft lips hit him hard in the gut. It took everything not to turn to her and take her mouth, staking his claim, his rightful claim, to this woman, his wife. But he held still.

"Thank you, Fran."

"Have a good day at school," he said. "I'll be right here when you finish."

She smiled at him again, mostly with her eyes. She removed her hand from his heart. It pounded in protest. Fran watched her until she disappeared inside.

CHAPTER SIXTEEN

Eva remembered each of her first days of school. The first day of kindergarten she'd come with a new outfit, her lunchbox, and shared her cookies with Mary Bennett. Her first day of middle school, she'd gotten a new backpack and had put her Trapper Keeper inside with colorful dividers for each of her classes. The first day of high school, she'd been in hand-me-downs and last year's binder that sported duct tape to hold it together. Lunch had been courtesy of the Free Lunch program. That was the first year both her parents had died.

She wore a comfortable pair of jeans and a new top today. It was a top she'd gotten when she'd purchased her wedding dress. She'd had a bit left over since she hadn't had to buy food for the week. She hadn't had to spend a dime on anyone but herself that weekend.

Fran had taken care of everything. From her living situation, to her siblings' care, to putting food on the table. Food, clothes, and shelter. And now he wanted to buy her a car. All of this and she wasn't even putting out!

She laughed to herself as she walked into the university's School of Science building. She wanted to put out for her husband. She wanted to know what it would be like to get lost inside Fran's arms, beneath his solid frame, maybe even on top of his big body.

Eva's cheeks heated. She'd never had such bold thoughts before. She'd never met someone who'd inspired them before. With just a few, likely chaste by most standards, kisses, and she was a wanton woman.

But she wasn't a wanton woman. She was a wife. She was a wife who wanted her husband.

Her phone buzzed. Reaching into her pocket, she pulled it out to see that it was a text message from Maggie wishing her luck on her first day.

Eva noted there was also a message in her email. It was a picture of Reed, Sean, and Xavier wearing glasses and holding books. In the first picture, they tried to look serious and failed hilariously. In the second picture, they made funny faces. The text below the pictures wished her a good first day.

She hadn't remembered giving any of them her phone number or email. But she supposed with men who were in the army, and one of them who specialized in technology, that it wasn't that hard to get her information. She was touched that they'd gone through the trouble.

They were more than just her new family; they were also her new friends. And that's what friends did for each other.

"Are you lost?"

Eva looked up to find a guy leaning against a doorway watching her. He looked like what could stereotypically be called a preppy kid with his collared shirt and pleated pants and parted hair.

"You had this faraway look in your eyes," he said, pushing off from the doorway. "I figure you're either lost or high?"

"I'm not high."

He raised his eyebrow.

"I don't do drugs."

"Me neither."

Eva didn't buy it. There was a spark in his eyes. But it was mischievous, not inquisitive.

"What room are you looking for?" He snatched the schedule out of her hand. "Oh, Professor Newton. He's a snoozer. But I know a guy who can get you his tests so you can ace the class."

"No, thank you." Eva snatched her schedule back.

"Why don't I walk you to class." It wasn't a question. He simply fell into step beside her.

"I'm good, actually."

"Just thought you might like a friend seeing that you're new."

Eva stopped in her tracks. She turned to face this guy. "I'm not lost. I'm exactly where I'm supposed to be. I don't buy tests; I do the work. And I have all the friends I need, thank you."

She scratched at her nose, even though it didn't itch. She let the ring finger of her left hand rub up and down her cheek a few times until the guy got the hint.

"You're married." The guy frowned.

"Yes," Eva confirmed. "Happily. And I'm about to be late to class. So, if you'll excuse me …"

She turned and marched down the hall toward her class. She found a seat near the front. There were quite a few seats open.

Professor Newton walked in with a folio of papers. Eva took out her pen as the lecture began. Five minutes after the lecture began, more students rolled in and took up seats, all in the back.

The professor wasn't boring. His voice was a bit monotone, but the picture he painted with his knowledge was fascinating. Eva's pen hadn't stopped moving for the whole class period. She noted that she was one of the only students using pen and paper, if they were taking notes at all. Most had laptops and were typing away as the professor spoke.

"Excuse me?"

Eva looked over to see a young woman next to her.

"Did you happen to catch what he said about coefficients? I got a bit lost."

"Oh, yeah, sure." Eva shuffled through her papers. She found what she was looking for and handed the document to the woman.

"Oh, no, no. Would you mind just repeating it back to me? I have a whole system of note taking, and I need to put it in its proper place. I know that sounds weird."

"No, it makes sense to me. My next class doesn't start for thirty minutes. You wanna grab something to drink and we can compare notes? Maybe a cup of tea?"

"I'd like that. I'm Jan Collison."

"Eva Lopez ... DeMonti. Lopez-DeMonti."

CHAPTER SEVENTEEN

"Steady there," Fran coaxed both animal and boy.

Carlos looked like a grown man from his perch on the horse. Fran was certain the boy felt grown up from his high seat there. There was something about being in the seat of a horse that changed a man's perspective.

Fran led the young man and his steed on a path through the ranch. So much had changed in a week. Fran spied Rosalee working in the garden alongside Sean and the dogs. Maggie and Dylan were necking on the side of the barn, believing no one could see them.

Carlos had taken to ranch life like he'd been born to it. The kid was up at dawn, doing chores before school. After he finished his homework, he was back out helping the other men with errands before sundown.

Rosalee was often out of the house and by her brother's side. All the signs of agoraphobia and social anxieties had all but disappeared.

That's what the ranch was all about. It healed everyone who came within the gates be they vet or civilian. The biggest change Fran had seen was with Eva.

There was a sparkle in her eye each morning when he met her at her bedroom door, or they crossed paths on the way to the kitchen.

She was relaxed, unguarded. She'd also stopped frowning and pursing her lips every time he brought a necessity or gift into the house.

The gifts were small things. He'd discovered what her favorite yogurt was, and he stocked up on two weeks' worth. He overheard her and Maggie talking about something called bath bombs. He ordered a month's worth online and stored them in the bathroom cabinet. She simply sighed when she saw them and then shut herself in the bathroom for an hour.

Fran spent that hour chatting with her brother and sister. He couldn't remember a single word that any of them had said. His mind and his entire focus were on the knob of the bathroom door where his wife was immersed in warm, sudsy, salty water.

"Look, Fran, I'm doing it."

Fran snapped his attention back to his young charge. Carlos was riding well. He'd figured out his balance quickly. He had control of the horse. The boy's self-esteem was soaring. They came back to the stables and Carlos dismounted on his own.

"Looks like you're getting your wish, soldier."

Fran turned to Dr. Patel. The man leaned on the railing as he watched Carlos. "My wish?"

"You wanted to help those kids back in Afghanistan. That's why you volunteered for the mission to build the school. Many of the inner cities of America are much like war zones."

That was the truth. The apartment complex he'd taken Eva, Carlos and Rosalee from had all the hallmarks of war; poverty, violence, firepower. Fran had saved two kids, but he thought back to the faces of the boys who'd perked up during his talk at the church. Could he save more of them? Perhaps he could try?

"I want to provide this for other children back in that neighborhood. I might not have the time to see it through. But I could get it started."

"You need to stop counting your moments and start counting your blessings," said Patel. "You have friends who literally would go to war for you. You've got these two kids who look at you like you've hung the moon. And you have a beautiful young wife who, as far as I can see, has put life back into you. Most people don't get that in a long lifetime."

Patel was right. Fran was blessed. His heart was overflowing with blessings.

"Thank you, Dr. Patel."

"For what?"

"For pushing us together."

"I'm sure I have no idea what you mean?" The man smiled with a twinkle in his eyes as he turned and headed toward the parking lot.

Fran shook his head as he watched the older man. Even before the edict came that all who chose to reside on the ranch had to be married, Patel had been pressing his case to match each of the soldiers. If Fran had listened, he might've had Eva in his life earlier. But he was happy she was there now.

She should be home soon. She'd had a late study session that evening and had taken his truck. He'd had to shove the keys into her hand and belt her into the driver's seat so she wouldn't think of taking the bus or a cab. He wanted to present her with her own car keys soon.

Fran helped Carlos put the horse up. Then the two of them collected Rosalee from the garden. They made their way to their home, the kids chattering along the way. His truck was in the driveway when they walked up to the door.

The kids pounced on their sister, regaling her of their day in school and at the ranch. Eva listened with a smile on her face as she set the table and placed a warm meal on each plate. She gazed up at Fran, brown eyes so full of warmth that his heart felt it was immersed in one of her bath bombs.

The two of them barely got a word in edgewise as the kids chattered on throughout the meal. It was Carlos's turn to clean up after dinner. But Fran took one look at the kid and his drooping eyes and sent him off to bed. Rosalee was equally as tired and hadn't argued when Eva suggested she turn in as well.

With the kids in bed and the dishes away, Fran plopped down on the sofa. A second later, Eva joined him. This had become their nightly ritual after the kids were in bed.

Eva scooted closer to Fran. He stretched his arm along the back of the couch. She immediately snuggled into the space between his shoulder cap and his breastbone. She'd claimed that spot the second night of their marriage.

Though theirs wasn't a physical relationship, he'd promised her hugs, as many as she wanted. They weren't innocent, platonic embraces and he didn't pretend they were. Fran's body was alive each time hers was near. But neither of them crossed the line of intimacy. These shared embraces were still well within the boundaries of friendship.

"How was your study session?" he asked.

"It was good."

The sound of her voice reached his heart before it reached his ears. Fran stared down at the top of Eva's head. The tendrils on the top of her head tickled his nose as he breathed in her scent. The smell of her, the feel of her supple body against his, each night it sent his heart racing.

Eva was saying more words to him, but Fran couldn't decipher them. His attention was rapt on her knees, which were resting on his thighs. She'd curled her bare feet under her bottom and her knees rested on his legs just as her head rested on his chest.

The *thump-thump* of his heart blared warning signs.

Eva laughed at something—something she'd said or something on the television, he wasn't sure. She threw back her head to look up at him. Her parted lips were a faded red, her lipstick had worn off through the day and then dinner. The muted red silenced the warning signs.

Fran couldn't take his eyes off her mouth. Her lips had stopped moving. A tremble quivered through the bottom one. She sighed and the sweetness got caught in his throat.

And still, his heart *thumped-thumped*. But the warning sounds, the warning signs, both were pointless.

Fran wasn't sure who moved first. It was likely a mutual decision.

They'd been deciding so many things together the last week. It was fitting they decided this next step in their lives together.

Their lives. Together. That was the only sound he wanted to hear, the only sign he wanted to pay attention to.

This kiss was even sweeter than the sole kiss they'd shared on their wedding day. That kiss had been the taste of something new. This kiss was the promise of something familiar.

He felt his blood boiling as he drank from this woman, his wife. Fran's heartbeat raced. Faster than he knew it should. And then there was pain. A blinding pain that robbed him of his breath and wrenched him away from her.

CHAPTER EIGHTEEN

It was inevitable. They both knew it. They'd been dancing around this moment for a week now.

Every night Eva came home from school. They put the kids to bed. Then they'd sit in this cocoon.

She fit so perfectly inside Fran's half embrace. The feel of his hand at her back was steadying. The divot in his shoulder had been made for her head. The sound of his heart was the sound that told her she was safe, protected, cared for.

Fran's heartbeats whispered promises. Promises that one day this easy friendship, this practical partnership, could turn into something more. Something the heart was made to do.

Everything in Eva told her that tonight that time had come.

She tilted her head back to see Fran. He looked down at her as she often caught him doing when he didn't think she was looking. For all he spoke of platonic and practicality, she knew he felt something for her. No man would go through the lengths that he'd done for her and her family without a bit of attraction.

And so when she reached up to taste his lips, she had her confirmation in his answering kiss.

Fran swept into her mouth just like he'd swept into her life. He pulled her to him, into the safety of his protection. His kiss only asked to give her pleasure. It asked nothing in return. His lips moved across hers, telling her that he just wanted to see her safe and cared for.

Eva had every plan to give this man not just her heart but her soul. It hadn't been love at first sight. It was better than that. It had been trust at first sight.

With just a glance, this man had gained her confidence. She had recognized this man was reliable and filled with integrity. Something she had found lacking in people since her parents' deaths.

Fran was able. He was strong. He was sure.

He was pulling away from her.

"Fran, I want this. I want you."

"Eva …" He breathed hard, likely from the passion they'd shared in the all-too-brief kiss.

"Fran, I love you. I do, and I want to be your wife in every meaning of the word."

"Eva," he gasped.

He was clutching at his heart and gasping for breath. The kiss had overwhelmed her too. But not to the point of pain.

Wait.

He was clutching at his heart in pain.

His heart.

"Fran? Fran?"

But he couldn't answer. His face was contorted in agony. He gulped down deep, lungfuls of air. Just the sight of him in pain sent Eva into the throes of agony.

"What do I do? Do I call the doctor? Oh, Fran, please. I don't know what to do."

She could call 911. Or she could call out to one of the other soldiers. But she was afraid to leave him. She wiped the hair from his face. She placed her hand over his heart.

Fran gripped her hand. Slowly his eyes opened, his breathing calmed. He gazed into her eyes. She'd never seen him look so vulnerable.

It scared her.

Fran was strong, unbreakable. But in that moment, he was weak and at the mercy of an enemy he could not strike out against.

His breath steadying, he tilted his head forward to rest his face against her cheek. Eva curled her arms around his neck. She held him to her, resting his head against her own heart.

"This is why this can't happen," he said, his voice was pain-laden.

"Are you saying that kiss made your heart hurt?"

Fran lifted his head to gaze at her. His eyes were filled with regret. "It's not the kiss. It could happen at any moment. It's set off by anything, by nothing. There's no rhyme or reason to why or when the fragments in my chest move. But one day they'll get too close to my heart and kill me."

"I know," she said. She'd been doing research on his condition. She knew that fragments often moved or became encased in scar tissue.

"That could be a year from now," she said. "It could be ten years from now."

"It could be right now, Eva." He pulled away from her.

She did not let him go. "That's why I don't want to waste any more time. I want to be with you."

"Eva …" He turned away from her, but he didn't leave from the couch.

Eva's palms came to rest over his heart. Fran clutched her hands in his, but he didn't pull away. He let out an agonized breath.

"You make my heart beat faster, Eva," he said. "But that's not what's going to kill me. What will kill me is not being here for you after, when you're hurting because of me. The idea of not being able to protect you kills me."

"Stop trying to protect me," she said. "I did just fine without you. But I do better with you. You do better with me. This may be your plan to keep me safe, but it was my choice to come here and be with you. It's my choice to stay with you. It's my plan to love you for as long as I can."

Fran hung his head. His grip on her hands loosened.

"Let me love you, Fran."

He rose from the couch. He didn't look back at her. Instead of going to his bedroom, he left out the front door.

CHAPTER NINETEEN

Everything hurt when Fran woke the next morning. Not just his heart. His back ached from sleeping on the hard, and at the same time lumpy, sofa. His neck spasmed from being raised high on the armrest which had elevated his head too high from the rest of his body. His left foot had fallen asleep from being exposed to the cold draft coming from the living room window.

He ran his hand over his chest. The raised scars weren't tender, hadn't been for some time. But they bothered him that morning.

Eva was fond of resting her head over that spot. She'd never come into direct contact with the scars. But every time she cuddled into him, Fran became aware of them. Even more so aware of what lay beyond them.

He wished he could reach inside his chest and pull out the fragments that kept them apart. He didn't want to jump every time his heart leaped at the sight of his wife. He didn't want to caution her against the affection he couldn't deny was growing between them. He didn't want to shut himself off from the love she'd offered up to him.

But the barrier remained. Distance was the only thing that would protect her. Perhaps he should move out of the house entirely now before the end came near.

"How'd you sleep, sunshine?"

Fran groaned at the sound of Reed's faux cheery voice. The man appeared in his bedroom door. He leaned against the frame with his good arm. The missing arm appeared as a stump in his t-shirt.

"Yeah, that's because you should be in your wife's bed," said Reed.

"It's not like that with me and Eva."

"Then you're dumber than I thought. You've got a warm-blooded, beautiful, intelligent woman who wants you. Although the fact that she wants you makes me question her intelligence. And you spent the night on my couch?"

"Getting involved with her like that, on a physical, intimate level would only hurt her more when I'm gone."

"Ah, so you'll just hurt her now. Yeah, that makes sense."

"I don't want to hurt anyone."

Reed sighed. He reached back in his room and grabbed his prosthetic. He began the process of strapping the limb on.

When the explosion had happened, Fran's first thought was to the men in his squad. Reed was closest to him. Fran had heard his cry of pain and was the first to witness his loss of limb.

He'd gone to the man, hefting Reed up and getting him to safety. Fran had been in the process of going back to look for more wounded when the pain in his chest stopped him in his tracks. He still didn't remember when the impact had happened, only its aftermath.

Fran had fallen to his knees as the cries of his friends and of the civilians whose lives he'd been trying to improve rose around him. He was paralyzed with his own pain, unable to do anything about theirs.

"A lot of the men and women I know walked into combat with a hero complex," said Reed. "You're the only one I knew who walked away a hero with a martyr complex. I don't think you can be both. You need to make a choice. Are you going to be the man who saves lives? Are you gonna be the man who dies for his beliefs?"

A knock sounded at the door. Fran closed his eyes, knowing who was on the other side. He was still raw this morning and would likely welcome Eva into his arms. Hell, he'd probably scoop her up into an embrace and not let her go, his thumping heart be damned.

More and more he wished there wasn't a wall separating them. Last night there had been whole houses between them. It wasn't far enough to escape the taste of her lips, the scent of her skin, the desire to get closer. But when the door opened, it wasn't her. It was her brother.

It was Saturday morning, so the kids hadn't had school. Fran had assumed they would sleep in. But Carlos and Rosalee had proven they loved ranch life and were up with the sun ready to get to work.

Fran lifted himself off the sofa and went out to the porch with Carlos. The two sat side by side looking out across the ranch as the sun lifted itself into the sky.

Fran knew this wasn't going to be an easygoing conversation by the strain at the edges of the kid's eyes. Neither was he sure what direction the talk would go in. So, he waited for Carlos to speak first.

"Are you guys getting a divorce?"

"No," Fran said more vehemently than he'd meant to. "When I married your sister I gave her my word. You know that a man's word is his bond."

"Yeah, but marriage is about love and you don't love her. I'm not a little kid. I don't believe in fairytales. I know there's no such thing as love at first sight."

Fran wasn't so sure. He knew it wasn't love when he first saw Eva. But he had the sense that his life had changed the moment he met her. He'd known she was meant to be in his world from that first hug at the church.

"I know you guys don't share the same bedroom." Carlos's cheeks reddened as he spoke.

Fran wasn't surprised he knew his and Eva's sleeping arrangement. Kids were nosey and Fran knew he and Eva weren't hiding that well.

"You were fighting last night," said Carlos. "I heard you raise your voices."

"It wasn't a fight. We had a disagreement."

"Isn't that another word for a fight."

Fran tried to shrug it off. "Married people fight, they disagree. It doesn't mean it's over."

"But you left."

Fran sighed. "I did. I shouldn't have."

"Why did you?"

"Because your sister wants something I can't give her. I want to give her what she wants, but I know it's not good for her. I felt like if I stayed close to her, I'd give in."

"So you ran away?"

Fran heard a chuckle from inside the house. He wanted to curse Reed. Here Fran was a decorated soldier, getting read the riot act by a kid. "Yeah. I was a coward. All right, here's the truth."

Fran looked down at the kid. Carlos looked so grown and so young at the same time. Fran knew he couldn't lie to Carlos anymore. Carlos would be the man of the house when Fran passed. Fran had to start preparing him for the responsibilities to come.

"I'm sick," said Fran.

"Sick?"

"I have a heart condition. There's shrapnel, fragments from a bomb, in my chest. They're close to my heart. They move from time to time. One day, a piece could move too close to my heart, and if it does, I'll die."

Carlos stared at Fran's chest. The kid took a deep breath. His hands balled into fists in his lap.

He was taking it far better than Fran had imagined. No tears. No whining. Just resolve.

"I knew it," Carlos finally said. "I knew I shouldn't have believed."

"Carlos?"

"You're gonna leave us just like my mom and dad."

Fran watched the kid shutter before his eyes. Fran felt trapped back in the middle of that blast in Afghanistan, needing to fight for his life so that he could save the rest of his squad. The pain was just as deep and halting. He couldn't reach Carlos.

"I knew I shouldn't have believed we could be a family forever. You're going to leave just like they did."

"Carlos—"

Fran reached for the boy, but Carlos shot out of his reach. Fran could chase him down, but to what end? The truth was the truth.

Another good deed, another life he tried to make better, and he'd only wound up hurting those he cared about. Again.

But no. Fran wouldn't let it end like that again. Carlos could still be saved. He could go after Carlos. He would do everything in his power to save the boy.

Fran leaped to his feet and ran.

CHAPTER TWENTY

Eva had tossed and turned all night. She hadn't gotten any sleep as she lay awake waiting for any sign of Fran's return. She'd spent the time planning out exactly what she wanted to say to him.

There wasn't a single, solitary word of acquiescence in her prepared speech. No. She'd made up her mind. This marriage would be the real thing for as long as they both drew breath.

She'd even considered moving into his bedroom that morning. But in the end, felt that was a step too far.

Eva knew Fran hadn't gone far. She'd watched him walk away from her last night. He'd only made it as far as Reed's small cabin.

She hadn't gone after him. She'd given him the time to cool off, to let his heart settle, before she pounced again. In the meantime, she'd done what any good student would do. She'd begun to research.

When she couldn't sleep, she'd fired up the spare laptop Fran had; the one which hadn't ever been used before. The one that had shown up the day after her first day of class. The one she thought she'd seen the packaging for go in the trash bin. She fired it up and went straight for the internet.

The first thing her research told her was that most victims of shrapnel to the body died of their wounds in battle. That wasn't promising. Nearly every case she came across where the fragments had landed near a vital organ was fatal.

But then she found what she was looking for. There were some cases where soldiers and victims of gun violence had survived shrapnel in the chest. There were even some cases where the shrapnel moved away from the vital organs over time. Or the body put a layer of scar tissue around the fragments.

That could happen to Fran. She wanted to talk to his doctor. Or maybe they needed to go to a specialist.

It didn't matter the money. For him, she'd drop out of school, take the partial refund, and put it all into his medical bills. She'd get a minimum wage job, two if it were necessary, to pay the bills to save his life.

Just as she was planning where to look for work, the front door slammed open. Eva looked up to see her brother. His face wasn't the cheery bliss of the past week. He was angry.

"Did you know?" Carlos demanded.

"Did I know what?" Eva said, closing the laptop.

"That he was dying."

"Who's dying?" asked Rosalee coming out of her room in brand new overalls that Fran had snuck into her room the other day. Rosie looked like a little farm girl.

Looking back over at her brother, Eva sighed. She'd spent years comforting her brother and sister after their father's death, during their mother's illness, from her relatives' inconsistencies and unreliability, from the violence of the neighborhoods they had no choice but to live in. This was something she couldn't hide from them.

"He's not dying," Eva said. "He has metal fragments in his chest."

"That could kill him at any minute." Carlos crossed his arms over his chest and glared. It was the same face he'd made as an adolescent when Eva tried to get him to eat his peas. His mind was set.

"Yes," she conceded. "But he could also live a long and happy life."

"Fran has something wrong with his heart?" said Rosalee, her voice tremored and her eyes grew large like empty saucers.

The door opened again, and the man in question walked in. Fran's gaze immediately tracked to Eva's. There was an apology, shame, worry, and wariness all rolled into one there.

He was out of breath. Heaving lungfuls of air. He doubled over at the threshold of the door.

Eva and her siblings looked at him. Eyes wide, mouths agape. No one moved as they watched him gulp down air. Rosalee began to wail. Carlos balled and unballed his fists.

Fran raised his head to her. That set her in motion.

Eva had him in her arms, taking the brunt of his large body with hers and urging him to the sofa. His gaze was so soft when it met hers.

"I'm sorry," he said. His voice was quiet as he labored to breathe. "I should not have walked out on you last night. It was cowardly. Please forgive me."

"You're forgiven. Please just try to calm down. Take deep breaths. You're going to be fine."

Fran tore his gaze away from her and found Carlos. Carlos came to him, sitting at his right side. "Men don't run from their responsibilities. We're family forever."

Carlos nodded, clasping Fran's hand. Tears burned at the corners of his eyes. The struggle to keep them in check was evident.

Fran turned his gaze to Rosalee. "Hey, princess."

"Please don't die, Fran," Rosalee wailed.

"I'm gonna try my hardest, okay?"

"Okay." Rosalee nodded.

Fran turned back to Eva. "Hey."

"Hey."

"I need you to call my doctor."

CHAPTER TWENTY-ONE

The pain was so intense that Fran couldn't speak. Eva leaned over him, concern etched on her pretty face. He lifted a hand, aiming to touch her cheek, to smooth away her worry. But his limbs shook with the effort.

He hadn't wanted to give up, not on his efforts to reach out to her, not on his desire to stay with her, to be with her for the rest of his life, however long that might be. But his body wouldn't cooperate.

Eva reached down to his trembling fingers. She curled them in her own. Lifting his knuckles to her lips, she pressed a kiss to each joint.

Fran felt her whisper into his palm. He felt the formation of the word *love* as her lips skimmed his palm. Her tongue rose to the roof of her mouth to make the L sound. He felt the burst of staccato breath that would make the ST sound and had to imagine she was begging him to stay.

He wanted nothing more. He wanted to be her hero. He wanted to be the man who raised a weapon to defend her. The man who went into danger to gather her sustenance. The man who wrapped her into his arms, not only for protection but for comfort. He wanted to be her everything. He didn't want to die to have to do it.

The moment she'd said that she would marry him, Fran had

buried himself in a mountain of paperwork. He signed everything over to her in the event of his death. She and her siblings would never want for anything for the rest of their lives.

But he'd gotten that wrong. They'd only ever wanted him.

As the gurney wheeled around a corner, Fran caught his last glimpse of Carlos and Rosalee. Carlos's stiff upper lip quivered as distance increased between himself and Fran. The young man wrapped an arm around his little sister's shoulder. Rosalee was a fountain of tears. Her hand reached out to Fran, but he was beyond her now.

Fran wanted to scoop the little thing into his arms and tell her he'd be back. That he'd be there for her. More than anything, he wanted to be there for them all. He hadn't wanted his death to be what saved them. He wanted to live for them.

He hadn't wanted to die a martyr. He wanted to live as their hero.

All around him doctors swarmed in. They parted Eva from him.

"I'm his wife," she insisted.

But her status didn't get her access to the operating room. A woman in a nurse's uniform barred Eva's entry. Reed put an arm around her waist and pulled her close as they wheeled Fran away.

Eva's body sank into Reed's. Her gaze never left Fran. He saw her eyes brim with worry and fear. Before the door's closed, her lips lifted in the smallest of smiles.

He knew it took a great effort for that smile. He could nearly read her mind. If this was going to be the last time he saw her, he wanted it to be with her smiling.

That woman. Thinking of everyone else even to the end.

Fran fought the pain that centered in his chest. It robbed him of his breath. He couldn't speak to her, he couldn't tell her the words he needed to say, the most important thing he ever had to say.

He couldn't shout the words, but he moved his lips to communicate the message.

The effort robbed him of his last bit of strength. The second the last of the three words were formed, he collapsed back down onto the gurney. And his world turned to black.

CHAPTER TWENTY-TWO

The waiting room at the hospital was packed. Dylan held a sleeping Maggie on his lap. Reed held a sleeping Rosalee on his lap. Rosie rested her head against Reed's prosthetic arm as he stroked her back with his other hand. Sean and Xavier took turns pacing the small space. Eva sat with her eyes glued to the door where she'd seen the doctors exit to talk with the family of the patients.

That door had opened three times in the last two hours. She'd overheard three conversations. Two of them had induced tears from the family. And not happy tears. Only one had brought on sighs of relief.

There were no other families in the waiting area now. Eva hoped the odds were in her family's favor that when the doors opened again, they'd be delivering sighs of relief. But the doors hadn't swung open in over forty-five minutes.

There was silence amongst the guys. No one offered her consoling words. They all knew the chances were that when the doors opened the next time, there would unlikely be any sighs of relief.

But they hadn't left her side. They'd surrounded her and her family, insulating them as best they could.

Carlos sat next to her, his eyes on the door just as hers had been for the last hour.

Eva opened her mouth to offer her brother consolation. But the words stuck in her throat.

Carlos turned to her. Her baby brother looked so old at the moment.

"I think we should pray," he said.

Eva blinked. Those were the last words she'd expected to hear from him.

"I was angry at God for a long time," Carlos continued. "I thought he'd forgotten about us when he took Mom and Dad. Then he sent us Fran. I never said thank you."

Carlos bent his head. After a moment, the others followed suit.

"Dear God, thank you for bringing Fran to my family. He taught me what I need to know to be a man. That a man takes care of his family. Moms and sisters do that too. Family takes care of family. I promise to do that from now on. If you have to take Fran tonight, please introduce him to my mom and dad so that they can take care of him the way he took care of us. Amen."

"Amen," their new family intoned.

A swishing sound brought all of their attention around. There was a man in a white coat standing in the doorway. The look on the doctor's face was grave.

The men rose. As a unit they moved in closer to Eva, standing at her side, at her back. Eva knew that no matter the news, whether tears or sighs, Fran had given her his love. He'd given her a family that would always have her back and never leave her alone. Still, she wished to have him at her back.

A tear slid down her cheek as the doctor opened his mouth to deliver the news.

CHAPTER TWENTY-THREE

A bright light shone on the other side of Fran's eyelids. He kept his eyes shut, not wanting to wake from the dream he'd been having. In the dream, he was sitting and talking with an elderly husband and wife. He knew the conversation had been long and pleasant. But at the moment, Fran couldn't recall a single word they'd exchanged.

What he did hold onto was the warm feeling in his heart, the smile of the wife, the look of approval the husband gave him. As they waved him off, Fran felt somehow empowered to take on the world.

But he still wasn't ready to wake up. So he stayed in the dream. In the blink of an eye, Eva was there. She stood in the sun, in a dress similar to the one she'd worn on their wedding day.

Fran walked up behind her. He slid his arms around her and pulled her body back into his. She was safe and content inside his arms. She tilted her face up, and he leaned down and kissed her.

Sunshine dawned in his heart. Rays of warmth spread as he sipped her in. He pressed her closer to him.

The light from the other side grew brighter, insisting he wake. Then Fran realized something; he could wake.

He wasn't dead. He was alive. That meant he could have Eva in the flesh.

He let go of his dream, and his eyes sprang open. It took a moment for his vision to adjust. When it did, he saw warm brown eyes gazing down at him. They weren't Eva's.

"You're gonna be okay," said Carlos. "I prayed for you. We all did."

Fran spied movement beyond the door. He caught sight of his squad. Their heads were turned, speaking to a man in a white coat. Reed caught Fran's eye from the other side of the glass. His friend winked.

"They said only two people in the room at a time," said Carlos.

Two people? Fran's gaze slid around. He spied Eva in a chair against the wall. Her eyes were closed, but he saw signs of stirring.

"She's been here all night. We've been taking turns coming in and sitting with you."

Fran couldn't take his eyes off his wife. He watched as her eyes fluttered open. They were hazy at first. When her gaze met his, the fog cleared, and she sat up.

"I took care of them all while you were asleep," Carlos continued. "I stayed by their side like a man does for his family."

Fran looked back at the young man. He lifted his hand and placed it on his cheek. "You did good."

Carlos nodded in agreement. Then he slid off the bed. He gave his sister a hug, and then he slipped out the door.

Eva made her way to Fran on slow feet. Fran wanted to sit up, to get up, to get to her faster. He reached his hand out to her. She took his fingers and sat down on the bed next to him.

"I'm sorry," he said.

"It's okay. You're okay."

"I promise you, I won't ever push you away like that again. I love you, Eva. I want us to be together, in a real marriage. I want to hold you. I want to kiss you. I want to fall asleep and wake up with you in my arms. If I only have another hour, I want to spend that time with you."

Fran brushed away a tear from her eye. She turned her face into his palm and kissed it.

"I love you, Fran. We're going to have more than an hour together. We're going to have a lifetime."

He'd let her believe that. He'd take every moment and treasure it.

"The shrapnel," she said. "It moved away from your heart. I don't really understand it all, but the doctor said that where it's moving, it'll likely form scar tissue that will hold it still."

Fran struggled to understand her words. They were too good to be true.

"They said you might feel more pain from time to time," she continued. "But the fragments are moving in a positive direction."

Fran wanted to laugh. He'd suffer an ache in his chest from time to time if it meant he got to have this love. Not just Eva's love, but the love of his entire family. He spied them all watching with grins on their faces from the doorway.

They all let out a cheer now that he knew the prognosis. Eva laughed. Fran did too.

He'd set out to save this woman and her family, to move them out of a danger zone and into safety. He hadn't expected them all to steal his heart and save his life. Now they had, the dangerous bits inside him had given way. Fran followed suit.

He turned to her, tugging her closer. Their lips met. It was nothing like the dream he'd just had. It was so much more because it was real, because this kiss, this love, this family, it would last.

EPILOGUE

Reed kept his eye on the bouncing ball as Xavier danced around the basketball hoop at the head of the driveway. He remained light on his feet as Xavier danced around, dribbling between his legs more like a backup dancer than a baller. Reed paid the performance no mind. He knew it would only be a matter of moments before his shot came.

He gave his shoulders a shake. Clenching and releasing the fingers of his sole hand, he lay in wait, ready to grab for his chance and steal the game-winning point. No one watching the game would think to consider that he had a lesser chance of winning due to the fact that he had only one fully functioning arm in a game where handling the ball was key. He and Xavier weren't evenly matched at all. Reed had the upper hand.

Watching his friend continue his fancy footwork, Reed kept calm and gathered the facts. That's all he'd need to turn the game to his advantage. His careful observations quickly panned out.

Xavier favored his left side. He kept the ball in his left hand more times than not. When he went for the shot, it would be with his right hand.

Reed squared up against his friend. Xavier faked a jab to his left.

Reed hadn't fallen for it. Reed attacked, using the stump of his special arm. With Xavier being on his subordinate side, it was easy to knock the ball out of his left hand.

Once the ball was free of Xavier's grasp, Reed stepped in. Using his body to block Xavier, Reed grabbed the ball with his own left hand. He pivoted his body, turning toward the hoop and made the shot.

The swish of the corded rope was louder than the applause of an NBA stadium at playoffs. But it was Xavier's groan that was music to Reed's ears.

"You've gotta be kidding me," groaned Xavier.

"Don't hate the player," said Reed.

"Let's go again. Best three out of five."

Xavier was a sore loser. But Reed was feeling pretty sore after two full out games. Before he could decline, the sound of a truck pulling up pushed the two men out of the driveway and into the yard. Once the truck was in park, Fran opened the passenger side door and stepped out.

Reed stepped up to the driver's side to hand out Eva. Eva smiled, grateful as she took his hand and hopped down to the ground.

"DeMonti," called Xavier, "think fast."

The basketball sailed through the air. Fran reached out his hands, but Eva smacked the ball away. Those same quick hands went to her hips, and her gaze shot balls of fury at Xavier. Reed's brows raised in shock. How in the heck had she gotten around the car that fast?

"Xavier Hunter Ramos if you over-excite my husband, I will tan your hide," Eva said.

Xavier straightened his back like the soldier he was. His shoulders snapped to attention and his head tilted as though he'd received an order from a commanding officer.

Reed's body reacted in the same manner. His right hand itched to rise to a salute.

"Are we clear?" Eva said to Xavier. Behind her Fran smirked at his friend.

"Ma'am, yes, ma'am," said Xavier.

"He is to have no excitement for the next few weeks," Eva said wrapping her arms around Fran's torso and placing her hand on his heart.

Now it was Xavier who smirked at Fran. Fran had been married for two weeks and there had been no excitement in his marital bed. Unlike Xavier who went out to get his kicks every weekend with a different girl.

"Come on, let's get you into bed," said Eva.

"Ma'am, yes, ma'am," grinned Fran.

"To rest," said Eva. "The doctor said you need to take it easy, Fran."

Fran hadn't argued. He'd placed a light kiss at his wife's lips and allowed her to lead him inside the house.

Reed watched after them. Soon that would be him.

The dating app had found him a woman with a compatibility rating of ninety-eight percent. Sarai Austin was perfect on paper. And soon they'd meet in real life, once she got back into the country from her overseas business trip.

Reed had chatted with Sarai online every day since they'd connected through the app. The more he spoke to her, the more he knew she was the one for him. He just needed to meet her in person to seal the deal. But for the second week straight, she'd been called out of town for business.

He admired her dedication to her job. And he was a patient man. But there was a deadline he was up against. The edict that he had to get married in just under two months. Reed just knew that if they could meet in person, everything would align. The data told him so.

The two of them had so much in common, and their conversations were so easy he'd swear he'd known her for years and not days. She'd seen his injury. He'd displayed images of him sleeveless with his stump, and his arm with a prosthetic prominently on his profile. She'd said she wasn't averse to it, and he believed her.

He just needed to look in her eyes. Then, just like Dylan and Fran, he'd have a woman who'd place her hand over his heart and fiercely protect that organ with all that she was. He'd have a woman tilt her head back, offering her lips to him for a kiss. He'd have a woman he'd wrap his arms around, a woman who knew his love was true and whole. Even if he couldn't quite lock her in an embrace, she'd never doubt that he'd hold her.

The moment Sarai touched down back on US soil, he'd have it all. Soon …

~

Wanna know a secret?
Sarai's not out of the country.
She's actually not far from the ranch.
It's just she has a little—well, big secret that she's not sure Reed will be able to accept.
Wanna know what it is?

You'll find out next in
"Offering His Arm"
the third book in The Brides of Purple Heart Ranch!

OFFERING HIS ARM

THE BRIDES OF PURPLE HEART RANCH
BOOK 3

CHAPTER ONE

"That makes no logical sense."

Typically, when Reed Cannon said those words they were out of frustration as he tried to use facts and figures to prove what was clearly rational. Not this time.

Reed found himself running the fingers of his right hand through his hair. His lips split into a grin. His shoulders relaxed as he leaned back and looked at the screen.

"Not everything has to make sense, Specialist Cannon," said the woman on the other end of the voice only call.

She was wrong again. But Reed didn't mind. He liked the sound of her voice and was happy to hear her speak more words. Even if they were groundless and implausible.

"Some things you just know," she continued.

She had him. Because this was something that Reed, somehow, someway, just knew. Sarai Austin, the owner of the sultry voice that was heating up Reed's speakers, made sense. She was the proverbial One that the love stories told of.

The two of them had so much in common from their educational backgrounds; where he had studied Computer Science, she had studied Web Design. To their tastes in food; she detested Brussel's sprouts and you couldn't get him near a stalk of cruciferous poison. And then there was the most important commonality; they rolled in the same science fiction television and film fandoms.

"The Weeping Angels would totally and entirely decimate The Silence," Reed insisted, championing the scary statue villains in the hit science fiction television show *Doctor Who*.

"Nah unh," Sarai disagreed. "The way a Weeping Angel kills is when their victim looks away. That's when the stone figure comes alive, uncovers their eyes, and moves closer. If an Angel looks away from a Silence they'd forget they'd even saw them. Hence, the Silence would win."

"Sarai, you are so wrong."

"Oh, really, Reed? You may have gotten me on the Kirk over Picard argument. I still don't concede on the Spike was better for Buffy than Angel debate. But I'm right on this one."

"The Angel would turn back to stone as soon as the Silent looked at it. But the Angel can still see the Silent while it's a statue, so it wouldn't forget. Then, the moment the Silent blinks, the Angel would move in and kill it."

Sarai sighed on the other end of the line. Reed was getting used to that sound. It wasn't a sound of resignation. No, Sarai didn't give up so easily. She was about to move in for the kill, and Reed couldn't wait to hear her rebuttal.

"Ah, but that's where you're wrong. If they looked at each other, they'd be locked in a staring contest forever."

"You know this is a nonsensical argument about fictional characters?"

"I know that when you no longer have a leg to stand on in a debate you call it nonsensical."

Reed chuckled. Just as he was learning her quirks and idiosyncrasies, she was learning his. The sound of her light laughter surrounded him in stereo, but the box on the screen where the video of her face would be was dark. He wanted it to light up with the technicolor of a movie screen.

Reed and Sarai had been in communication for weeks on the

dating app. Unlike many of the sites out there that had users swiping left or right depending on someone's attractiveness, this app was designed by sociologists, behavior scientists, and psychologists. The app matched users on levels of compatibility.

Sarai and Reed had earned a 98% compatibility score.

They'd gone through the seven stages of chatting via messenger. Then recently moved onto chatting over the voice feature of the app. It took four conversations to unlock the video feature. This was their fifth conversation.

The video feature's red button had changed to green with their last conversation, but neither of them had engaged it. They had no idea what the other looked like.

Reed wasn't fooled enough to say it didn't matter. He knew it did. The last three women he'd chatted with had balked when they'd seen what had become of his left arm. If he were honest, he'd admit that he'd rushed those relationships. Eager to get to the big reveal to see if they'd accept him.

He'd seen their rejection the moment the video went live. Two of them had tried to play it off that his prosthetic arm wasn't a big deal. One had ended the call immediately. Those other two never called back after their play acting.

Reed had taken things slow with Sarai. Mainly because of their high compatibility score. But also, because he liked chatting with her. Now they were outside a chat room and talking. But he couldn't delay it any longer. She had to see him. He just hoped that she accepted what came up on the screen.

"Sarai, you know what would make sense right now?"

"What? That the Cybermen could take out Daleks?"

Reed chuckled at the absurd idea, but he kept the conversation on track. "The video feature is available. Do you think maybe it's time we both went live on screen?"

The pause that ensued was deafening. Reed leaned back in his office chair. His office consisted of a desk shoved into the corner of the dining room he shared with no one. Reed wanted to share his dining room. He wanted to share his life. He felt certain that this was the woman who should be sitting next to him in this empty room.

"Why?" Sarai asked. Her voice was so tiny and small. So unlike the big personality that came through her text messages and voiced arguments.

"There's something about me that I think you should know. You have to see me in order to do that."

"Is this about your arm?" she asked. There was a note of relief in her voice. "You wrote that you have a prosthetic clear as day on your profile. It doesn't bother me."

"Women have said that to me in the past. Then when they see it, they sing another tune."

Reed leaned forward, getting closer to the dark video dot at the top of his screen, even though Sarai couldn't see him. "I really like you, Sarai. I'd like to take our relationship to the next level. A level where there are pictures. Unless … you're not interested in going any further."

"No, no. It's not that. It's just …"

Reed pulled close to the speakers listening intently as she inhaled. Still no resignation in her breath. She wasn't giving up. She was going to launch into another argument.

And he was going to give in. If she didn't want to see him live, or if she wanted to wait longer, he'd let her have her way. It didn't make sense, but something told him he'd have to be patient with this woman.

"All right. We can turn the cameras on."

Reed's heart pounded against his chest. He felt an itch in the palm of his hand. The itch was in the palm of his left hand which was no longer a part of his body. Phantom feelings came to him from time to time. Right now, the phantom fingers of his left hand wanted to reach out and click the button to turn on the feed that would finally bring him closer to meet his match. He reached out his right hand and flipped the switch.

CHAPTER TWO

The green button flashed at Sarai, daring her to click it and show all of her imperfections to Reed. Sarai had used many dating apps over the last couple of years. This was usually the time that she typically closed her laptop and ran.

Well, not physically run. More metaphorically. Because Sarai Austin was in no shape to run. At least not any longer.

Just three years ago she'd strutted her stuff on some of the hottest runways in the world. Now, she rarely left the house or got out of her pajamas. Her life was spent entirely online, from keeping up with her various makeover blogs, to chiming in on fandoms, to socializing on various platforms with virtual friends. She'd gone to college online, earning a degree in web design, which came in handy with her current line of work.

She'd even had a couple of virtual boyfriends. Sarai was always careful to choose men who lived far enough away from her that it would make a weekend getaway cost-prohibitive. Her last relationship was with a guy in Russia. But he'd gotten tired of their chat room talks and unfriended her. The guy after that, he'd lived in Australia. When he'd wanted to FaceTime her, she'd ended the relationship.

What other choice did she have? She wasn't about to turn on the live feed so that they could see that her profile picture was three years old and thirty pounds lighter than she was in the present day. No, she didn't need that kind of rejection. She'd had enough from the modeling world.

So why was her finger hovered over the accept button to engage her video camera with Reed?

Because she looked forward to their chats every night. Because he made her laugh, genuinely laugh. And he made her think, and stretch her mind when she went toe to toe with him in one of their debates.

Also because he had no idea what she looked like, neither in the past nor in the present.

Sarai had made her way around nearly every dating app out there. They all required a photograph as part of the profile. But not this one.

Instead, it engaged its users on a final exam about their life, asking questions about every facet of their being then matching potential couples based on an algorithm. Most of the guys Sarai had been matched with had been slightly over fifty percent. But she and Reed were a near perfect match at ninety-eight percent.

Maybe … Just, maybe?

The computer screen blinked. The dark square that had been black filled with the face of a man. A handsome man. Sarai leaned in and wiped her monitor just to make sure all that perfection was real.

There were no wayward smudges on her lens. Reed Cannon was the stuff of a girl's dreams. He was handsome with his sandy blond hair and evenly tanned skin. His intelligent, dark eyes pierced her through the colored monitor. His lips were stretched in a cupid's bow that aimed straight for her heart. He looked like a young Luke Skywalker. All he needed was the lightsaber.

And he wanted to date her. So there had to be something wrong with him. She just couldn't figure it out.

Then she saw it; his prosthetic arm. He thought that would deter a woman? If anything it clenched the comparison to the young Jedi in her mind. What fan of the Star Wars franchise wouldn't find the loss of a limb in combat just a little hot?

"Sarai? Are you there?"

"Just a second."

Sarai took a deep breath. She could do this. She wanted to do this. She wanted to continue her conversations with Reed. And if they had to happen on screen, then so be it. She reached to click the mouse.

But before she did, she readjusted the camera to ensure that it only showed her from the shoulders up. All the weight she'd gained was in her belly and hips. She had a good collarbone. And the angles of her face were still attractive.

She'd made up her face, of course. What woman didn't immediately put on makeup after rolling out of bed in the morning whether they were receiving company or not? She wasn't a complete sloth.

She'd penciled in a smoky eye to accentuate the lift of her lids. She'd learned to kohl her eyes back in middle school under the tutelage of her Persian mother. As always, Sarai added some golden sparkles to bring out the hazel flecks in her green eyes.

Her lips were Autumn Red, a shade that highlighted the hints of red in her skin coloring. She'd kept her blonde hair up in an intricate knot that looked effortless, but she'd taken forty-five minutes to sculpt it. Her blonde tresses and green eyes were the only physical traits she'd gotten from her dad's side of the family. Everything else spoke to her Middle Eastern roots. All bundled up together, it made her look unique.

Well, it made her face look unique.

Checking once again to be sure that the virtual connection between her and Reed was disconnected, Sarai stood. She readjusted her shirt. The scoop neck flattered her collarbone making her look slimmer, but when she stood the shirt rode up exposing the rolls of her belly.

Her flesh wasn't on display. She'd double-Spanxed herself into the top. But that hadn't stopped the bubbles of her belly from rising up beyond the spandex. And the double-Spanx always made laughing, and talking, and breathing tricky. But beauty was pain, right?

Looking into the monitor, Sarai saw herself framed for the view. From the neck up, she had no trouble admitting she was a beauty.

Once upon a time, her face had gotten her booked into the high end of fashion. It was just the rest of her that was a fat mess.

Her boobs, which had always been large, now had an equal amount of flesh under her armpits. Her arms now had an extra layer of fat that wiggled when she raised them. Her belly jiggled when she walked as if she were doing some belly dance from her ancestral homeland. And don't get her started on her thighs. She was sure Thor trembled when she walked.

Sarai took a deep breath. In her mind, she took those negatives statements and picked them apart. She was not the number on the scale. She was not solely what she saw reflected back in the mirror. The positivity technique she'd practiced in therapy helped to calm her nerves. But it didn't change her mind. Therapy had helped her cope, but it hadn't cured her. She would never be truly cured.

"Sarai? Has our connection gone bad?"

Sarai closed her eyes. She didn't want the connection she had with this man to break. But to keep it intact, she'd have to reach out and grab the other end of the knot.

Sarai clicked the button.

On the other end of the connection, Reed blinked a couple of times. Sarai chewed her lip as she waited for his verdict. Were her arms in the shot? Could he see the flab? Oh no, she hadn't contoured her cheekbones to perfection. Surely she looked like a chipmunk with a store of winter's nuts in her jowls.

"Wow," Reed whispered.

Sarai's hand shot to her cheek. Was it that bad? What had she been thinking? She reached for the mouse to turn off the camera. The fat wobbled at the backside of her bicep as she did so.

"You're beautiful." Reed's smile stretched across his face. His dark eyes were crystal clear as he gazed at his screen. He didn't look disgusted. He looked pleased.

Maybe the camera subtracted a few pounds? There was the whole compression thing that happened as information traveled across the ether. He'd called her beautiful. It was nice to hear. But still, Sarai had a hard time believing it was the truth.

"*You're* beautiful," she parroted. Those words she believed. Reed could've easily broken into the modeling world with his looks.

"Not without all my parts." He held up his prosthetic arm.

"Nonsense." Sarai barely gave it a glance. She was more intent on the light in his eyes as he looked at her in the monitor. For the first time in a long time, she didn't mind her own reflection. "Put on a black glove, put a lightsaber in it, and I'll probably swoon."

Reed threw his head back and laughed. Sarai had loved eliciting laughter from him over the voice calls. Watching it happen in real time and in color was the most beautiful thing she'd ever seen. Suddenly, she couldn't remember why she'd waited so long to get to this step? If this was the sight she'd see at the top of the mountain, then she'd happily climb to get here.

"I know the protocol says to have four video chats before meeting in person," said Reed. "But I'd love to take you out to dinner."

Sarai felt herself falling off the high mountain at the mere thought. Dinner and date; two of the most feared words in her vocabulary. Reed wanted to not only see her in the flesh, he also wanted to watch her feed the excess amount of flesh on her person.

No, this wouldn't do.

Her hand reached for the disconnect button. Her index finger pointed at the END button on the screen. But she couldn't do it. She didn't want to lose the sight of his face. Or the twinkle in his eye as he looked at her. But neither could she see him in person the way she was.

"Come out with me, Sarai."

"I can't."

Reed's face fell. The light in his eyes dimmed. "Why not?"

"Because ..." Sarai looked out the window at the Montana skyline. One of the compatibility points was proximity. She knew Reed lived in the same state as her. He was only thirty minutes away. "Because I'm headed out of town. Out of the country, actually. I'll be in Paris for a couple of weeks doing makeup for my friend's photo shoot."

"A couple of weeks?" He looked devastated.

"But maybe we can see each other when I get back? That is if you're still interested."

"*If* I'm still interested?" He raised a brow and then leaned into the camera. "Would a Weeping Angel mute a Silent?"

Surprised laughter spilled out of Sarai. "Wait, we haven't come to an agreement on that."

"Then I suppose we'll have to keep debating it and settle it when we meet in person."

Reed's grin was contagious. Sarai found herself matching it, no longer concerned if her cheeks were puffing out. She had a plan.

There were plenty of weight loss programs that touted drastic changes in just thirty days. She'd start one tomorrow, and then, next month, she'd settle this fictional argument in real life with this man straight out of her dreams.

CHAPTER THREE

"How in the world did coffee spill inside the tower?" Reed crouched over the soggy computer terminal atop Dr. Patel's desk. The smell of fried wires and dark roast hit his nose.

Beside him, Soldier gave the wet ground a sniff. The little Chihuahua had been Reed's shadow for the last few weeks. His literal shadow as the small dog sported only three limbs like his human companion.

"Everything was going fine," said Dr. Patel. "And then the coffee holder suddenly retracted."

"Coffee holder?" Reed looked around the edge of the desk. There was no coffee holder. He knew that for a fact.

The interior design and functionality inside the medical suite had been his responsibility. That had included ordering the furniture and putting things together. It would be a feat for a one-armed man, but Reed was up for the task. He knew the job would take multiple days so he'd ordered the computer hardware and the office furniture to come in on separate days.

But somehow the computers and office furniture had all arrived on the same day. He was sure one of his fellow soldiers had interfered with his order, or simply held up the packages until they were all here at the same time. That way Reed couldn't refuse their help in putting things together when everything came at once.

Xavier and Sean had set about screwing in and hammering at the office furniture while Reed had focused all of his attention on the computers. When it came to computers, the other two men were pretty useless.

Reed couldn't stand being useless. Or worse, having someone think he was useless. Just because he'd lost a limb didn't mean he'd lost out on life. He still did all the things he loved.

He played video games. He played tabletop games. He played sports. He dated.

Nope. Not having his arm wasn't holding him back in the slightest. What was standing in his way, at the moment, was just an ocean.

The Atlantic Ocean stood between him and Sarai. That body of water was keeping Reed from achieving his goal of meeting her, courting her, wooing her, proposing to her, and then marrying her all within six weeks' time. Six weeks was the deadline for when the land the ranch sat on would change its zoning so that only families could live there daily. If Reed wanted to stay in this place where he was accepted, this place where he was useful, this place that had given him and his fellow soldiers a new purpose after exacting a pound of flesh from each and every one of them, then he'd have to get married.

That was why he'd been on the dating apps. He was looking for a bride who'd be compatible for him. If he could get the right woman to say yes in time, then he could stay for the rest of his life.

"Where exactly did you put your coffee cup, Dr. Patel?" Reed turned back to a problem he could solve.

He'd been a technology specialist in the armed forces. He was still able to perform all the tasks necessary to operate a computer. However, his disability status cut him out of a lot of the jobs he'd once been qualified for; namely those in combat zones. What was left for him were jobs he was overqualified for, jobs that didn't use 10% of his skillsets, jobs that would leave him bored to tears behind a desk all day long.

Reed turned to Dr. Patel as the older man pointed to the computer tower. Reed frowned. There was no coffee holder there.

Dr. Patel pressed a button. Soldier let out a stream of yips as a whirring sound emitted and the CD disk drawer opened. Both man and dog stared speechless at the dripping compartment meant for outdated circular disks. Then they both swiveled their heads to look up at the degreed man who sat in the office chair.

Last week, the psychologist had called Reed into his office. Dr. Patel had frowned at him insisting he'd called Reed for help with his computer problems ages ago. Reed was meticulous about appointments and being mindful of people's time. When he insisted he never got the message, Dr. Patel said he'd pressed the F1 button on his computer days ago. Reed had tried to explain that that particular HELP function wasn't connected to him.

Reed hadn't laughed at the older man. It was par for the course with the good doctor and technology. When he'd first come to work at the ranch, Dr. Patel had asked Reed if he could reboot the internet because it was running slow that day.

"How is it you developed the dating app that has likely changed my life, but you have more trouble with technology than anyone I've ever met?" Reed asked as he sat down to work on the sopping wet terminal. He didn't have high hopes that the computer would survive. If it did survive this attack by the good doctor, its days were still numbered in this office.

"I didn't develop the app." Dr. Patel reached down and brought Soldier into his lap. The dog balanced on his hind legs as he stretched his small head up to receive scratches. "Only the compatibility questionnaire. That, I wrote out on paper. So, it's working well for you? You've found some matches."

"I found THE match. We're a 98% compatibility."

"That's wonderful. I'm so pleased to hear it. I suppose you'll be bringing her to the ranch soon? Possibly wedding bells in the near future?"

Reed hadn't told Sarai about the necessity for wedding bells yet. He hadn't told her he needed to get married in under two months if he wanted to keep his home and his livelihood here on the ranch. He'd had enough rejection when he'd been discharged from the army.

"She's out of the country for a couple of weeks," said Reed. "But we've been talking every day for a while. Now we're video chatting and FaceTiming."

"Sounds like things are progressing. Pretty much like how I courted my wife. We wrote to each other and spoke over the phone before meeting face to face."

Dr. Patel had had an arranged marriage, and he'd been happily married for decades. He'd arranged many other people's marriages, including two other soldiers on the Purple Heart Ranch. Reed had thought about recruiting the doctor for his love life too, but he'd become gun-shy about meeting women in the flesh when he had some flesh of his own missing.

The app, which allowed two potential partners to get to know each other based on compatibility, was a much more palatable idea. And it had worked. He'd met Sarai who hadn't once balked at his lost limb.

"She's out of the country for weeks, you say?" asked Dr. Patel. "That'll be cutting it close. The zoning changes officially in just under two months."

"Yeah, I know." But Reed also knew that Sarai was it for him. He'd never met someone he'd had so much in common with. She was the one. He just knew it. "I guess I'll just have to get her to fall for me over the internet."

The computer before him sparked and whizzed. Reed jumped back toward safety. Soldier hopped down from Dr. Patel's lap and ran out of the room. The wires connecting the terminal to the router smoked. Looked like the terminal's number had come sooner rather than later.

CHAPTER FOUR

Sweat dripped down Sarai's face as she pumped her arms and marched in time to the beat. Coordination was not her strong suit. Unless it had to do with accessorizing.

Her latest blog post had been on pairing the right bracelet with the right lip gloss and then moving day to night with the look. It had garnered her over a thousand likes in an hour. She was now a quarter hour into the new aerobic phase of her life and beads of sweat were her only companion.

Sarai's heart pounded as she tried to mimic the so-called easy movements of the skinny women in scant spandex on the screen. This workout promised it was simple enough for the very beginningist of beginners to succeed. So far she was succeeding, even if out of breath.

"Now, deep breath in," said the cheery leader on the screen.

The fitness expert's rock hard abs glistened with oil that made Sarai squint as she looked at the flat screen TV. Sarai looked away from the leader's example to the girl next to her. The carbon copy of the leader had been pointed out at the start of the video as the one to follow for a low-impact version of the exercises. Second fiddle's abs were cut and glistening too. Neither woman was breaking a sweat or grunting or grimacing like Sarai. Sarai couldn't help but wonder why no one on these videos looked like the people who pressed play at home?

It was no matter. The skinny leader had just told everyone to take a deep breath. That had to mean she was at the cool down portion of the workout. They'd stopped moving and were all taking deep, soothing breaths. Oh, thank goodness, it looked like it was over.

"And another deep inhale," said the workout leader. "Great job. You did it."

Sarai had done it. She'd made it through the entire workout. She was out of breath and a sweaty mess, but she'd done it.

"That completes the warm-up."

Sarai froze. Her arms had been stretched up in the inhale posture. Her head had been tilted up toward the ceiling, as though she were lost in a prayer of gratitude. Her head dropped down until she was looking square at the television screen to make sure she'd heard the skinny leader right.

Warm up?

That was the warm up?

Sarai dropped her arms to her sides. The flesh of her arms landed against the flesh of her love handles with a splat and a squish. She picked up the remote control and killed the power on the television set. The world turned to black, erasing the glistening abs of the trainers.

Thirty days. The cover on the DVD promised she'd lose up to twenty pounds in twenty days and become her best self. But Sarai couldn't make it twenty minutes in the program.

Outside, the beautiful Montana sky was darkening. She'd told Reed that she was out of town. It was the only reason she could think of to keep from seeing him in person while still seeing him virtually. Because she wasn't quite ready to give him up. She wasn't sure if she could ever give him up.

What was a guy like him doing on a dating site anyway? He could have any girl he wanted with his looks and his intelligence and that smile. Oh, that smile.

Sure there was the reality of his missing limb. But Sarai forgot about it every time she spoke to him until he brought it up. Which he always did.

It was as though he wanted to shove it in her face. As though he wanted to make sure she caught it and that he wasn't hiding it. But it didn't matter to Sarai. So much about him outshined that one fault.

Unlike with her where there was so much of her to spread around. Sarai flopped down on the sofa. Her wide load displaced so much air that the magazines on the coffee table fluttered pages open. Spread in the center of the fold were girls she'd known in her modeling career. Their abs were even flatter than the fitness experts.

Models weren't meant to have a six-pack. Flat was better than bumps. For years, Sarai had striven to meet that imperfect ideal. But her body kept expanding in ways that were unacceptable to the powers that be in the industry.

The last straw had been when a casting director had ordered her to consume nothing but water the entire twenty-four hours before she was set to do a shoot. Sarai had done as she was told. She was welcomed onto the set the next day. The clothes hung off her frame in a way that showed her emaciated frame. And then, twenty minutes into the shoot, she collapsed.

That had been the last time she'd been on a set or walked a runway or even taken a selfie. She'd thought that had been her rock bottom when she'd hit the floor. She'd been wrong.

Her stomach grumbled at the memory. Or possibly from all the calories burned during that ten-minute warm-up of torture. Sarai hefted herself off the couch and went to the kitchen.

The contents of the fridge were a forest of green. Fresh, leafy greens. Green smoothies. Green tea. Her stomach grumbled again, this time in protest at the sight. No, that sound was her computer.

She had an incoming video call. She knew it couldn't be Reed. He believed she was in Paris, which would mean it was around two in the morning for her in France.

But this call was from France. The only people who'd be up in

France at this time of night were the chic clique coming from a fashion show's after party.

Sarai shut the fridge and went over to her laptop. She didn't bother framing the camera to only show her face. She flopped back in her office chair as her spandex let her rolls hang out.

"Hey, girl," Sarai said.

"Hey, girl," came a deep voice from across the web. A flash of light filled the dark frame, then a beautiful male face came into view.

Mason Lee had cheekbones that every woman would die for. His eyes were outlined in sparkling blue liner exaggerating the curve of his Asian features. His glossed lips were spread in a smile as he leaned in toward the camera as though he could peer into the screen.

"What are you wearing?" he asked.

"Spandex."

His bottom lip pushed up toward his top lip as though forming the top of a question mark. "Why?"

"I told you I was starting that exercise program today."

Mason's bottom lip pressed harder, curving even more. "Why?"

Sarai clucked her tongue at him, but his lips still remained in their curved question mark. She fluttered her hands up and down the tight fabric encasing and suffocating her body. "I'm finally trying to lose the weight."

"Sweetie, how many times do I have to tell you? Women pay to have the curves you have."

"Not in the modeling world, they don't."

"Well, you're not in this world any longer, are you?"

"Because I'm too fat."

Mason lips reformed their shape. There was no question this time. He was about to start a full-blown inquiry.

Sarai scrambled to correct her language. "It's just that time of the month. I'm not feeling like myself."

Her best friend didn't look convinced, but he did drop the crease between his brow. Sarai didn't need him to become concerned about her. She wasn't backpedaling into harmful behaviors. She was just having a bad day.

"You were always far too real to meet the unrealistic ideal of these idiots," Mason said.

"Says the man who models for a living."

"It's different for guys, and you know that. They want men with muscles and six-pack abs. They want women who look like little girls or little boys. You look like the full-grown woman you are. You are healthy, and your body functions exactly as it's meant to."

Sarai knew Mason was doing what BFFs did, trying to make their bestie feel good about themselves. He also knew the things to say and what not to say to trigger her disorder. She wasn't triggered, just disappointed in her performance with the workout program.

"Well, you look like you worked up a sweat. How did it go?" he asked.

Sarai hung her head. "I didn't make it past the warm-up."

Now Mason's lips formed an O. But not one of surprise. It was a wince of commiseration. It hurt Sarai's brain just thinking about Mason's hours-long workout regimen.

"Wait a minute," he said. "Is this for that soldier?"

She twisted her lips instead of responding. Unfortunately, since the video was live her bestie saw the expression and read her correctly.

"Sarai, honey, you need to stop hiding behind your laptop. Just go and meet him."

For the first time in a long time, Sarai wanted to. She wanted to get dressed up and go out. She wanted to sit across from a man and feel all the jitters and excitement of a first date. She felt that every time she sat down with Reed at her laptop. What would it feel like to sit across from him in real life?

"You've never talked about a guy this much before. And didn't you say he has no idea what you look like? That means he likes you for you."

"We video chatted the other day."

Mason squealed with delight. "Rai Rai, if this guy is as great as you say he is, he'll accept you for who you are, not what you look like."

Sarai chewed the inside of her lip, but she didn't answer. Her grumbling stomach filled the silence. She reached out to hit the mute button too late.

"What have you eaten today?" Mason asked, his lined eyes turned to inquisitive.

"I just finished working out. You're supposed to eat afterward."

Mason glared at her.

"The fridge is stocked with greens." Sarai's stomach grumbled again at the thought of the unappetizing green foods awaiting her.

"Sweetie, you have a habit of going to the extremes sometimes. I just don't want you to do that now."

"I'm good," Sarai said. "I'm not going down that path again."

Mason glared some more. "I worry about you when I'm not there."

Sarai and Mason had shared this townhouse for just under a year. But he was rarely at home with all of his bookings around the world. Sarai often forgot she had a roommate.

"I just don't want you falling back to old patterns," Mason was saying. "Maybe you should schedule some appointments with that doctor you used to see."

"Mace, I'm going to eat now. I don't need to see a shrink."

"Okay, okay." He held up his hands, but his lips were pressed up in that curved question mark again.

Sarai decided she'd rather cut the conversation short over going down the dark path of her past. "I'm gonna go eat, and you need to go get your beauty sleep."

"Sleep? Sweetie, I'm in Paris. This city never sleeps. We're headed out for the after-after party. I'll call you tomorrow to let you know who got drunk and who slept with whom."

They were laughing again as they disconnected the call. Her bestie had nothing to worry about. Sarai had no intentions of taking things to an extreme. But neither did she want to turn the exercise program back on. She got up from her office chair, on wobbly legs that still burned from the ten-minute contortions she'd endured, and made her way back to the forest inside the fridge.

CHAPTER FIVE

"I can't believe there's such a thing as a beauty blog." Reed leaned back in his desk chair as he looked at his computer screen. "And you make a living from it?"

"Yes, I do. I make a full time living hiding the flaws of women and …" Sarai's smile warmed the low resolution of the screen. She leaned in conspiratorially. Reed found himself pitching forward too. "… and some men."

Reed threw his head back and laughed. He was used to being the one telling the jokes, and he did with Sarai. She laughed at all his jokes which was another point in her column. Reed was keeping score.

The dating app's algorithm said they were a 98% compatibility match, but Reed wondered if it were actually an even 100%. Sarai was smart; she hadn't made a single spelling mistake or grammatical error in her profile. She was prompt; she always showed up a couple minutes early for their scheduled chats. And she was capable; she ran her own business and, by all accounts, was quite successful at it. Even if Reed didn't entirely understand it.

Yes. She was a perfect fit to be Mrs. Reed Cannon. Or Mrs.

Austin-Cannon, if she preferred. Whatever she wanted to call herself, she was definitely taking his name.

"So, Sarai with an I …"

"Yes, Reed with two E's?"

He looked up at the screen and smiled again. They'd only known each other for three weeks but they already had a running inside joke. Instead of the traditional spelling of Sarah with an H, her name ended in I. Reed was more often a last name instead of a first name, and traditionally it was spelled with an I instead of two E's.

In her profile, Sarai explained that her mother was of Middle Eastern descent; Saudi Arabian to be exact. And that's where the nontraditional spelling came from.

"You know," she said, "I almost didn't click on your profile when I saw that you were a vet. I didn't think you'd want to date anyone with my heritage. Even though I was born here in America."

"I hold no ill will to the people of Afghanistan and Syria or any country in the Middle East. The peoples' countries have been taken over by radicals. Many of those citizens are just good people trying to live their lives."

When Reed had joined the army, helping people wasn't the first thing on his mind. He enjoyed the order that was inherent in the armed forces. The chain of command made sense to him. With the analytic mind he had, they'd put him in charge of tech. He'd been in Afghanistan helping to set up the communications system in a rebuilt community. He'd been working on setting up the new school for the children when the explosion happened that took his arm.

He crossed one arm over his chest. His fingers rubbed at his forearm, then caught the stump of his injury. "I was helping set up the internet when this happened."

Reed held up the stump to the computer's camera. He watched Sarai carefully as her gaze shifted on the computer screen. She blinked slowly and cocked her head slightly. Reed held still under her perusal. He felt the phantom sensation of his left-hand clenching into a fist.

"Does it hurt still?" Sarai asked.

Reed shook his head, wishing he could make his nonexistent fingers unball from a fist. But in his mind, his nails dug into his palm and the pain was real. "I didn't feel it when it was severed. And I didn't feel much after."

Sarai's gaze shifted back to center. She was looking directly at him again. She said nothing. She only waited.

He liked that about her. She didn't fill any silence unnecessarily. She didn't say anything cliché. It was another point in her favor. She was an excellent listener.

"Is that a dog barking?" she asked.

Reed bent down and scooped Soldier into the palm of his hand. The little Chihuahua weighed so little that it was easy to balance him in his palm. "Sarai meet Soldier. Salute, Soldier."

Soldier balanced on Reed's lap. He sat back on his hind legs and lifted his solitary front paw. Like Reed, Soldier had lost his left arm, allowing him the ability to still salute.

Sarai giggled with delight. "How did you two find each other?"

"He's not my dog. He belongs to the wife of one of the other soldiers here. We kinda took to each other."

"I can see why," Sarai said, leaving a long pause before filling in the silence. "You both have very serious faces."

Reed chuckled. He liked this girl more and more. Soldier stuck out his tongue and panted. Reed understood the sentiment.

"Listen, Sarai," Reed began again, trying to determine the right order of the words to ask her the question he'd been dying to ask since their first typed chat. Even then, with only characters standing in, she'd captured his full attention. "I'd love to see you."

Her gaze dipped down. Her smile loosened. "You're seeing me now."

She'd said she'd been burned before by the world of online dating. He had too. Women who were not who they said they were were a dime a dozen behind a computer screen. Then there were those that said they were okay with his shortcoming, as he liked to call it. Then they showed up and couldn't stop staring. Or they asked ridiculous and sometimes lewd questions, like what could he attach to his arm.

He'd taken his time with Sarai. But his time was running out. Reed had less than two months to court Sarai, woo her, and convince her to marry him.

He'd said on his profile that he was looking for a serious, long-term relationship. But he hadn't said how soon. Nor how serious.

"I want to take you out," he said.

"I told you, I'm out of town."

"But when you get back next week?" Reed watched her throat work. He wasn't imagining their chemistry. He knew they could be something more, something real if they could just meet in real life. Unless there was a reason they couldn't meet in person. "Sarai? Is there someone else?"

Her eyes flashed up to the screen. Indignation in the light green of them. "I wouldn't do that."

A small smile played at the edge of Reed's mouth. "I'm sorry. I just really like you, and I want to take this to the next level." Heck, he wanted to take it to the final level.

"We can see each other when I'm finished -I mean. We can see each other when I get back."

"So, next week?" Hope filled his heart.

She squirmed on the screen. "It might be a little longer. I'm working hard, trying to … finish. But that doesn't mean I want to stop seeing you online, while I'm here, in this place."

Reed sighed. It would have to do. He could wait another week, a couple weeks if necessary. The moment she set foot back in Montana, he would sweep her off her feet. Metaphorically speaking since he only had one arm. Because he knew, without a doubt, that he wanted there to be nothing more than a hyphen between them.

CHAPTER SIX

Sarai leaned back in her ergonomically correct chair. It squeaked, springs protesting the move. She ignored the sound in light of her new progress.

She hit post on her latest blog entry about finding your perfect shade of blush. Her last entry got over five thousand likes in just a week. She had a couple hundred comments on the post as well. Sarai had a knack for helping others enhance their outer beauty with the perfect shade or right accessory just by looking at their profile pictures.

She was feeling good today. She'd been doing well this whole last week. She'd made it further and further through the exercise video. Last night, she'd even made it to the end and was still standing … leaning against the sofa was more like it. But she was on her feet.

The greens in the fridge hadn't spoiled. She'd actually eaten them. They'd just needed a bit of spice, and olive oil, and a pinch of honey. With a bit of Middle Eastern flare, the field fare was edible. She'd even begun practicing mindful eating again like her doctor had taught her too.

Food was nourishment for the body, mind, and soul her psychologist used to tell her. But she'd be the first to admit that it tasted better with a bit of curry powder and cinnamon.

Her stomach grumbled now in the middle of her work day. Sarai saved her work and rose from her chair to answer its call. Mason had worried she would slip back into old, destructive patterns. He had nothing to worry about.

Coming from a world where she had to fit into the small sample-sized dresses made for mannequins, Sarai was often surprised she'd made it out of the modeling world with only a few scars. Unlike the other models during her tenure, Sarai hadn't developed bulimia or anorexia. Her affliction had been a bit different.

She passed Mason's bedroom door on the way to the kitchen. The door was ajar, likely the wind from last night. Mason liked to sleep with the windows and curtains thrown wide open. He never minded being on display.

Sarai reached in to pull the door closed when she caught sight of someone in the room.

There was a woman she didn't recognize standing in front of Mason's floor to ceiling mirrors. Her skin was tanned golden, as though she'd just come from the sands of Arabia. Her shoulders were elegant and proud, holding up a full bust. Her waist curved inward and then her hips flared out like the belly dancers her mother used to socialize with in Sarai's youth.

Sarai gasped, surprised to see that she was looking at herself. Had she changed so much since the last time she'd stood before a mirror? She'd learned in therapy that she didn't see herself as others did. She hadn't been in front of a full-length mirror in years.

It was only when she looked in a mirror that she had a problem. That's why there was only a hand mirror in her room and no full length mirror in her bathroom. Mason, on the other hand, had mirrors everywhere in his room, which was why Sarai avoided her roommate's private sanctuary like it was a bawdy house.

Intrigued by what she saw, Sarai took another step into Mason's room and then another. She walked on the balls of her toes, tiptoeing quietly into the room, as though afraid to spook her own reflection.

Sarai stood before the mirror and stared. It was like looking at a long lost friend. Granted, her top was flattering as it displayed her angular collar bones. And the leggings she wore held the rolls of flesh at bay. She wasn't flat everywhere as the photographers and designers desired.

Still, she looked … slimmer.

It was working. The change in her diet. The daily exercise. It was all working.

Making an impulsive decision, Sarai turned on her heel. She stepped away from Mason's wall to wall mirrors and opened another door. Inside Mason's bathroom was a scale. It sat catty-corner to the toilet as though it were simply a stepping stool for someone to do their business.

It had been at least three years since she'd stepped on a scale. The memory of the number it had last flashed at her still haunted her dreams some nights. But this was a new day. She'd seen her new reflection. Things were improving.

Sarai hesitated for a second. Then she took a leap. She stepped onto the scale … and wished she hadn't.

The number the needle landed on was higher than the last time she'd weighed herself years ago. Sarai's sucked in her gut, but it did no good. She felt nauseated as she peered down. The world spun as the needle rocked back and forth, landing at a higher number each time.

She reached out to the wall to steady herself. Then she decided to stop the torture and stepped off the scale. The needle fell like a stone back to zero, as though it had been straining under her massive weight, gasping for relief.

This was a disaster.

The mirror must've been a trick. Mason had probably gotten one of those slimming mirrors that department stores, and circuses, used to trick unsuspecting customers. That's the only explanation.

Sarai still felt the rolls on her abdomen. Her thighs still rubbed together creating enough friction to start an electric storm. The flesh at the back of her arms still flapped like wings that would never lift her bulk off the ground.

There were birds that couldn't fly because they were fat. What were they? Ostriches? Yes, ostriches. Funny looking, long neck, fat-bellied ostriches.

There was no way Reed would want to kiss an ostrich. He couldn't get his arms around the bird's belly. He'd take one look at her flabby wings and run in the other direction.

Sarai's limbs felt heavier. Her gut felt bloated. She turned out of the bathroom, sure to avoid looking at the trick mirror. The ground shook at her retreat as the sliver of confidence she'd built over the last few days shattered.

Outside, a cloud settled over the once sunny day. Sarai's heart sped up even though her workout had been hours ago. Her limbs felt leaden. She just wanted to lie down, but her stomach continued its grumbling protest.

She couldn't face the bland greens today. She needed something to warm her insides and soothe her sad soul. She didn't get out much, preferring to interact with the world through her keyboard instead of face to face. But she was in need of some comfort, and food was the only friend she had to turn to.

CHAPTER SEVEN

Reed thumbed at the condensation on his mug. The frothy foam sat atop his drink. Tiny bubbles burst as they rose to the surface. He lifted his glass to meet the others around the table. The mugs crashed and the froth spilled over and onto the dining table.

"Here's to Dylan," said Xavier. "Our fearless leader."

"Hear, hear," came a chorus of male voices. Sean sat to one side of Reed. His shades were off, but he made sure that his scarred side was to the wall and not toward the diners in the restaurant. It had been like pulling teeth to get the man out of the house and off the ranch tonight.

The group was a sight when they went out in force. Xavier and Fran got head nods from men and longing gazes from single women. Their wounds weren't possible to see out in public.

Sean, with his scars, got stares. Dylan, with his prosthetic leg, which he no longer bothered hiding under pants now that he had the love and admiration of a good woman, and Reed, with his prosthetic arm, got pointing and whispers.

Reed didn't let it get to him. Like all the men in his squad, he'd served his nation with honor. He'd left the people of his country a little safer and it had only cost him half a limb. Others had fared far worse. Some even paid the ultimate price.

"Much like the bomb that altered our lives," Xavier continued his boisterous toast. "Dylan had one moment of brightness, then he dimmed, and left behind a lot of smoke."

"You're terrible at this, you know?" said Fran.

"Oh, I'm getting to you," said X. This wasn't just Dylan's belated bachelor party. Francisco had gotten married shortly after Dylan took the proverbial leap. "And here's to Frances. Who followed behind Dylan into the belly of the institution of marriage."

"X," Reed cautioned his fellow soldier, but he knew it was a moot point. The guys loved to razz one another any chance they got.

"Don't get me wrong," said Xavier. "Marriage is a wonderful institution. I'm just not crazy enough to go inside."

No one laughed at Xavier's pathetic jokes. They all knew how he felt about marriage. The man was already eyeing the girls at the next table. And they were eyeing him back.

The five of them had all gathered for a rare night off the ranch for Dylan and Fran's belated bachelor parties. Both of their marriages had been so sudden that there had been no time to plan. Dr. Patel had insisted that they have a meal at his family restaurant on him. They were finally getting around to taking him up on it.

"Let me take this," said Reed, raising his glass once again. This time there was no crashing of mugs. The froth stayed inside everyone's container. "Dylan, we owe you our lives. You continue to lead us through dark times and show us the way. Not just on the battlefield, but in life. You came through adversity and were able to find the love of your life. I only hope I can do the same someday."

Dylan pressed his lips together and nodded. Gratitude was clear in his blue eyes. Reed turned his attention to Fran.

"Fran, your ability to plan, and your vision of a better world, has touched more lives than you'll ever admit. You are a role model to the children now in your care, and to the children that will come onto the ranch for learning and healing. I am proud to be your brother, and hope that I can be half as good of a man to the family I plan to have someday."

Fran's throat worked. His Adam's apple bobbed up and down before he managed to swallow. Satisfied that he'd paid the proper tribute to his brothers, to his family, Reed raised his glass higher.

"To Dylan and Fran."

Xavier and Sean repeated Reed's words. But as soon as they were sipping at their brews, Xavier broke the moment, which wasn't a surprise.

"That's enough out of you Donna Reed," said Xavier. "As I was saying—"

"We're good, X, thanks," said Dylan. "Thank you, Reed. Those were powerful words."

Fran nodded his agreement. They both lifted their glasses to their lips again and drank. Each of their wedding bands caught in the low light of the restaurant.

Reed felt a pang in his heart and an itch on his finger. Though he no longer possessed his left hand, he still wanted to sport one of those bands.

"Looks like you're up next," Dylan said to Reed. "How's the online search for a wife going?"

"Things are going well," said Reed.

He'd been looking online for a while. There had been some time when he'd had plenty of horror stories to tell the guys about the desperate, unhinged, unsavory women trolling the interwebs. Story time hadn't happened for a while though.

Sarai had been in the first batch of online matches. Even though they'd been a near perfect match, she'd been hard to pin down. She still was. But like any problem, Reed knew there had to be a solution.

"You don't have a lot of time left," said Dylan. "It's less than six weeks before the zoning goes into effect on the ranch. It's going to take a year to fight it and get it changed after that deadline."

Reed nodded. He knew what was at stake. He was working on it. There were other women who were available as solutions. He just couldn't stop thinking about the one who was closest to him in every way but physically.

"Did we just hear you correctly?" said a feminine voice. The coeds who Xavier had been eyeing all night turned around to face their booth. "Did you say you have to get married to stay on your ranch?"

"Yes." Xavier pulled on a somber look that any cognizant woman would be able to see was fake. "We'll lose everything if we don't find brides."

These two girls, however, widened their gazes and cooed at the predicament. Reed knew that Xavier had been using this pickup line on unsuspecting women for weeks now. These two were just another group to take the bait.

"Wow," said one of them. She was curly haired and petite. "It's like something out of a romance novel."

"Did a grandfather write in his will that you can't inherit unless you get married by a certain age?" said the other. Her hair was long and bone-straight.

"Or are you all here in the country illegally?" said the one with the curls.

"No," said Reed. "We're all Army vets. It's a zoning issue."

The women's faces fell at the less than romantic legal issue the guys were facing.

"But," said the straight-haired one, "he just said you all need mail order brides."

"*We* don't." Fran held up his ringed finger.

Dylan followed suit, holding up his left hand.

Sean looked away.

With three out of five men off the table, the women looked Reed's way to even up their numbers. Reed didn't have a piece of metal on his finger. He had a metal arm. He held up his prosthetic.

If the women glanced at it and didn't screech in horror, they might be worth his time.

"Oh, my God," said Curly Hair. Her screech was loud enough to force the cook to poke his head around the corner. "What happened to you?"

Her straight-haired friend reared back as though Reed might reach out and give her cooties with his metallic attachment.

Reed had just said that he was a veteran. Couldn't they put two and two together? Apparently not. "Alligator attack."

"Whoa," the two said in unison. Quieter, though.

Airheads weren't his cup of tea. Intelligent, humorous fan-girls were. Reed palmed the phone in his pocket. "Excuse me."

He got up from the table as Xavier crossed over to the girls' table.

Reed made his way to the back porch of the restaurant. A sappy country song about lovers constantly missing meeting each other played on the radio as he did. He dialed Sarai's number. He'd only dialed it one other time when their internet connection had been choppy.

It rang. Then rang some more. He was about to hang up when she answered.

"Reed?" She was a bit out of breath as she said his name.

"Hey," he said. His smile stretched wide just at the sound of her voice. Then he cursed under his breath. "It's midnight there, isn't it? I'm so sorry, I didn't consider the time difference."

"It's okay. I was up. I didn't know we were chatting tonight? I didn't have it on my schedule. I thought you were busy."

Just another thing he liked about this girl. She kept an orderly calendar.

"We're not. I am. I … I was just thinking about you."

There was silence on the other end of the line. He heard traffic through the connection. Was she outside? Had he interrupted her evening? Was she with someone else?

She could be. She had every right to be. They'd never claimed exclusivity. He couldn't even call her his girlfriend.

"No, it's fine," she said. "I was just headed out to grab a bite."

"If you're on a date or something …" Reed kicked at a pebble on the wood patio.

"I'm not seeing anyone else. I mean …"

"Neither am I." Reed rushed to fill the silence, hoping he could close even more distance between him and this woman. "I don't want to see anyone but you."

There was more silence from her end, but he distinctly heard her breath catch. Had he gone too far? He didn't want to push her, even though his time was short. This thing between him and Sarai was too important to mess up over a zoning deadline.

"I'm sorry," said Reed. "I'm not trying to rush you. I just … am I the only one who feels something here?"

"No."

Her voice was so quiet; he wasn't sure he'd heard her until she repeated herself.

"No, you're not."

There was more silence on the line. But it was a comfortable silence. It was the silence they'd shared a couple of times online when she'd caught him gazing at her. There was a hint of embarrassment in her tone, but also pleasure.

"Listen," said Reed. "I don't want to hold you up from your meal. I just wanted to hear your voice."

He could practically hear her smiling through the phone. He knew exactly what that would look like. Her beautiful face would stretch over perfectly straight, white teeth. Her eyes would crinkle at the corners. She might run her hands over her ear to brush away a nonexistent stray hair.

"I'll call you tomorrow."

"Okay," she said. "Goodnight, Reed."

"Good morning, Sarai."

"What?"

"It's already a new day there, in Paris, right?"

"Oh. Right. Of course."

Reed chuckled. He loved getting her all flustered. She'd look away from the screen when she did, giving him a moment to stare at her without shame. Soon he would be able to tilt up her chin when she looked down.

Reed hit the END button on his phone. But he knew that wasn't the end. It didn't matter when it started, but he knew he wanted to begin with this girl and never end. Even if that meant he'd have to leave the ranch.

CHAPTER EIGHT

Sarai hit the END button on her phone. The cool night air slapped her in the face. She hated lying to Reed. Heck, she hated lying to herself.

She'd promised herself that she'd get the weight off in the next few weeks so that she could be confident when she presented herself to him. So that she could be the girl she used to be before it all came crashing down one day on a photo shoot.

But here she was; Week One of her promise, and she hadn't even made any progress. In fact, she was a few steps back. What was she going to do?

Her stomach grumbled again, letting her know what it wanted to do. The smell of curry and spice didn't warm her as she'd hoped it would. The thought of putting the rich cream and carb-loaded rice in her body made her want to puke.

She couldn't go in there. She couldn't eat that food. The day of the photo shoot, she'd met the designer's weight goal after only consuming liquids. Maybe if she just did a little abstinence from food, for just a few days, she could get on track.

Her phone rang at that instant. Mason's made-up face popped on the Caller ID, like a virtual angel on her shoulder hearing her naughty thoughts. Sarai hit DECLINE.

She wasn't regressing into old, harmful ways. She had tools. She knew how to manage her food intake. But it would be okay if she took a day off or two. Fasting was entirely safe if done correctly.

The sounds of a country song of two lovers constantly missing meeting one another sounded into the quiet of the night. It was a peculiar thing to hear the crooning of a cowboy coming out of the doors of an Indian Restaurant.

"Sarai, is that you?"

Was everyone checking up on her tonight? First, Reed. Then Mason, and now her former psychologist.

Sarai turned a model bright smile on, complete with smizing of the eyes—as Tyra Banks liked to say—as she turned to greet Dr. Patel. "Dr. Patel, hi, I thought you spent Wednesday nights at church."

She'd counted on that. She'd learned her mindful eating at Patel's Family Restaurant. Back when Dr. Patel had diagnosed her, one of the treatments was to come dine with him and his family there on Thursday nights.

At Patel's, Sarai had learned to take comfort in curries and chutneys. She'd learned that bread wasn't the devil and a warm piece of garlic naan was sweeter and more satisfying than a bar of chocolate. She'd learned to take thirty minutes just to eat a bowl of rice, reveling in each grain as it hit her tongue.

Mindful Eating, Dr. Patel had called it. It was how Sarai had reclaimed her life after the incessant rejection of modeling had changed her perception of herself. It was how she'd learned to use food to heal and not harm her body.

"It's been too long." Dr. Patel opened his arms up to her. The man was a hugger. But he was also a good listener with a great memory.

He didn't bring her into a hug. He rested his hands lightly on her shoulders and gave her a squeeze. After years of being nothing more than a mannequin for clothes, makeup, and accessories, Sarai still didn't take to people touching her without her permission. She'd given Dr. Patel this permission long ago. Still, he was not one to cross boundaries. He'd wait until his permission was renewed.

"Are you coming in to eat?" he asked.

"I …" Sarai opened her mouth and caught the whiff of the spices that had warmed her from the inside out when she was healing. But she also caught sight of her reflection in a car window. "I was just passing by. I thought you were in church on Wednesdays."

"It's a special day. Some good friends of mine are having a celebration. Why don't you come inside? I'd love for you to meet them."

Sarai was already backing away. "No, I was just out for a walk."

Dr. Patel nodded. But though his head acquiesced, his eyes saw deeper. "How are you adjusting to everyday life?"

"I'm doing okay." Sarai shrugged. The movement might've been hard to see in the voluminous hoodie she was wearing along with the two-sizes too big sweatpants. Dr. Patel wasn't looking at her body. He looked in her eyes.

"How is your heart?" he asked. "Are you getting out? Meeting new people?"

"I'm dating." Not exactly getting out, but online dating was the new age version of going to bars and clubs to meet people.

"How does this gentleman make you feel?"

Sarai smiled thinking about Reed. "He gets me. He listens to me. He's so easy to talk to."

"There it is." Dr. Patel put his index finger under her chin and lifted. "You glow just talking about him. The way you feel inside lights you up outside."

Sarai did feel warm inside when she talked about Reed. She just wished that warmth inside her would burn some extra calories.

"I can't say I'm not disappointed," said Dr. Patel. "I wanted to set you up with a young man who I thought would be perfect for you."

Sarai cringed. Soon after she'd completed her treatment for her eating disorder with Dr. Patel, he'd begun talking about how she now needed to heal her heart. He'd wanted her to come to his church to meet people then. Sarai had demurred then, still getting used to the new her.

"It looks like I'm too late though," said Dr. Patel. But he didn't sound the least bit put out. He smiled when he admitted his defeat. "I can't wait to meet this young man who's stolen your heart."

CHAPTER NINE

After a year of ranch-style living, a three-story walk-up seemed like a hassle to Reed. Standing in the one-bedroom apartment, he crossed the linoleum floor to the barred window.

Outside, the view was nothing but concrete. There were no rolling pastures like on the ranch. No sounds of animals roaming about or calling to each other. Instead, the honks of horns and walla walla of the inner city yelled at him.

Instead of looking out to see Xavier and Sean shooting hoops, Reed saw skinny, young boys with pants hanging low on their hips and angry tattoos on their bare, bird-like chests.

He didn't catch Dylan and Maggie sneaking a kiss behind the barn, or Fran and Eva holding hands as they walked down the lane. Nope. Instead, he saw young girls in too much makeup and too tight jeans talking to grown men twice their age.

Instead of a pack of tame disabled dogs rambling about at the feet of a group of humans who cared for them, Reed looked down to witness young boys holding dogs on short leashes as the canines gnashed their teeth and snarled at one another. Life off the ranch was truly a different world.

"Now we do have wheelchair access. But it's around the back."

Reed turned from the window to face the landlord of the complex. The man was short with a beer belly and ketchup stains on the collar of his shirt.

"There's nothing wrong with my legs," said Reed.

The landlord glanced at Reed's pants-covered legs. A second too late, the man jerked his gaze back up, skirting over Reed's prosthetic. "Well, of course not. I wasn't implying that there was. I just want you to know that we are up to code with the Fair Housing Act and all that mumbo jumbo."

The Fair Housing Act was not mumbo jumbo. It was the law. A law that the federal government deemed necessary to put in place to protect the rights of people of different races, color, religion, national origin, gender, familial status, and ability.

Reed had been around the back of the complex to use that particular entrance, not because he needed it. He'd seen an elderly woman with two bags of groceries. He'd offered his help, but when she'd caught sight of Reed's arm, she'd hesitated. Reed, in his typical fashion when someone was uncomfortable with his wound, made a joke.

"Don't worry, I can handle the bags. I'm all right." He waved his fully intact right arm.

The old lady didn't get it. But she did offer him her bags.

As they made their way up the concrete ramp of the handicap entrance, Reed noted all the cracks in the walkway. Someone in a wheelchair would have great difficulty navigating this place. Someone who needed a cane to get around, someone who had to watch their step to avoid a fall, would face the same challenges.

The law wasn't just for those missing limbs or who had challenges with mobility. Clearly, the landlord had done the bare minimum and called it a day. Whether he put down a deposit on the apartment or not, Reed would definitely be filing a complaint in the morning.

"You'll be happy to know there's a bus on the corner, son. In case you were worried about getting around."

Just as much as Reed hated being underestimated, he hated being called son by anyone he wasn't related to. He'd endured it with a few drill sergeants and other superiors in the service. He'd never balk against the chain of command. But it still got under his skin.

"I can drive," he said to the landlord as he made his way towards the bedroom.

"Really? Is that safe?"

Reed didn't answer. He looked into the bedroom.

"Now, son, any other modifications you have to make, like something to hold you up while you take a shower, you'll be responsible for putting in and taking down when you leave."

"I don't need to make any other accommodations. It's just my arm."

Reed held up his fully functioning right arm. That confused the landlord, who again looked at his prosthetic. Then immediately jerked his gaze away.

Reed didn't expect the man to get the joke. He didn't expect that anyone in this neighborhood would understand him. They'd likely ask a lot of questions or stare and point. He'd stick out like a sore thumb because he only had one.

Still, Reed sighed and took the application the landlord offered. He didn't have many options. Even if he moved off the ranch, he'd still have to commute there every weekday. That's where his job was. Finding a job for a one-armed computer tech was going to be a stretch, and he knew it. The money he got from the government, coupled with what he earned from his work on the ranch, wouldn't afford him any luxuries.

Reed ignored the few stares he got as he made his way back to his truck. It didn't stop his new neighbors from looking at him as though he were less than a man. All because he was missing one of his four limbs. They couldn't see that there wasn't much that limited him. The only thing holding him back in his life was not proposing to the woman he fully expected to spend the rest of his life with.

Reed and Sarai had been talking every morning for the past week. They spoke early in the mornings due to the time difference. Every day he'd wanted to bring up the zoning issue on the ranch and casually work in his need to get married. But he didn't want his proposal to hinge on the zoning issue. He was convinced he wouldn't find a better woman for him than Sarai, not in the cyber world or the real world. So, he'd wait until she came back.

He had to postpone their talk this morning to take this appointment. She hadn't protested, saying she had work to do and could use the time. But they were back on schedule tomorrow. He would broach the topic with her then. Not about the zoning. But definitely about their relationship status.

Could he claim her as his girlfriend even though they hadn't met in person? Maybe he could even fly over to France this weekend. It would cost him the deposit on the apartment, but it would be worth it to see her in the flesh.

Reed's phone rang and his heart pounded at the sound. Could it be her? Was she calling him in spite of their later date? He fished the device out of his pocket hoping to see Sarai's smiling face in the caller ID. Instead, he saw Fran's mug.

"Yeah?" Reed leaned against the passenger side of his truck as he pressed the phone to his ear.

"Hey, you still in town?"

"Just about to head back."

"Eva's got a flat. I'm all the way on the other side of town. Do you think you could give her a hand changing the tire?"

The knot that had lodged itself between Reed's shoulder blades during his apartment visit and tour of his new neighborhood loosened. He felt the phantom pain in his long-lost hand relax. "You know I've only got one of those."

Fran made an impatient sound. "I'm serious, man."

Reed knew Fran was serious. His brothers didn't think twice about his ability to do what was necessary. Something as simple as changing a tire, a feat which most four-limbed human beings couldn't do with two hands, they thought nothing of asking a one-armed man to perform.

"I'm on my way to her," Reed said. He disconnected and hopped in behind the wheel.

He found Eva fifteen minutes later. She was parked near Patel's. Reed greeted the petite brunette with a grin and a hug.

"I told Fran that I could've called Triple-A," she said.

Reed made the same impatient sound that Fran had made a quarter hour ago over the phone. Eva was fiercely independent. She was slowly learning that all the men on the ranch would move heaven and earth for each other and the ones they loved. Reed wanted Sarai to experience the same devotion.

Sarai had told him that her parents traveled a lot and they didn't spend time together. Reed had assumed her parents were divorced but was surprised to learn that they weren't. They simply crossed paths whenever their work put them in the same country.

He couldn't understand how that worked. Once he and Sarai were on the same continent he was determined to have her close by his side. The idea of flying to France was looking more and more appealing to him each moment.

For now, Reed set to work changing Eva's tire. But when he pulled out the spare, he saw that it, too, was flat.

"We can wait for Fran to bring another spare. Or we can leave it here and come back for it tomorrow."

"I just got this car," moaned Eva.

"Yeah, but you insisted on getting a used car with your own money instead of letting your husband buy you a brand new one."

"I don't need a new car."

Eva was a notorious penny pincher. Fran had a habit of telling his wife something was used or discounted when it wasn't just to weaken the fight he'd get out of her. Reed suspected this new used car would stay here on the side of the road, leaving Fran the perfect excuse to buy his frugal wife a brand new model.

"I'm so sorry to take you out of your way," said Eva.

"You know it was no trouble. And I'd never leave you stranded."

"You've got crud all over your shirt because of me." Eva wiped at the grease stain on his shirt.

Reed caught Eva's fingers in his hand and tugged her to move forward. "Why don't you pay me back with dinner. Patel's is just around the corner."

"Deal. Thanks for coming out. You're my hero." Eva pecked the side of Reed's cheek.

Reed leaned into her affectionate embrace. Eva was maternal to her core. Reed would miss her and Maggie fussing over him daily. But he wanted his own wife to fuss over him.

He placed Eva in the crook of his good arm and they fell into step with one another. As they turned the corner, another woman bumped into his chest. The bag of food she'd been carrying fell out of her hands and splattered onto the ground. The smell of curry and other spices wafted through the air.

"I'm so sorry …" Reed began and then trailed off. It couldn't be. He was hallucinating. "Sarai?"

CHAPTER TEN

Sarai's entire life flashed before her eyes. She saw herself at seven when her mother first pushed her onto the stage at beauty pageants when she just wanted to hang out with her friends playing Barbies. She felt the ache in her jaw at seventeen from smiling at casting call after casting call where she was poked, prodded, pinched, and spoken about as though she wasn't there. She smelled the rancid smell of coffee and cola and cigarettes at twenty-one as she crammed her body into dresses a size too small and heels too narrow.

As the scenes of her short life flashed before her eyes, Sarai felt the agony of drowning in tears of the rejection, of the loneliness, of the constant hunger of modeling. That pain of not being good enough had been clawing its way back into her consciousness over the past week as she tried and failed to exercise. As she tried and failed to eat mindfully. As she tried and failed to lose the weight she'd learned to accept was normal and healthy.

She'd taken to looking in the mirror at the evidence again. She'd taken to stepping on the scale and seeing the cold hard facts. She'd thought she'd gained a new lease on life during her therapy. The truth was that all she'd gained was weight.

Her reflection in the glass, the numbers on the scale, they told a different story. They told the story of a once beautiful girl who had let herself go. All she'd gained over the last couple of years was weight. The weight that wasn't coming off. The weight that would keep her from receiving the real live affection of any man, including the one who was now standing in front of her.

"Sarai, is that you?"

Was it her? Was this woman standing before him the real Sarai Austin? She didn't feel like herself. She'd been fasting for the last five days. When she'd stepped on the scale this morning it had gone up two pounds instead of falling even a single ounce. Devastation didn't begin to describe how she felt.

She had to face facts. She wasn't going to lose this weight. She'd let it hang around too long. And now it weighed her down heavily on the sidewalk outside of Patel's standing in a puddle of curried rice and buttered chicken that she wouldn't even get to eat.

And Reed was standing there, looking down on her. Standing with a petite, skinny woman with a bright smile and big eyes. Her waist was small and her hips flared. She wasn't model tall, but she had the kind of figure men were now clamoring over on social media. And she was in Reed's arms.

Sarai couldn't muster the energy to run. All she could do was stand there with the late day sun glaring brightly in her face.

When a cloud moved in she saw clearly. When he said her name, she knew for sure. The life she'd been trying to carve for herself by shaving off the pounds, that life was over.

"I can't believe it," Reed continued.

Sarai waited for the shouting to start. Surely his anger would burst forward now that she'd been caught in a web of lies. Or worse, what if he simply recoiled from her, walked around her, and never spoke to her again. It would be a far worse rejection than any agent or fashion designer or photographer. Because she did want to stand in Reed's light.

"Is this why you couldn't talk today?" he asked, "Because you were flying back?"

Sarai hadn't been able to talk with Reed today because she was under a work deadline that she'd put off all week. It was highly unlike her to miss a deadline, but her body image and weight issues had consumed her. The only time she had felt a semblance of normality was in her morning talks with Reed. And the more she talked to him, the more guilty she felt.

It was a vicious cycle. She'd been spinning around so fast that she just needed for it all to stop.

She'd spent the entire day yesterday in bed. Then, this morning, she'd woken up and forced out a blasé post about choosing the best toner to contour a thin nose.

The art of contouring was just a diversion away from the truth. At the end of the night, the makeup came off, and the big nose would be revealed every time. She wasn't fooling anyone. She was still waiting for her readers to call her out on it. But as yet, no one had.

"This is the best surprise," said Reed. He was smiling at her, not sneering, not glaring, not even frowning. His handsome face was even handsomer in person. And then she was in his arms.

Reed let go of the petite brunette and pulled Sarai into a one-armed hug. But even with that single arm Sarai felt enveloped. She felt surrounded by him.

Her arms came around his back as her sneakered feet squished in her ruined dinner. Reed's shoulders were broad. He smelled like a fresh breeze and warm bread. Sarai wanted to take a bite.

He wasn't angry with her. He thought she'd just returned from her fake trip. He still didn't realize she'd been here all the time, hiding because she was ashamed of the way she looked.

Then she realized. She still looked the way she looked. Even worse, she was in an unflattering sweat suit with minimal makeup.

Of course, she'd put on blush, mascara, and a bit of gloss. She wasn't a savage. But she'd done no contouring, and she had on no eyeshadow.

She was a mess. And the guy of her dreams was gazing down at her. But he wasn't looking at her sweatshirt where her uniboob made an impression in the cotton. He wasn't looking down at the baggy sweatpants that made her look two sizes bigger.

No, he was looking at her face. He was looking into her eyes. And he was smiling with a smile huge enough for her to fall in.

"I'm so happy to see you, Sarai."

And at that moment, Sarai no longer wanted to hide. She didn't care that the flesh of her arms flapped against his back. She didn't care that her stomach pushed against the elastic of her waistband. She didn't care that if she moved her thunder thighs would crack the pavement.

All she cared about was standing under Reed's smiling gaze. And she'd do anything to stay in this exact spot for the rest of her life.

CHAPTER ELEVEN

It was like one of those moments when he was dreaming and he knew he was dreaming and he could direct the course of his dreams. Reed had been dreaming about Sarai for weeks. Nothing X-rated. Just dreams of being in her presence, holding her, talking to her, sitting beside her, holding her hand. Most of the dreams didn't even end with a kiss.

This—the embrace he held her in right now—this was a dream come true. He didn't want to wake up. He didn't want to let her go.

If he'd had any doubts about her, which he didn't, he was certain now. The reality of Sarai, the smell of her, the feel of her, the small gasp she let out as he gave her warm body a squeeze, let him know that this was the real deal.

"I'm so happy to see you, Sarai," he said when he finally was able to let her go. "I can't believe you're standing here in front of me."

"Yeah. Yeah well, as you said, I couldn't talk to you this morning because I was coming here. Home. I've come back home. Unexpectedly. And it looks like I've surprised you."

She had surprised him. But why had her voice taken on a sour note? Reed noticed that Sarai's gaze had slid past him and was now darting at something behind him. At someone behind him.

Eva stood watching the whole exchange with interest. Reed knew this whole incident would be spread around the ranch in just a matter of seconds once she whipped out her phone and texted Fran. That was the payoff for living in close quarters.

He didn't blame Eva. He'd do the same if he had a juicy tidbit about one of the others. It was something Sarai would have to get used to when she came into their group.

A thought entered Reed's mind. A thought he hadn't dared to consider until now. There was time.

There was enough time to convince Sarai that they were right for each other. Not for right now but for always. He had just over a month to take her on a few dates, sweep her off her feet, and then pop the question. Not because he had to, but because he wanted to.

Reed didn't knock arranged marriages and marriages of convenience. But this—what he felt for Sarai—this was something else. He couldn't call it love at first sight. Even though this was the first time he was seeing her live and in the flesh. He'd fallen for her just through their conversations, and he believed she'd done the same.

So why was she fidgeting and not meeting his gaze? Because her gaze was still darting behind him. At Eva.

She couldn't think that— That he could possibly— Didn't she know that he wasn't the kind of guy to lie or cheat?

Reed reached back with his prosthetic and motioned to Eva. "Sarai Austin, I'd like you to meet Eva DeMonti, Fran's wife."

"Fran's wife?" said Sarai.

Reed heard the relief rush through her voice. She had doubted him. He couldn't understand why. He'd have to work harder to make sure she knew how much she meant to him.

Eva stepped forward with a welcoming, non-threatening smile of a woman who was not after a man. The two women shook hands. Then Eva's eyes went large.

"Wait?" said Eva. "Sarai Austin? The model?"

It was almost imperceptible. Reed probably wouldn't have noticed it except he was staring so intently at Sarai. He saw her shoulders hunch at Eva's recognition.

Reed had known Sarai was a model. She'd mentioned it in her profile. But he couldn't remember them talking about it in any of their conversations. She'd only ever mentioned her beauty blog.

"That was a lifetime ago." Sarai wrapped her arms around her figure as though she were trying to hide herself.

"I know," said Eva. "Now you do a makeup blog. You taught me how to do the smoky eye."

Eva waved her fingers in front of her eyes and widened her gaze. Reed hadn't noticed that there was coloring on the lids of Eva's eyes until just now.

"It looks really good," said Sarai, a small smile on her face as she narrowed her gaze at Eva's eyes. "You have a really nice tilt to your eyes. You should elongate the corners with a thin pencil to accentuate that."

"Good tip," said Eva.

Reed had no idea what the two women were on about. He only knew he wanted to spend more time with Sarai, preferably alone so he could start his campaign to win her hand.

"Maybe you could show me how sometime?" Eva continued. "If you ever come to the ranch."

Sarai looked uncertainly at Reed.

"Yes, you should come out to the ranch," said Reed. "I was just about to take Eva back. You could come with us."

"Oh, I'm not dressed to go out," said Sarai.

She looked beautiful to him. Even in the jogging pants and the oversized sweatshirt. Besides, the ranch wasn't a place for fancy dressing. But he didn't want their first time in each other's presence to be spoiled by meeting his entire squad and their even more meddlesome wives.

"Why don't you come to grab a bite at Patel's with us," said Reed. "It's the least I can do since I'm responsible for ruining your dinner."

"It's okay," she said, looking down at the curry-stained paperbag on the sidewalk. "It wasn't for me. I mean, I shouldn't have gotten it anyway."

Reed frowned at that statement. Instead of pursuing dinner at the restaurant, which she did not seem open to, he decided on another route. "Can I give you a lift home?"

Sarai blinked at him, as though she didn't understand the question. Her gaze slid down his arm, his prosthetic arm.

"I do have my driver's license." He felt his jaw tighten and tried to loosen it.

But Sarai didn't look at him in shock. Realization dawned in her green eyes. A small sigh escaped her lips. He knew that sigh. It was the sound she made before she launched a counter-attack on whatever debate they were having.

"Oh, no," she said. "It's just that I'm not that far. I live in walking distance."

"Well, can I walk with you?"

Sarai took a deep breath this time. This sound was new to Reed. It sounded to him as though she were summoning courage. He couldn't imagine what there was to be brave about.

She squared her shoulders, stepped back, and opened her arms. "Are you sure?"

Reed didn't hesitate. "Of course I'm sure."

Sarai's hands dropped to her sides. Reed couldn't see her curves due to the excessive cloth covering her skin, but he knew they were there. He was more intent on looking into her eyes. He could get lost in her gaze.

With her arms at her sides, she still looked at him as though she were confused. But then she nodded in acceptance. "Okay then."

Reed turned to Eva and handed her his car keys. "Order mine to go. I'll be back in a bit."

"Take your time." Eva grinned.

Reed turned back to Sarai. He offered her his arm. His heart stopped when she hesitated again.

But she wasn't looking at his prosthetic. She was looking into his eyes, searching for something. He supposed she found whatever she was looking for because she slipped her hand in the crook of his elbow where he still had flesh. Reed's entire body came alive with just that small touch.

CHAPTER TWELVE

Sarai kept her arms wrapped tight around her middle. She hoped against hope that the maneuver had a slimming effect on her rotund body. But she doubted it.

With every lift of her foot, she felt the jiggle of her upper thighs rubbing together. With every foot placed in front of the other, she heard the ground shake. Could Reed hear it too?

He must have with the way he was fidgeting. He tugged at his ear with his right hand. Then he adjusted a mechanism on his prosthetic.

Sarai marveled at how realistic the fingers looked. The only thing that gave them away was the fact that they weren't twitching like the fingers of his right hand. Reed reached the apparatus out to her and Sarai jerked, embarrassed that she'd been staring.

"I'm sorry." Reed pulled his hand away. "It's just that you're walking on the outside of the sidewalk and closer to the cars. My father beat into my head that a gentleman always puts himself in front of danger for a lady."

Sarai hadn't been considering her safety when she'd chosen which side of the sidewalk to walk on. She'd only been considering her angles. Her right side was her best side. She'd learned through her years of modeling. She needed every advantage she could get.

But she allowed Reed to cross over to the left side of her. He placed both his arms behind his back as they walked. Sarai busied herself trying to angle her body as she walked so that he got a view of her right side, her better side. Her machinations had her walking straight into a pole.

Reed put his prosthetic arm out in front of her, between her and the tree stump of a pole. Her belly impacted the prosthetic and bark scraped against the fake arm.

"I'm so, so sorry." Sarai stepped back, rearranging her sweatshirt to hide the evidence of the rolls. But she knew he'd already felt them. Or if not felt them, he had to have felt the impact. There were wood chippings along the arm.

"Did I hurt you?" he asked.

Shouldn't she be asking him that question? But he simply flicked the pieces of bark from his prosthetic and focused his gaze on her. Again, on her face, not her body.

She wasn't even wearing full makeup, but he didn't seem to notice. She'd never believed that about guys, that they didn't notice makeup. But it must be true with Reed. His smile was bright and genuine and … interested.

"How was your flight?"

Sarai gulped before she let loose the lie. Her tongue was feeling heavier than her frame. "It was fine."

"Nasty airplane food? Is that why you were at Patel's?"

"I shouldn't have gone there. I'm on a diet."

Reed frowned down at her, finally looking somewhere that wasn't her eyes.

Sarai held her breath. She sucked it in. But who was she kidding?

Reed shook his head. "I've never understood the concept of diets. It must be a girl thing."

Sarai stared at him. Maybe he was blind? Did he not see the colossal weight she was carrying around?

"I'm sorry, was that sexist?" he said with a deprecating smile. "I just don't believe in depriving myself. That's why I wanted to see you sooner rather than later. You know I was actually contemplating flying out to Paris this weekend?"

Sarai's heart quickened, faster than it had when she'd been moving along to that exercise video. Could falling for a guy be considered as a workout? Because if so, she would lose the weight in no time under Reed's attention.

"Anyway, Patel's is one of my favorite restaurants," he said. "I'm there all the time."

"I used to go there all the time during therapy."

"Therapy?"

Her racing heartbeat slowed as her chest tightened. She didn't want to tell another lie. They were starting to weigh her down more than her weight. "I told you that I was a model. I had to deal with a lot of rejection. So my parents sent me to a psychologist."

"Rejection? I don't see how when you're so beautiful."

"Are you blind? I'm not even wearing blush."

Reed peered down at her cheeks. "Would that make a difference? Maybe I am blind. They say the physical vanishes when you see a person for who they are inside."

And now she was out of breath. Yes, falling for Reed Cannon was definitely a workout. If not the pounds, she would surely lose her heart to this guy. "It was called food therapy. Mindful eating."

"That sounds like something Dr. Patel would make his patients do."

"You know Dr. Patel?"

Reed nodded. "He works on the ranch. And he's my psychologist."

"Mine, too. Or at least he was. I finished therapy a year ago."

"How do we have all these connections in real life and yet we meet online?"

"It's crazy, isn't it?"

"Obviously must be if we've both needed a psychologist," he grinned. "Dr. Patel helped a lot with my PTSD and coping with the loss of my limb."

He held up his prosthetic arm. He was watching her face again, carefully. Sarai wasn't sure what he was looking for. She only hoped that he found it.

"This is me," she said as they came up to her place.

"It suits you," Reed said looking at the townhouse she shared with Mason.

Sarai wasn't watching where she was going again, and she stumbled as she came to the stairs of the stoop. Reed reached out for her with both arms. She felt the hard, cold material of his prosthetic at the fleshy parts of her side.

Oh, no. Her sweatshirt had ridden up. Reed was touching her fat. Sarai jerked away.

Reed pulled his prosthetic arm away from her and then placed it behind his back. "I'm sorry."

"No, I'm sorry. This isn't what I planned. It's not how I planned to meet you. I thought there would be more time for me to prepare for this."

He looked down at his arm. "I understand."

But Sarai didn't think he did. He deserved to know the truth. She didn't want there to be any more excess layers between them than there already were. She needed to come clean.

"Listen, Sarai, there's something I haven't told you."

And she would come clean. Right after he did. It was polite to take turns.

"There's a reason I went to the dating site in the first place. It was to find a wife."

He paused and in his pause Sarai blinked her eyes rapidly searching for clarity. She would've tugged at her ears to be sure she'd heard him correctly.

Did he just say that he was looking for a wife?

"I need to get married to stay on the ranch," Reed continued.

"You're getting married?"

"I'll need to if I want to stay there."

She knew it was too good to be true. The guy of her dreams was getting married. Her heart should've slowed to a complete halt.

Instead, it continued to race as though it could run after him and hold onto him for herself.

"Anyway, I've got six weeks," he said. "I need to find a bride in a little less than six weeks or move."

Need to? As in present tense? So he hadn't found someone? She wasn't too late? "Six weeks?"

"I know it's fast. I know it's sudden. But I think there's something here, between us."

"Us?"

"Yes, us. My plan was to date you, to woo you, and then to pop the question."

Sarai couldn't swallow past the lump in her throat. She tried to force out something more than a single syllable but failed.

"I realize that six weeks is too sudden," Reed continued. "So, I've decided that I can wait."

The words burst out of her now. "Wait? Why? Why wait?"

"I just … Well, you don't think it's too soon for us? We literally just met."

"You were thinking of asking me to marry you?"

"Well … I … it's just that we're so compatible. Statistically speaking, I won't find a better match than you. So, it just makes sense on an analytical level."

Now her heart did stop. Her breathing stopped. She stopped blinking. Sarai held entirely and completely still in this moment, committing every detail to memory.

The way Reed chewed at the corner of his lip. The way he ran his right hand through his hair. The way his left arm was behind his back, as though he were prepared to bow like a gentleman of old days. And the way he looked at her like she was something special.

No one had looked at her like she was something special in so long.

"And," he continued, "there's the fact that I really, really like you."

Sarai nodded. She took a deep breath in as she contemplated his words. When she had her answer, she spoke slowly and surely. "If you ask me in six weeks, the answer will be the same. So, logically, you might as well ask me now and be able to stay on the ranch."

Reed stared at her. He took a step back, looking her up and down. Sarai began to squirm and fidget under his perusal. Was he finally coming to his senses?

No. He was going down on bended knee.

"Sarai Austin, you captured my attention with your profile blurb. Then you held it with our chats and conversations. Will you do me the honor of becoming my partner IRL?"

This was happening. It was really happening. Sarai pushed past the lump in her throat and managed a choked yes.

Reed's smile was so big, so huge. Sarai wanted to make him smile like that for the rest of her days. And she would. She would be the woman he deserved to have. Inside and out.

Six weeks had been unrealistic for such a life-changing event. They had time now. She had time now. Time to be the woman she knew she could be.

CHAPTER THIRTEEN

One thing that was hard for a one-armed man to do was to tie a knot. On this big day, for Reed, a clip-on simply would not do. Xavier wound the fabric around Reed's neck and made a noose.

"You sure about this?" asked Xavier as he tightened the tie.

"I've never been more certain." Reed held still as his friend perfected the knot. He tilted up his chin so he could glance in the mirror at his reflection.

"You just met this girl. Are you sure you know everything you need to know about her?"

"I've known Sarai for almost a month. That's longer than Dylan knew Maggie, or Fran knew Eva and looked how that worked out for all of them. Then there's the math."

"Right, the math." Xavier gave a tug of the knot. "The basis of every good relationship."

"Math doesn't lie."

"Math is quantitative," said Xavier, "not qualitative. What do you really know about this girl?"

"We have a lot in common."

"The fact that she knows obscure facts in the Whoverse does not necessarily make you compatible."

"She gets me," said Reed. "I get her. Neither of us is perfect. But what faults may come about either of us, I'm still ninety-eight percent sure she's the one for me."

"Not one-hundred?"

"It's statistically impossible to get a perfect score."

From the corner of the room, Soldier barked as though he agreed. Reed bent down to the dog and offered his hand. The dog hopped up on his hind legs and tapped Reed's open palm with his sole front paw in their version of a high five.

"I am not going to be upstaged by a dog." Xavier held out his palm and Reed clasped it in his own. "All right. I'll have your back."

With his free hand, Xavier gave Reed a firm pat on his back. Reed didn't return the favor. That's where Xavier's scars were. They weren't painful any longer. But like all of the soldiers that came to this ranch, Xavier was cognizant of his own wounds.

"I know you've got my back, bro," said Reed. "I just wish you'd consider staying here."

Xavier shook his head. "You know marriage isn't for me. But don't worry. You'll still get shared custody of me. You guys will have me on the weekends."

There was a knock at the door. Reed thought for a second that it might be one of the other soldiers, but he dismissed that idea. None of them would bother to knock. They'd just barge in.

Dr. Patel poked his gray head in the door with his fatherly smile. "Good morning, Specialist Ramos. Might I have a private word with the man of the hour?"

With one final adjustment of Reed's tie, Xavier headed out the door. Dr. Patel came in, closing the door behind him. He didn't take a seat but stood smiling proudly at Reed.

Dr. Patel had made such a positive impact in everyone on the ranch's lives. He'd worked tirelessly and patiently to ensure the men were healed from the inside out. He'd officiated Dylan's and Fran's weddings. And now, he would join Reed and Sarai together in holy matrimony.

"Is it time?" Reed heard the eagerness in his own voice.

"Almost," said Dr. Patel. "I just wanted to have a little chat with you."

Neither Reed's or Sarai's parents could make it to the ceremony on such short notice. Neither parents were particularly happy about the quickness of the marriage. Well, his parents weren't. Sarai had mentioned that she'd emailed her parents but hadn't heard back yet.

Reed had proposed just two days ago and it had been a whirlwind of preparations since. He'd hardly seen Sarai during that time as Maggie and Eva had insisted on shopping trips with his bride.

"You know, for someone who is so … not tech-savvy, I can't believe your app worked," said Reed.

Dr. Patel chuckled. "I had nothing to do with the computer side. Only the science of compatibility. It worked because you and Sarai are two compatible spirits."

"Yeah." Reed felt a phantom tingle in his left palm. "We share a lot of the same views. We like a lot of the same things. That will make for lots to talk about in this relationship."

"No, you misunderstand me," said Dr. Patel. "I mean in the core of your soul, where your wounds lie."

Reed's brows squished together. That was not what he expected the good doctor, the man about to perform his marriage rites, to say about him and his betrothed. Their wounds matched?

"You both see yourselves differently than the world sees you. Your perceptions affect your actions. Sarai had a tough time with modeling. There's a lot of rejection in that industry."

"I know," said Reed. "She told me."

"That's good." Dr. Patel pressed his lips together, as though he were trying to hold something inside. It was very unlike the man. He either spoke his mind directly or made his feelings clear as he bore into his patients. "But I'm fairly certain she hasn't told you everything."

Sarai had shared a lot with him. But Reed wasn't fooled enough to think there weren't some things they both held back. There may have still been secrets between them, but there was a lifetime for them to tell each other everything.

"I won't break patient-doctor confidentiality," said Dr. Patel. "I'll just tell you to accept yourself. But accept her, too."

Reed frowned, certain he was missing something. "I do accept her, just as she is."

"Good." Dr. Patel patted him on the shoulder. "Just be aware that she might not believe you when you tell her that."

"I think she believes I accept her. She is marrying me, after all."

"That's because Sarai is a smart girl," Patel smiled. "Don't let her hide who she truly is from you. And you don't hide either."

Reed wasn't one for trying to solve riddles. He liked hard truths and logical facts. His brain couldn't comprehend when Dr. Patel spoke philosophically.

This wasn't a conversation about facts. It was clearly one of those advice talks that a father would give his son before he walked down the aisle. Reed appreciated Dr. Patel for the gesture. But he was ready to get on with the main event.

"I don't see any faults now," he said. "But if and when I do, I'll keep my vows and the promises I'm ready to make to her."

Dr. Patel nodded. "Yes, I believe you will."

CHAPTER FOURTEEN

Years in modeling made certain that Sarai learned her best angles. She turned to the right and left in the mirror. She turned all the way to the back and looked over her shoulder. The angle didn't matter. She was a hot mess dressed in white.

When she'd been dress shopping with Maggie and Eva yesterday, they'd all had a fantastic time. Eva and Maggie were two bundles of joy that chattered and smiled and laughed and made Sarai feel as though she'd fit in for the first time in a long time.

On the drive into town, they'd regaled Sarai with their own shotgun marches down the aisle. Though each of their weddings was quickies, their marriages were both solid as rocks. And the two women were the happiest people Sarai had ever met. She wanted some of that, and it was possible with her and Reed.

The women had filled in more details about the ranch and the men, particularly Reed, over lunch. Maggie, the aspiring veterinarian, had had a turkey burger, while Eva, the college student, had had pasta. Sarai had picked at a salad, moving the leaves around her plate as she listened to stories of Reed and his antics with the other soldiers.

All too soon the women had gotten down to business. They pulled up at a wedding dress shop and the torture began.

Sarai hadn't looked directly in the mirror as she'd tried on the proffered dresses. She did not trust the store's glass after her encounter last week. So, she had decided to rely on the other women and their judgment.

Big mistake.

When Maggie and Eva's eyes had lit up at their first sight of the third dress, Sarai thought maybe she had a winner. Looking at herself in the mirror now, she saw nothing but disaster.

The dressed was ruche city. Ruching on the bodice, ruching over the hips, ruching on the backside.

Every model knew that the art of ruching fabric was designed to hide the body's flaws. The gathering of the cloth was designed to flatter a less-than-flat tummy. It was laid out to loosen the roll of love handles. It was blocked out to bury a big backside. Each of Sarai's flaws was hidden behind the carefully crafted textile and everyone would see.

"You look so gorgeous."

Sarai turned as Maggie came into the room. How had she taken Maggie's kind and complimentary words for the truth? Sarai knew girls complimented each other but didn't really mean it. That behavior was rampant in the modeling industry. Girls would smile in each other's faces and, a second later, go behind the other's back to get a skinny leg up.

"She does, doesn't she?" Eva came up behind Sarai, placing her hand on Sarai's back. "I would kill for your hips. You look like Marilyn Monroe."

Maggie nodded in agreement. Both women gazed with wide eyes and wide grins at Sarai's form in the reflection. The forced smile on Sarai's lips was so brittle she was certain it would crack at any minute.

Marilyn Monroe had been a size sixteen in her life; size twelve by today's standards. That was not a compliment in high fashion where size six was considered plus size. Sarai hadn't let herself go that far —yet.

She was still clinging to a size eight. The wedding dress was a size nine. She hadn't looked when she'd tried it on. But she'd caught a glimpse of the tag today.

"Oh, sweetie, are you crying?" Maggie pulled a few tissues from her purse.

Before her new friend could wipe away Sarai's tears, Sarai grabbed the tissues from the other woman's hands. No way was she letting anyone near her carefully made-up face. Her dress might be a disaster, but her contouring was on point.

Sarai had khol'd her eyes and accented the sharp tips with a dusting of gold glitter. Her blush also had hints of gold glitter. The effect brought out the red of her Middle Eastern skin tone. She might be ashamed of her weight, but not her heritage. Not even on a ranch filled with US Army vets.

She'd expected a bit of animosity, but there hadn't been even a hint of it. Each man had welcomed her with a smile, a hug, or a peck on the cheek. The peck had come from Xavier Ramos, the soldier Reed had told her to watch out for. But the caution had been given with a quirk of the lip and a roll of the eyes, not a frowning glare.

Everyone on this ranch cared deeply for one another. Reed had told her stories about each person on the ranch in their chats. But seeing it in real life, seeing the support and the friendship and the care, it made Sarai ache at an emptiness somewhere other than her belly.

Maybe Maggie and Eva truly believed this crimply, concealing dress was pretty? Maybe their smiles were genuine? Misguided though they might be, Sarai didn't believe their compliments. Even though she wished they were true. The woman they spoke about and praised and said was beautiful, Sarai simply didn't see that woman reflected back in the mirror.

"Oh, Miss Sarai, you look like a real live princess." Rosalee's eyes were big and bright as she stared at Sarai's form. Eva's little sister was coming in the door, so she couldn't see Sarai's reflection in the mirror. What Rosalee saw was Sarai in the flesh.

One thing Sarai knew; kids didn't lie. They could be brutally honest little beasts, as she discovered in grade school. Sure, they could fib. But not when it came to compliments. Sarcasm was a learned skill that took years to master.

"When I get married," Rosalee continued, "I want to look just like you."

Sarai turned away from the mirror so that she met the little girl's gaze. Rosalee's brown eyes were open so wide with wonder that Sarai saw a reflection there. What Sarai saw reflected in the depths of Rosalee's eyes was someone she didn't recognize. The woman dressed in white was indeed beautiful. So much so that it took Sarai's breath away.

"It's time," said Maggie.

Rosalee turned toward the door and the vision was gone. The little girl pulled open the door, and Sarai was blinded by a bright light.

It was sunlight. That light encouraged her to leave her old life behind. It beckoned her on to a new life.

Sarai stepped out into the light. When she did, a sea of faces greeted her. Each of them was smiling. There wasn't a single sneer or smirk or pinched brow. Each face gazed at her in appreciation, in awe, in admiration.

Reed stood at the end of the walkway. He looked like something out of a catalog in his dark suit. When he found her gaze, he clearly mouthed the words, *you're beautiful.*

Nothing made sense to Sarai any longer. And that was fine. The sun on her face warmed her. The breeze in the air cooled her skin. The steps she took were in the right direction.

CHAPTER FIFTEEN

Reed almost didn't recognize the woman that walked toward him. That must be a product of getting to know someone's personality first, seeing the beauty of who they are on the inside and coming to care for and respect that aspect of a person before they have a chance to present themselves physically.

He had already believed Sarai Austin to be a beautiful person. Her intelligence knocked him off his feet. Her wit took his breath away. Her sense of humor made the butterflies rise from his gut to his chest.

Even before he'd seen her, he'd known she was a beauty. Walking toward him, dressed all in white, with the sun shining down on her, she was positively breathtaking.

His legs buckled, and he reached out for something to hold onto. Luckily, Sean stood beside him and had his back. He caught Reed by the shoulders and gave each of his biceps a steadying squeeze until Reed could stand on his own two feet again.

It was just in time because Sarai, his bride, his wife to be, had arrived.

She reached out to him. Without thinking, Reed offered her his left arm as she came to stand on the left side of him. Sarai wrapped her fingers around his prosthetic forearm. Reed could have sworn he felt the heat of her fingertips on the flesh that was no longer there.

She smiled up at him. There was a look there, something he'd seen before in her eyes. Underneath the heavy kohl of her lids was a hint of doubt mixed with a tinge of fear. He'd seen it the first time they'd engaged the video chat feature.

Sarai was nervous. He'd rushed her back then to turn on the camera. Was he rushing her again?

Reed leaned down and whispered in Sarai's ear, "Are you sure?"

He felt the intake of her breath at the side of his cheek. Had he called it correctly? Was she regretting the speed at which things were moving between them?

And then she sighed. It was the little exhale of breath that he knew so well from their audio-only chats. The sound that told him that she was not resigning. She wasn't one to give up easily. She was about to move in for the kill, and Reed couldn't wait to hear her rebuttal.

When he pulled away, she was smiling at him. The doubts and fear were gone. Trust and hope sparkled in her gaze. It was all the answer he needed.

He turned them both to face Dr. Patel in his role as pastor. The man eyed the couple with that small smile that said he knew more than he let on. Pastor Patel began the ceremony, and before Reed knew it he was reciting his vows.

Reed turned back to Sarai and repeated the words that Patel had prepared for each of them. With such a quick wedding, neither had a chance to write their own vows. But with both Reed and Sarai having a history with the man officiating their union, they trusted Patel to choose vows that suited them both.

"Sarai, I will love you no matter what. I will always be honest with you, kind, patient and forgiving. I give you my hand and my heart as a sanctuary of warmth and peace. I pledge my love, devotion, faith, and honor as I join my life to yours. I take you to be my partner for life, promising above all else to live in truth with you and to communicate fully and fearlessly."

As vows went, these ones were spot on. With each word that left his lips, Reed felt the truth in them. Their relationship had begun with communication, honest discussions free of any physical distractions. It would continue that way as they set out as partners who lived fully and fearlessly.

"On this day," Reed continued to parrot the pastor with words that were spoken straight from his heart, "I give you my heart, my promise, that I will walk with you, hand in hand, wherever our journey leads us, living, learning, loving, together, forever. This is my sacred vow to you, my equal in all things."

A tear ran down Sarai's cheek. Reed lifted his right hand to brush the tear away. When he did, it left a smudge at her cheek rendering her makeup job imperfect. It didn't matter an iota to him. She still looked perfect.

"Reed," Sarai began her recitation of vows as prepared by her former psychologist. "I will pay attention to your physical and emotional needs. I will grow with you, not apart from you. I will take care of my health so that I can be here with you as long as possible."

She stumbled over those last words. Her head dipped slightly. But only for a second. She inhaled and let out that sigh he knew so well.

"I will always show you with my words and my actions that I am yours alone forever. I take you to be my partner for life. I promise above all else to live in truth with you and to communicate fully and fearlessly. You are my true counterpart. I will love you, hold you and honor you. I will respect you, encourage you and cherish you in health and sickness, through sorrow and success, for all the days of my life. This is my sacred vow to you, my equal in all things."

Listening to the woman he would spend the rest of his life with making these solemn promises to him, Reed came to a realization he never thought his logical mind would deduce. It was entirely logical that a person you knew for a short time could become your entire world. Sarai was that for him now; his entire world. He would spend the rest of his days holding up to those promises he'd just made.

"You may now kiss the bride."

Reed's hands itched to take hold of her. He reached both out. Only to pull back his prosthetic.

Sarai wrapped her fingers around those fake digits. She stepped into him, lifting his left hand and placing her cheek in the palm of his fake hand.

Reed swore he felt the softness of her cheek in his phantom palm. He couldn't wait any longer. Some part of their duties as husband and wife would hold. But not this part. Not this taste of her. Not this moment where he would claim her as his own.

He pulled her to him, fitting her lush curves against his hard chest. It was just a press of the lips. A chaste kiss by any standards. But Sarai's lips were a starburst of joy. Her sweetness overwhelmed him, and he decided he would not ever let go.

At some point, their lips broke apart, but he did not relinquish his hold on her. At some point, they were announced as a new union, but he felt like they'd never been apart. At some point, they were pulled apart for congratulatory hugs, but she still felt connected to him.

Sarai was a part of him legally and spiritually. But she felt a part of him physically. Like his phantom limb brought back to life.

CHAPTER SIXTEEN

Sarai held tight to Reed's prosthetic hand. Her grip was so absolute that she was glad his fingers weren't flesh and bone, otherwise, she was sure she'd break them.

That kiss had nearly done her in. She'd been kissed before. Some of Europe's most practiced playboys had sought her out thirty pounds ago. They all paled in comparison to the heat of Reed's lips against hers. The warm, spicy gust of his breath as it brushed her cheek. The flutter of his lashes against her forehead. She was left lightheaded and dizzy in the face of a kiss that could run on daytime Disney.

She didn't let go of him when they paraded down from the gazebo to greet his friends as husband and wife. She held tight to him as he led her to the makeshift dance floor outside the barn. She kept her fingers laced around his forearm when they sat to eat, and he heaped food onto her plate.

The sight of the fried chicken and the smell of the barbecue sauce made her stomach churn and grumble at the same time. She was able to ignore those diverging feelings. But her heart fell into her gut when Reed held up his fork to her with a choice bit of meat.

"I couldn't eat a thing," she protested.

Reed lowered the fork with a frown. "I thought you loved chicken."

"I do. I'm just all nerves right now." Sarai took a deep breath. She let out a slow sigh as she prepared a better excuse for her unsatisfied appetite.

"But you have to smash the wedding cake in Uncle Reed's face," said Rosalee. The little girl was perched across from them on the other side of the table. Her plate was heaped with fried foods, barbecue sauce, and chips.

Down at the other end of the table, Sarai caught sight of the two-tiered cake that Dylan and Maggie had picked up from the local grocer. One of the first things Sarai had learned was that her new friend, Maggie, wasn't ever allowed near a kitchen. Just looking at the sugar-laden, calorie-packed, preservative rich cake made the buttons at her back strain.

To one side of the cake, Sarai caught Dr. Patel eyeing her. He said nothing with his mouth. He was busy helping himself to the barbecue and macaroni salad. But his eyes spoke volumes.

That's one thing Sarai didn't miss about therapy. The scrutiny.

Dr. Patel never put her down or judged her outwardly with harsh words. But his quiet, compassionate gaze that said *I care*, said it way too loud.

She didn't want Reed to hear that look. She didn't want any of these new people that were eager to be her family to see the judgment in Dr. Patel's eyes. Sarai's entire body tensed. Her fingers clutched Reed's.

He winced and twisted his hand inside hers. She was sitting at his right side now, and she was holding on to his flesh and bone.

"Sarai looks too beautiful to have cake smushed in her face," said Reed.

"Probably 'cause you want to kiss her face," said Carlos, Rosalee's older brother. No sooner had the words left the teenager's lips did he immediately turn red.

A chorus of manly chuckles and feminine giggles spread around the table. The dogs, who sat at everyone's feet, barked and yipped with glee.

The cake was handed out. There was inevitably a bit of smushing. Carlos smashed a piece in his sister's face. Rosalee ran after her brother threatening a sweet treat in retaliation. Sarai relaxed inside of Reed's embrace as she watched the cake move farther and farther away from her.

"How did I get so lucky?" he whispered in her ear.

She wanted to tell him that she was wondering the same thing. She couldn't remember ever being this happy. Not when she got her first modeling contract. Not when she took her first steps on a Parisian runway. Not when she booked her first magazine spread.

From the moment she walked to Reed at the altar, he hadn't let her go. He hadn't stopped telling her how beautiful she looked. And she was starting to believe him.

The afternoon turned to dusk, and she never left his arms. They sat and talked. They swayed on the dance floor. They stood and they laughed with others. Reed introduced her to all the dogs, including Soldier who danced between Sarai's heels. As she and her husband danced and laughed, Sarai forgot to feel self-conscious in her dress.

Soon, Sarai and Reed left their friends, the dogs, and the food behind as they walked the path to his house. Her new home. Her new life.

"I'm sorry no one from either of our families could be here," said Reed.

Sarai shrugged. "I'm excited to get to know the family that showed up."

The residents of the Bellflower Ranch, or as they preferred to call it, the Purple Heart Ranch, were all proving themselves to be a group of genuine individuals who truly cared for one another. And, over the last two days, it seemed they were open to bringing Sarai into their caring circle.

"They can be a handful." Reed's tone was ominous, but the smile on his face softened the blow.

"I don't mind."

"Famous last words." Reed chuckled.

Sarai felt the rumble of his laughter as it rolled through his body and straight to her heart. She'd heard him laugh many times during their talks. Watched it a couple times when they'd video chatted. Today, she'd felt it rush through her, over and over again as he sat next to her, held her in a loose embrace, and now walked beside her.

It was an addictive feeling. One that she planned to glut herself on. Unlike her relationship with food, this addiction wasn't one that could hurt her.

Reed would never hurt her. Of that, Sarai was sure. She just needed to make sure she didn't disappoint him.

"This is us," said Reed as they stopped in front of his door, their door.

Reed turned the knob. It was unlocked. There was no reason for it to be locked on a ranch where everyone was family.

Sarai looked down at the threshold. It was customary for the groom to carry the bride into their new home. She certainly hoped Reed wasn't thinking that. Not with her weight.

He reached out his arms as though he were going to attempt it.

Sarai stepped back. "Reed, don't you dare."

"I could," he looked defiant. "I could carry you in my arms. This thing is plenty sturdy." He held up his prosthetic.

Sarai tried to hide her grimace. It was the first direct mention he'd made of her weight. But as comments went, it wasn't the worst she'd ever heard. "I am a big girl. I don't want you breaking your back over some silly tradition."

"Hey?" He chucked his finger under her chin, lifting her gaze to meet his. "I don't want you to ever feel you're settling for less because you married someone with only one good arm."

Again he held up his prosthetic, indicating that was the good arm. It did the trick. A bemused grin made its way onto Sarai's face.

"Sarai, I'm going to get everything I ever wanted because you married me."

They held for a moment. His finger under her chin. Her head

tilted back. It was the perfect moment for a kiss. It was the logical thing to do in the circumstance. Her husband did not disappoint.

Reed tilted Sarai's head back a bit more. Then he leaned down and covered her lips with his. This kiss wouldn't make it past the Disney censors. Not when Reed's tongue slipped out to taste the top of Sarai's lip.

A warmth began in Sarai's gut. It was a powerful hunger. It pushed and shoved its way up her chest and into her throat. When Reed broke the kiss, her craving made itself known with a long, gluttonous sigh.

"Let's go inside," he whispered.

Sarai gulped. She continued to tremble. Not because of the cold air. Not because of the after-effects of the kiss. It was the anticipation of what happened next.

She was no virgin, but she hadn't been with a man in years. Certainly not while in her present condition.

But this was Reed, her husband. He couldn't back out of the relationship now that they were married. Not even when he saw her thunder thighs or her love handles or the flab at the backside of her arms.

"Today was amazing," he said, as he led her down the hall toward the bedroom.

"Yeah." At least she thought she said yeah. Her mind was fixed on problem-solving.

Perhaps she could convince him to keep the light off? Maybe she could feign modesty and ask him to leave the room while she changed? Then she could sneak under the covers and he'd be none the wiser.

"Wait?" They came to a halt, and she jerked back to the present. "This isn't your bedroom."

Reed's bedroom was across the hall. She knew because she'd peeked in there earlier this morning when she'd arrived.

"I know," he said.

"So … we're … you …?" She didn't know what question she was trying to ask.

"This is technically our second date," Reed said. "I don't know about you, but I'm not that easy."

His response was so unexpected that Sarai blurted out a laugh. He was right. This was only the third day that they'd been together in real life. In her past dating life, even in the fast and loose lifestyle of a fashion model, Sarai had never slept with a guy after only a handful of dates.

"I told you," Reed said. "The plan is to meet you—check. Then to woo you—"

"Trust me, I'm wooed."

"I've already married you. I just need to check off courting you from the list. Can I take you out tomorrow, Mrs. Cannon?"

"Yes, Mr. Cannon."

"We may have rushed the marriage, but we're not going to rush the relationship building. We'll build a strong foundation. This is forever. So, we've got a bit of time."

And with a light peck at the corner of her mouth, Sarai's husband left her standing there hungry for more.

CHAPTER SEVENTEEN

Why? Oh, why had Reed left his new wife at the spare bedroom door last night?

Because she'd been nervous through the ceremony and reception. Because she'd stiffened a couple of times while they were dancing when he'd pulled her close. Because she'd trembled when they'd crossed the threshold to their home, and he'd hinted at lifting her into his arms.

Dr. Patel's warning came to his mind as the new day's sun broke into his bedroom window. There was something about her that he didn't know, something she hadn't told him. Reed had no idea what that could be? He'd bared his soul to her. Didn't she trust him to tell him any and everything, no matter how dark?

Apparently not. But that was okay. For now.

He'd just have to work extra hard to make sure she knew there was nothing that would scare him away. He'd let her keep her secret for now. Whatever it was wasn't putting a wedge between them.

Reed didn't want anything coming between them. He wanted nothing more than to pull her closer. To hold her in his arms. To press his lips against hers.

Sarai had enjoyed the kiss that had turned them into an official union. She'd sighed into their second kiss as well. She'd been disappointed as much as she'd been nervous when she'd realized they wouldn't be sleeping together on their wedding night.

Reed knew consummation of a union was a requirement for marital legitimacy. It was necessary to sleep with one's spouse or face grounds for divorce. That didn't worry him. He had no doubt that this marriage would only be dissolved by death. He and his wife would only get physical once there was total trust between them and that included his wife telling him all of her secrets.

With that thought, Reed rolled out of bed. He left off the prosthetic today as he dressed. There was no need to hide who he was. He'd lead by example for his family.

Reed opened his door at the exact same time that Sarai opened hers. She was dressed in track pants and a sweater. She looked lovely even though her curves were hidden.

The two newlyweds stared at one another. Then grinned. Then looked away.

"Hi," he said.

"Good morning," she said.

With the pleasantries out of the way, Reed didn't know what to do next? Should he go up and kiss his new wife? Should he only hug her? Should he keep his distance since this day, the first day of their marriage, would ostensibly be their third date?

They both took a step forward at the same time and nearly collided. So, they both took a step back. This waltz of uncertainty was getting them nowhere.

Finally, Sarai stepped up. She reached for his hand. Without thinking, Reed lifted the left one. Before he could pull his stump back, Sarai placed her hand on his flesh. Warmth flooded through his entire body. Until she jerked her hand away.

"I'm sorry," she said. "Is that okay?"

"Of course it is."

He offered his stump again, and she placed her hand gently on his mangled flesh. With his right hand, Reed pulled his wife into a hug. Sarai fit him so perfectly. There was nothing between them. In his mind, Reed began revisiting his courtship plan and its duration. For now, he planted a kiss at her temple.

"I was just about to make breakfast," Reed said.

"Oh. I'm not hungry. I'm not really a breakfast eater. Just gonna have some juice."

She twined her fingers with his. Reed pressed their palms together and felt that sense of deep connection that he'd felt when they'd said their vows. It was the most satisfying intimacy he'd ever experienced before in his life.

He regretted losing the connection as he opened the fridge. Sarai pulled the orange juice out of the fridge while Reed grabbed the eggs. She had her glass of juice in hand and was sipping her beverage while he was still assembling everything he needed.

"Can I help?" she asked.

"No, I've got it."

It took him longer to do simple things, like making an omelet. He never wanted his wife to doubt that he was capable of not only the simple domestic tasks but the larger ones as well.

He cracked the egg in one hand without any shell spilling into the pan. He scrambled the eggs with the spatula. Placing the utensil down, he sprinkled on some cheese. Then picked up the spatula again to serve up his breakfast fare.

Joining Sarai at the breakfast nook next to the window, Reed asked, "So, what are we doing today, Mrs. Cannon?"

He would never get tired of the way she smiled shyly when he called her that. His wife shrugged in response as she sipped her juice. "Doesn't matter to me. I'm just happy to be here with you."

The only reason he didn't lean across the table to kiss his wife was that he had a mouthful of eggs. "Do you have to work?"

"No, I scheduled my posts for the next couple of days. What about you?"

"If I try to do any work around here this weekend, the guys will take my other arm."

She laughed at that. He loved that he could joke with her about his arm. It showed him that she truly didn't look down on his injury.

"Can we just stay in?" she said.

"I'm pretty sure that's what's expected."

Again she blushed. No, blushed was the wrong word. When her cheeks heated, Sarai glowed.

"We can veg out on the couch and watch the idiot tube," he suggested.

"That sounds lovely."

"I'll grab some snacks."

Reed placed his dishes in the sink. Then he turned to the cabinet filled with chips and sweets. Opening things could be a challenge for Reed, especially bags that required a two-handed grip. But he'd had gotten pretty good at using his teeth. He ripped the bag of chips and put them into a bowl.

When he presented his offering to Sarai she grimaced. "There's a lot of calories in that."

"Don't tell me you're still on a diet."

She squirmed as she curled her feet under her bottom at one corner of the couch.

Reed placed the bowl of chips on the coffee table and sat down in the center of the couch. "You should know I think you look perfect."

"I'm not perfect."

"Of course, no one's perfect. I was attracted to what was on the inside of you. And now that I see the outside …"

He saw her breath catch. She held it instead of exhaling while she waited for his answer.

"Sarai, you're beautiful inside and out."

She swallowed but looked like she was having a tough time doing so.

Reed rose from the couch, taking the chips with him. He chucked the chips in the trash. Going back to the snack cabinet, he reached for a bag of popcorn. "Empty calories. Better?"

She smiled and nodded.

He came back to the couch with the approved snacks. Sarai had moved from the corner and now sat in the center. Reed shared the cushion with his wife. They sat in a companionable silence for nearly five minutes before Reed noticed that they stared at a black television screen.

"What do you want to watch?" he asked.

Sarai shrugged. Her shoulder bumped his, and he felt heat flare through him. He scooted closer until their shoulders touched. She didn't shy away from his arm.

"I have the complete *Star Trek* series on DVD starting with the original series," he offered.

"I've never seen the originals. I did watch a few of the Next Generation with Captain Picard."

Reed pulled away from his wife and squinted down at her. "Picard?"

Sarai leaned back as well. Her gaze flicked Reed up and down in challenge. "What's wrong with Picard?"

"He's not Shatner," Reed snorted.

"Shatner always reminded me of a dirty, old grandpa." Sarai wrinkled her nose.

Reed's hand went to his heart. "How did I not know this about you?"

"What? It's not a big deal. I'm more of a *Star Wars* kinda girl than *Star Trek*."

Reed shuddered. "This marriage is doomed."

Sarai poked Reed in his chest. "Are we having our first marital fight?"

"Yes, we are and it's a big one, and now it's gotten violent." He caught her hand and laced their fingers together.

"Why don't we go to neutral ground then. How about something we both like?"

"We missed the latest episode of *Doctor Who* yesterday since we were, you know, getting hitched."

"I've been dying to see that episode."

Reed let go of his wife's hand and reached for the remote, then hesitated. "Wait, are you all caught up? I figured you wouldn't have seen the last few episodes since you were in France."

Sarai's body tensed beside him. "They actually show them in Europe first. It is a British show after all."

"So, you've already seen the latest episode already?"

"No. I've been so busy."

"Too busy for the Doctor?"

"Maybe I was waiting for the right person to watch with."

The electric strings of the high pitched Theremin sounded through the television speakers. The familiar tune raced, keeping pace with Reed's heart. He stretched his stump and rested it on the back of the couch behind Sarai's head.

Sarai shifted.

Reed immediately lifted his arm, certain she was trying to get away from him. He was wrong.

His wife scooted her body closer to him. Then she rested her head and snuggled into the nook of his shoulder. Reed relaxed his arm. As the show droned on, he realized he'd need to watch it again. He was so intuned to his wife that he didn't hear anything after the opening music died away.

CHAPTER EIGHTEEN

Sarai woke the next morning. The grumbling of her stomach woke her before her alarm clock.

She'd spent the day with Reed watching *Doctor Who*, then movies, at some point she'd fallen asleep. She vaguely remembered Reed leading her to her bedroom. She clearly remembered the feel of his lips on her forehead.

She was so tired that she couldn't lift her arms to bring him under the covers with her because that was certainly her dream; staying in bed all day and night with her husband. But neither of them were ready for that. Sarai wasn't sure she'd ever be ready to be completely bare in front of her husband in body or soul.

He'd told her she was perfect to him. He'd called her beautiful inside and out. It wasn't the first time he'd said that to her. The more he said it the more she believed it just might be the truth.

Sarai wrapped a thick robe around herself, gathered her toiletries, and made her way to the shared bathroom at the end of the hall. Reed's door was shut and the living room was empty. He must be either still asleep or already out. She wasn't sure which as she didn't know her husband's schedule outside of their daily video chats.

Inside the bathroom, Sarai took a quick shower. The steam from the hot stream fogged the mirror, which was a good thing. She didn't need to see herself today. But as she patted her body dry the fog cleared. Sarai looked up into the mirror and caught a look at herself. Her reflection in the glass was hardly recognizable. She looked, not exactly thinner, but definitely different.

Was it possible? Had Reed's words changed her view of herself so much that it was manifesting physically? Her gaze dipped down away from the mirror to look at herself in the flesh.

There was still the cellulite on her inner thighs. But she had to stare before she could see the lines clearly. Her belly looked a little less like the top of a muffin, but there was not one single pack visible, let alone six. But there was a difference.

Then, looking down near the toilet, she saw it. A scale. It was a cheap store bought platform that was likely inaccurate.

Did she dare?

Sarai let the towel drop to the ground. Then she picked it back up making sure to wipe away every single drop of water that held onto her skin. Once dry, she hung the towel on its rack.

She closed her eyes and took a tentative step. Once balanced on the scale she still couldn't get her eyes to open. This was a bad idea. She did not need the disappointment today; the second day of her marriage to the man of her dreams.

She was going to step down. Her eyes opened so that she could see where she was stepping. Of course, her gaze fell on the needle of the scale. Sarai gasped at what it told her.

Five pounds? That couldn't be right. She stepped off the scale, then stepped back on again. It told the same story.

She was down five pounds.

Five. Whole. Pounds.

She wanted to dance. She wanted to shout. It was working.

Rosalee had said she looked like a princess. Eva and Maggie had said she'd looked pretty. The guys had all looked at her with appreciation, not leering like men did when she was a model. It was respectful.

And then there was Reed. Reed who thought she was beautiful

inside and out. Reed who said she was perfect. She could be perfect. She just needed to stay the course she was on.

She was consuming foods. Just not solids. Only liquid. It had worked for her last photo shoot. It was working now. Just a few more days, maybe a week or two, and she would be even closer to her goal weight.

Sarai stepped off the scale and came back face to face with her reflection. It might be the steam but looking in the mirror it did look like her love handles were a bit flatter. She wondered if her arms were still flap-tastic. She lifted the left one slowly and—

"Sarai? You in there?"

Sarai dropped her arm with a *thwap*. She grabbed for the towel and flung it around her work in progress of a body. She might be improving but she was not ready for primetime, especially not in the daylight hours.

"I'm just finishing up," she called.

"Meet me in the kitchen when you're done, I'm making breakfast."

Sarai waited until she heard the sounds of her husband walking away from the bathroom door. Then she slipped out quickly and darted into her room.

The wardrobe she chose today was sure to flatter all her best parts and hide what still needed work. First thing was first, two layers of Spanx were a necessity. Over the Spanx, she pulled on her best jeans, the ones that molded her backside into an upside down heart. The shirt she chose was long sleeved to hide any possibility of flabby wings.

"Hey," Reed said looking up at her when she came out of her room. "Wow, you look beautiful."

Sarai took in a deep breath, but it didn't fill her lungs. The air only just made it down to her diaphragm which was constricted by all the spandex.

"I was thinking I could show you around the ranch today? Maybe you could help me with my chores?"

"Farm work?"

"You're a ranch wife now. You'll need to understand how things work here."

"Will this have anything to do with manure?"

"We won't muck out the stalls today, but you will need to put on a good pair of boots."

Sarai looked down at her silver boots. She pointed her steel-plated toe and lifted the heel. "These are Givenchy."

"Whatever they are, they won't make it back alive. You can put on a pair of running shoes for now. We'll head into town and get you a sturdy pair later."

"Fine." Sarai went back to her room and looked for a pair of sneakers that matched her outfit. She'd cleaned out her closet back at the house she and Mason had shared, but she still had a few storage units of clothing that were sample-sized. The best she could do was a pair of Gucci tennis shoes. But they were from two seasons ago. They were castoffs from Mason, so she didn't mind if they got scuffed.

"Morning fuel." Reed held up a glass of fresh squeezed orange juice to her when she came back into the room.

"Where'd this come from?" She'd seen how he'd had to maneuver yesterday as he'd prepared his breakfast and the snacks. Working with one arm proved more challenging than she'd imagined, but Reed handled it all in stride. She'd never heard him once complain or make a fuss.

"We have a juicer."

Sarai looked over to see a disassembled contraption in the sink. There wasn't an orange rind or gut to be found. Reed had made the drink and done the clean up all with only one arm and no assistance.

The sweet citrus of the fruit juice hit the back of her throat and raced down to fill her empty stomach. Sarai ignored the rumble of her stomach as she marveled at the abilities of this man she'd married. Again, she reaffirmed her vow to be the woman he deserved in body as well as in mind.

CHAPTER NINETEEN

Reed escorted his wife around the ranch on his arm. It was like they were back in a time of gentlemen and ladies. Soldier nipped at their heels as they walked.

Well, the Chihuahua nipped at Sarai's heels. The moment Reed and Sarai had stepped outside of the house, Soldier had taken one look at Sarai and offered his single front paw. Sarai had squatted down and accepted his paw and then a series of amorous licks. Soldier hadn't stopped gazing up at her since. Reed understood the sentiment.

Sarai wasn't dressed for the real chores he had to do this morning, and he'd assumed she wouldn't be up to his real duties just yet being that she was a former model and now a makeup blogger. So, he'd already gotten up and mucked out the horses' stalls earlier this morning. He'd saved the fun bits for her.

Reed watched Sarai's eyes light up as she fed the baby goats. The furry kids all crowded her as she held out food. As they passed by they left little presents all around the ground. Yep, those fancy, poor excuse for sneakers of hers weren't making it back into the closet. But she didn't seem to mind.

When the goats were fed, Reed took her to his favorite part of the ranch. His favorite chore. He took Sarai to the garden.

Reed loved the feel of the fresh soil in his hand. He loved working the earth, taking something from a seedling, feeding, watering and nurturing it until it grew into something tall and proud that he could then consume. Having Sarai work the earth with him was one of the most satisfying experiences in Reed's life.

But when he saw her perspiring and constantly dabbing at her head, he decided it was time for a break. He extended his arm to Sarai. As she came to her feet, she wobbled.

Reed pulled her close until she was steady. It felt good to have her body pressed against his. But concern for her health outweighed his desire for her.

"You okay?" he asked.

"Just stood up a little too quickly." Her eyes were closed, and she took deep breaths.

Reed held her to him. Mostly out of concern. But a huge part of him just loved that he could finally touch this woman in the flesh. She was his perfect match. Even if she wasn't a Trekkie. He had time to work on that minor discrepancy.

He had the woman of his dreams in his arms. And he never planned to let go. Sarai took a deep breath and opened her eyes.

Her gaze was foggy at first. Soon they sharpened on him. Reed saw vulnerability reflected back at him, and so he pulled her closer.

"Better?" he asked her.

"The best." She breathed out a sigh and offered him a smile.

And just because he could, Reed bent his head down and brushed his lips against his wife's. Sarai tasted of salt and oranges and his.

"Get a room," he heard Xavier call.

Reed was tempted to make a lewd gesture to let his friend know exactly what he thought of his interruption. But his hand was filled with something precious. So instead, he turned his wife in the opposite direction and walked away.

"Tell me more about your time as a model," said Reed, breaking the tranquility of the moment.

"Why would you want to hear about that?"

"Because you never talk about it much. And it's a part of your life. And I want to know everything about you."

"It was a rough time in my life. Sure, I got to dress up, wear pretty clothes, and travel to exotic places. But they don't treat you like you're a human being with feelings. You're just a mannequin for their clothes or accessories or makeup. They're allowed to say mean things about you and you're just supposed to take it. Not only that, you're supposed to do something to change the mean things they point out about you, or you won't have a job. There's a lot of rejection."

"Dr. Patel mentioned that."

Sarai stopped walking. "Were you and him talking about me?"

"No. Yes. Not in a bad way. We were discussing our vows. He gave me a bit of a fatherly talk."

They picked up walking again. The breeze that was constantly present during the morning had left and only the rays of the sun touched their faces. Sarai was quiet for a minute as they walked on. It felt like she was leaning a bit more into him as they walked. Which was fine by Reed. He wanted her to know that she could lean on him for any and everything for the rest of their lives.

"I went to him to deal with the rejections," she said after a long pause. "My parents made me. It was the best decision in their otherwise poor parenting. I think they only did it because they wanted me to get better so that I could come back to work."

"Did you get better?"

She shook her head. "I left modeling. That helped the most."

"So, why did you do it for so long?"

Sarai shrugged. "It helped pay my family's bills. My mom was a model. My dad too."

"Your father was a model?"

Sarai nodded. "Now he's a photographer, and my mom is a fashion show director. They travel a lot now. That's why they couldn't come to our wedding."

"There's still so much I don't know about you," said Reed. "I want you to know that you never have to hide from me. Not anything. I accept you no matter what."

A storm of emotions played across her beautiful face. Then she let out a small sigh. Though it was small, Reed knew it was the harbinger of something big.

"I had an eating disorder," she said.

Reed's expression remained patient and accepting. Her confession didn't surprise him. It was a common issue with models. But now his mind rewound back to this morning when she only had orange juice for breakfast. Then it rewound earlier to the previous day when she didn't touch a single snack he'd placed on the table. And even further back to their wedding day when she declined the cake.

"Do you have anorexia?" he asked.

"No, it's not that. I don't have bulimia either. It's hard to explain."

"Whatever it is, know that I accept you for who you are. It doesn't change my mind about you. I ... Sarai, I love you."

Reed was becoming addicted to her small gasps. She did it when he surprised her. She did it when she was about to make a point that would unravel his stance on an issue. She did it each time just before he kissed her. And now he saw that saying those three words would elicit the response he was coming to cherish. He'd be saying those words a lot for the rest of their lives.

Even with the gasp, a storm of emotions played across Sarai's face. First the vulnerability. Then a flash of disbelief. Finally, a hint of acceptance.

Her eyes glistened. Her mouth opened. Reed braced himself to hear his words repeated back to him from her heart.

But before she could utter a single syllable, tires screeched up the driveway. Reed didn't recognize the fancy car. But he got the notion that Sarai did.

She squinted in the high noon sun. And when she pulled her hand away she gasped. But this was a big gasp.

"Mason?"

A man stepped out of the luxury car. At least Reed thought it was a man. The guy was tall and lanky, but with a muscular top build that slimmed into a small waist. He wore a pink silk shirt and purple leather pants. And … was he wearing eye makeup?

"I tried to get here earlier Rai Rai," the man—Mason—said.

Mason held his arms open wide. Reed felt like he was in the crowd watching a seventies rock star prepare to perform. Instead of belting out a rock opera, Mason squealed as Sarai came into his arms.

"What are you doing here?" asked Sarai. "I thought you booked the McQueen show?"

"I told that queen I'd catch him on the flip side. I had to see my girl get married. But it looks like I missed it by two days. And this must be the man of the hour?"

"Reed, this is Mason Lee, my best friend, and former roommate. Mace, this is Reed Cannon, my husband."

"Charmed, darling," said Mason.

Reed extended his hand. Mason did the same. But instead of a shake, Mason wrapped his fingertips around Reed's and presented his knuckles.

Reed wondered if he was supposed to kiss the man's knuckles? If so, that wasn't happening. He considered himself socially progressive, but that was going a bit too far.

Reed dropped the man's hand and put his arm around his wife. "I'm sorry you missed the ceremony."

"Don't be, darling. I was there for the whole courtship."

Sarai had talked with Mason about Reed? Reed couldn't remember if she'd talked much about Mason, her best friend, with him. He thought he remembered hearing the name once or twice.

In fact, now that he thought about it, he did remember. Sarai had said she was in Paris helping her friend at a fashion show. This must be that friend.

"You're looking amazing," Mason said to Sarai. "Marriage definitely agrees with you. You definitely have brightened since I saw you last month."

"Last month?" said Reed. "Weren't you guys together in Paris a few days ago?"

CHAPTER TWENTY

The heat had been beating down on her all day. From the moment Sarai got out of the shower and came through the steam, she'd started sweating. She was certain the goats would at some point ignore the food in her palms and reach up to lick the sweat off her brow. Or worse, start chewing at the fabric of her shirt and expose her flesh.

But she'd escaped all that. Reed didn't see her sweat or her fat or her imperfections. He'd nearly pushed the thoughts from her own mind as he constantly looked at her without judgment. As he looked at her with adoration. As he looked at her with only love reflected in his eyes.

She knew it was love because it was what she felt for him. It was a feeling deep inside her. A feeling she'd been afraid to bring forth into the light of day. Until he unveiled his own feelings.

She'd been about to do the same when Mason pulled up. Now, she stood under the glaring sun with nowhere to hide. She couldn't hide her lies under fabric or with makeup. She was laid bare and exposed.

Sarai forced herself to look at Reed. He still looked at her with the same love shining through his eyes. There was only a small cloud of confusion there. Sarai lacked the strength to shove those wisps of doubt away with more lies.

"Sarai?" Reed asked. "What's he talking about?"

Sarai looked to Mason. Her BFF sighed but gave her a look that said he'd have her back in this lie. The look also said that he wouldn't like it, and she'd get an earful as soon as they were alone.

Mason had been there through her ups and downs in her modeling career. He'd been there right after she'd fallen down and out of the spotlight. He'd been there through her treatment and after.

Mason stood by her now. He said nothing. He waited for Sarai to speak.

Sarai opened her mouth but felt nauseous. She closed her lips and tried again. All that came out was the truth.

"I wasn't in France."

She opened her eyes and watched as the light dimmed in Reed's gaze. Clouds grew. Her own vision of the truth went hazy. But she continued with the facts.

"I was here the whole time."

"Here?" said Reed. "In Montana?"

She nodded. Or she thought she did. The movement felt heavy.

"But you said you were in Paris." Reed stepped away from her. "You lied to me?"

Sarai felt entirely untethered as her husband removed his arm from her back. She could step over to Mason, and he'd support her. But she wanted to stand beside Reed.

"You lied to me," Reed repeated. Clearly, he was trying to work out the problem in his head and not coming to a solution. "Why would you do that?"

Reed looked to Mason.

"Is there something between you two?" he asked.

"No," Mason and Sarai both said at the same time.

"I don't play for your team, soldier," said Mason.

Reed looked back to Sarai. "You didn't want to meet me? Is it because ..." He held up his arm.

"No," she insisted. Why did he always bring things back to his disability? "It's not you, it's me. I didn't want you to see me like this."

Confusion still clouded Reed's face.

"Look at me," said Sarai. "Really look at me."

Mason sighed. Sarai ignored him. Her best friend never understood what it was like to be a female model. The pressure was ten times worse for the girls than the boys.

Reed just stared at her, still not seeing the truth that was clear to see in front of him.

"This isn't the real me," said Sarai. "I'm not who you believe I am under all these layers of clothes and makeup." Her makeup was melting off under the glare of the sun. The double Spanx was squeezing the life out of her.

"Who are you?" Reed asked.

Who was she? That was a good question. She could see that the answer was coming clearer to her husband with every second the sun glared down on her back.

What she saw reflected back in Reed's gaze was something she recognized. She saw her flabby, pathetic self in his eyes. Reed's gaze was darkening, shutting her out. His rejection was imminent. He was finally seeing her as she truly was.

What had she been thinking?

She knew what she'd been thinking. She'd believed the app. She'd believed the logic. She'd thought that she and Reed were compatible on a deeper level, a level past the physical. She'd been so starved for affection, and now she would be denied any of it from the one person she wanted it from.

Sarai's head was so full but so light at the same time. There was almost no more fight in her. Almost. With her last bit of energy, Sarai reached out to her husband.

Reed pulled his prosthetic arm away from her.

It was too late for her to pull back. She found herself falling forward into the empty space he'd left.

The world was going dark. She thought she heard Reed call out her name. But the last thing she remembered was hitting the ground hard. Then all was black.

CHAPTER TWENTY-ONE

Reed's world was spinning. The sun glared down on his back as he stared at this woman, his wife, as she stood before him with her lies exposed.

He'd given his heart to Sarai. He'd opened up and let her in. Not just into his mind and heart, he'd let her into his arms. And she'd lied to him.

He couldn't understand it. She'd been here the whole time in Montana?

What did she mean this wasn't the real her?

What layers?

He'd spent weeks peeling back her layers, getting to know the woman she was. He knew who she was.

Didn't he?

They were a 98% match. The math was on his side. But it didn't calculate the lies and omissions.

But here stood this best friend whom he didn't know much about. There was also the eating disorder she'd only just mentioned. And she'd been here the whole time?

"Who are you?" Reed asked.

Sarai sighed, but this sigh was filled with defeat. She reached for him. But he pulled away from her.

He'd offered her his arm. He'd laid his wounds bare. And she had lied to him. This wasn't the girl he fell for. Who was she?

Sarai kept coming forward. But she no longer had her feet under her. Her gaze was unfocused. Instead of the green of her eyes, he saw only the whites.

Her eyes had rolled back in her head. Her body had gone stiff. She was fainting. She was falling.

Reed sprang into action. But it was too late. He reached out to her, but she slipped down his stump and through his hand. His fingers caught the edge of her shirt, but it wasn't enough of a hold, and she hit the ground.

Reed dropped to his knees beside her. He checked her pulse. It was there but shaky. He checked her breathing. She was still getting air. But she was unresponsive.

"We have to get her to Dr. Patel."

Reed put his hand under his wife. He gathered her back to him, but without a second hand, he couldn't lift her.

He looked to her friend Mason who stood paralyzed in shock. For all his muscles and build he didn't look like he could actually lift a woman.

Reed called out to Sean and Xavier. Within seconds, the two came running. Xavier lifted his wife effortlessly and carried her to the doctor while Reed trailed beside them uselessly. He'd vowed he'd be there for her. The first moment of crisis and he'd failed her.

Once inside Dr. Patel's office, they laid Sarai on the therapy couch. Dr. Patel set about examining her. He was patient. There was no sense of urgency. Reed paced the length of the floor, running the carpet ragged.

"When was her last meal?" Dr. Patel asked.

"Breakfast," said Reed.

"What did she have?"

"Orange juice."

"And? Is that all? What about dinner?"

Reed told the doctor the food diary he'd cataloged moments before she fainted. Dr. Patel nodded as he listened to the sparse list. Then he looked past Reed as though he'd find more answers over his shoulder. Reed turned to see Sarai's best friend.

"She'd been doing good, doc," said Mason. "She hadn't had a relapse in almost a year. I've been out of town for a few weeks. But we talked every couple of days on the phone."

So had Reed and Sarai. But she hadn't told him about this issue. What else hadn't she told him?

"Did she tell you she has an eating disorder?" Dr. Patel asked Reed.

"She just did. Just a few minutes ago. But she's a healthy weight."

Reed looked down at his wife's body. She was curved in all the right places that a woman should be in just the way that would drive a man wild. Her shirt had ridden up over her midriff. Instead of flesh Reed saw black spandex. No, actually there was one blue layer of spandex covered by a black outer layer.

Was that a body shaper? Why would she think to wear something like that? And out in this heat?

Reed had no clue about women's sizes, but he knew Sarai was nowhere near what could be considered overweight or plus sized. Her waist was slim and he could see that her covered abdomen was concave beneath all the layers she wore.

She'd begun to tell him she had an eating disorder. That it wasn't the ones he knew about. What was this eating disorder?

"It's called body dysmorphia," said Dr. Patel. "She doesn't see her body the way others do. She sees imperfections where there may be none. She'll try to control her intake of food or work out excessively to achieve an unrealistic ideal."

Reed had thought he knew her so well. How had he not known this? How had he not seen the signs?

"I'm going to get some fluids in her and then have a chat," said Dr. Patel. "Why don't you give us some space?"

But Reed didn't want to leave her side. He'd already let her slip through his fingers once. He had to be here when she woke up so that she knew he was still by her side.

"I'll come and get you when she's ready," Dr. Patel assured him.

Reed stepped out the door. But he didn't leave. He intended to wait until his wife woke up.

CHAPTER TWENTY-TWO

Darkness surrounded her. Sarai saw nothing, not even a pinprick of light. But she was conscious and aware.

Her body ached all over, but mainly on the left side. The skin on her shoulder stung as she shifted and the material of her shirt rubbed against the torn skin. Her jaw ached when she winced from the pain of her shoulder. Her hip throbbed when she tried to curl into the fetal position seeking comfort from the pain.

She'd hit rock bottom again. Literally this time. But the pain didn't only radiate from her skin and bones. It went deeper. She felt it in her gut. Sarai was desperately hungry.

It went beyond her stomach needing food. Her soul felt starved. Her spirit felt famished. Her heartfelt ravenous. Only one thing would satisfy her.

"Can I see her?"

Reed.

His voice broke through the darkness like a lightsaber coming to life. Her first instinct was to shield herself. To cover up the imperfections that ran rampant all over her body.

Her first thought was to check her makeup. What was she wearing? How did she look?

"I need her to know I'm here."

Sarai forced her eyes open. She didn't think she could feel any worse. But coming to and seeing that she was alone in an empty room did the trick.

Reed wasn't there with her. She was alone. But he was near, she could hear him. He was just beyond the door.

She tried to lift her head but it stung. She tried to move her arms but they felt leaden. She knew she wasn't trapped, that nothing held her down. But her body refused to do what her mind demanded.

Wasn't that irony.

Her illness caused her mind to play tricks on what she saw of her body. Her dysmorphia had driven her from her career, from her life, from her friends, from the man she loved. It had made her believe that she'd gained too much, and so she'd endeavored to lose what she could. Now her mind wanted to reach out and claim what she'd lost. But her body, her flesh and blood, was too banged up and bruised to cause any change.

"I didn't catch her when she fell," said Reed. "She needs to know I'm here for her."

The pain in her husband's voice caused Sarai to whimper in pain. Her fall had left real bruises on her body. A fall that happened because she'd slipped back into old and dangerous habits.

Her illness had only ever caused her harm. Now it was hurting the man she loved. Reed deserved better.

"I just need her to know that I love her."

Sarai did know that. Despite every ill-conceived perception in her mind, that one truth she believed. Because she believed in Reed. He'd never lied to her. He only told her the truth. He was telling it now.

He deserved the truth from her. He needed to know that they couldn't be together with the way she was now. She was not well. She needed to be better.

The door opened. For the first time in a long time, Sarai didn't scramble to cover her body. She didn't try to shield her unmade face. It was painful, but she was determined to face the truth. Instead of Reed's face, she saw Dr. Patel.

"You're awake," he sounded surprised. "How are you feeling?"

"Awful. Inside and out. I need help."

"Good. Your husband is outside. Would you like me to get him for you?"

"I don't want to see him right now. Not like this. Not yet."

She had one more makeover to do. This one, hopefully, would be her last one.

CHAPTER TWENTY-THREE

Reed popped up from a dark dream. Sarai fell through his arms again and again. Every time he closed his eyes to sleep, it happened again. And again. She slipped through his grasp.

He woke up with his heartbeat racing. His mouth was dry. His throat was sore as though he'd cried out in real life.

Reed scratched at the tightness in his chest. He knew he wasn't going back to sleep again. Adrenaline rushed through him. He had to do something. There was only one thing he wanted to do.

The sun was blinking a few rays of its light over the horizon. Reed rolled out of bed. There was no need for him to dress as he'd never taken off his clothes from yesterday.

Unclean, unshaven, and unkempt he marched over to the medical suite on the ranch. Dr. Patel had insisted that Sarai spend the night there in the small clinic for observation. Patel and his daughter, Ruhi, had taken turns watching over her through the night.

Sarai hadn't wanted to see Reed when she came to. That had gutted Reed. It was the hardest, most jagged pill to swallow. Dr. Patel had told him to give it a day, to give her the time she needed to work out a few things.

It was a new day. Time was up. She was his wife. They should face all their problems together.

As Reed pulled the door of the suite open, he saw both Patels speaking quietly in the corner. Their backs were to Sarai's door. Reed crept in with the stealth he'd learned in combat zones. He should've known he was no match for Dr. Patel.

The man's gaze lifted as his daughter flipped through paperwork. Patel glanced at Reed. His face was expressionless. When his daughter handed him the clipboard of papers, Dr. Patel's gaze went to it.

Reed took that as a green light. He turned the knob of Sarai's door and slipped in. Belatedly, he thought he should've knocked. But he knew there was no way he wasn't going inside.

He'd endured chats over the computer, calls over the phone, the barrier of a video camera. No more. His relationship with his wife would only ever from this day forward exist in reality.

Inside, Sarai slept peacefully. She was beautiful even in her sleep. Whatever her treatment would be to combat this illness would not involve them being apart.

Reed sat down on the twin mattress. He reached out his hand and brushed a sliver of hair from her face. There was a slight abrasion there, likely from her fall, and she winced.

"Reed?" Her eyes blinked open. She stared at him for a second, her gaze coming into focus, and then she started. "I'm not wearing anything."

She was fully clothed in pajamas. A sheet covered her midsection. But she didn't reach for the sheet. She covered her face with her hands. Just as soon as she covered her face, she pulled her hands away.

"I'm sorry," she said. "It's really hard for me to be exposed. Dr. Patel diagnosed me with body dysmorphia. It means I don't see myself-"

"The way that others see you," he finished for her.

"Yeah."

"How can I make you believe that I think you're beautiful?"

Sarai looked into his gaze. There was turmoil in her green eyes. "I don't know?"

"This is what Patel told me on our wedding day; that we needed to see each other as we are. And not let the other hide. You accept me for who I am?"

He lifted his stump and brushed the side of her face that wasn't bruised.

"I do," she said, leaning into his touch. "I do accept you, wounds and all."

"I accept you for who you are. We'll need to help each other out with our own perceptions."

Sarai hesitated but she didn't pull away from his embrace. "I love you, but I don't love myself. I don't think we can be together until I learn to."

Reed pulled her to him with this right hand, locking her into his embrace. "I'm not letting you go. I'll close my eyes and not look at you if that's what you need. But I am not letting you slip through my hands."

She turned her face into his chest. Reed felt the wetness of tears permeate his shirt.

"Sarai, I want you to look at me so you know the truth. I want you to see the proof."

She lifted her teary-eyed gaze to him. She didn't wipe away the tears. She let him see her raw emotion. It was a start.

"I got angry and confused yesterday," he said.

"Because I lied to you?"

"No. Yes." He took a breath and began again. "Yes, when I learned that you'd lied, that felt awful. I'd opened myself up to you, only to learn that you'd closed a part of yourself off from me."

"I won't lie again, I promise."

"I believe you. And when I learned more about your illness, after talking with Dr. Patel and Mason, I came to understand why. I spent the night studying it. The first thing I did was to take all the mirrors and the scale out of our home."

Reed ran his fingers around the abrasion on her cheek. Sarai closed her eyes as he did so. The sigh wasn't one of resignation. He knew then that she wasn't giving up on them. She was ready to fight.

"I can wait to share a bed with you. But you can't keep yourself from me, Sarai. You can't not talk to me. You are my addiction. I need you in my life. For better or worse, that was the deal. Sickness and health."

He pressed a kiss to her wounded flesh. Only a light kiss. But he needed his wife to know that he loved her despite any real or imagined flaws she might have.

"Please believe that I love you despite your wounds," he said.

"I do. I know that one thing is true. It's everything else I have a hard time trusting."

Sarai tilted up her head and met Reed's gaze full on. Her gaze was open, vulnerable. But at the edges of her green eyes, Reed saw certainty.

"I'm going to get treatment," she said.

Reed winced. "Is it inpatient?"

"Since Dr. Patel is here, I can see him on the ranch."

Reed sighed in relief. "I can wait for anything so long as I get to hear your voice, see your face, hold you in my arms. I swear, I will never let you fall again."

"I'm going to work hard to love me too."

"I believe you'll do it. Once you see how amazing you are. Just keep looking into my eyes. Trust the reflection you see there."

Sarai gazed into Reed's eyes. Her lids narrowed as she focused on the reflection in his gaze. After a moment, a small smile tugged at her lips.

Reed leaned down and captured her lips. He drank in that smile and tasted acceptance. He tasted love. He tasted commitment.

With one final brush of his lips against hers, Reed tasted who Sarai truly was. As he pulled away, he left behind his true essence. When he looked into her eyes he saw reflected who they would become together.

EPILOGUE

It was another day in paradise. Sean Jeffries held up his hand, shielding his face from the sun. Up in a tree, a male bird sang a song to a female perched on at the edge of a branch. His notes were strong and pure, but Sean noticed a couple places on its wing where it looked like it had been pecked and a few feathers pulled loose.

Still, its song was intriguing enough for even Sean to hold still. With each note, he hopped closer and closer to his chosen mate. At the last note of the song, another male with bright, unmarred feathers swooped in. His song was a squawk, but his bird-body was perfect. He stole away the ladybird and they flew off together, leaving the wounded songbird alone and defeated.

Sean wasn't surprised. He knew that outward appearances mattered more than what was on the inside. The last year had taught him that truth which contradicted all the self-help books he'd read and seminars he'd attended in his life.

He lifted his hand and knocked on the door he stood in front of. He was sure to turn to his left side, placing his scars in the shadow as he did. He had no song to sing to this lady, but neither did he want to spoil her morning with his ruffled features.

"Good morning, Sean," Sarai said as she pulled open the door to the home she shared with her husband. "Reed's not here. He went out to help the others a couple of hours ago."

"I know. He sent me to take you to your appointment." Sean stepped aside and indicated the golf cart they sometimes used to get around the ranch.

Most of the men preferred to ride horses to their destinations on the property, but he knew that Sarai lacked the confidence to ride. She thought she was too big to fit on a horse. It was an unfounded idea. The woman weighed far less than Sean who rode for hours with no problem. But Sarai was still working on her body issues. With the help of her husband and everyone on the ranch, she was making progress.

"Really?" Sarai cocked a hand on her hip. "He sent you to drive me less than halfway across the property?"

Sean shrugged. He would've done the same had Sarai beeches wife. The men on the ranch treated their wives like the precious treasures they were. And there was the fact that Sarai had collapsed in the heat shortly after her wedding. They weren't taking any chances with her health.

Sean handed her into the golf cart and they took off across the ranch. He would never tire of the beauty of this place from the rolling hills in the distance to the green pastures that stretched as far as the eye could see. But he would have to give it up soon.

"It's just a few weeks until the zoning deadline," said Sarai. "Are you headed down the aisle soon?"

"No. I don't have any prospects for matrimony."

"I find that hard to believe. A smart and handsome guy like you? Girls must be lined up at the gates."

They weren't. Sean rarely left out of the gates of the property. On the ranch, he didn't get constant stares at his scars.

"Have you tried online?" asked Sarai. "Reed and I were a ninety-eight percent match, you know."

Sean knew. But he also knew he wouldn't find the perfect match online, like Reed. Or bump into her at church, like Fran. Or have her fall into his lap, like Dylan. Those routes were closed to him.

As they pulled up to the medical suite, a small, energy efficient car that was just a touch bigger than the cart pulled up too. Ruhi Patel stepped out. When she did, Sean swore that the sun narrowed its rays on her casting her in a golden glow. The birds joined in chorus to sing the sweetest song ever heard. Flowers spontaneously bloomed as her feet touched the earth.

"Good morning, Sarai. You're looking healthy today."

"Good morning, Nurse Patel," said Sarai. "I love that shade of eyeshadow on you."

Eyeshadow? Sean hadn't noticed the artificial coloring just under Ruhi's brow. He'd always assumed it was her natural, inner glow.

"Sean. Sean?"

Oh no. She'd been speaking to him and he hadn't responded. He knew he hadn't been caught staring. He'd perfected his peripheral vision so that he would appear to be looking away from someone, but in truth, he'd be free to take in an eyeful. Sean always practiced that tactic when Ruhi was around.

He lifted his gaze to find Ruhi looking directly into his eyes. She was smiling at him. That smile often caught him off guard. So much so that his lips cracked a grin, a rare occurrence with him because when he did it further increased the grooves in his right cheek.

Ruhi's gaze slid to his scars and she cocked her head to the side. Sean didn't shy away from her perusal. Ruhi was the only person he held still for. She didn't pretend she didn't see his wound. She stared openly, challenging it to defy her healing prowess.

"I thought we weren't seeing you until tomorrow?" she said. "You doing okay?"

Ruhi lifted her hand to his face. Her index finger caught Sean's chin and she tilted his head so that she could get a better look at his wound. He allowed it. He shied away from everyone but her. She was the only good thing that came out of this cursed scar.

"Just dropped off Sarai for Reed."

Ruhi rolled her eyes but didn't let his chin go as she examined him. "The machismo on this ranch is so thick you could cut it with a butter knife."

Like Sean, Ruhi had come from a traditional family with traditional values. Sean had gone through a rebellious phase as a teenager, but it hadn't lasted long. He ached for a wife to call his own, and children to run after, and a home to look after.

Ruhi was still rebelling against her upbringing. If it was a valued tradition, she turned the other way. As she turned to go into the building, a packet of papers fell out of her purse.

Sean bent to pick up the documents. His gaze settled on bold words; Doctors Without Borders. Sean knew of the program. It placed doctors in faraway places to help those in need. The documents were filled out in pen with Ruhi's slanted scrawl.

"You're leaving?" As the words left his mouth, Sean felt his throat closing.

"If I get in." She took the pages from him and placed them back in her bag. "This is the last stage of the application process. I'm on a short list now. I'd get to travel the world and help those most in need. It's a dream come true. Wish me luck."

Sean clenched his jaw. He watched her walk into the medical suite beside Sarai. The two women chatted away as they disappeared down the hall.

Sean's heart thudded and then it stopped beating. He hadn't planned on getting married, which would've meant he'd have to leave the ranch. But he'd planned to stick around. If Ruhi left the ranch, there would be no reason for him to do even that.

A cloud moved in front of the sun. In unison, the flock of birds that had gathered at Ruhi's arrival took off into the air. Sean turned his scarred face back into the shadows and took off into the gloomy day.

∼

That's only the beginning!

You know a romance novel guarantees an HEA.
Can't wait to find out how Sean and Ruhi get theirs?
The story continues in
His Permanent Scar
Book Four in the Brides of Purple Heart Ranch series!

HIS PERMANENT SCAR

THE BRIDES OF PURPLE HEART RANCH
BOOK 4

CHAPTER ONE

*D*ust kicked up the gravel as the yellow school bus pulled up the drive to the Bellflower Ranch. Though no one called this place by that name. All the residents and inhabitants had christened the sprawling land the Purple Heart Ranch due to the wounded warriors who came there to find healing both inside and out.

Sean Jeffries watched the bus as it came to a stop beside the mess hall. The hall was a converted barn where the veterans took their meals. Well, those veterans who weren't married took their meals in the barn. The number of single men on the ranch was dwindling fast. Only two were left, and Sean was one of them.

Pretty soon there would be no single men residing on this ranch. The zoning regulation that deemed the ranch could only be inhabited by family members was due to take effect at the end of the month. When that day came, both Sean and the other last single soldier standing, Xavier Ramos, would have to hightail it off the land. It was a day Sean was not looking forward to. But there was nothing he could do about it. He had no plans to get married anytime soon, if ever.

Instead of thinking about his own fate, Sean focused on the future of the ranch. That future was stepping out of the school bus. One by one, the scraggly boys hopped off the bus. Some had wide eyes as they looked around the ranch. Others had narrowed gazes filled with suspicion. Some formed groups and stood close. A few others stood apart and solitary.

Sean didn't blame either group of boys. It wasn't how he'd looked his first day of basic training for the army. He'd been entirely trusting of his superiors, of his fellow soldiers, of the entire process. That trust had served him well in training. But when he'd finally gotten out into the field and right into the trenches of war, that training had failed him and nearly taken the lives of his brothers at arms.

The sun glared down at him in the afternoon sky. Sean slunk back into the shadows of the barn. Being in the spotlight, having the heat of the sun on him, brought back the nightmares of the explosion. With his eyes wide open, he saw the horrors of that day played out again.

Men working together to build a school for their community. Women offering aid to give their families a brighter future. Children running around in excitement at opportunities they would soon be receiving. And one child standing off to the side with a secret that would send it all crashing down.

Sean clenched his fists. His hands were empty of his weapon. He'd laid down his weapons after his mistake that day and hadn't armed himself since. He also kept his distance from strangers in general, but innocent-looking children in particular.

At his side, Scar sat on her rump breathing heavily in the midday sun. The pug scratched at her skin, her nails gnawing at the missing patches of fur on her back. A couple of the other ranch dogs waited eagerly for the new humans to step off the bus, likely hoping to get new playmates. But Star was a cautious little beast. She'd been scorned one too many times by humans to trust them immediately.

The kids that came off the bus were mostly black and brown. They were all from the same inner city neighborhood. Sean's childhood neighborhood hadn't been so homogenous. He'd grown up in a racially and culturally diverse neighborhood; the true American Dream where people who'd come from money and people who'd bootstrapped themselves up to success lived in relative harmony.

Much like the veterans who occupied the ranch and were now extending a helping hand to these boys in need.

"Welcome to the Purple Heart Ranch," said Francisco Demonti. "You twelve have been chosen to participate in our youth program because you're having some trouble at school. That could be trouble with grades, trouble with social interactions, trouble with authority, or all three."

Since the ranch opened a year ago to rehabilitate wounded soldiers, this had been a dream of Fran's and Dylan's. Neither had been a troubled kid in their youths. Sean suspected that both meant they were subconsciously gearing these kids toward a life in the service.

Even with the scars they'd all gained, the limbs they'd sacrificed, and the friends they'd lost, Sean did not regret his time in the service. The U.S. Military had made him the man he was; a man with loyalty and honor. A man who knew that not all militaries held the same values and could make monsters out of men.

Sean also knew that it didn't have to be a government-run army that could turn men and young boys onto the wrong path. Some streets in America were meaner than those in Syria and Afghanistan. Better these kids went into the service than get caught up in a street gang.

But the kids weren't listening to Fran. Their attention was diverted elsewhere. Two men rode up on horses.

When they got to the gathered group of boys, Dylan swung his prosthetic leg over the horse and climbed down. Beside him, Reed Cannon also dismounted. When his feet struck the ground, he kept his prosthetic hand on the reigns to the mare.

"Man, this is a place for cripples," he heard one kid stage whisper loud enough to be certain he was heard.

Sean hung back in the shadows with Star. The pug looked up at him with her scarred face. The dog had a face that only a mother could love. The same could be said about Sean. Sean reached down and gave the dog a scratch under her chin to reassure her. The dog lolled her tongue in ecstasy at the gesture.

Sean didn't patronize the dog by telling her it was what was on the inside the mattered. Sean knew all too well that people judged the outside first and often didn't make it to look at someone's character.

"Look at the dogs," another boy snickered and pointed.

Soldier, the three-legged Chihuahua, and Spin the wheelchair-bound Irish Terrier sat panting, waiting eagerly for the go-ahead to mingle amongst the boys and make new friends.

"Yo, man, check out Quasimodo over there," said another of the boys. His stubby finger was pointed into the shadows at Sean.

Sean had to give the kid props. At least he knew his literature. Sean was a disfigured man lurking in the shadows. The scar on his face was a souvenir from his time in service, just like Dylan's missing leg, Reed's missing arm, and the shrapnel buried in Fran's chest.

Fran whistled loud to get the kids' attention. The boys didn't all straighten their backs, lift their heads, and stand tall as a soldier would when called to attention. But they did quiet down and turn their gazes over to Fran.

Fran didn't address the boys' comments with words. Like all the soldiers on this ranch, Fran was a man of action. He would show these kids the meaning of the word respect, likely in the horse stalls.

A small smile cracked Sean's lips at the thought of what Fran had in store for them. But as he smiled, his skin pulled and tugged and rippled uncomfortably. His scar limited his ability to express himself, which was fine since there were few people Sean wanted to show emotion to.

When he turned to head in the opposite direction of the group, he came face to face with one of the kids. The boy could have been a smaller version of himself. The kid stood back in the shadows. His shoulders were hunched to be unassuming. His body language said stay back, I'm not friendly.

"Does he bite?" the kid asked.

It took Sean a moment to realize he wasn't asking if Sean bit. The kid was asking about the dog. Star lifted her nose and gave the kid a tentative sniff. The pug must have found the kid to be okay because she reached out her tongue and gave the kid's hand a lick. That answered the kid's question.

Star was entirely docile. She just looked mean because of her smooshed mug and the patches of skin missing from her back. But give the dog a scratch behind the ear, show her a bit of kindness, and she would be your devoted friend for life.

"Aren't you supposed to be with the others?" Sean asked the boy.

The kid shrugged as he scratched Star's ears. He opened his mouth to speak but a fit of coughs came out instead. "I have allergies."

That didn't sound like allergies to Sean. The cough was too deep. The kid struggled for breath as the fit overtook him.

"How long have you had that cough?" asked Sean.

The kid shrugged. "Couple weeks maybe?"

"Have you been to the doctor?"

"We can't afford health insurance. My dad says it'll go away once the seasons change."

A whistle sounded from across the way. Sean, Star and the kid stood to attention at the call of Fran's whistle. Fran motioned to the boy.

The kid sighed, clearly wanting to hang with the dog more than he wanted to go and join the other humans. He gave Star one more pat. Without so much as a nod to Sean, he turned to go to the others. But before he took his first step, another series of coughs wracked his body. Once he caught his breath, he made his way over.

Sean almost stopped him, but he let the kid go. It wasn't his responsibility. The kid's parent would take care of it. Or not.

Sean would never be responsible for another child, or another soul. After facing off with a child soldier back in Afghanistan, he was happy to stay away from children for the rest of his life.

CHAPTER TWO

Contrary to her family and friends' beliefs, Ruhi Patel believed in love. Love was a scientific, provable fact. Beyond the data, she'd experienced it happen many times with her own five senses.

She'd seen it in her father's glances at her mother. She'd smelled it in the food her brother, Kabir, cooked for his wife, tasted it in the curries her sister-in-law made for her extended family. Ruhi had heard it in the songs her sister, Anika, sang for her husband. But Ruhi had never felt it herself.

And that was fine. Ruhi wasn't looking for love. Not exactly. She was far too practical and grounded. But she did harbor a hope that, like her parents and siblings who'd all fallen in love at first sight, love would sneak up on her and knock her off her feet.

"Ruhi, we have to talk."

Those words certainly knocked Ruhi back on her feet. But it was in the wrong direction. It wasn't what she was expecting to hear from the guy she'd been seeing for the past five months.

Ruhi had been spending most weekends at Dr. Michael Paskiewicz's place. So, this talk could go either way. Either he wanted to end the relationship or he wanted to move it forward.

They were seated in a small cafe in the trendy district in town. It was a place just outside the free clinic they both worked in; she as a nurse practitioner and he as a doctor. The entire clinic often came to this place before their shift started to get a mug of dark brewed energy, or for lunch to get refueled with a protein-packed sandwich.

It was after work now and Ruhi was having a tuna salad. Admittedly, it wasn't the best choice while on a date, and her stomach had grumbled a bit at the choice. But she and Michael were past the impress-me stage. The trouble was she didn't know if they were moving on up from there or taking a detour to a dead end.

Ruhi leaned back in her chair. For the first time in a long time, she considered; What did she want? Did she want to progress or get off this ride with Michael? And if they did progress, how far was she willing to go?

She'd always proclaimed she wouldn't get married or have a family until her career was well underway. She wasn't exactly where she wanted to be with her career today. Her soul was satisfied helping the less fortunate at the free clinic, as well as working with wounded veterans alongside her father at the Purple Heart Ranch. Still, there was more she wanted to do.

She'd applied to work with Doctors Without Borders, an organization that provided medical aid where it was most needed and often not accessible. It had always been her dream to travel and offer her services to those who needed it most. Unfortunately, she was still waiting to hear back about her application to the organization. If she got the job, it wouldn't be conducive to a relationship.

"We've been seeing each other for four months now ..." Michael was saying.

It was actually five. But who could expect the guy in the relationship to keep track? Michael probably wasn't counting their first few weeks of dating. Or all the times when they'd gone out in a group but stuck close to one another.

"... and I think you feel it too."

It? Did she feel *it?* She supposed she felt something for him. And apparently, he felt something too.

He didn't reach across the table for her hands. He retracted both of his hands below the table. Ruhi looked down and saw a bulge in his pocket.

This was it. He was going to do it. He was going to propose … something. That they move in together? That they join their assets? That they get engaged?

Her gaze stuck to the bulge. Was it big enough to be a ring? Or maybe a spare key? No, it was too fat to be a key. It had to be a ring.

Oh, God. It was happening. She was getting proposed to. But did she want to be proposed to? Did she love him? Did love truly matter in these days?

She and Michael were entirely compatible. Even though everyone in her family had fallen in love at first sight, they'd all had their unions arranged based on compatibility. Her parents were matched based on their personalities and goals. Kabir and his wife were both in the food industry and loved classic literature. Anika was a singer and her husband wrote film scores.

Ruhi and Michael were both in the same field. They were both health conscious and environmentally responsible. He had a compost bin and a rain barrel in the back of his townhouse, which was seriously sexy. And he drove a Prius.

Dr. Michael Paskiewicz was perfect for her in every way. She would be a fool not to say yes to his proposal.

Michael tilted his gaze up to hers, and suddenly, she felt it. That *it*. The butterflies in her stomach. But they felt a bit more like bees buzzing around and stinging her.

She felt some of the fish bubble up in her throat as though it wanted to break free. Oh, no! Was she about to barf?

She couldn't. Not now. She had to hold it in. This would not make for a great story to tell their children about how daddy proposed to mommy.

"Yeah, I can see you feel it too," said Michael. "There's just not that spark between us."

Ruhi blinked. She opened her mouth … and burped.

Michael reared back. He wrinkled his nose. She'd had extra onions on her sandwich, so not only did he get a whiff of the sea, he got the pungent smell of an earthy weed.

Ruhi's hands shot to her mouth, and she caught a whiff herself. But the embarrassment of her bad breath paled in comparison to the embarrassment of her assumption. "You're breaking up with me?"

"Breaking up?" Michael's nose relaxed and his brows pinched. "We weren't exactly a couple. Were we? I just thought we were hanging out. Being casual. Isn't that what you said you wanted?"

It had been what she said. Five months ago. But by the third month, she'd assumed they were a couple. Who wouldn't have?

"I feel that we're better off as just friends," he said.

Translation: *I don't want to commit to you but I'd still like to come over in the middle of the night on a weekday if that's cool.*

"I'm going to take some time and work on myself," he said.

Translation: *I'm going to go off and be selfish and self-centered and everyone else can take a hike because I won't notice.*

"It's not you, it's me."

Translation: *It was totally her, and he didn't want to see her anymore.*

"We're on different paths," he said.

Translation: *You're a slacker, and I'm about to climb a rung up the ladder of success and leave you in the basement.*

Michael reached in his pocket and pulled out the thick bulge. It wasn't a key. It wasn't a ring. It was an envelope. He pulled out a piece of paper.

"See? I got accepted to Doctors Without Borders."

Ruhi's stomach twisted the knot it had tied itself into in the other direction. "I didn't know you applied."

"I got interested when you talked about it. I applied on a whim, and I got in. I leave in a week."

"Wow. That's just …"

Not only was he dumping her after their casual, five-month-long, exclusive relationship. Wait? Had he been monogamous?

She couldn't ask now. She wouldn't get a key or a ring, and he was stealing her dream job. Her stomach untwisted, and she lurched again. Her hand covered her mouth in time, and she tasted bile. She had to get out of there.

"We'll still be friends, right?" said Michael.

That was the last straw. There was a votive candle on the table between them. Ruhi picked up her water glass and tossed it in his face. It doused the candle and the rest of the tuna sandwich. But mostly it soaked Michael's face and his shirt.

"Oh, my bad," she said standing up. "Thought I saw a spark."

And with that, she marched out of the restaurant without looking back. She made it all the way to the alley before bending over and giving up her meal to a gutter.

CHAPTER THREE

Sean rode the horse at a gallop. It was the only time in the world he felt free, in command.

He'd driven tanks in the army. He'd been in foxholes waiting for insurgents to appear. He'd jumped out of helicopters and into danger zones. None of that compared to commanding a horse.

The feel of the wind biting his face made him forget about the tug of the scars when he smiled. It was the only time he smiled, because the feel of the wind on his face negated the tug of the scars on his cheek.

Equine therapy had given Sean back his life. That and the healing touch of a certain nurse practitioner. But Sean could ride horses every day. He could only see Nurse Ruhi on their appointed days, and he could never tell her how he felt about her. He was sure her professional relationship prohibited her from dating any of her patients. But besides that, Ruhi was seeing someone else.

Dr. Pasteurizer, as Sean had dubbed him, appeared to be the perfect partner for Ruhi. But something about the man had always rubbed Sean the wrong way. The few times the man had been on the ranch helping out, he'd never looked directly at the people in his care.

He was one of those doctors who focused on the charts and not the patient. Where Ruhi always insisted Sean hold his head high and look her in the eye when he was under her care.

It was the main thing Sean would miss about the ranch. When he moved off the ranch next month, he would have to change health care providers. He knew Ruhi worked at a free clinic, but the government took far too good care of him to qualify for those services, and Sean would never take away a spot from those in need.

So, after next month, he'd only see Ruhi in passing when he visited the ranch. Or when he managed to catch her at her family's restaurant. He'd gone to her apartment for her birthday a couple of months ago, but that had been as a group with the others.

He was certain he couldn't just show up there to hang out and have to tilt his chin up so that she could look at his cheek as she examined him, see in his eyes as he answered her questions.

He had no inclination to marry anyone else to stay on the ranch and continue to see her. It wouldn't be right to offer his hand to someone else when another woman held his heart. And Sean knew Ruhi wasn't interested in his heart, only his healing.

Which was enough. It had to be. He brought the horse to a trot as he saw signs of others up ahead.

In the distance, he saw the young boys of the after-school program. They were split into two groups. One boy in each group was blindfolded and wandering around.

It was a trust game from his army days. It was designed to teach the team members to watch each other's back and keep them out of harm's way.

The coughing boy was one of the two who wore a blindfold. At the moment, he was headed into a pile of firewood. No one from his group was warning him. Instead, the boys of his team were covering their mouths to keep from laughing too loud.

Standing off to the side, Dylan watched it all go down. The Sergeant did not look happy. But neither did he intervene. Sean knew a hard lesson was about to be learned.

As expected, the kid walked into the pile and fell. The others around him tore their hands from their mouths and burst out laughing.

The kid tore off the blindfold. His dark face was screwed with confusion, and then betrayal, and then anger. He got up and raced for one of the bigger boys. The smaller kid tackled the big kid to the ground before Dylan could intervene.

Both kids were out of breath as they were separated. The little kid coughed and kept coughing. Then he doubled over and coughed a bit more, struggling for breath. They all waited for the kid to right himself. When he did, it was clear the fight was far from over.

"This team is on stable duty," announced Dylan.

The boys groaned. Sean would've too. Cleaning out the horses' stables was his least favorite job on the ranch.

"You did not have your brother's back," Dylan continued. "You work together as a unit and succeed. Or you all fail. If one man falls, you all do."

Dylan turned to the little cougher. "What's your name, kid?"

"James."

"And yours?" Dylan turned to the kid who'd taken the hit.

"Maurice."

"Maurice, take James to go see the nurse."

"I'm fine," wheezed James. Then he gulped down air before launching into another coughing fit.

The kids weren't laughing anymore. In fact, Maurice's face was screwed up in worry. He turned to Dylan.

"I don't know where the nurse is?"

"I'll show him," said Sean. He handed the horse's reins to Dylan and motioned for the kids to follow.

"I don't need his help," James managed between coughs.

"Look, I'm sorry," said Maurice. "I thought it was funny. Don't take it so serious."

"Whatever," said James. Then he turned to Sean. "The cough isn't serious. It's just allergies."

That was not allergies. Sean had no patience to entertain the kid. He pointed them both in the direction he wanted them to head toward. The medical suite where Ruhi was on duty today.

The other kid, Maurice, was ready to turn on his heel and head back to join the group. But before he did, he caught Sean's gaze. The judgment in Sean's eyes must've turned him around.

"Come on," Maurice said to James. "Let's go."

"I said you don't have to come with me. I don't need your pity."

"I gave the Sergeant my word. Whether you like it or not, I'm gonna do what I said."

Part of Sean wanted to cheer the kid. The other part of him wanted to roll his eyes. But it was a start. He marched behind the two as they headed into the medical suite. They walked past Dr. Patel's offices and straight to the back where Ruhi's exam room was tucked.

Sean listened to hear if she was in with another patient, but he knew she wasn't. He likely knew her schedule better than her planner. She had no appointments at this time unless someone came in with an injury. And there was silence coming from the room. Only the scratch-scratching of a pencil against a clipboard.

But as he drew nearer, that sound stopped abruptly. It was followed by a heaving sound, as though someone was about to be sick. Sean stepped in front of the two boys to get into the room.

And there she was. The sight of her was always a blow to his solar plexus. But this blow went straight to his gut. Ruhi was leaning over the sink, rubbing her stomach and grimacing.

"You okay?" Sean said coming into the room and standing by her side.

"Just something I ate." Ruhi straightened and pulled on a smile.

Sean's mouth itched to do the same. Aside from being on a horse, she was the only one who could elicit a grin from him. Even when she was on the cusp of being sick, she made his heart beat faster.

Sean was used to sensing and containing danger. But whenever he was around her, he only felt peace. He didn't know how he'd manage without that constant smile in his life.

"What can I do for you guys?" she asked, looking past him at the boys.

Before Sean could speak, James started coughing again.

"That does not sound good," said Ruhi.

"It's my fault," said Maurice. He stepped forward as though physically taking responsibility. "I played a joke, and he fell down and hurt himself."

Ruhi shook her head. "That's not a fall down cough. That sounds like there's fluid in your lungs."

She motioned James into the room and began her examination. Sean took the opportunity to openly gaze at her. Her golden skin looked a bit sallow today. There were slight bags under her eyes as though she'd either been crying or not sleeping well. There were no jokes or attempts at light-hearted banter in her conversation with James. The air about her, which was usually charged with electric energy, felt depleted.

Something was wrong. Maybe she was sick? She looked a little green around the gills.

"It's bronchitis," Ruhi pronounced sometime later.

"Is it my fault?" asked Maurice. Remorse was clear in his eyes.

"No, sweetie," said Ruhi. "It's an infection. James will be fine so long as he takes care of himself. He'll need some medicine."

"So, I'll have to stay home from school and the ranch?" James asked. To Sean's surprise, he did not seem happy about the option of a day off from school.

"No, if you're up to it, you can go to school, and you can come to the ranch. You just have to take it easy. You're going to feel tired a lot."

"But I won't be able to participate in the activities?" James asked. "I'll be a drag on the team?"

"Not if you have help," said Sean. He looked to Maurice.

"I'll help," said Maurice.

"I don't need you to," wheezed James. He hopped off the exam bed and squared off against Maurice.

"Well, you're on my team, so I have to." Maurice met him toe to toe.

With a sigh, Sean got between the two. With a stern look from him, they both backed down. Ruhi tore a piece of paper from her prescription pad.

"Give this prescription to your mom," said Ruhi.

"My mom isn't with us." The kid looked away as he said it.

The way he said it made Sean think that his mom was alive, just not physically present. She could be in jail, rehab, or skipped out on him entirely.

"Your dad?"

James nodded. He took the note from Ruhi, holding it carefully as though it were expensive lace. "How much is it gonna cost?"

"It's not too expensive," said Ruhi. "If your dad needs help paying I know some charitable organizations who will help."

"We're not a charity case."

Looking at the kid's clothes, Sean begged to differ. He was also smaller than the other kids his age. Sean wondered if the kid had been born addicted to drugs?

James folded the piece of paper and shoved it in his pocket. With a hunch of his shoulders, he headed out of the room. Maurice waited a couple of steps and then trailed after him.

Sean turned to Ruhi. "Should we call social services?"

"What for?"

"He said earlier he's been coughing for a couple of weeks. His parents might be neglecting him."

"Let's keep an eye on the situation first," she said. "We don't know the whole story."

"My parents would've rushed me to the hospital at the first cough."

"Your parents could afford it and had the resources."

Ruhi lifted her hand to pat Sean on his back. But her hand wavered. Instead of landing on his back, she put it to her belly. And then to her mouth.

"Ruhi?"

But she dashed away from him and back to the sink in the back of the room. Ruhi doubled over. Her body was wracked by retching sounds. Sean made it to her in time to gather her hair from her face and hold it away from the sickness that overtook her.

"I'm fine," she choked out.

But she didn't sound fine. Aside from a bit of sick on her face, there were also tears streaming down her cheeks. Despite still looking beautiful, she was most definitely not fine.

CHAPTER FOUR

This could not be happening. No. This was not happening.

Ruhi's stomach disagreed with her as it squeezed out the orange juice she'd drank that morning. But no, even that small bit of citrus was gone. Only bile coated her tongue.

This was not food poisoning as she'd hoped. That tuna salad sandwich that she'd thrown up yesterday was long gone from her system. So she knew it wasn't that.

She couldn't bring herself to say what it could be. Instead, she did what any medical professional would do. She went through the symptoms.

Her bra irritated her, and her breasts were super sensitive. She'd been visiting the bathroom more times than she cared to count over the last few days. She was tired as soon as she woke up, and she'd closed her office door to take a nap twice this week. There was also the nausea without vomiting. And the last two days of nausea with the vomiting.

All those symptoms could point to the flu. Or pneumonia. Possibly mononucleosis. Even meningitis. Oh, how she wished she had meningitis.

But the calendar didn't lie. Ruhi was almost a week late for her monthly visitor. She was never late. Not since her first visit at the ripe age of twelve. Her body was like clockwork. Still, she couldn't give her diagnosis voice.

How had this happened? She'd been careful. She was always careful. But contraceptives weren't foolproof. There was always a slim chance. How had she beaten the only odds she didn't want to?

"Ruhi?"

Sean's voice sounded behind her. He'd pulled her hair from her face as she'd lost the contents of her stomach, just like a good girlfriend would do. But Sean was a grown man, and he'd seen her puke in the sink. Would embarrassment leave her alone for a just a day?

"I'm fine."

She closed her eyes as she tried to straighten. She didn't want to see her reflection in the mirror. She didn't want to see herself like this. She didn't want anyone to see her like this.

But she wasn't fine. Her stomach told the truth and twisted. She retched over the sink again, more bile leaving her body.

Her eyes opened as she came up for air. But she didn't see herself. The first thing she saw was Sean's scar. The angry gash wrinkled his brown skin.

And just like that, she suddenly craved a Hershey bar. Then the thought of any food made her sick, and she retched again. Only this time, instead of bile, tears rolled down her face. She was too tired to hide, and she let them flow.

Sean's hand came to her back. It was the first time he'd ever touched her. She'd touched him multiple times over the past year as she'd treated him. The feel of his hand at her back instantly calmed her stomach, but it made her feel even more tired. She had the urge to curl up in his arms and go to sleep. To let him hold her and shut the world out.

Ruhi straightened her back. She was not that type of girl. To lean on a man? No, thank you. Look at what that had gotten her.

"I'm fine," she insisted. But the moment she left the comfort of Sean's arms her stomach protested again, and she turned back to the sink.

When she was done, too tired to hold her body weight, she slumped down onto the floor. The cool ceramic tile was nice on her skin. But even nicer was the feeling of Sean's fingers moving up and down her spine as he sat beside her.

Ruhi leaned her forehead against his shoulder. And they sat like that for long moments. In silence. Sean had never been much for words. His smiles were hard to come by, but he always had one for her.

"Should I get your father?" he asked.

"No."

That was the last thing she needed. Her parents were proud of her professionally. But she knew they worried about her in her social life. They were all smiles with each academic or career advancement. But with each new relationship, those prideful smiles slipped. With this news, she was certain she'd get alarmed looks and frowns.

What was she going to do? Being a single mother had never been in her plans. Her father would insist that Michael handle his responsibility. But Michael had already made it clear where his priorities lay. He was likely packing his bags, and maybe even bagging some other girl right now.

No. She would do this on her own. She'd tell Michael about the baby, of course. But not until she had everything figured out and well in hand first.

"Why don't you come lie down on one of the exam beds?" Sean offered.

"I'm fine. Just something that disagreed with me."

Sean's eyes said he didn't believe her. He was a watchful one. He always saw more than he let on beneath that hooded gaze of his. But Ruhi knew he'd never give voice to any suspicions.

"I'm fine," she insisted. "I'm going to be fine."

Sean brushed a stray piece of her hair back behind her ear. He offered her one of his small smiles. Ruhi's breath caught. She knew he was handsome, but she'd never looked at him that way. She was always more concerned about his healing.

The skin on his cheek wrinkled and Ruhi knew it pained him to do so. She had the urge to brush her thumb across that skin to smooth it out. But she didn't.

Sean pulled his hand back as though it had made the move on its own. "Is there someone else you want me to call?"

Ruhi closed her eyes. Though he didn't say it exactly, it was clear Sean suspected what was truly going on inside her. Soon everyone would.

Ruhi had spoken of Michael. He'd been to the ranch a couple of times to pick her up or drop her off. He'd even consulted on a case or two. She knew that was the someone Sean was referring to when he asked if she wanted him to call someone.

"No, I don't want to talk to him."

Sean's gentle face transformed in an instant. As a soldier, a man of action, he might assume that violence had entered the picture.

"No," Ruhi held up her hands. "It's not like that. We broke up."

Sean's brow raised. Then his gaze lowered, looking pointedly at her flat belly.

Ruhi closed her eyes, unwilling to deal with the reality. "Sean, please. Just, please."

"Should I call your father?" he said again.

"Oh, God, no." Ruhi shuddered. When she did her face snuggled deeper into the nook of Sean's shoulder. Lifting her head felt like such a chore that she decided to simply stay there.

"Okay," he said. "Whatever you need."

Sean shifted and Ruhi heard the sound of water running. A cool cloth touched her mouth and she sank even deeper into Sean's embrace.

"Whatever you need."

Ruhi leaned into him as he pressed the cloth to her face. She wasn't sure how long they stayed like that. But the soothing, cool warmth was exactly what she needed.

CHAPTER FIVE

The feel of the heat on his back was real. But just like in reality, Sean knew he had to push forward. He had to find Xavier and get him out of danger.

It was just a dream. Sean knew he was dreaming, but that didn't stop the nightmares from tormenting him, trapping him in the darkness and making him relive the gruesome explosion over and over again.

The sounds of children crying deafened his ears. The sound of women wailing pierced his conscious. He had to duck as the bricks they'd laid earlier fell all around him. He had to watch his step as the splintering of wood that gave up the fight and joined the raging flame.

There were so many bodies around him. Some called for help, but he couldn't get to them. Others were silent and still. But their accusations rang loud.

This was Sean's fault. It had happened on his watch. If he could take back that one second of hesitation … would he?

No matter his choice, the kid would always die.

The smell of burning flesh, the screams that were shrill and then instantly muted like a radio being turned off, Sean pushed through it all to find Xavier. Dylan and Fran had been outside when the suicide bomber had depressed his weapon. After his second of hesitation and the worst had happened, Sean had sprung into action.

He'd managed to get Reed out and to safety while others worked on his injury. But when Sean did a head count of his unit, he hadn't seen Xavier. He'd only heard Xavier call out that there was danger. And then his friend was gone.

Sean had to wade through the wreckage of brick, wood, and bodies. He had to watch the light go out of the eyes of people he knew he couldn't save. All because he had looked into the once innocent eyes of a child and hesitated.

In the dream, he found Xavier as he'd done in reality. Xavier had been lying face down. Flames encroached in on him, preparing to consume him as they had the school that had been filled with hopes and dreams. The fire's heat had already licked off the back of Xavier's shirt. When Sean touched his back to grab hold of him, the man woke and screamed and started swinging from the pain of the burns.

Sean fell back into the wreckage. A piece of metal slapped him in the face, leaving a mark to forever remind him of that day and what war could do to the most innocent of human beings.

Sean and Xavier managed to get out before the building collapsed around them. But the smell stayed with Sean. The sounds stayed with him. And the scar would never let him forget.

It had been a child who'd done this. Just a boy of thirteen, radicalized by his father and sent off to become a weapon of war. That morning, a father had strapped a bomb to his son's body and sent him off to certain death, while he'd stayed behind.

There had been a tear in the boy's eye before he'd done what his father told him to do. It was the tear that made Sean pause in his perch.

Just last week, Sean had played soccer with that kid out in the street. And now, his rifle was trained on the boy's heart. He'd seen the threat under the boy's clothing, but the tear in his eye made Sean pause his trigger finger. That single second cost more than Sean had in his account. It robbed Sean of his faith in humanity.

They caught the father within days. The man was tried and

convicted. As he was led away, he went proclaiming his pride in his son for the sacrifice he'd made for the cause.

That turned Sean's stomach every time he thought about it. Whatever it was called, that wasn't love. It was cowardice and perversion. No god would ever have a father murder a son in his name.

The tendrils of the nightmare slowly loosened their grip on him. But he still wanted to lash out. His hand itched for a rifle to hug close. He wanted to push away anyone who got near him.

Even as dark and gruesome as the nightmare was, Sean kept his eyes closed. He was not ready to face this day. But the sun had other ideas. And so he opened his eyes.

Sean's whole body felt as though he'd been cast into the fire and pulled out. His skin felt brittle and tight. It hurt to move his limbs. Still, he preferred the dream to his current reality.

Ruhi was pregnant.

The possibility of being with Ruhi, in reality, had always been a dream. A dream he could only access during his waking hours. Those dreams never came true.

He knew that Dr. Pasteurizer, or whatever his name was, was all wrong for her. Sean had been certain she'd break up with him sooner or later. He was glad that it had come sooner. But the guy had gone and broken up with her after he'd gotten her pregnant.

Just as Sean couldn't fathom turning a child into a weapon of war, he couldn't understand a father who would abandon a child.

In the modern world, there were far too many single moms for his comfort. Too many women that had the title shoved on them, not by their own choice. Sean wanted to find Ruhi's ex and put his fist down his throat.

But it wasn't his place. Ruhi was his nurse. He had no business interfering in her personal life.

However, holding her in his arms had been the first time in a long time that he didn't feel the constant heat at his back. As she'd settled her head against his shoulder, the constant screaming in his head had stopped. As he'd run the cool cloth over her face, he'd only smelled the fresh floral scent of her skin lotion.

It had been the only peace he'd had in a year. He wished he could have more of it. But he knew better. Love was not in his cards, not with a scar on his face and inside his soul.

Sean dressed and headed out to greet the day. He wasn't the only one up. The soldiers of the ranch were used to early mornings as part of their duties. It was another reason ranch life suited them so well.

Sean fell into work beside his squad. The men had been proud of their work as they'd built the school. The loss of the building had been a blow to their spirits as much as the explosion had taken a pound of flesh out of each of them.

But this ranch had given them all back their purpose. Working with the therapy horses, tending to the farm animals, tilling the soil, watching things grow and prosper under their care, all of this work had brought each man back from the horrors of war.

"The school called and told me that kid, James, the one with bronchitis, he stayed home from school today," said Dylan. He held the wood of a broken fence as Sean pounded in a post.

"Do you think we should stop by and check on him?" asked Fran. He hefted the other end of the new railing.

Dylan shrugged as he fit the wood into place. "She said he misses a lot of days from school, but his grades are always great."

"Do you think we should talk to his parents?" asked Fran.

"I gave the counselor the number to the ranch."

Sean stayed mute during the conversation. He supported the youth program, but he wanted no active part in it. Yesterday was his one and only starring role.

The sun rose higher in the sky. The rays licked a trail up Sean's back. Sean took a deep breath, trying to shove the memories of war away. But the sun's rays were relentless under the Montana sky.

"Jeffries," said Dylan. "Don't you have an appointment with Dr. Patel today?"

He didn't. But Sean got Dylan's meaning. The other soldiers never spoke of his PTSD. They didn't really speak of their own, except with Dr. Patel. Each man knew the warning signs. And Sean was clearly displaying them now under the heat of the sun. Without another word, Sean handed the hammer over to Fran and took off toward the medical suite.

When he arrived at the doctor's office, Dr. Patel's door was closed. The walk and the cool air had done him good. Sean's thoughts were his own again. And his only thought was of Ruhi.

He made his way down the hall and to her office. But when he got there, he saw that her door was also closed. The lights were off, and the room vacant.

That was odd. Sean knew her schedule. It was her day at the ranch.

"She's taking the day off." Dr. Patel came up behind Sean. His steps were slow; his hands were visible. The psychologist knew better than to sneak up on a soldier, especially a trained sniper. "I didn't realize you had an appointment with her today."

"I don't. I was just … I had a question and …"

Dr. Patel eyed him with that patient smile. Sean didn't talk much in his sessions with the psychologist. And still, the man was able to tell exactly what he was thinking.

"There was a sick kid yesterday," said Sean. "And she helped him. I just had a question about his treatment."

Dr. Patel nodded. "Ruhi said that her stomach disagreed with her."

This was one of those times Sean was happy he had a limited range of facial expressions. He didn't smile or frown or nod. He kept his face perfectly immobile.

"But I think it might be personal troubles."

Again, Sean held his tongue and his facial muscles still.

"It's hard being a father in these days, especially with girls pushing for the equality of the sexes. I think it confuses men because there are some things that men should do for their wives and their families. But my Ruhi, she thinks she's supposed to do it all by herself."

Sean sure hoped she wasn't trying to raise this child all by herself. But he also hoped that the baby daddy would stay out of the picture.

"Listen to me," chuckled Dr. Patel. "I've turned into a psychologist who tells my woes to a patient. But you have that kind of face." Dr. Patel winked.

Sean managed the smallest of smiles. Only Ruhi and her father could get him to lower his guard enough to stretch his facial muscles.

No. That wasn't true. The guys could in rare moments. And Maggie was always saying something that made him shake his head if not crack a smile. And Eva always invaded his space with her maternal hugs. And he found he liked watching *Doctorx Who* episodes with Sarai.

Sean was going to miss the women of the ranch when he had to move. He would be smiling a lot less when he was gone. There would hardly be any women in his life that he would feel comfortable sitting next to or hugging. A woman whose hair he didn't mind holding back as she let the contents of her stomach wash down a sink. A woman who he'd love to sit in silence with on the cold tile floor.

"I was going to take Ruhi some Mulligatawny soup after work, but I have to run to the church which is on the other side of town."

"I can take it."

"You sure it's no trouble?"

"None at all."

Sean followed Dr. Patel back down the hall to his office. The doctor handed him the Tupperware. It was warm in his hands, and he welcomed the heat.

CHAPTER SIX

The white stick fell to the linoleum floor with a clatter. Ruhi was surprised it didn't shatter into a million pieces because that's how she felt. Her life, her plans, her future, were now all scattered in pieces by something so small as a little white stick.

There were no lines to count on the stick. No pink or blue colors. This test was digital. It told her in black and white.

She was pregnant.

It had told her twice. She'd brought a two-pack just to be sure. The first one had said the same thing. There was no such thing as a false positive when it came to pregnancy. If the hormones were there, then a baby was in the oven.

Ruhi's hands went to her abdomen. There was something living in there, someone. A little person that she was now responsible for. They'd been there for some time now, likely a few weeks, and she hadn't known about them.

Oh, no! She'd had at least three bottles of wine over the last month. And she'd gone out dancing in a smoky club at least four times. And there was that tuna salad the other day. Wasn't tuna bad for babies?

Great. She was already off to a great start as Mother of the Year.

She had neglected her child for weeks, exposing him or her to all the wrong elements. And to top that off, they wouldn't get a dad as part of the deal.

Ruhi looked up on her mantle. There was a picture of her standing between both her parents on her graduation day. She knew that each of her siblings had a similar picture. Her parents had given each of their children the same amount of love, or more, when it came time that they needed the extra attention.

Ruhi had never once felt neglected or alone, even when she wanted to be by herself. She'd known her whole life that her family, especially her parents, would be there for her before she knew she needed them.

Her child wouldn't know the same. Unless …

She looked down at her cell phone. Maybe she should give Michael a chance to be a dad? It wasn't exactly an option. He was the father. He could choose to not be in their child's life, but that wouldn't change the fact that he was the child's father.

It wasn't as though she were trying to get back together with him. He'd made it clear there was no spark. The problem was there had been a spark, and it was growing in her belly.

Ruhi picked up her phone. Her stomach rumbled, but nothing came up. She just had a sick feeling that settled there.

Michael was still in her number six spot, after her parents and siblings. She hit the little heart next to his name and listened while the phone rang. And rang.

Finally, it clicked over and Ruhi nearly threw up.

"Hello?" said a feminine voice. The voice was sleep riddled.

Had he already moved on? It had barely been two days. And his new chick was answering his phone. She'd never pulled that while they were together.

Ruhi quickly disconnected the line. Humiliation filled her gut but unlike anything else she tried to keep from coming up, it stayed down in there.

A knock at her door had her jerking to attention. It was probably her father. She'd called in sick that morning. He or her mother was sure to be by with some spicy soup to cure her.

But she didn't have a case of a common cold. She had a case of the stupids. The only known cure was not repeating past mistakes.

Ruhi tossed her phone to the side. Then she picked it back up and deleted Michael's number. Not only from her favorites, but from her contacts.

Ruhi went to the door. She opened without asking who it was. It didn't matter if it was her mother or father, she'd have to tell them sooner or later that she was pregnant out of wedlock and would be raising the child on her own.

Her hand halted on the doorknob. She turned back to the picture over the mantle. They were smiling proudly at her there. The next picture wouldn't be filled with pride. There would be a look of disappointment on their faces when she told them her newest accomplishment. It wouldn't be the first time.

They'd tried setting her up for years for an arranged marriage with a parade of nice Indian men that they'd vetted thoroughly. It wasn't that Ruhi was determined to marry outside her race. She just was suspicious of any Indian boy that showed her interest, certain they were a plant by someone in her family.

Eventually, her family took the hint and left her to her own devices in her dating life. But she didn't miss their telling glances that said though they supported her, they disagreed with her track.

Dating wasn't the only track they disagreed with her on. They didn't understand why she stopped at Nurse Practitioner and didn't get her Doctorate degree.

They didn't always see eye to eye with her recycling, environmentalist, and health choices. But they indulged her.

Could they indulge her being a single, unwed, career mom?

She knew they would. But there would be that period of disappointment at the edge of their smiles, in the corner of their eyes.

Maybe she should call Michael back? If she showed up with a husband they'd be less disappointed. But no. She had her pride. If he'd moved on, then she would too.

Besides, she was swearing off men for the foreseeable future. That was a guarantee now that she'd have a child in tow. Kids were known to put dampers on a woman's social life.

Ruhi took a deep breath and pulled open the door. "What are you doing here?"

Standing on her stoop, in the dim light of the hallway was Sean Jeffries. He held up a covered soup bowl she recognized as her mother's. "Your father sent me with soup."

Ruhi sighed. She wasn't sure if it was because of the soup or because she had a reprieve for a little while longer before she told her parents about her predicament. A predicament that only she and Sean knew about.

"How are you feeling?" he asked.

Ruhi waved him in. "I haven't thrown up today. But my stomach isn't sure about spicy foods."

"I also brought crackers and a banana. I hear that's good for … you know."

"You can say it, Sean. I'm pregnant." Ruhi tugged open the container filled with her mother's spicy soup that would always warm her heart when she was under the weather. The moment the curry hit her nose, she slammed the lid shut so that the smell couldn't travel any further into her queasy body.

Sean seated himself in the center of her small love seat and watched her beneath his hooded gaze. He made certain to turn the right side of his face away from her. Ruhi walked over to the right side of him and sat. The warmth coming off his body reminded her of being tucked in on a winter's night by her mother, of sipping chai tea with her father on Sunday afternoons.

Before she knew it, she'd tucked her legs underneath herself and settled into the nook of Sean's shoulder. She was too tired and too comfortable to feel any shame about leaning on him. Though she was certain this wasn't the most professional of moves, Sean was the only person in her corner right now.

And besides, he wasn't complaining. He sat beside her, his arm wrapped across the back of the sofa. He'd always been the perfect gentleman. All of the soldiers on the ranch had been since the moment she turned up to help with their healing. Not one had made a move on her, not even Xavier who was a notorious skirt chaser. It was likely out of respect for her father. But more likely it was how these veterans were built, to protect and to serve.

Or was that police officers? Ruhi couldn't be bothered. The warm comfort and cozy silence were all she cared to focus on.

"Have you told … him?"

Ruhi shook her head. When she did, her nose brushed against Sean's shoulder. He smelled of wood and outdoors and a hint of the spices from her mom's soup. For some reason, the smell of the spices on him didn't bother her stomach one ounce.

Ruhi lifted her gaze. Her eyes glanced over Sean's scar. When she'd first seen the deep grooves, she'd thought they made him look angry. But she'd never once in an entire year heard Sean raise his voice. She couldn't remember a time when he'd looked directly at her for more than the second it took to answer her litany of health questions.

He gazed down at her now, and she saw that he had golden flecks in his hazel eyes. The cruel scar highlighted the gracious curve of his upper lip. She'd touched the scar numerous times and knew it to be stiff and unyielding. She'd never touched his lips. She'd bet they were soft as velvet.

Ruhi sat up straight. The motion made her nauseous. Sean's hand at her back instantly quelled the sick feeling.

"Michael was otherwise engaged with someone else when I called. He's the one that ended our relationship. He's already moved onto someone new."

Sean shook his head, anger clear on the grooved lines of his face. "I'm not his biggest fan. Still, the child deserves a father."

Ruhi wrapped her arms around herself. "I just wish the father were someone else."

Sean's arms came around her. She didn't brush him away. She hadn't realized she was so starved for affection. When was the last time Michael had simply held her?

"What if it was?" Sean's words were spoken so quietly she thought she'd imagined he'd said anything at all.

"What if what was?"

He turned to her. His gaze wide enough for her to see his hazel flecks. He tugged at his chin before he spoke again. "What if the father were someone else."

"What do you mean?" she asked.

"What if it were me?"

Now not only her stomach was playing tricks on her, but Ruhi was also hearing things. "I'm sorry, what?"

Now, Sean avoided eye contact. "It just seems that we might be able to help each other out. I need a wife to stay on the ranch. You need a father for your child."

She stared at him. Because of his scar, Sean couldn't make the normal range of facial expressions. He always looked serious, some would even say angry. But Ruhi could always tell what was on his mind by what she saw in his eyes.

Slowly his gaze slid to her, and she saw that he was completely serious.

CHAPTER SEVEN

$\mathcal{I}$t was too late to take them back. Sean's words were already out of his mouth and in her ears. And, oh boy, had she heard them.

Ruhi stared at him. Her lips parted, her eyes wide. Her hand was on her abdomen, as though she were protecting her baby from the ludicrous idea.

Sean had no idea what had gotten into him.

Wait. Yes, he did. It was the feel of her resting against his shoulder. It was the vulnerable, lost look in her eyes as she'd gazed up at him.

It had all felt so right. And if she married him, even in name only, she could feel free to do that every day.

She could come home from a long day at the office taking care of others, and he would take care of her. He would bring her comfort foods to nourish her. He would listen to her as she told him all of her secrets and worries. He would hold her as she rested and take on any load that she bore, including the one she carried in her belly.

But it was a pipe dream; a self-destructive mission. Instead of a vest containing an explosive, Sean had opened his heart. His misguided efforts had just blown up in his face.

Ruhi was turning the proposal over in her head as she stared at him. She obviously thought it was the most ridiculous idea ever. He should've delivered the soup and turned to go without breaching her threshold.

"I'm sorry," he said rising from the couch. "It was a stupid idea. I was just trying to help."

He took a few steps to the door. She didn't stop him. She didn't move. She was still frozen in the same position that he'd left her on the small love seat.

Had the idea of being with him disgusted her so much? Now she wouldn't be comfortable treating him. He'd ruined everything, and she wouldn't want to see him professionally anymore.

"I just want to be sure you understood I wasn't suggesting we behave like a real married couple," he said. "It would be platonic. Would've been, I mean."

Why was he still talking? He couldn't remember the last time he'd talked this much. For the last year, he had been a man of few words to even those who were closest to him.

One reason was because every time he opened his mouth, he felt the traction of the scarred skin on his cheek. And so he kept quiet and let the scab lie. Now he barely felt the scar, and he couldn't seem to keep his mouth closed.

"You wouldn't have to be a single mother. You'd have a partner. I could stay on the ranch. We could raise the child there around a huge family who would have each other's back. But it was a ridiculous idea."

"That doesn't sound ridiculous at all." Her voice was so quiet he nearly hadn't heard her. Slowly she turned to him. Her gaze lifted and so did the hope in his heart. "Platonic?"

"I beg your pardon?" Sean took a step toward her. It was a careful step, as though he were making his way through a live minefield.

Ruhi stood. Her steps were just as cautious as his. "Our relationship? We'd be platonic? Equals? Sharing all the duties of the household, finances, and parenthood?"

Now Sean's jaw decided to clench. He swallowed, trying to get moisture to the inside of his mouth. When he was able to open his jaw he swore he heard the creak of hinges. "Of course."

"What if you wanted to date?" she asked.

A harsh breath left his nose as he laughed. Date? He hadn't thought of dating anyone but her in a year. But he didn't dare tell her that. His heart had already been put through enough tonight.

"I'm not looking to date anyone," he said. "Not looking like this." His hand lifted and motioned to the side of his face.

Ruhi followed the direction of his fingers. She cocked her head and frowned. Sean hadn't felt self-conscious when she looked at him since the first time she'd rested her fingers on his chin and lifted his gaze to meet hers. Now, all his insecurities rushed in. Consciously, he angled the right side of his body away from her. But her next words had him dropping his guard entirely.

"You don't realize how handsome you are," she said. "That the goodness in you shines through."

No. No, he did not realize that. He did not believe that. "I'm not a good man."

"I don't believe that. Not for one second." She took a step toward him. More sure and less cautious this time.

Sean took a step back. "I've done … things, Ruhi."

She nodded. She knew about his PTSD. It was part of his medical chart. Though they'd never talked about it before. She likely knew where much of his stress stemmed from. Still, she took another step toward him.

"You protected people," she said. "The innocent civilians in other countries, and all of the people in your country."

She stopped moving when she was standing before him. She took a deep inhale. Her hand came to rest on her belly.

Sean held his breath. He didn't breathe again until she exhaled.

She looked at him. Her eyes filled with so much vulnerability that he took another step toward her. But her outburst of laughter halted him. For the second time tonight, Sean felt as though his heart had been blown to bits.

"This is crazy," she said. "I can't do this to you. I can't ruin your life just because I screwed up mine."

She thought marriage to him would ruin his life? Not hers? For the second time tonight, his heart sewed itself back up and reached toward hope again.

"You wouldn't be ruining my life," Sean said. "You helped to heal me. You are the reason I can get up in the morning and face the day looking like this."

She opened her mouth to protest, but Sean held up his hand. This confession was the closest he'd ever get to telling her his true feelings.

"I've never told you how much what you do for me means to me. If this is how I can show my appreciation, by coming to your rescue in your time of need, I would be honored to be your hero."

The moment was ripe for him to get down on his knee and propose. But he knew better. He knew that wouldn't impress Ruhi. And so, instead, he offered her his hand.

"Ruhi Patel, I would be honored to be your partner in raising this child. Please consider taking my hand and being my partner in life."

CHAPTER EIGHT

For the first time in days, Ruhi woke without immediately rushing to bend over the toilet. Her stomach grumbled with hunger instead of upset. She felt light instead of foggy.

Her hand rubbed over her abdomen. Her belly was still flat, but she felt different. She had the knowledge that a new life was within her. And she, herself, was starting a new life.

She was getting married. Or at least she thought she was getting married. She hadn't given Sean a final answer. She'd told him she'd think about his proposal.

Lying in bed after he'd left, she'd thought of nothing else. It would solve so many problems. The first being her desire not to raise a child alone. Then there was the waiting disappointment that would dawn on her parent's face when they learned her news. But with Sean by her side, they wouldn't frown.

Her parents loved each of the soldiers. Anyone of them would've been on their husband-approved list for their single, professional daughter. That included Sean; the gentle soul whose gaze was haunted by the ravages of war.

Sean didn't attend church services, but Ruhi had seen him more times than she could count out in the field with a Bible in his hand.

Her father had mentioned that they had prayed together in a few of his sessions. Sean preferred his fellowship in private.

He was a practical man, not given to romantic overtures. His marriage proposal hadn't been poetic. It had been practical and well thought out. She hadn't been swept off her feet. But she had found it thought-provoking.

It made sense. She couldn't think of a single reason she shouldn't consider Sean's proposal seriously. Love obviously wasn't coming her way in this lifetime. She'd dated enough to know that the spark would likely never ignite in her heart. It was high time she stopped looking for it.

She now had another life to care for besides her own. She had to start thinking practically. But could she spend the rest of her life with Sean in a platonic relationship? Could he? Could a man be platonic?

Ruhi wasn't so sure it was biologically possible. She'd never seen Sean with a woman the entire year he'd been on the ranch. He rarely left the grounds. He rarely lifted his gaze to any of the women who worked on the ranch. Except for the other wives, and her.

She and Sean got along fine. He was a decent man, loyal and kind. He was even funny every once in a while. He respected what she did and trusted her judgment. They both were financially stable.

Heck, she'd been having the best relationship of her life and hadn't even known it.

The only problem was that there wasn't any love between them. But was that really a problem? If love hadn't found her in all these years, it probably wasn't paying her any mind. Not everyone married for love. The vast amount of pairings were business arrangements, and they worked. Why not hers?

And in a few years, if Sean wanted a divorce because he found someone who'd love him, someone whom he loved in return, then she'd honor that and let him out of the marriage. It was just a contract, after all. There would be no need to hold him to it if the arrangement no longer served him.

With that thought in mind, Ruhi dressed and headed in to work. She wasn't due at the ranch until later in the afternoon. She did her rounds at the free clinic quickly. Even though the clinic urged twenty minute max visits, quickly and free often clashed.

There was a mom of five and each of the children had pink eye. A sixteen-year-old boy came in with what Ruhi confirmed to be an STD. A fourteen-year-old came in and was diagnosed with the flu instead of the pregnancy she suspected. She couldn't turn any of these people away with a doctor's note and a thank you for your patronage. Each deserved her undivided attention and a heartfelt talk.

So Ruhi didn't walk out of the clinic until well after lunch. When she pulled up to the Purple Heart Ranch she saw the bright yellow school bus carrying the boys of the youth program pulling in as well. The last kid straggling off the bus was coughing.

Ruhi recognized him as the kid she'd diagnosed with bronchitis. James, he'd said his name was. Ruhi made her way over to the kid before he headed into the fields with the others.

"Hey, James," she called out. "Feeling any better?"

The kid looked around as though he wasn't sure she was talking to him. "Oh. Hi. Yeah. I'm fine."

Ruhi had been saying the same thing for a couple of days, and she wasn't. Not until just this morning when she felt she'd worked out a new five-year plan. One that included a marriage of convenience, a hunt for the best preschools, and perhaps her own practice. Montana was one of the few states that allowed a nurse practitioner to practice on her own. Then she could spend as much time as needed with her patients to treat their ailments from the inside and the outside.

"Were you able to get that medicine I prescribed?" she asked the kid.

"Oh, my dad said he'll get it today."

The shiftiness of the kid gave Ruhi pause. Clearly, he wasn't telling the truth. Hadn't it already been two days since she'd seen him? If left untreated, bronchitis could develop into something worse.

"I may have some cough syrup in my office. Why don't you come and get it?"

But he was already shaking his head and backing away. "I gotta go catch up with everybody else. I already missed a day. But I'll come before I go."

"Okay." She could do nothing but watch the kid go. For the moment. She'd give the school nurse a call when she got to her office and see if there was anything that could be done on their end.

"We're having trouble with that one." Dylan parted from the shadows and came to stand beside her. "He's a loner. Doesn't like anyone seeing him as weak."

"Yeah, I know the type," Ruhi said. "Hey, have you seen Sean?"

"He was in the stalls. He drove over to your place yesterday?" There was a lift to Dylan's eye.

That was the only thing she wasn't looking forward to about living on a ranch. There was very little privacy, even when your doors were shut. But just the same as everyone put their nose in everyone else's business, loyalty and devotion ran deep. Ranch families were real families.

Still, Ruhi wasn't ready to have her business divulged just yet. She shrugged, evading Dylan's prying blue gaze. "I wasn't feeling well. He brought me some soup. I just wanted to thank him."

"Hmm."

Ruhi ignored the loaded sound that Dylan made and headed to the stalls. She found Sean inside mucking out one of the stalls. She called his name, but he didn't respond. She could see the wires of earbuds hanging from his ears. Shouting would do no good, so she went up and tapped him on the back.

Sean spun around, rake held high like a bat. Ruhi instantly raised her arms to cover her face. Through her fingers, she saw Sean's eyes go wide.

He dropped the rake and doubled over as though he were going to be sick. "Oh, my God. Oh, my God."

Ruhi straightened and went to him. She reached out her hand and then withdrew it at the last minute. "Sean?"

His eyes were closed tight. His hands balled into fists. "You can't sneak up on me like that." His voice was so quiet, so broken.

Ruhi had never had the occasion to seek him out. He was always waiting for her at her office door. "I'm sorry. I'll know better next time."

"Next time?"

The tremor in his voice shook something deep inside her. Ruhi didn't like to see people in pain, especially not those she cared about. Sean had been there in her time of need, and now, somehow, she'd hurt him.

Sean looked from her eyes, then to her belly. "No. There can't be a next time. What was I thinking? I could hurt you or the baby."

"You would never …"

"Not on purpose, no. But what if I get surprised or startled. What if the baby wanders in my room at night and I'm having a nightmare and …"

"Sean, I know you. I trust you. You would never hurt anyone."

"I have hurt people."

"In the service."

He stared at her. There was so much vulnerability in his gaze. She wanted to wrap him up and protect him. Instead, she turned away and looked out the door at the midday sun.

Was she making the right decision? She'd never come face to face with Sean's demons. That look in his eyes, however brief, when he didn't recognize her, that had scared her. Was she making a mistake putting her child under the same roof with this man?

She turned back to him just as he was taking a step to her. Somehow they collided. As she teetered toward the ground Sean rotated his body so that he landed on the hard ground with her on top of him.

That cinched the deal for Ruhi. Despite what he may think, Ruhi had no doubt that Sean would do whatever was necessary to make sure she and her baby were taken care of and out of harm's way.

With his hard body under hers, she also began wondering how long the platonic part of their plan would last. By the way he gazed at her lips she wondered if he were thinking the same thing. Again the thought raced through her mind; maybe this was a mistake. But for a different reason.

"Ruhi?" her father called out. "Dylan told me you were in here. I have a surprise for you."

Her father pulled the doors to the stables open, letting in the full light of the day. The surprise was that her mother was with him. Her parents looked down at Ruhi who lay on top of Sean.

No one moved. Not her parents framed in the doorway. Not Ruhi or Sean tangled on the ground. The silence in the barn was deafening.

"It's okay," Ruhi said. "We're getting married."

CHAPTER NINE

Sean had been caught by parents before with girls. It had never been more than kissing. The parents had never been too upset when they found their daughters in his embrace. Sean was a great student, came from a great family, and had a great future ahead of him.

That was then.

This was now.

Dr. Patel steepled his fingers on his large desk. They didn't sit in the arranged chair and chaise lounge like when Sean was at his therapy sessions. This wasn't a session. This was an interrogation.

"So," began the doctor. "You and Ruhi?"

That was it? That's how Dr. Patel planned to start this conversation. Where was Sean supposed to take that? There were so many directions.

So, he and Ruhi were caught in a compromising position.

So, he and Ruhi were a thing.

So, he and Ruhi should consider entering a pie eating competition.

"It wasn't what you think?" That seemed a safe bet.

Dr. Patel waited patiently for Sean to tell him what to think. What did Sean want the father of the woman he was secretly in love with and was about to enter into a marriage of convenience with, to be the beard for her deadbeat baby daddy ex-boyfriend to think? Anything out of his mouth would be a lie.

"I care very deeply for your daughter."

That was the truth. Sean wouldn't sully his relationship with this man who had helped him with anything but the truth.

"I know," said Dr. Patel.

Of course, he knew. Dr. Patel knew everything. Sean and the others long since held the belief that the man had a direct line to God. Sean was certain the two chatted about the inner workings of everyone's lives and God sent Dr. Patel to do his good work on earth while He remained in heaven.

"And that's what worries me," Dr. Patel continued. "My daughter has very non-traditional ideas of relationships. I know you come from a traditional family. I know, despite what you may think of yourself, that you want a wife and children for yourself. I'm not sure that Ruhi will ever want those things for herself."

Wow. For the first time likely in his entire life, Dr. Patel got it wrong.

Sean did want those things. He wanted a family of his own. He wanted a wife to come home to every night. He wanted children to toss into the air and teach life lessons to. The problem was the only woman he saw himself having any of those things with was Ruhi.

"Being a father is the hardest job," Dr. Patel continued. "I thought being married was hard work, but a husband and wife always work toward a compromise. A father and his children, that's a different relationship. You can guide them, but inevitably you have to let them go off and make their own decisions. It's hardest when you know the path they're on is not the best."

Sean knew that. His own family, who he loved dearly, urged him to come home after he was discharged from the service. But Sean knew that being back in civilian life, even surrounded by the people who loved him most, wouldn't help in his healing. He knew he needed his fellow soldiers around him, men who would understand and not be offended when he needed to go quiet and be alone.

"I would be thrilled if my daughter married someone like you. I would be over the moon if it was, in fact, you that she chose. Freud would say she's rebelling against her parental ideal. But I don't think she's happy. I know she's not happy. I worry for her, but I have to let her walk this path and hope that she ends up in the place she's meant to be. The problem is, Sean, I don't want you getting hurt along the way."

Sean couldn't help but crack a smile even though it hurt his face. This man would be his father in law. He couldn't ask for a better role model, a more solid patriarch than the father he already had. But Dr. Patel could easily stand next to his old man.

Sean scooted the chair away from the desk. He ran his hands over his jeans to smooth the fabric as he stood. "Dr. Patel, I have something very important to ask you. I would like to ask for your daughter's hand in marriage."

Dr. Patel frowned. "Haven't you been listening, son?"

Son. Sean liked the sound of that. "I have. I've already asked Ruhi to be my wife, and she's said yes."

Sean had never seen Dr. Patel at a loss for words.

"I would've asked you first but it all happened so fast."

"Forgive me, but why? I know she cares for you, but not in a romantic way. Meanwhile, I've seen the way you look at her. That is most definitely in a romantic way."

Sean rubbed at his chin. Dr. Patel was right. Sean was in love, while Ruhi was only in trouble.

"Does this have to do with the zoning?"

Sean sat back down. He nodded as he did so.

"I can't say I'm not surprised that she would help in that matter. I assume you two have some kind of short-term agreement in place?"

They'd never discussed a duration to the arrangement. Sean wanted it to last a lifetime, even if it remained platonic. Just being near Ruhi made him feel alive.

"But you have real feelings for her?"

"I do," Sean admitted.

"Does she know that?"

"I don't think so." He couldn't tell Ruhi's father that their marriage would be platonic. Especially not with a baby already growing inside her.

"What about… what was his name?"

That said something if the girlfriend's father couldn't remember the boyfriend's name. "Michael. He's leaving for a job overseas."

"Oh." Dr. Patel didn't look put out over that. "I'm worried about this arrangement, but I'm also pleased. I meant it when I said I can't think of a better man for her."

"You're not worried about my … episodes?"

Dr. Patel took a deep breath. "There are some protocols we can put in place for your nightmares. But I trust you."

Ruhi had said the same thing. Sean would do everything in his power to keep their trust even in this relationship that had its roots in a lie.

CHAPTER TEN

"I thought you were dating Mitchel?"

Ruhi looked over at her mother as she mispronounced her ex's name. Deeksha Patel was dressed in colorful pants and a bright shirt. You could take the girl out of New Delhi, but you can't take New Dehli out of the girl.

"His name was Michael," said Ruhi. "And we broke up."

Why could no one remember his name? They'd dated for five months. Okay, they'd been casually seeing each other for four months. But she'd introduced Michael to her family and friends. Hardly anyone could remember his name. True, Ruhi wanted everyone to forget they ever knew him now.

"So you and Sean are casual?" Her mom grimaced when she said the word. There was the disappointment at the crinkle of her eyes.

"Sean and I are … a bit more than casual."

And there it was. Her mother's eyes lit up. Ruhi tried not to let that light get to her, but she couldn't help it. She loved being in the light of her parents' praise. It had been a long time since that had happened.

She'd gotten great grades in school. She'd done well in sports. But all of her accomplishments were largely over. She'd hoped getting the

Doctors Without Borders position would gain her another bout of praise, but that career opportunity had been stolen out from under her by that Mitchel-guy.

Ruhi knew this pregnancy would get a crinkle of disappointment when her parents learned it was another man's child. A man whose name they couldn't even bother to remember. But with her pact with Sean did they ever need to find out?

There was also her impending marriage to Sean. She knew her family wanted to see her settled. Despite how much her parents pushed her and her siblings to advance in academics and their chosen profession, Ruhi knew they both believed that marriage and family were life's ultimate goals.

"I told you," said Ruhi. "We're getting married."

"So, that wasn't a joke back there in the barn?"

"No, Mommy. I was completely serious." She was also whining like a child whose parents thought she was fibbing. "He asked, and I said yes."

The air gushed from her mother. Her mother's arms flew around her. She squeezed Ruhi so tight Ruhi thought she might burst.

A girlish giggle escaped her mother as she released Ruhi from her hold. "We'll get on wedding planning straight away and ..."

Oh, no. The pride of marriage and being in a union Ruhi could take. But a traditional Indian wedding that lasted days? No. There she was putting her foot down.

"We're just going to go to City Hall, Mommy."

The pride and joy and giggles came to a scratching halt, like a needle careening off a record. In an instant, her mother's joy of her announcement was washed away. Deeksha Patel took a deep breath to begin what Ruhi knew would be a long diatribe that would only end when Ruhi gave in.

"You are my last child."

"I know, Mommy, but you got to do this two other times already."

"Don't you want to celebrate your union to Sean?"

"It's not about the celebration, Mommy. It's about the vows we make to each other. The commitment. That's what I want to focus on."

Where did that come from? It wasn't as though Ruhi had never planned to get married. She didn't ever see herself having a huge wedding. She didn't like being the center of attention. She just liked having her family's praise. That was all she needed, her family around her as she went through this.

And Sean.

Sean had been her rock over these last couple of days. He'd infiltrated all of her plans for the future. How had he become so integral to her life?

What she did know was that she couldn't do this without him. She didn't want to. And she also didn't want to make a big fuss over the start of their union. She knew he wouldn't want that as well. Just like her, Sean didn't like the spotlight.

"Sean and I are both private people. We don't like to have a spectacle around us."

"Oh," said her mother. She rubbed at her cheek, the right side of her cheek. "I see. He's worried people will stare. But he's so handsome."

Sean was handsome. The scar added to that. It gave him an air of mystery. Ruhi watched some of the other women working on the ranch give him a few lingering glances. Sean never noticed, of course. He was always too busy looking down and hiding his face.

But not with her. He looked at her. Mainly because she forced him to when she was treating him. But he also gave her his smiles, which she knew was hard for him because it was an uncomfortable gesture.

"Ruhi?"

Ruhi blinked as her mother called her name. She'd been lost thinking about Sean's smiles. She quickly brushed those thoughts off. That was not a path she was going down.

Sean might keep giving her smiles, she was sure he would. But they would always be friendly. She couldn't handle anything more than that. There'd been too much rejection in her life. She just needed to focus on her baby. And her plan.

"Don't worry," said her mother. "I'll plan everything. You'll have the wedding here, like the other soldiers. And we'll only invite a few family members."

Ruhi inhaled, ready to put up a fight. But as the air traveled down her lungs, she realized that she was tired. There was no fight left in her today. "Of course, Mommy."

Her mother's eyes lit up. She wrapped her arms around her daughter. Ruhi heard no more of her mother's planning, which quickly went beyond the small affair she'd just promised. Ruhi just nodded and went along and let her mother take care of everything.

CHAPTER ELEVEN

The colors were so bright that Sean had to shade his eyes. Mrs. Patel said she invited a few people, just close family, and friends. All the seats were taken at the gazebo and a crowd stood for rows behind them. All in vibrant colors.

He'd been told this was the small family ceremony known as the *ganesh pooja.* This intimate ceremony happened on the first night of a traditional Indian wedding. A typical wedding, he'd learned, lasted three days.

Ruhi had lost many of the battles over the planning of their wedding. The only two she'd won were having the wedding on Saturday of this week, and she had insisted that they condense everything into one day. Mrs. Patel had grumbled but assented. Sean assumed Ruhi hadn't gotten a look at the latest guest list.

They'd both wanted something small. But their parents had other ideas for their children.

Mixed in with the bright sari's, Sean saw his parents and their friends. The men were in suits and the women wore their best church hats, Sunday crowns, and lacy fascinators. The two families were mingling in what was called the *sangeet,* which usually happened the second evening of the traditional Indian wedding.

Sean admittedly was feeling overwhelmed. It had been a while since he'd been around that many people and that much noise. He focused on his breathing and the sound of his heartbeat.

"Sean?"

Dylan made sure to announce himself before placing a hand on Sean's back. Sean still tensed. Not from his friend's gesture. Sean tensed because he'd been found in his hiding place.

"How are you holding up?" Dylan asked looking out at the gathered crowd. "It's not exactly a small affair."

Mixed in with his and Ruhi's families and friends, Sean saw his ranch family. Reed was introducing Sarai to Sean's parents. Sean saw Xavier chatting with his older sister—he'd have to go put a kibosh on that. But Fran was already stepping in between the two and introducing Sean's sister to his wife. Maggie was making the rounds amongst the Patel side of the family with her dogs in tow.

"You ready for this?" Dylan asked.

Sean wasn't sure if his friend was asking about the marriage, or the wedding, or his future? He was trying to concentrate on Dylan's words and not the cacophony of sounds. He was trying to stay in the shade so the sun wouldn't beat down on him and remind him of the feel of the fire. He was trying to pick out the familiar faces and not be on the constant lookout for a threat.

Looking out, even though Sean didn't recognize some of the faces, he knew there was no threat there. Everyone's faces were filled with joy and anticipation. And it was all in support of his union to Ruhi.

These were all family and friends. No one was there to hurt anyone. Everyone was there to celebrate. Still, his heartbeat refused to settle.

"We've got your back," Dylan said. "You know that."

Sean nodded. "I know that."

"Say the word and we can make the ceremony private."

Sean shook his head. Mrs. Patel and his mother had gone to so much trouble to make this ceremony happen in just a matter of days. He was getting what he wanted, the woman of his dreams' hand in marriage. He could give their families what they wanted, a big gathering to celebrate. He could do this.

"I just need a minute alone."

Dylan nodded and stepped out of Sean's way. The moment his friend was out of sight, Sean slunk around the corner. He made his way back toward the living quarters. He was unconsciously headed towards Ruhi.

He knew he'd found her when he heard a lot of feminine giggling. They were in Maggie and Dylan's house, the largest on the lot. Ruhi had been by his place— their place—to drop off her things, but she hadn't yet spent the night in their home.

Sean knocked at the screen door. "It's me. Sean. Can I have a word with Ruhi?"

"You can't see her before the wedding," Mrs. Patel called out. "It's bad luck."

"I know. I just want to talk to her for a minute. Alone if possible."

The women came to the front door. Mrs. Patel looked up at him with a pinched expression, that instantly softened. She lifted up on her tiptoes and planted a kiss on the left side of his face. It was a move that only Ruhi had attempted, but Sean held still for Mrs. Patel. It was uncomfortable, but he allowed it.

"Don't you dare turn around," warned Mrs. Patel.

Sean stood in the doorway with his back to his bride as the women walked out of the house and onto the porch. Sean's gaze focused on the gathered crowd. He couldn't help but look for threats again. He found none in the giggling girls all dressed in colorful fabrics.

A hand at his back made him jump. Ruhi gasped and Sean turned. And then he gasped.

She was a vision. She didn't wear the traditional white wedding gown. She was an explosion of colors from deep reds to royal blues to lush greens. Her skin was decorated with brown henna in swirling patterns that drew the eye. Sean forgot the danger behind him and focused on the treasure in front of him.

"I'm so sorry," she said. "I snuck up on you again after I said I wouldn't."

He couldn't answer. All he could do was stare.

"Sean? Is everything all right?"

Sean gave himself a shake. "I'm sorry. It's not you, it's me."

Her face fell. Her hand went to her belly, and she began backing away. "Oh, God, no. No, no, no."

"Ruhi? What's wrong? Is it the baby."

"You can't do this to me. It's my wedding day."

"Do what?"

"Break up with me."

"I wouldn't. I'm not."

She paused. Her hand moved from her belly and balled into a fist. "Then what are you on about? Why are you here?"

"I just … I just got overwhelmed standing out there with all those people."

She stepped back and wrapped her arms around herself. "So you want to call it off?"

Sean held up his hands, moving toward her. "No. I don't want to call it off. I just needed to get away from all of them. I just wish it could be us, just us."

Her face softened, and she dropped her arms from her middle. "I know. I'm sorry." She walked past him, peeking out the door. "But trust me, this is small."

Sean closed the door. He rested his head back against the frame and allowed himself to gaze down at her. "I just needed a minute alone."

"Were you having flashbacks?"

"Not exactly. My mind starts looking for the danger, and I couldn't stop assessing, even though I know they're all family and friends here to support us."

"So you came and found me?"

He swallowed, but the lump wouldn't move past his throat. So, he came out with it. "You're my safe place. When I came to you for treatment …" He shrugged. "I just knew I could trust you. Whenever you touched my scar, I didn't jerk away from your touch."

"Unless I sneak up on you." She wiggled her eyebrows.

Sean smiled down at her. He was too tired to try and hide what he was feeling. He knew she saw it when she had a small intake of breath. She lifted her hand slowly and cupped his cheek. He hadn't felt the skin around his wound tug when he smiled. In her hand, he felt no irritation at all.

"I trust you too," she said.

He placed his hand over hers. The connection sent a wave of heat through him, but he felt no danger. Suddenly, he wanted this woman to belong to him. If a piece of paper would do that, then he'd brave the entire crowd in the heat to make it happen.

"Our parents went through a lot of trouble to put this wedding on," he said. "We should honor that."

"True, but we can still do it our way."

"What do you mean?"

Ruhi removed her hand from his face. She laced her fingers with his. "Let's walk each other down the aisle. Together."

CHAPTER TWELVE

Ruhi didn't care about the gasps as she and Sean walked hand and hand down the aisle. There were parts of this ceremony that were traditional and parts that were all Sean and Ruhi. This part, the part where they came into this marriage of their own free will, this was all about them.

Sean's hand engulfed hers, giving her warmth. She squeezed back to show him that she was with him under the gazes of those gathered. She couldn't explain how much it touched her that he'd sought her out during his time of need.

More so it shocked her how hurt she felt when she thought he was breaking up with her. She'd been trying not to get caught up in the preparations of the wedding, but the little girl inside her was bouncing on her toes when she put on her wedding *saree*.

Her breath caught when her mother wrapped her in the fabric. Her hands shook as her sister applied the henna. Her heart raced when she heard Sean's voice at the door.

He'd looked devastatingly handsome from the back as he stood in the entryway. Ruhi hadn't cared about tradition, she wanted to see him. But she'd also wanted him to see her.

She didn't doubt that she'd made the right choice in partner. Sean would be an excellent husband, father, and partner in life.

Already he was discussing things with her. She'd told him some of the details of her five-year plan. Mainly the parts that dealt with the upbringing of the baby. She made no mention of the offer of an exit plan for him at the end of the time period. He'd made no remark about wanting a way out as she told him of her plans.

Instead, he offered her guidance on some of the finer details. He offered input where she was unclear of her direction. He'd stood by her when she put her foot down on somethings their mothers had insisted on in the wedding. He'd also commiserated with her at other points when their mothers asserted their will over their children.

Yes, they were a great team.

And now they were walking down the aisle together to make it official.

It would seem her mother would get another portion of a traditional Indian marriage. Though Ruhi's parents wouldn't be giving her away as they would in the *kanya daan* portion of the ceremony, Sean and Ruhi were performing a version of the *mangal phera* ritual. In that ritual, a couple would join hands and walk circles around a fire. The couple walked hand in hand through their gathered guests toward the sun.

They came to stand before her father who would be officiating the ceremony. Her dad was all smiles as he looked down at his youngest daughter and the man who would promise to take care of her for the rest of their lives.

"Friends, family, canines."

The dogs yipped as her dad announce their breed. The humans chuckled. In the distance, a bird called out a song. It would seem everyone and every beast was excited at the impending union.

"We are gathered here today," her father continued, "to witness the union of this fine man who will soon be my son in name and deed and my youngest treasure."

Ruhi felt tears sting her eyes as her father gazed down at her with more pride and joy than she'd ever seen. Sean, still holding her hand, gave her fingers a squeeze. Ruhi held onto Sean through much of the ceremony. She found herself unable to meet her father's gaze. Not because she was ashamed at the farce, but because it didn't feel like a farce.

She felt a connection growing to Sean. True, there was no spark of love. But she didn't really miss it.

Finally, she'd found someone who would have her back, someone who would seek her out, someone she could depend on. It was enough. It was more than enough. It was almost, nearly … everything.

"Sean, will you repeat after me?"

Sean turned to Ruhi and repeated the vows her father had written for them. "Ruhi, you are my reason. You are the reason I face the day. You are the reason I brave the night. You are the reason my weaknesses turn to strengths. You are the dream I want to live. I pledge my life to yours, that your dreams become my dreams. No matter where life leads me, I know that your light will always bring me out of the darkness back to you, where I'm meant to be."

Through his hands, Ruhi could feel Sean's pulse racing. Or perhaps it was her own pulse rate. Her father had a gift for vows, but those cut deep, slicing open her heart and pouring out every emotion she ever had. She had to take many deep breaths before she could begin her recitation.

"Sean, I could promise you in sickness and health. I could promise until death do us part. But I won't. You have been sick, and I have brought you back to health. You have seen death and I refused to let you part. For our lives, I will be your healer, I will be your light. Whatever life may bring, I know that I have your loyalty, your protection, your service. And you have mine."

Ruhi watched as her tears were mirrored in Sean's gaze. One escaped and fell down his cheek. She reached up to wipe it away. Her hand stayed, and she cradled the side of his face.

With their written vows to each other complete, they took the *saptapadi*, a vow to support each other in life which required them to take seven steps apart from each other. When they came back together, Sean applied a red powder to the center of Ruhi's forehead and tied a black beaded necklace around her neck. It symbolized that she was now a married woman.

But they weren't done. There was one more tradition that they had to perform. A broom was placed in front of them. This was the African-American tradition of jumping the broom to signify that man and woman were now a union.

Ruhi reached for Sean's hand. They nodded at each other then they jumped over the broom's handle together. On the other side, the two laughed. It was the loudest and most cheerful she'd ever heard Sean.

She liked this side of him. She wanted to see more. And she would in the life that they were about to share.

"You may now kiss your bride," her father said.

There was something weird about having her father tell her to kiss a man. After all the display, and the emotion, and the tears, it was the first time Ruhi had blushed. It was also the one part of the ceremony she hadn't thought to negotiate with her mother.

Ruhi turned to Sean. There was something in his hazel gaze, something bright. Like little tiny sparks.

She stood mesmerized by them as Sean put his hand to her face. Ruhi felt her chin burn where his palm touched. His descent was slow, as though he were allowing her to back out at any moment.

She didn't. She held perfectly still. Those bright tiny lights burned brighter and brighter the closer he came to her. At the last second, Ruhi grew impatient. She closed the distance between them and captured Sean's bottom lip with both of hers.

That's when she knew she was in trouble.

Her heart rate increased. Her stomach did flips. Her palms itched to be filled with more of him.

Sean was soft and firm at the same time. He was sweet and spicy. And he was warm, all warmth. A warmth that infused her body all the way down to her toes.

Five years definitely wouldn't be long enough to get her fill of this comfortable and cozy place. She could stay inside the cradle of his embrace for the rest of her days. And then he broke away.

Sean was close enough that she could lift her head and capture his mouth again. In her heart that was what she wanted to do. But in her head, she knew better.

This was a marriage of practicality, not a love match. Sean was a good guy doing a good thing for her. And he was getting something out of it too.

Now the deed was done. The ink was dry on the marriage certificate. All the rituals had been performed to bond them together for life. There was no backing out now.

CHAPTER THIRTEEN

Sean clenched his hands into fists over and over again. Squeezing hard, he curled his fingers and dug his nails into his palms. He barely registered the pain. There was too much pleasure running through his body. If he didn't get himself under control, he'd surely reach for Ruhi again and repeat that kiss.

It had been chaste by all standards. His fourteen-year-old-self had kissed Cindy Bartlett longer and more firmly than that. He'd perfected the French technique with Lucy Tucker at sixteen, but that too paled in comparison. Just the slightest touch of his lips against Ruhi's, just for a matter of seconds, and he felt the world shift.

With that shift of his inner axis, Sean could take the brightness of the sun. The clapping of the people gathered, which would have made him wince and retreat into the shadows, didn't bother him so much with Ruhi by his side. He would've never left her side with any potential of danger. But these were all family and friends and they were cheering their union.

Since he couldn't kiss her again, he contented himself with nibbling at his lips, searching out any remaining hint or trace of the momentary sweetness she'd gifted him. He knew that would be the only time they'd kiss. This was to be a marriage of convenience, not one of love. The only passion was on his side.

But it was enough. All he needed was to keep Ruhi by his side where he knew she'd be safe and cared for. Her and her child.

Music began to play and the makeshift dance floor cleared. Ruhi turned to him. Her gaze apologetic for putting him on further display.

Sean didn't care. If it meant holding her in his arms again, he didn't mind at all. He would walk through a minefield just to stand in her shadow.

Sean took Ruhi's hand in his. He gave her a slight tug, and she came to him. She placed her head against his right cheek, over his scar as they began to sway.

Had she done that on purpose? She knew he didn't like it when people stared at his wound. Now they'd be staring at her instead of his scar.

"Thank you," she said, only loud enough for him to hear over the music and the murmur of their guests.

"For what?"

"I don't know if you realize it, but you've just taken on a lot. You see how my mother likes to celebrate. You'll be expected to be at many more of these family celebrations."

"I don't mind," he said. And, truly, he didn't. "I like your parents."

"You've also agreed to become an instant father."

There was that.

Sean had always been good with kids. Until the blast. Now he shied away from them.

But a baby? An infant was innocent. An infant he could help mold and grow.

He would teach this child the right things. Just as his father had taught him. Just as Ruhi's father had taught her. Was that a tickle of hope he felt?

"I won't lie," he said. "I'm nervous about …"

He looked down at her silk covered belly. His gaze lifted to meet hers. Ruhi's lips were pursed. Was she holding her breath?

"But we make a great team," he said. "Don't you think?"

Her lips relaxed into a smile. "I do. We do. But you're the one who has to put up with me."

"I like you."

Did he say that too quickly? Was his tone too vehement? Did his hold on her tighten slightly? Had she heard the truth in his statement?

He may have said the word like, but he meant love. Sean loved Ruhi. He had since the first time she'd put her healing hands on his cheek. He knew she didn't feel the same, but she didn't have to.

He would protect her. He would look out for her. He would eliminate any danger before it could get to her. Whether she liked it or not.

"I like you, too," she said.

There was a sparkle in her eyes. It looked to Sean like hope. For the first time in a long time, Sean felt like a hero again. Under her gaze, he was. He would not only slay dragons for this woman, he would not only run into burning buildings for her, he was prepared to change a dirty diaper.

That was true devotion.

"We're gonna be okay, aren't we?" she asked. "This was the best decision for both of us?"

"Yes, I believe that."

"I'm probably going to stink at being a good wife, but I know I'm a good partner."

He didn't believe that. She was good at everything she did because she put her heart into it. But Sean wasn't able to let her know his opinion on that particular topic. They had incoming.

"Uh oh, here comes my dad."

Apparently, the missives were coming from both sides. "And here comes my mom," said Ruhi.

"I'm sorry," they both said in unison.

"I'm cutting in son." Luther Jeffries offered his gnarled, work-worn hand to Sean's new wife. "I want to dance with my beautiful new daughter."

"And I want to dance with my new son," said Mrs. Patel moving into the space Ruhi vacated. "Oh, Luther, the beautiful grandbabies they're going to give us."

"I can't wait to bounce them on my knees."

Both of their parents spoke over Sean and Ruhi. Ruhi's smile wavered. Sean's tightened.

"But we'll have to wait," said Mrs. Patel. "My daughter has a five-year plan, isn't that right, Ruhi? No babies until you've checked everything off your career list. We'll have to be patient."

Sean watched Ruhi tense in his father's embrace. His father didn't notice. His grin and his pride were so palpable, Sean doubted anything could bring the man down. Sean knew his parents worried about him. They'd been over the moon to learn he was marrying, and marrying Ruhi to boot. They'd met and liked his nurse last year.

"You dance beautifully, Mrs. Patel," said Sean, twirling the older woman in his arms. His father could be distracted. But he doubted the psychologist's wife would turn so easily. And so he turned her away from her daughter.

"Oh, my dear, you must call me Mommy. All my children do."

"Yes, ma'am—Mommy."

"I want you to know I truly don't think my daughter could've done better than you. My husband has a lot of respect for you, as do all the men here. I know you're a man of faith, though a private one. Still, I wish you would join us at church. Let people see how beautiful your spirit is, both inside and out."

"Thank you, Mrs. -Mommy. I promise I'm going to make your daughter very happy."

"The secret to a good marriage is honesty. You be honest with each other and you'll last a lifetime."

"Yes, ma'am." Sean twirled the woman again as he answered.

Mrs. Patel frowned as she came out of the turn. Oh, no. Did she suspect something? Did she know they were already enmeshed in a lie? "Yes, what …?"

Oh. "Yes, Mommy."

CHAPTER FOURTEEN

The party lasted into the night. Between the gospel and soul music from Sean's side of the family, to the Bollywood tunes from her side of the aisle, the partying, the praising, and the dancing, it didn't look like it was going to stop until dawn. But Ruhi was exhausted before midnight.

Before she knew it, Sean's hand was at her low back, and he was steering her away from the festivities. He said their good nights as they went. All Ruhi had to do was lean into his shoulder, which she did.

She was his wife, after all. This was definitely a perk. She didn't have to stand on her own, she would be expected to lean on him a bit, if she were tired. And she was tired.

Between the ceremony, the cake, the curried chicken, the fried chicken, the barbecue chicken, and rice and potato salad, she was ready to be rolled down the lane. And there was still the fact of the growing being inside her who zapped her energy every other second.

Luckily, zapping energy was all the baby was doing. Ruhi had been able to eat and keep the food down. But having to constantly tell small lies and stick to a story made her mentally exhausted. Everyone wanted to know the story of how she and Sean fell in love.

They'd concocted a simple enough story that stuck as closely to the truth as possible. After her last break up, Sean was there to pick up the pieces. They realized they had feelings for each other that had been growing over the year they'd known each other. They knew that it was right, so they decided not to wait.

Each person they told the story to bought it hook, line, and sinker. Though the soldiers assumed the speedy marriage was due to the zoning issue. Her side of the family didn't have any issues with quick marriages. Ruhi and Sean had thought his parents would need more convincing, but they had met Ruhi before and were thrilled at the union.

Telling the story wasn't a real hardship. What truly bothered Ruhi was having to fib about was her love for Sean. She liked Sean, more and more each day. But love?

She wanted to tell everyone that that emotion wasn't in the cards for her. Michael had been right. She'd never felt that spark for him. She'd never felt it for anyone. Now she had to pretend it was there with Sean.

Sean deserved a spark. He deserved a romance. He deserved a girl who would look at him with stars in her eyes. He'd never get that with Ruhi.

An even worse thought entered her mind. What if he sparked with someone one day during their marriage? What if it was Ruhi who stood in the way?

But she was too tired to think of that. Sean's hand at the small of her back was far too comforting. All she wanted to do was stay in the crook of his arm and rest. Before she knew it, they were back at his place.

Sean unlocked the door to his cabin. She'd been inside briefly today, but only long enough to drop off her necessities. The rest of her things were still back in her apartment. This house was still foreign to her.

She'd visited Dylan's cabin to have dinner with him and Maggie shortly after their wedding. She'd visited Fran and Eva's home when Rosalee had come down with a bad cold. She'd had no reason to be in the other guys' homes. Sean, Reed, and Xavier each had lived alone in their two-bedroom bunkhouses. Now one of those bunkhouses was her home.

"I set up an office in the breakfast nook for you," he said turning on a light.

In the small space, the illumination showed a small desk with a computer and a filing cabinet where a breakfast nook must've once been. It was cozy and quaint and so thoughtful.

"Sean … thank you."

"There are only two bedrooms, but I figure that's fine for now and the baby's first year. We can decide if we want to add on to this house or build something new in the future."

The future. When she was a mother. All of her plans were out of whack. She still had more revisions to make with her five-year plan. She'd have to consult Sean in those plans. But she definitely wasn't doing it tonight. She just wanted to rest.

"You're tired," said Sean. He steered her down the hall. "It's been a long day. We can talk about this at another time when you're thinking clearly. We'll do what you think is best."

"Me?"

"Of course. I know we agreed to be equal partners, but this affects you most. You take the lead. I'm behind whatever you want to do."

His hand was still at the small of her back. It was the only thing holding her up. Standing in front of his spare bedroom door, Ruhi turned and wrapped Sean up in her arms. Slowly, tentatively, his arms came around her.

Belatedly, Ruhi wondered if she'd overstepped her bounds? Was she being too affectionate with him? Too familiar?

"And there's something else," he said as his cheek rested on the top of her head. "I think the balance of duties will be skewed for a bit with you being pregnant twenty-four-seven for the next year. So, I'm taking on a majority of the household chores. I insist."

Ruhi didn't know what to say. Sean was practically the man of her dreams, offering her everything she ever thought she wanted in a relationship. Except they weren't in a relationship.

"Thank you," she said into his chest. She was tempted to fall asleep with her cheek resting against the cushion of his right pec. "I couldn't do any of this without you."

"I told you, I wouldn't have come through this past year without you. I'm in your debt."

He pulled away from her then. She wanted to whimper in protest as his warmth fell away from her. The moment his hand left her back, Ruhi felt weak. But she didn't dare show it.

With just these few gestures Sean proved to be the best boyfriend she'd ever had. And once again, he was not her boyfriend. But he was something better.

He was her partner.

She just wished it was acceptable for him to lie down next to her with his hand supporting her lower back until she fell asleep. But that wasn't part of the deal. So Ruhi closed the door to the spare bedroom behind her and found herself as she always was; alone and on her own.

CHAPTER FIFTEEN

"Sean, you don't have to do this."

Sean gazed down at his new wife. Her lips were pursed to one side of her mouth. It was her thinking face. He'd found the facial gesture endearing when she'd first started treating him. He'd soon learned it was the expression she made when she was unsure of something and would have to go and consult a chart or a medical text.

"This is now part of my responsibility," he said.

Ruhi pulled her car into the doctor's office and put the car in park. Sean had loved the surprised look on her face when he'd opened up the driver's side door for her and then hopped into the passenger seat. He knew Ruhi liked her independence, and Sean had no need to take any of it away from her.

He didn't think letting a woman into the driver's seat, or a man cooking for a woman, or either of them picking up a dustpan made him any less of a man. Real men did what needed to be done. His father had taught him that.

And his mother's bark was not worse than her bite. His mother's bite stung. Though Sean had only felt her bite a few times in his life, because he rarely misbehaved.

He liked strong women. They were overflowing in his immediate as well as his extended family. He'd also been surrounded by that particular breed of women while in the service. The only people threatened by strong women were weak people. Weak men and weak women.

Sean didn't doubt his strength. He and Ruhi had spent the weekend in relative quiet. The guys had moved her items from the apartment to the ranch. She'd unpacked while Sean helped. He enjoyed putting up her things in their shared space.

No one commented on the fact that they had separate rooms. Though Sean was certain when their parents came to visit they would have questions. But that would hold for some time.

Though he'd had no problem with Ruhi driving, he did hop out of the car to hand her out of the driver's side. He was an evolved man, but he was also a gentleman.

"I just don't want you to feel obligated to do this stuff," she said.

"If I had to go to the doctor's outside of the ranch, would you come with me?"

"That's different. I'm your nurse."

"I'm your husband."

That remark made her hold her tongue. He hadn't said that out loud. This was the first time, and he liked the sound of it.

Sean placed his hand at the small of Ruhi's back, preparing to guide her across the street. He looked left and right for any signs of danger as he waited for her next protest. There were no cars coming in either direction. There also was no argument coming from her lips.

Instead, she leaned into him and allowed him to guide her into the building. As much as he liked this strong woman beside him who could stand on her own, he loved it when she took solace in his embrace. He chalked up her lack of fight to the pregnancy. He'd be certain to take advantage for the next eight months.

Sean kept his arm around her as they waited in the waiting room. He joined her in the exam room, turning his back as she undressed to step into a hospital gown. The doctor joined them shortly after.

Sean had been surprised to find that the OB/GYN Ruhi had chosen was a man. He would've been certain that a modern woman such as herself would want another strong female delivering her first-born. Ruhi had shrugged and said she wasn't a sexist.

It was her first visit with the OB/GYN, so the doctor didn't know any of their particulars and that included their relationship.

"We're recently married," Ruhi said. "Just this weekend."

"By my calculations, you're six weeks pregnant," said the doctor. His gaze went from Ruhi to Sean.

"That's about right," said Sean. He watched the doctor's shoulders relax. Sean wondered how many times that math had broken couples up?

"Would you like to hear the baby's heartbeat?" asked the doctor.

Ruhi hesitated. She looked to Sean. Sean took her hand in his. He lifted his brow. The decision was hers. Ruhi turned to the doctor and nodded.

The doctor lifted the hospital gown to reveal Ruhi's belly. Sean felt he should avert his gaze. But he was her husband, and for all intents and purposes, the one who put the baby in there. So, he looked.

There was a translucent splat of jelly on her flat belly. Then the doctor pulled out what looked like a back massager. He put the bulbous head on her belly and began moving it around. Both Ruhi's and the doctor's gazes turned to a black and white monitor. Sean didn't look away from his wife's belly. Not until he heard it.

The sound pounded into his ears like a soldier's march. It crackled like the interference in a two-way headset. He expected the screams of trapped civilians to come next, followed by the pants of desperation of those he could not save trying to snatch his attention away.

Sean felt his palms go sweaty. His jaw clenched tighter and tighter as the PTSD began to tug at him. Instead of the panic that would set his trigger finger itchy, something tugged at his hand.

"Sean?" Ruhi's fingers curled into his palm, grounding him back into reality. "Do you hear it?"

Slowly the pounding softened. The crackling dissipated. The pulsing vibrations evened out until they became a single note. A delicate beating.

This was not the sound of death. It was the sound of life. A new life that was growing.

It was so small. So precious. So delicate.

For the first time in a long time, Sean wanted to run toward the pounding. He wanted to protect it, to hold it to him, to save it.

This heartbeat, this life, was the work of another man. But Sean was stepping up to the plate. He would help this child grow. He would help mold it. He would be its hero.

CHAPTER SIXTEEN

The missed period, the morning sickness, the positive pregnancy test, all those hadn't truly made Ruhi know she was pregnant. Hearing her baby's heartbeat made it all real. That tiny little sound is what let her know that she was a mom.

She wasn't going to be a mom. It had already happened. There was a living, breathing, beating life inside her. It was growing fast and it was depending on her.

The realization clicked the second she heard her child's heartbeat. The second she saw the monitor come to life with the evidence deep in her womb. And when it did, all her carefully thought out plans went out the window.

This was a lifetime job. In one year, she'd be holding a baby in her arms. In five years, she'd be doing the same. Any job, any mission, any adventure would have to involve and revolve around her child.

And Sean.

Ruhi had fought so hard to prove she was independent her whole life. But in an instant, she couldn't imagine the rest of her life without these two beings. One she hadn't met yet. One she'd known for a short while who'd become integral to her wellbeing.

She handed Sean her car keys as they exited the doctor's office. He walked around and opened the passenger side door. She'd never liked that gesture, a man opening doors for a woman as though he was the key to her passage through. When Sean held the door open for her, or pulled out her seat for her, or held out his hand to her, it made her feel that he was making way for her to experience something she'd never known before. And best of all, she knew she wouldn't do it alone.

Ruhi stepped into the passenger side of her car. She settled into the seat. She strapped in as her partner in life took the wheel.

"Are you hungry? Tired?" Sean asked.

Ruhi shrugged. She was content to let him figure out the agenda for the rest of the day. She didn't doubt he'd get her exactly what she needed. And so she closed her eyes. When she opened them, they were back at the ranch. She smelled spicy foods, but she was still inside the car. A bag of take-out sat in the back seat.

Ruhi smiled. It was exactly what she needed. Rest and food.

She waited for Sean to come around to the passenger side and hand her out. With the food in one hand, she took his other hand. Once she was out of the car, he rested his free hand on the small of her back. Inside their home, Sean settled her on the couch with a TV dinner tray. He pulled the food out and placed the cartons before her.

"You're spoiling me," she said.

He only smiled. "You've taken care of me so long, it's time someone took care of you. Just for the day. You can boss me around tomorrow."

"Am I bossy?"

Sean paused, looking down at her. "You're assertive. You know what you want. And you're smart. Most of the time I assume you've thought things through so I'm happy to follow along. That's important to a soldier. You want to trust the person in your squad. You're in my squad now."

"I trust you, too."

His lips parted, but he said nothing. Ruhi's heart beat in her ear. Her cheeks flooded with warmth. The moment was so ripe for a kiss.

If they had that kind of relationship. Which they didn't have. Which they couldn't have.

The last thing Ruhi wanted was another man telling her he felt no spark for her. Sean wasn't in love with her. They'd known each other for a year. If love was going to show up between them, it would've done it months ago.

What was between them was a warm and cozy friendship. She could lean on him. Better yet, he had proven he wouldn't buckle under the weight or turn from her if the load got too heavy.

She'd kissed men that she hadn't felt a spark with, hoping something would kindle and grow. When she'd kissed Sean there had been no spark. Only a sense of rightness. He was the right man for her.

Maybe kissing didn't have to stay off the table in this relationship? Maybe they could enjoy each other physically someday? She certainly enjoyed his embraces. Just the simple nearness of him.

He was young and virile. Surely he couldn't go without the comfort of a woman for the rest of his life. They had time. She would broach this subject in the future. Maybe after the baby was born.

"I know you have the rest of the day off," he said. "But I'm going to go check on a few things around the ranch. I won't be long."

"Okay."

He leaned down toward her. Ruhi held her breath. Her mouth watered as he came nearer. Maybe the physical things could start between them sooner?

Ruhi tilted up her head. Sean's lips didn't make it past her forehead. Warmth spread through her as he planted a light kiss between her brow. Not an explosion. Just a pleasant hum of heat.

"Call me if you need anything," he said when he pulled away.

"I'll be fine," she smiled.

He rose and headed out the door. Ruhi watched after him. Her mouth watered even more as she watched the backside of him go out the door. She still felt that burning hunger when the door clicked shut. Finally, she registered the buffet before she attacked the food.

She was partway through her second carton of takeout when her phone rang. When she looked at the caller ID she dropped her fork.

It was Michael.

What did he want? It didn't matter. She didn't want to deal with him now.

But she should answer. She should tell him about the baby. He had a right to know. Even though she was certain he'd shuck his responsibilities.

By the time she reached for the phone, it had stopped ringing. Maybe he'd call back. If he did, she'd tell him. If not, she'd call him later.

By the time she'd cleaned the takeout boxes, Michael hadn't called back. Sean hadn't returned either. Ruhi didn't feel like waiting for either of them and so she took a nap instead.

CHAPTER SEVENTEEN

S ean aimed to rush through his chores and get back to his wife. His last sight of Ruhi tucked in on the couch gazing up at him was all he could think of. He was having a hard time convincing himself that there was nothing between them with the way she'd looked up at him. Perhaps, the more time they spent together, the more this could become something that resembled a real marriage.

With Scar at his heels and Ruhi on his mind, Sean grabbed the liquid fertilizer instead of the weed killer to tame the wayward grass in an overgrown patch of field and didn't realize his mistake until Scar ran away whining. That's when Sean looked down to see that half of the patch was covered with the growth treatment. He caught himself as he grabbed the chicken feed just as he entered the horse stalls. Finally, he decided it was best if he stayed away from the animals and headed to work with the inanimate objects on the ranch.

Luckily, the addition of the youth program had lessened the amount of work he had to do. But with Dylan and Fran focused on the boys in the program, that did leave Sean on his own to handle some of the duties that would be faster if he had another adult at hand.

Xavier and Reed were off in the city picking up supplies. The three women who lived on the ranch each had taken on their own duties. Maggie worked alongside the trainers to take care of the animals. Eva, who was excellent with numbers, took over the books. And Sarai was hard at work on the ranch's website.

Sean grabbed a hammer and some nails. There was always a fence that needed mending on a ranch. It was tougher to do the work on his own, but at least he wouldn't accidentally hammer another person's thumb to a piece of wood in his distracted state. With the pesticides back on the shelf, Scar returned to join him.

The sun was behind the clouds and stayed off his back as Sean worked. Scar quickly fell asleep on a patch of grass. In the shade, Sean was able to hide from any memories of the explosion. So, when he heard footsteps approaching he wasn't caught off guard. He assumed it was one of his brothers coming to give him a hand. The coughing fit that accompanied the footfalls told Sean he was wrong.

"Aren't you supposed to be with your group?" Sean asked the kid.

James bent down to scratch Scar behind her ears. "I just slow them down. I don't understand why we have to be a unit anyway. I just want to work with the animals."

Sean stood and the kid kicked at a stone with his worn shoes. He shoved his hands into pockets which rode the hem of his jeans up enough to show his socks above his ankles. His shirt had one too many stains that looked like they were older than the kid. Was there no one taking care of this kid?

"Come give me a hand," said Sean. "You take one end of the rail, and I'll take the other."

Sean still wound up taking most of the weight, but it was less wieldy than when he was holding the wood by himself. He quickly nailed in one side and joined the kid on the other.

"I could do that on my own," he said. "But with two people it moves easier and faster."

"Yeah," said the kid. "But you can ride a horse by yourself."

"When we take you out to herd the cattle, you can't do that by yourself."

"Can't you use a dog?"

"You would have to train the dog. Then you and the dog would be a unit."

James pursed his lips at that. He shoved his hands back into his pockets. Sean clearly saw the outline of each of his fingers in the threadbare fabric.

He made a mental note to ask Sarai to look into getting some clothes for kids. He knew the former model still had some contacts in the fashion world. After the kids' hesitancy to take charity money for the prescription, Sean assumed that James wouldn't take the hand out of clothing. Sean had managed to sneak some cash into the kid's backpack the last time they were on the ranch. It was enough to pay for the prescription. Sean hoped the kid had used it for that.

"You need someone to watch your back," Sean said. "The friends you make will watch your back. But you need to watch theirs too."

Speak of the little devil, Maurice made his way through the fields towards them. He didn't look pleased as he came up to James. "Hey, you just left me back there."

"Sorry," said James. He kicked at a pebble on the ground and shoved his hands deeper in his pockets. "I was just giving Specialist Jeffries a hand."

"We're supposed to be stacking the hay bales together. I turned around, and you were gone."

"The hay was making me sneeze and …" James opened his mouth and let out a string of wheezing coughs. He wheezed so hard he was sucking down air in strained gasps.

Sean wasn't sure if he should go to the kid? Were there rules about touching the kids, even if only to pat them on the back? What if he had to give the kid CPR?

As Sean hesitated, Maurice stepped up and rubbed his hand on James's back. "I thought you went to the doctors."

"I did."

"Did your dad get you the medicine?"

"Yeah, I just forgot to take it." James kicked at another pebble. "I will when I go home."

He shoved his hands in his pockets and kept his head down as he turned to go. Scar trailed after her new ear-scratching friend. Maurice looked to Sean and shrugged before turning to follow James. Sean knew bronchitis could last weeks, months even. But with medication, it should be getting better and not worse.

Clearly, the kid didn't have the medication. If it had been in his system for a couple of days now, he'd be improving. How could this father not do what was necessary to take care of his kid? If Sean had heard that cough come from his kid, he'd move heaven and earth to make it stop.

The reason these kids were all here was because their parents neglected them on some level. Why else would they be acting up or getting bad grades or falling ill? It was criminal to treat a child with so much neglect, nearly as bad as indoctrinating them to harm others.

"For a newlywed, you don't look too happy."

Sean turned to see Fran walk up.

"It's a crime how some of these parents are treating their kids," said Sean, motioning to the kids still walking in the distance. "When our child gets here, I'll move heaven and earth to make sure they have everything they need."

"Your child? Wait. Is Ruhi pregnant?"

Sean froze. His tongue had loosened in his anger. There was no way he could take that outburst back, or distract Fran with something else. But that wasn't even the worst to come.

"But you two only just … Oh."

Fran had obviously done the math in his head and came to the baby daddy conclusion without Maury Povich's blood test results.

Fran whistled, tilting his head back to the sky. Then he dropped his gaze to Sean's, a serious look on his face. "I know how you feel about her. But another man's child?"

"He left her," said Sean. "What kind of man does that when a woman is carrying his child? I'll be here for them both. I'll be the best husband and father."

The title role of Best Father he wasn't worried about. He'd had great examples of that in his life. The title role of Best Husband?

There he worried. He was married to the woman he was in love with, but he had to hide the depth of his feelings on a daily basis. Well, at least the pregnancy was one less thing he had to hide.

"Look, Fran, we're keeping it quiet."

"Of course." Fran nodded.

But Sean knew that by the time he got home it would be all over the ranch. Including to the medical offices where Ruhi's dad would be tomorrow. And then they'd all start doing the math.

CHAPTER EIGHTEEN

Ruhi felt exhausted in her dream. She knew that morning had turned to afternoon because she could feel the sun on her cheek. But she was cold. Why was it so cold?

Her eyes refused to open. Until a trail of heat touched her brow. Her awareness tracked that heat. Across her forehead, down her jaw, back behind her ear. Then it was gone.

Ruhi blinked her eyes open in search of the heat and found Sean. His brown skin positively glowed in the afternoon sunlight. His hazel eyes were like stars shining solely for her. She wanted to curl up and burrow deep in his feather-light embrace. But he jerked his hand away from her face, and he looked down, shutting off her view of the twin stars.

She blinked a few more times. Light was all around him, strands of sunlight coming through the window, like sparks. It had been Sean. He'd warmed her through with the slightest touch.

"I'm sorry to wake you," he said. "You looked so peaceful."

"It was. I am."

He lifted his lashes to look at her. And there it was again, that light in his eyes. Fireworks bubbled in her belly. But she didn't feel sick.

Lightheaded, yes.

Dizzy, a bit.

Breathless, definitely.

These weren't pregnancy symptoms. These were the things people said about falling in love at first sight. But that wasn't happening. Not between her and Sean.

She'd known Sean for a year. If anything were to spark between them, it would've happened by now. So, this couldn't be love.

Could it?

It was the first time she'd seen him in this light. Before it had always been under the harsh glare of fluorescent light in the clinic. He'd never been looking down at her. She'd always been looking up at him or eye to eye as she examined him. But her heart was doing funny, fluttery things under his gaze.

Ruhi knew love happened immediately as well as over time. It had just never happened like that to anyone she knew, certainly not anyone in her family. Everyone talked about it being in an instant, or shortly after the first meeting.

She' been in too many relationships where she stuck around to wait and see if something would catch. It never did. Hadn't she given up on that?

She had. But something was happening inside her. Something itched. Something burned. One moment it wasn't there. And the next it was.

"Ruhi, we have to talk."

In another instant, she felt sick. The lightheadedness, the dizziness, the breathlessness swung across a spectrum that pointed to nausea.

"The cat's out of the bag," he said. "Or rather, the bun is out of the oven."

"What?"

Ruhi sat up. The change in altitude sent her head reeling. She reached out for something to hold onto, and Sean was there.

He wrapped his hand around hers, and she felt grounded, but not secure. Sean slid onto the couch beside her, and like a magnet, her body snapped into place inside his embrace. If he was breaking up with her, he'd have to figure out how to pry her out of this spot because she just didn't have the energy or the inclination to move.

Instead of pushing her away, his arms wrapped around her. One came to rest at her low back. The other cradled her head.

"How are you feeling?" he asked.

"Warm," Ruhi said into his chest. "I was so cold. And now I'm warm."

"I'm so sorry about that. I keep the thermostat low in here. I thought the blanket would be enough to keep you warm."

"It was. But this is better." Since he wasn't pushing her away, she decided to snuggle deeper into his chest.

They sat quietly for a long moment. Sean stroked his hand in circles on her low back. Ruhi took slow breaths that filled her with his scent. If this was how he broke bad news, she was willing to get used to it. But the moment he started talking her stomach tied in knots again.

"I have bad news," he began.

Ruhi took a deep breath. Slowly she lifted her head to look her fake husband in the eye. But she did not leave his embrace. He owed her some comfort if he was about to pull the rug out from under her.

"Fran guessed that you're pregnant, and he figured it wasn't mine. I'm sure everyone knows by now, and your father will likely find out tomorrow when he's here."

It took Ruhi a moment to comprehend what he was saying. She was so focused on listening for the familiar breakup phrases. Her mind went over Sean's words again and again. When she couldn't pick out a single break up cliché, her heart settled. Her breathing evened. Her head cleared.

"You're not breaking up with me?" she clarified.

Sean blinked. The light in his eyes dimmed and then burned brighter. "Breaking up with you?"

He had to force the words out. They sounded so foreign on his tongue. Ruhi could see him turning his words over and over in his mind just as she'd turned over what he'd said to her.

"Never," he concluded.

"Never?" she asked.

He unwrapped himself from her and slid from the couch. Before she knew what was happening, Sean was down on his knees. He reached for her hands. Ruhi was so stunned at the turn of events that she gave them both over.

"There's something you need to know," he said. "Something I should've told you before we got married. I'm … I'm in love …"

"You're in love with someone else?" She finished the sentence for him. She forced the words out with a choke. She knew it.

"Ruhi. I'm in love with you. I have been since my first appointment with you."

"With me?"

Sean nodded, his gaze open and vulnerable. As those flecks twinkled at her, she saw it. He'd looked at her like that countless times. How had she not seen it?

"I didn't want to make you feel uncomfortable, but you should know it if we're going to be together. There should be no secrets. I was in a dark place when I came to you. I felt my heart come back to life when you lifted my chin to heal my wound."

"I was so focused on healing you, I didn't look at you. I didn't realize it was even there."

"And now?"

"Now …" She lifted her hand to his cheek. "Now, I see it. Now, I feel it."

She cupped his face with both her hands, running her thumbs over his cheeks. She was close enough to taste the warm spice of his breath.

"A spark."

Ruhi leaned down as Sean pulled her to him. Their lips touched softly, but it was an explosion of sensation. The impact of his bottom lip against her top stole her breath. When he tilted her head to gain more access, Ruhi's entire world went off its axis. She felt her world shatter as Sean's lips claimed her own. She felt put back together as he held her firmly inside his arms.

It was a new state of being. She no longer felt that she was an independent woman. She'd become more. She'd grown and was now a rock solid unit.

CHAPTER NINETEEN

Warmth surrounded him. He felt the heat radiating from his chest. There was a lightness in his limbs and a tingling in his hands. Absent was the cold, steel hardness of a weapon.

Sean waited for the panic to settle in. He was defenseless in a dark, hot place. But his heart was calm.

The warmth moved up to his face. He felt it creep and crawl through the grooves of his cheek where the wound lay. In the nightmares, he never had the scar. Not until he woke up and ran his hand over his face. That was the only way he knew he was out of the dream world and back to the harsh reality.

The heat left his face and quickly migrated to his back. This was more like the regular nightmares, the ones that mirrored the horror of what he'd faced back in a combat zone. The pounding in his ears started next.

Only, there wasn't just a deep, hollowness with the drumming sound. It went from a single heartbeat to multiple and back again. From out of the darkness, the sound of cries rose. The high-pitched wail of an infant's cry quickly drowned out all the other voices.

Sean inhaled to calm his heart's beating, trying to gain control of himself. This was a dream, a nightmare. He just had to wake up, to open his eyes.

But the bodies fell around him. The child's cry rang louder in his ears. The trilling wail of distress threatened to break his entire being in two.

He managed to open his eyes, but he was still in the dream. Shards of light broke through. It was the light of the flame. Red, hot, angry sparks leaped out at him. They lashed at his skin, licked up his spine, smacked him in the face.

But he didn't fall. He couldn't. He knew the only way out of the dream was to find Xavier. But the man's prone body was nowhere to be found. Then he saw it.

At the end of the tunnel, he saw Ruhi, a child in her arms. Her child. Their child. His child.

The child screamed in distress. Ruhi called out in fear. She was calling his name.

Desperation tore through Sean like a missive finding its target. Sean pumped his legs. But the faster he moved, the farther away they appeared to get. And still, Ruhi called out his name.

He was close. He was so close. A dark figure moved into view behind Ruhi and the baby.

The figure was small, half Ruhi's size. It was a young boy. The boy wore what Sean knew to be a suicide vest. Tears streamed down the kid's face.

"Sean?"

Sean had to act. The boy's life or his family's lives He'd never wanted to make this decision again. But here he was, and he was hesitating again.

"Sean?"

He felt the cold, hard steel of a gun in his hands. He lifted the weapon. He cocked the gun. He aimed and—

"Sean, it's a dream. Wake up."

His eyes tore open. His hands reached out, searching for his weapon. Instead of steel, he found flesh.

Ruhi's eyes were wide. Her breaths came in anxious pants. Her face ashen in the dim moonlight. Her palms faced him, fingers straining upward in a stop motion. Sean saw his own fingers wrapped around her wrists.

She was frightened. She was afraid. Of him. The nightmare was nothing to this reality. This was hell.

"Oh, God. Did I hurt you?"

Sean released her hands and scooted away from her. They were still on the couch in the living room. He remembered that after their shared kiss, they relaxed back on the couch, content to stay in each other's arms. They both must've fallen asleep.

"No," she said. "You didn't hurt me. Are you okay?"

He didn't take her word for it. He reached over and turned on a table lamp. Under the fluorescent light, he did a visual scan of her body, searching for any wounds he may have inflicted on her while the nightmare had him.

He found none. This time. "I could've hurt you."

"You never would." Ruhi lifted her hand to his face.

"On purpose—never. By accident, that's very possible."

"I know about the nightmares, Sean. But just now, you were reaching for me, and I'm right here."

Sean looked down at his hands. "I grabbed your wrists."

She shook her head. "When you woke up. But before that, you were pulling me toward you. Holding me tight. I think you were protecting me."

Ruhi brushed her thumb over his cheek. Then her index finger lifted his chin so that he met her stare. There was no fear in her gaze.

There was warmth in her brown eyes. Compassion laced her heavy lashes. There was also a spark of something else at the corner of her eyelids. For the first time in a long time, Sean wished he had a match to fuel that flicker into a flame.

When he'd confessed his feelings to her, she hadn't said she loved him back. And that was fine. A spark was fine. Though he'd kept himself in the dark cold for so long, he did know how to feed a fire.

He was happy to spend the rest of his life adding kindling to Ruhi's heart in hopes to make love grow.

"I know better than to startle you," she said. "But I needed you to know that I was safe. That I was with you."

Sean's chin fell to his chest. Not out of shame. Out of exhaustion. He'd been holding himself so tightly together. But she'd unraveled him in just a second.

"I know your PTSD is real and has real consequences. But we'll face them together."

"Heat's a trigger," said Sean.

"Oh, that's why it's so cold in here all the time." She shrugged. "I'll wear thermal underwear."

Thinking about Ruhi's underwear only made him get hot under the collar. "We're not sleeping together. Not until I get a handle on these nightmares."

"Oh." Her shoulders sank, and she let out a weary sigh. "Great."

She was disappointed. That was a great sign. "I want to," Sean insisted.

"Me too."

She was kneeling on the couch facing him. Both of her knees brushed up against his thighs. It would be so easy to pull her onto his lap. But not yet.

"I just need to be sure," he said. "I need to trust myself with you."

"So you're asking me to wait a while?"

"I promise to be worth the wait."

He did pull her close then. Not onto his lap. He pulled her chest against his heart.

This time, Sean took Ruhi's face in his hands. He cupped her chin, rubbing his thumb over the bottom lip he planned to capture again and again between his own lips.

Ruhi's breath was warm against his palm. Her heat and her nearness were having a triggering effect on him. Only he was far from hell. This was heaven.

Sean tilted Ruhi's face. He locked in on his target. His aim was true as he closed in on his quarry.

The chime of a cell phone broke them apart. Sean glanced down at Ruhi's phone on the coffee table and froze. He saw her ex-boyfriend's face. Followed by a text that read. "Got your message. You up?"

CHAPTER TWENTY

"Why is your ex sending you a booty call text message at one in the morning?"

Ruhi shut her eyes to try to regain balance. She was caught between a haze of want and a fog of annoyance. What she wanted was for Sean to finish what he'd started and kiss her senseless as he'd done before she'd fallen asleep safe in his arms. She wanted to test the bounds of his resolve to keep her at arm's distance while they sorted these nightmares. Ruhi had every plan to conduct those tests while inside his embrace.

When he'd been caught in the snare of his dark dreams, her first and only instinct was to let him know that she was there for him. The way he'd been there for her this whole time. Sean had never once wavered since he'd come to her aid. He'd never stepped back as she increasingly came to lean on him.

Ruhi was determined to do the same for him. Whatever he needed to manage his PTSD, she would do. As long as it didn't include leaving the comfort of his arms, or giving up his heart-melting kisses. Those were all non-negotiable.

Unfortunately, Michael had impeccable timing. She'd called him earlier in the day before Sean had come home. It had taken him all day to respond.

Come to think of it, he never got back to her immediately during their relationship. She'd always felt like an afterthought when it came to his daily agenda. She'd often been pushed aside when a new opportunity presented itself.

Still, Michael was now and would forever be the father of her child. She had to set the record straight with him. But first, she had to tell her husband the full truth.

"Sean, there's something Michael and I need to talk about. Something you and I have to talk about first."

"About the baby?"

Ruhi nodded.

Sean released her face, but he didn't move away from her. He rested his hand on the back of the couch. With his free hand, he took Ruhi's hand in his. "Do you think he's changed his mind? Do you think he wants to be a part of our child's life now?"

Our child. How had she not seen the amazingness of this man for an entire year? He'd come to her every week for a year.

She'd stared directly at his face, straight into his eyes. She'd seen his strength; she'd seen his resilience. She knew he was trustworthy and honest. But that mutual respect that shone through as he regarded her, that immediate acceptance without judgment, those qualities finally pierced through her prescriptive mind and lodged inside her heart.

Ruhi wished she'd opened her eyes to him last year. She wished she'd allowed him into her heart sooner. Then this would be their child in spirit as well as in blood.

But she couldn't hide the facts. By now everyone on the ranch would know. They'd know she was pregnant, and Sean wasn't the father.

Her parents would know by morning, and would likely be crushed that they weren't the first to know. She'd screwed it all up. Even worse, Michael, the child's father, would be the very last to know.

"Michael can't change his mind until he has all the information," she said.

Sean's brows drew in confusion. But his gaze remained patient. The small smile on his lips still spoke of trust.

"I never told him I was pregnant."

Now he pulled away from her. His fingers released hers. His arm that had lain on the back of the couch pulled out of the half embrace. "You never told him about the baby?"

"I found out I was pregnant after we broke up and he was preparing to leave the country. He was already sleeping with someone else when I tried to tell him."

"Ruhi…" He didn't look at her. He looked down at his hands. The hands that had been holding her a moment ago, bringing her into his embrace, into his protection, into his heart.

"I know, I know. I was just so humiliated. But I called him again this morning. He's just now getting back to me."

Sean lifted his gaze. His hazel eyes dark, his jaw tight. "And if he wants to get back with you?"

"Trust me, he doesn't."

"Do you want him to want you?" Sean wrung his hands together, clenching and unclenching his fingers into fists.

"No." Ruhi laughed at that. "Not at all."

She had wanted Michael to want her. But being wanted by Sean was far better. So why was Sean getting up from the couch?

"Sean?" Ruhi rose to join him.

"A child needs both their parents."

"This child will have a mother and a father regardless of what Michael decides."

"I thought I was stepping into a vacant spot."

"You did," she insisted. "You stepped into my heart."

Sean's gaze raked over her. Ruhi felt exposed under the heat of his perusal. She felt her soul was laid bare as her husband judged her past decisions and present actions.

Sean didn't have a wide range of facial expressions, but Ruhi knew his face so well. He was hurt. He was confused. He was disappointed.

"Sean?"

"It's late. You should get your rest."

He held his hand out to her. But when Ruhi reached her fingers to his, he ducked his hand around her back. All week long when he'd rested his hand at the small of her back, she'd felt anchored, grounded. Now she only felt the weight of the world pulling her down.

Sean walked her to her bedroom door. He turned the knob and handed her inside. "Good night, Ruhi."

"Sean?"

"Let's talk in the morning."

And with that, he shut the door with a quiet snick. A moment later she heard the same small snick of his door shutting her out. He hadn't said the words, but Ruhi felt that somehow they'd just broken up.

CHAPTER TWENTY-ONE

The sound of his name on her lips reverberated in his ears again and again. It muted the sounds of screams and cries of his nightmare. It left him feeling cold. He couldn't close his eyes in bed. But keeping them open he could only stare at the shut door.

He'd had her in his arms. He'd tasted her lips. He'd admitted to his feelings and she'd reciprocated. It had been everything he'd ever wanted. And it was all based on a lie.

Not the lie they told together. That lie was different. It had been for the greater good. They'd done it to protect the child. Only now it might have been for nothing.

What if Michael wanted to be a part of the baby's life?

Ruhi had said she didn't want her ex back. But if he wanted to be a part of the baby's life, she couldn't exclude him. So where did that leave Sean?

Whether he'd known about the baby or not, Michael had tossed Ruhi aside when he'd dumped her. Sean knew the breakup hadn't been consensual. Most weren't. She clearly hadn't expected it, hadn't wanted it when it happened.

Sean would never toss Ruhi to the side. He wanted her back in his arms right now. He didn't want Michael anywhere near her. His every instinct told him to go to her door and tell her so, to gather her back into his arms, to press his lips against hers and not let even the daylight between them.

But there was so much between them. Lies, babies, baby daddies, nightmares.

There was no way Sean could sleep. But he couldn't stay in his room with so much pent-up energy. His only choice was to leave the house.

It was just before dawn when he arrived at the stables. He saddled up one of the horses and went out for a ride. Power surged through him as he drove the horse hard, but Sean couldn't outrun his demons.

As Sean slowed the horse to a walk to cool it down, he realized he was still worked up. The ride had done nothing for his energy levels. He decided to turn his attention to some manual labor.

The sun was up now, and the inhabitants on the ranch were waking to greet the new day.

Sean looked around for something to do that wouldn't require him interacting with another person. Most of the work required another set of hands. Except the fencing.

Mending fences was best performed with another. On one's own, it proved a difficult, but doable, chore. That was precisely what Sean was looking for.

He picked up the necessary tools and set off to work. The banging of the hammer was the best therapy, especially when he imagined the nail being Michael's face. Pretty soon the sun was high on Sean's back and he heard someone approaching.

"Excuse me."

The unfamiliar voice caused Sean to stop mid-hammering. He turned to look over at the man. He was dark skinned with a well-worn face. Sean could tell the man wasn't old, a few years older than Sean possibly. But he had that aged look about him. The look of a hard life, likely once filled by drugs.

"Are you Sean Jeffries?"

"Yeah."

"I need a word with you about my son."

"Your son?"

"His name's James Ezra."

So, this was the neglectful father who couldn't be bothered to take his kid to the doctor. He'd made his way out to the ranch. But he couldn't take his kid to the pharmacy. Sean wanted a word with him too. That was why he'd called DFACS yesterday.

"I appreciate what you all are doing for my boy by bringing him out here after school," said Mr. Ezra. "What I don't appreciate is sicking child services on me. My kid needs his dad not foster care."

"He needs you to be present in his life. He needs clothes for school. He needs medication when he's sick."

Sean dropped the hammer as he approached the man. The two stood at opposite posts of the broke down fence.

"Who are you to tell me how to be a parent?"

"James has been sick for a while. You haven't done anything about it."

"I'm doing the best I can. The free clinic has a waiting list. I called when he started coughing but they couldn't give us an appointment until next month."

"He was seen here by the nurse. She gave him a prescription. It was never filled."

"What prescription?"

"We gave it to him last week. I gave him the money to get it filled."

"What money?" But no sooner than the words were out of Mr. Ezra's mouth than he closed his eyes and swore. "That's where that wad of cash came from."

Mr. Ezra pressed his lips together. He ran his hand over his brow and then over his heart. It took him a couple of tries before he could speak. It was clear the man was choked up.

"I was short on the rent this month. It's not the first time, and I thought they were finally going to evict us. But then the money showed up." Mr. Ezra choked again on the last words. "I thought I'd misplaced that money and it was my lucky day when it showed up in my drawer. But it was James."

What was he saying? Had James slipped the money Sean had

slipped into his backpack into his father's dresser? Had the kid sacrificed his own health to try and help cover the bills?

"His biggest fear is going into foster care," Mr. Ezra continued. "That could happen with an eviction. We've had Social Services watching us before. You see, I was an addict. James's mom, too. But the moment I met him, held him, I never touched another drug. I can't say the same for his mom. I'm not giving up on her. You don't give up on family. I do the best I can for him. I keep a roof over his head, food in his belly. I would've gotten him the medication."

Sean wasn't sure what to say. His family had never had to make decisions like that one had. They never had to choose comfort over health.

"Are you a father?" asked Mr. Ezra.

Sean hesitated. Was he? The child with Ruhi was not his blood, but he felt a connection to that life growing inside her. Not just because he loved the unborn child's mother, because he'd been the first to know of the baby's existence, because he'd started making plans, because he'd altered his life for the child. Sean had stepped up, and he didn't want to back down.

"I can see you are," said Mr. Ezra. "So you understand you do what's necessary to protect your kid. I fall short on a lot of things. But I will never stop being there for him."

Sean understood that. He wasn't sure he could back away from the unborn child. He definitely wasn't backing out of his marriage.

"Listen, I'll pay you back. I don't need the charity."

"It wasn't charity," said Sean.

Mr. Ezra shook his head, but Sean held up his hand.

"The moment you stepped on this ranch you became family," said Sean. "You get no choice in the matter. Family doesn't give up on family. You just said so yourself."

Once again, Mr. Ezra's lips pressed together. He ran the back of his hand over his brow. Sean could see he was wearing the man down.

"I heard James say you're a mechanic? We've got a tractor that needs a look."

After a moment's hesitation, Mr. Ezra said, "I can take a look at it. But no family discount on the pricing."

Mr. Ezra cracked a smile as he held out his hand. Sean chuckled as he clasped the man's hand. This ranch had a way of collecting new family.

As Sean and Mr. Ezra turned to head toward the barn where the broke down tractor was parked, a Prius drove down the lane. The man behind that wheel was not a family member that Sean wanted to collect. The car belonged to Michael.

CHAPTER TWENTY-TWO

$\mathcal{A}$ stabbing pain in her gut ripped Ruhi from her sleep. Her breaths came out quick and raspy. Her pulse raced, and her heartbeat thrashed in her ears. No sooner had the pain stabbed her, did it disappear entirely. What it left behind was a desolate ache in her chest.

Ruhi scratched at her chest, certain she could feel a tear. The more she rubbed, the deeper the wound felt. As a medical professional, she knew that heartbreak was real. The emotional stress caused by a breakup or stress on a relationship could appear as real, physical symptoms.

Sean had only held her for a few hours. But the loss of his arms around her, supporting her, felt like the loss of a limb. Is this what it was like to fall in love?

She'd risen to love and the ascent had been perfect. Now she'd fallen flat on her rear and it hurt worse than anything.

Sean hadn't exactly broken up with her. But his silent reproach was worse than any of the breakup lines she'd been fed. His disapproving gaze cut deeper than her parents' grimaces about her dating choices.

Ruhi did not want to live her life without his hard-earned smiles.

She didn't want to walk any farther from his warm embrace. She had to figure out how to win him back.

A knock sounded at the front door. Ruhi rushed out of her bed to get it. But her steps slowed as she came into the living room.

Sean wouldn't knock on his own front door. On her bedroom door, sure. It was unlikely he lost his keys to his home. Even if he did, the inhabitants on this ranch didn't always lock doors, especially not during the day.

Ruhi didn't want to talk with anyone else. Especially if it was going to be a discussion about having one guy's baby while marrying another. Looking through the peephole, she definitely didn't want to face the man on the other side of the door. But she had to come clean.

She pulled the door open to reveal Michael.

At the sight of him standing in his collared shirt and casual slacks, Ruhi felt a dull pain in her lower back. Her heartbeat remained steady. Had her heart ever flip-flopped in his presence? She couldn't remember a single missed beat.

Michael turned on his thousand-watt smile. Ruhi squinted up at it. There was no spark. There hadn't been any chemistry between them, just compatibility.

After a moment, his smile turned to a frown, and he reared back from her. "You look awful."

She was sure she did. Her eyes were swollen from all the tears she'd cried last night. Her cheek was puffy because she'd slept on her side with her cheeks in her hands. She'd done that partly to recreate Sean's gentle touch, but also because laying on her back had become uncomfortable. And she was certain her hair was only a smidge above a rat's nest.

"You live here now?" Michael said as he came in.

Ruhi wiped a hand over her face before answering. "Yes, I just moved in the other day."

"And you're engaged?" Michael's eyes were glued to the ring on her left hand.

"Married," she confirmed.

Michael shook himself, pressing his fingers to his temples and then making an explosive gesture. "We broke up less than a week ago and you're married?"

"And pregnant." Ruhi nodded. Then she just decided to rip the Band-Aid off. "I'm six weeks pregnant."

Michael's mouth fell open. His jaw worked as though he were about to say more. Then he blinked. And blinked again.

Ruhi watched as Michael did the math in his head. She knew he'd carried the one when he took a step back from her. Just like she'd assumed he would.

There was a small part of her that had hoped he would've stepped up. Not because she wanted to be with him. Because she did want their child to have the chance to know their blood father.

"Don't worry," she said. "You don't have to have any responsibility for this baby if you don't want it. My husband is an amazing man. He will be an amazing father."

"Wait." Michael held up his hands. "Just wait a second. You're throwing all of this at me. You've known for at least a week that you're pregnant with my kid."

Well, at least he wasn't denying parentage. That gained him a point in her favor.

"You've had the time to move and get married. But not call me to let me know that I'm … I'm …?"

Michael looked from her face to her belly and back again. No matter how many times he traversed the track, he still couldn't manage to spit out his new title.

"Ruhi, this is a lot. You gotta give me at least a few minutes to process."

Michael padded from one side to the other in his leather shoes. He flicked a few glances her way, then he closed his eyes and picked up the pacing again.

Ruhi took a seat. He was obviously going to be at this for a minute. And she didn't blame him. It had taken her days to accept her condition. And that was in the midst of nausea.

Thankfully, her morning sickness had only lasted a few days. Only a dull ache remained. She was sure that would be cured once she reconciled with her husband.

But the ache was starting to get more urgent. More prickly. Almost like it was stabbing her from the inside out.

"You know, the main reason I came here was because Doctors Without Borders has been trying to reach you," said Michael. But his voice sounded far away. "You weren't answering your work or cell phone for the past few days. They reached tout o me because they knew we were colleagues. They want you too …"

Ruhi didn't hear the rest of what Michael said. Her entire being focused in on the sharp pains radiating from her low back. Her brain had been foggy all night and morning, but as the symptoms mounted her medical brain made a clear diagnosis of what was truly happening to her.

"Ruhi?"

The pain hit her so sharply that she'd doubled over and was panting for breath. "It's the baby. Find my husband."

CHAPTER TWENTY-THREE

ean paced up and down the tiled floors of the hospital's waiting room. Reed and Sarai sat in one set of chairs. Maggie and Eva sat across from them. They were all hunched over, worry heavy on their shoulders. Dylan, Fran, and Xavier were still at the ranch, but they checked in every half hour and planned to come over as soon as they got the chores done and the kids of the youth program back on the school bus.

Dr. and Mrs. Patel sat on a couch pushed against a wall that faced the swinging doors where the doctors had taken Ruhi over two hours ago. Where everyone on the ranch knew the score of exactly what was between him and Ruhi, her parents were still clueless. Sean had had to explain the entire situation to them, from her pregnancy to the baby's true parentage, to the arrangement he'd made with Ruhi.

He expected the Patels to be angry, upset, disappointed. They'd been surprised, most certainly. But not a single line of anger or betrayal wrinkled either of their facial features.

Dr. Patel clapped Sean on the back and then gave his shoulder a squeeze. Mrs. Patel embraced him tightly, and kissed him on his scarred cheek. Then they both retreated into the corner to wait.

Michael stood looking out a window, sneaking not so discrete glances at his watch.

Sean walked over to the man. "If there's some place you need to be, don't let us keep you."

Michael frowned as he put his hand in his pocket. "She didn't tell me, you know. I just found out. It's a life-altering event."

Sean knew. But he hadn't hesitated when he'd figured out Ruhi's condition for himself. He'd stepped up even though it wasn't his place.

"I have other plans," Michael continued. "I'm not ready to be a father. Probably ever."

At those words, Sean waited for the relief to rush through him. This would mean Michael would be out of their lives. Sean was glad for what that meant for his marriage. However, he didn't relish what that would mean for the innocent, unborn child.

"I don't want to be cast as the bad guy here," said Michael. "I'm just caught off guard and unprepared. I haven't had a chance to consider my options and make a plan."

This man was so like Ruhi with his need to arrange all the details of his life. Life didn't always work according to plan. There was that old saying after all. Sean was sure God was laughing at them both. Sean was sure He was laughing at them all.

Sean didn't mind the laughter. God could enact whatever plan he chose was best. So long as Sean got to keep the kid and the woman.

"Look," said Michael. "There's nothing between Ruhi and I. We were just casual. I mean, I'm not after her."

"Well, I am," said Sean. "I've got her. And I'm not letting go. I'm holding on to the kid as well."

Something flickered in Michael's eyes. Sean wasn't sure if it was relief?

"But this is a big family," Sean continued. "There's room for you if you choose to be a part of your child's life."

Sean held out his hand. Michael stared down at it for a full minute, confusion and uncertainty on his face. Finally, the other man reached out and clasped Sean's hand. But his grip wasn't firm.

Over Michael's shoulder, Sean saw Dr. Patel smile approvingly. Sean had thought that he and Michael were far enough out of earshot that the others couldn't hear. But of course, everyone was paying attention.

"That extends to us too," said Mrs. Patel.

"Us too," said Reed.

Michael looked over at the small crowd of Ruhi's family and friends. His expression screwed in what looked like discomfort at the outpouring. This wasn't likely a part of his plan either, not this big of a family.

The double doors swung outward and the doctor who'd taken Ruhi back emerged. The white-haired woman looked down at her clipboard and not up at the group of people who rushed up to her.

"Who is the child's father?" the doctor asked.

Both Sean and Michael stepped forward. But his step was unsteady and he fell back in line with the others. Sean came to stand before the doctor.

"How's my wife?"

"She's going to be fine."

"And the baby?" asked Mrs. Patel.

"The baby is fine. Just a bit of cramping. It's not unusual, but Mrs. Jeffries will need to stay on bed rest for a while."

"Can I see her?" asked Mrs. Patel.

"She asked to see her husband," said the doctor.

Sean heard his own footsteps as he walked down the hall to Ruhi's room. His palms were sweaty and empty. Then cold steel gripped him as he turned the doorknob.

Ruhi lay on the bed looking out the window. Her hand slid up and down her belly absentmindedly. She turned to him, and he saw a spark in her gaze. He felt it ignite his body. The door closed quietly behind him.

"Sean."

She reached for him. There was so much resonance in how she said his name. Relief, vulnerability, hope. Love.

Sean didn't hesitate. He raced to her and pulled her in his arms. "I'm so sorry for walking out on you last night."

"I should've told you about Michael. I should've told Michael about the baby. I have now."

"I know. We worked it out."

"You? We? Who?"

"Me and Michael. We agreed. I get full custody of you."

She narrowed her gaze at first. Then realization dawned. She threw back her head and laughed. The sound was like magic. It flooded his body with a warmth that made him feel safe, certain, rescued.

"He thinks he got the better deal," Sean said.

"What about the baby?" Ruhi asked.

"Worst-case scenario, this kid will have one father, half a dozen aunts, and uncles, and more people than they could ever count to care about them. This baby will want for nothing, just like his or her dad."

"I need you to know that I choose you," she said. "Over and over again, I choose you. I want to spend my life with you. I want to raise this child with you. I want to plan my life with you. I've fallen hard for you. But I don't want to do it again. It hurt. Now I just want to rise with you."

"I'm not sure what that means, but if you want it I'll give it to you."

"It means I love you."

Sean closed his eyes, savoring the sound of those words. She would be his beacon in the dark. Ruhi's light, her love. He knew he had a long way to go to manage his demons, but he now had an angel in his corner.

"I love you, too," he said, gazing down at his wife. "I promise to reach for you and not run or walk away from you again."

Ruhi put her hand to his face. He would've sworn that her touch healed him. But his wounds had hardened on the outside. Ruhi penetrated into the depths of him, and his pulse raced to pull her close to him, to have, to hold, to protect for the rest of his days.

She was his permanent mark.

EPILOGUE

"*I* don't understand why we had to come all this way to buy music. Couldn't we just download it from the internet?"

Xavier sent up a silent prayer for today's youth. Kids like Carlos were so used to having everything at their fingertips with the click of a button. "I don't want a digital song. We're at this store to get the album."

Carlos' face pinched in confusion.

"You do know what an album is, don't you?"

"Yeah. It's a collection of songs that are, like, grouped together. They're in a list under an album title and you can buy them all together in one download."

All Xavier could do was shake his head. Most kids today had never heard the scratch of a record playing, the touchdown of a needle on vinyl, the squeak is a part of the record skipped. They heard everything as a pristine replication of ones and zeros, no analogous waves.

"Whoa, this looks like something out of an old-time movie," said Carlos.

Xavier put his truck in park outside of the small mom and pop record store. It was one of the last in the entire state, likely one of few remaining in the entire United States. Just like independent bookstores and home movie stores, music stores were disappearing fast in the modern world of online retail, subscription services, and free downloads.

Xavier wasn't entirely averse to the digital takeover. It made getting the obscure music he liked to listen to easier. He had a healthy iTunes library of purchased music. There was a library of CDs in his home. But Xavier was a traditionalist in this sense. When he could get the physical album, he'd jump at the chance. Even if that meant driving an hour out of his way to do so.

He hopped out and went into the one-story building. On the right of the record store was a small diner with very few customers. On the left was an electronics store. Unfortunately, all the lights were off inside. It had likely gone out of business some time ago as handheld devices took over the technological world.

Inside the record store, a pretty woman stood behind the counter. She had earbuds in her ears and was looking down at the cell phone. She didn't look up as he came up to the counter.

"Excuse me?"

She didn't respond and he had to repeat himself twice, getting louder each time. When he finally caught her attention, her brows pinched in annoyance. Until they landed on his face. Then the telltale smile of interest lit her features.

Xavier was used to women showing interest in him based on his looks. He would've distracted himself with her attention, but for the long drive, and the preteen browsing the aisles.

"I called ahead," he said. "You should be holding an album for me. *Songs of Faith* by Aretha Franklin."

She went behind the counter and came back with the album. "Is it for your mom?"

"No."

Xavier didn't offer more. He reached out for the album with greedy hands. He'd been searching for this for years and finally, he had it in his hands again.

"It's over a hundred dollars for this," said the clerk. "You know you could get it for ten bucks on Amazon."

Xavier jerked his gaze up to her, disgust clear on his face. What was she doing working in a record shop if she pushed people to the competitor? It didn't matter. He'd found what he was looking for and now it was time to go.

But after paying, he couldn't bring himself to leave immediately. There was something about a record store and the musty way it smelled. He found joy flipping through albums looking for a treasure. It reminded him of his youth and his time with…

He shook his head. He didn't think about that time. Or her. Those memories were all in the past. Perhaps he should go back and talk to the disloyal cashier. She was so unlike her that it would certainly take his mind off of his past.

Carlos had found the sheet music section and was busy looking for the notes to Final Fantasy. He'd recently joined the school band. The kid had settled on drums to the dismay of all the early-rising residents of the ranch.

Xavier looked up at the cashier. Yeah, she might be a good distraction for a few minutes. Just remind him of how much he'd changed since his younger years. How much he didn't deserve a girl in a floral dress who smelled of lilacs blowing in the wind.

Xavier took a step towards the clerk but there was something tethered to his leg. He looked down to find a child with her stubby arms wrapped around his right leg.

"Sorry," said the cashier. "That's the other cashier's kid. She doesn't speak. She usually doesn't even interact with people."

Xavier stared down at the child. She had a round face, like the cherubs on the stained glass windows of his hometown church. She smiled up at him with the most angelic grin. But it was her eyes that caught and held him. They were steel gray with royal blue at the edges. It was like he was looking in a mirror.

In the distance, he heard a door open. Voices trailed out. One of the voices was filled with distress, but the tone of it was so familiar it brought memories he'd long tried to bury back to the surface. Xavier inhaled to push them away and the smell of lilacs on the wind nearly knocked him over.

"I'm sorry, Mr. Adams. It won't happen again. I'm looking for a new sitter for Alex now and… Alex? Alex?"

The little girl let go of Xavier's leg and raced over to the woman calling out frantically. Once the woman saw the child, she breathed a sigh of relief and scooped the little girl into her arms.

"Alexandra where did you go? I told you to sit in the chair until mommy was finished her meeting."

Alex grinned and pointed to Xavier who was only standing because he was leaning against the rack of records. The sigh of relief that had just left the woman's mouth turned into a gasp of dismay when she met Xavier's gaze.

"Xavier?"

"Cassie?"

He wasn't sure if he said her name aloud. It had been over two years since he'd uttered the name of his first and only love. Nearly five since he'd last seen her.

And now she was standing in front of him. Holding the hand of a child who couldn't have been more than four. A child who had his eyes.

≈

Can you say secret baby?
You won't want to miss Purple Heart Ranch's notorious bad boy reconnect with the good girl who got away. Even more importantly, you won't want to miss why these two had to part ways. And then witness their journey back to each other.

That's what's coming up next in the next installment in
Having His Back
Book Five of The Brides of Purple Heart Ranch.

HAVING HIS BACK

THE BRIDES OF PURPLE HEART RANCH
BOOK 5

PROLOGUE

$\mathcal{X}$avier picked his way over the dilapidated structures littering the patchy field. Interspersed with the discarded rubbish, rubble, and refuse of the junkyard there was broken concrete, dangling wire, and rotted wood. The place was a virtual landmine waiting to ensnare a booted heel, tennis shoe toe, or the instep of a flat heel. He stepped carefully to get through it in order to get to the treasure on the other side.

"Oomph."

Xavier turned, immediately on guard. In addition to the treasure he sought before him, there was precious cargo behind him. "You okay?"

Darkness cloaked them inside the fenced in land of rejected items. But Cassandra Butler was a bright ray of sunshine to his eyes. She had been since the first time he'd seen her walking down the street humming an old spiritual tune.

Xavier had stopped walking that day he'd first heard Cassie sing. Cars had honked interrupting her melodic song. He turned to shout at them to stop all the noise so that he could only hear her pure voice, only to realize he'd stopped walking in the middle of the street and the light was now green. Xavier had quickly crossed out of harm's way and trailed behind the songbird.

Cassie trailed behind him now, picking her way over scrap and debris in her sandals. He'd told her to dress practical for their date, but he supposed this was practical to Cassie. She wore a long sundress with a cardigan covering her shoulders.

As part of her religion, Cassie never wore pants. All her shirts were buttoned up, and if her shoulders shown, she covered them with a sweater in the cold months or a cardigan in the warm months. In the eight months they'd been dating, he'd never seen her bare shoulders. The sight of her bare toes in the sandals made his mouth water.

"I'm fine," Cassie said, wrapping her fingers around his bicep.

Just the touch of her fingers and the fact that she was leaning on him for support made Xavier feel ten times stronger. He'd had his fair share of women before he'd turned twenty last year. Fast girls and loose women flocked to the dark haired boy with the golden brown skin, the gift of gab, and the mischievous twinkle in his light gray eyes.

Xavier had welcomed them all with wide open doors. Until that fateful day in the street when he'd been rendered immobile by this innocent, untouched, shoulder-covered songbird.

His gift of gab hadn't swayed Cassie when he'd caught up with her. She'd turned away from the twinkle in his gaze and looked down at the ground. But even worse, she'd stopped singing.

Xavier had followed, pursued was more like it. She'd given him one-word answers intent on dissuading any further communication. He was undaunted until she turned a corner that he didn't care to follow.

It was into a church. Xavier had nothing to say to God. But he wanted to talk to the girl again, and so he'd waited.

But after twenty minutes of waiting outside the church, her voice rose and called him inside. Xavier's feet moved before he'd thought about it. Inside the church, she'd stood out amongst a group of people, a choir. In the center of the choir, she shown bright singing the most beautiful song. Xavier had taken a seat in the back row.

He'd led many a girl astray in his young life. For the first time, a girl led him down a righteous path. She was like the sirens in the Greek myths. But instead of bashing his head into a rock, Cassie stole into his heart.

"We're almost there."

Xavier pulled her to him now. He kept Cassie close, urging her to walk in his footsteps as they made their way through the junkyard and to the surprise on the other side.

It had been weeks since he'd last seen her. Now he couldn't look his fill of her. His hands ached to span across her back, to hold her cheek. He wanted to bend down and taste her. But he held back.

As a man who'd never had to temper his appetite for the fairer sex, Cassie was a meal that was not on the menu. Surprisingly, that hadn't deterred him. Not even during their long absences from one another.

He lifted her up and over a discarded muffler. When her body pressed against his, part of him wanted to take advantage. But his heart cooled his carnal desires. Mostly.

She slid down his front as the temperature rose and his mouth watered. He allowed himself a small taste of her lips, savoring the sigh that escaped her perfect mouth as he pressed his advance. As he pulled her closer, her thigh pressed against the protrusion at the front of his pants.

Xavier placed her on the ground and cleared his throat. He put distance between them, not wanting her to question that particular bulge until the time was right. He'd been planning this night for weeks, and he wouldn't let anything go wrong.

He wrapped his right hand around her left, toying with the bare fingers of her left hand. He smiled under the cover of night with a secret she would soon know. If things went his way, that hand wouldn't be bare much longer.

In the clearing, they came to the place he'd wanted to show her. A white gazebo with lace trellis. The structure was like something out of a fairytale at the end of a dark and forbidding forest.

"Oh, Xavier," Cassie sighed. "It's beautiful."

At the other side of the gazebo was a field of wildflowers. Xavier led Cassie up the steps where he'd set up a blanket, a picnic basket, and a cell phone with speakers playing an old gospel tune. The singer was the only songstress who could rival Cassie's voice.

Cassie had introduced him to Evangeline Taylor's music. In the times when he couldn't hear her sing, Evangeline had kept him company. But the gospel singer was a pale comparison to his Cassie's voice.

Cassie glanced over the setup, but when she looked up and out, her mouth rounded into an awed O. Looking out over the gazebo, beyond the flowers, was a cliff where the Montana mountains met the stars.

Xavier came up behind her, wrapping his arms around her. "They say this is what it looks like out in the desert. You can see where the mountains meet the sky. This is the sky I'll be lying under and thinking of you for the next nine months."

She turned to him, a tear in her eyes. Cassie didn't like talking about his deployment. He'd first spied Cassie just a few weeks before he reported to Basic Training. They'd spent nearly every day together after she'd let her guard down. Then he was gone.

They weren't able to communicate. There was plenty of high technology like video chatting and email in the Army. But Cassie's strict parents didn't allow any of that. There was also plenty of low technology communications like phones and letters. But her parents had not approved of him the one and only time they'd met him.

So when Xavier left town for training, they had no contact. But he thought of her every day and night. She was surprised when, nine weeks later, he returned to find her. But once again, their time was short and he had to leave just a few weeks later for his Advanced Individual Training. The moment he was able to leave, he came running back to her.

And now that his training was complete, he had only a few days before he reported for his first deployment overseas. This time, they'd spend nine months apart. He didn't doubt that his feelings would increase in the long time span, and he needed her to know it. He had just the way to prove it to her and it was wearing a hole in his front pocket.

"I'm going to imagine you singing to me under this sky," he said.

"I will," she said. "I'll sing for you every night."

Xavier pressed his lips to hers. He'd kissed a lot of girls, but no one had ever been as sweet as Cassie. He'd dabbled in recreational drugs in the not too distant past. But after a taste of Cassie's lips, nothing ever gave him such a high, and he quit every substance. Except her.

"There's something else," he said when he pulled away from their kiss.

He led her to the blanket he'd laid out and the picnic basket. Cassie loved romantic things like this. She wasn't into jewelry and gifts like other girls. A simple walk in the park while talking, or a picnic and she would give him the biggest smile. Well, she was getting both tonight. The picnic and a piece of jewelry.

Xavier sat her down on the blanket. He fumbled in his front pocket, pulling out the box. Cassie gasped as she looked down at the jewelry encased inside.

"Cassie, I've never felt this way about another person in my life. You mean everything to me. The only reason I joined the army was because I didn't know what to do with my life. Then I met you."

She looked up at him with that twinkle in her eyes. The twinkle shone bright even as her eyes glistened in the moonlight. Xavier swiped the tears away. The drop fell into his hand and instantly evaporated at the center of his warm palm.

"When I come back, I'll be able to provide for you," he said as he presented the ring. It was a modest piece of jewelry he'd picked up from a pawn shop. The navy blue gem reminded him of Cassie's eyes. "You don't have to answer me now. I just need you to know what my plan is and that my intentions are-"

"Yes."

"Yes?"

She threw her arms around him, pulling him close, and squeezing him hard enough to elicit a cough.

Xavier caught her and held on. He didn't think it was possible to be this happy. But the happiness in his heart kept growing and growing. This little church girl, this preacher's daughter, had swept him off his feet and nearly knocked him on his back.

Cassie took the ring and aimed it for her left ring finger. But Xavier stopped her.

"You know your father won't approve now. Not when I have nothing to offer you but my word."

"Your word is good enough for me. I trust your word. I believe in you."

God, this woman. She was the reason Xavier began calling on God again. If He could bring such a perfect treasure into his life, then surely the higher power existed and was looking out for him.

"Xavier, I love you. Nothing my father says will ever change that."

"Cassie, I love you too. I'm going to prove myself worthy of you."

She shook her head and pressed a kiss to his lips. "You're already worthy of me. I am yours. Now and forever."

She pressed another kiss to his lips, deeper this time. Cassie's kiss was urgent and unending.

Xavier had learned to temper himself in the last two months. He'd never been without company since discovering the pleasures of a woman. He hadn't touched another woman since that first day he'd seen Cassie and heard her sing nearly a year ago.

When she'd allowed him to hold her hand, his body had ignited with desire. But he felt no urge to go further, no urge to press his suite. He would wait forever for this girl.

At the same time, he was still a man. Cassie's kisses were getting very insistent, and her body rubbed against his in a way he hadn't experienced for many, many months.

"Cass." He held her away taking a deep breath. "Slow down there."

She shook her head. "I don't see the need. You just promised yourself to me forever. In the eyes of God, we're already married."

Xavier's breath caught as he looked down at this girl who'd stolen his heart and changed his life. She was right. Even though he was deploying in just a couple of days, the nine months they were about to spend apart wouldn't change anything in his heart. He was hers, and she was his.

Forever …

CHAPTER ONE

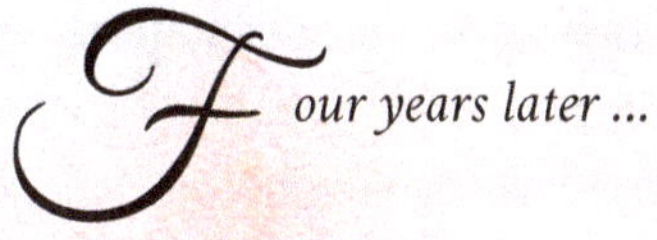

Four years later ...

"I'm sorry, Cassie, but there's nothing I can do. It's beyond my control."

Cassie Butler didn't even have the energy to sigh. Her shoulders were so used to being rigid that they didn't slump at the news. She barely even blinked her eyes because she was so tired that her eyelids couldn't be bothered to take the journey downward only to come back open at the top. So they simply stayed open as her boss delivered her the news.

"When is the store closing?" she asked.

"The lease is up at the end of the year, but I can't afford to even stay that long. So I'll have to pay a penalty fee for breaking the contract. I have to close at the end of the month. I'm sorry, but that means I can only pay you for last week."

He looked devastated. Cassie knew she should offer him compassion. It's what her God-fearing parents would demand she do. Well, they'd demand she do it for strangers, but they'd offered no such compassion to their own daughter when she found herself in a bind.

It so happened that Cassie didn't have any compassion extra in store. She was too focused on her own plight to think of the fate of poor Mr. Adams and the record store he'd pumped money into during the age of digital downloads. Cassie was low on cash. She was out of a job. And she didn't have enough to cover next month's rent.

Nope. All she could think about was what was she going to do?

She couldn't go home to her parents. Those doors had closed four years ago when she'd discovered that she was pregnant out of wedlock. Her parents hadn't bought into the idea that He Who Shall Not Be Named had given her a ring and promised to marry her in nine months upon his return from deployment. Nine months had come and gone, and that person, whom she longed to forget, had never returned. She'd finally had to admit that she'd just been another notch on his bedpost.

Instead of showing her compassion, her parents had punished their youngest daughter for her poor decision making and loose morals. They'd sent her to a home for wayward girls who'd found themselves in a family way. Cassie hadn't been allowed to read the books, but she was sure the best way to describe Saint Agnes's House was akin to something out of a Victorian gothic novel, minus the locking girls in closets. But only barely.

Cassie had only spent a few nights in that house of horrors before running away to a women's shelter. She'd been living on borrowed time, borrowed beds, and borrowed couches ever since. Just once in her life, she wanted to feel secure once more. Be it in a home of her own, a room of her own, or even a bed with four posts and not a box spring on the floor.

None of those simple dreams would happen in this moment and this time. Her time here, just like her time at St. Agnes, and her time in the shelter and her time in various rented rooms was up. And just like all the other times, she'd find a way.

Her shoulders straightened even more. Her eyes blinked once. But when they opened, she still didn't have a plan. What she knew for sure was that there was no use hanging around here. There was nothing left for her here at the record shop.

She'd thought she could earn money and dip her toe in her passion for secular music. But no. It was not meant to be.

She'd have to go back to retail or fast food work where she'd only make enough money to cover rent and childcare. But that was going to be her life, and she'd just need to suck it up. She'd made this bed of choices, and she would lie in it.

Forever.

Cassie stood and turned to go from the office. "Thank you for giving me a chance. I wish you the best."

After all, it wasn't Mr. Adams's fault that he'd taken a gamble on opening a record store that sold only gospel and secular music out in the middle of nowhere Montana when music could be downloaded to a phone or computer from the comfort of the modern consumer's phone. Cassie had had more far-fetched dreams herself, like believing the word of a soldier who likely had conquests all over the world. If he had even been a soldier. For all she knew, that could've been another one of his lies.

On the other side of Mr. Adams's door, Cassie looked down at where she'd left her daughter. The seat was empty. She didn't panic. Rebecca was at the front. She wouldn't' have let Alex go out the door. She was probably just walking around the stacks of music.

In one corner of the shop, Cassie spied a young boy frowning at the records as though he didn't know what they were. That was another reason the record store was going under. Aside from not listening to praise music, young kids listened to digitized music they could carry around in their pockets.

"Alexandra, where did you go? I told you to sit in the chair until mommy was finished with her meeting."

The only other person in the store was a tall man. He had golden skin and a dark head of hair. He held an album in his hands. Even from this distance, Cassie could tell that it was Evangeline Taylor's first album. She was surprised that someone so young, and a man at that, would be interested in the classics. It was likely for his great-grandmother. He was lucky he'd gotten the album since the store was going out of business. It wasn't an item an online retailer would easily have in stock.

The man was looking down, but as Cassie approached he looked up. Cassie was caught by the lightest gray eyes. Just like her daughter's. Just like …

Oh, no. Oh, no no no.

This could not be happening. She'd always told herself if she ever saw him again, she'd just cross the other street. She wouldn't confront him and be humiliated. She needed to find Alex and get out of there.

And then her worst nightmare came true. Her daughter was hanging on her father's legs, looking up at him like he'd hung the moon.

"Cassie?" He whispered her name as though it were an answered prayer.

"Xavier." She whispered his name like it was a punch to her gut.

Cassie took the steps toward him, careful not to touch any part of him as though he had the plague. She swooped up her daughter in her arms. Then she made a mad dash for the door as Xavier called her name again.

She'd parked at the curb outside of the store since it was her day off when Mr. Adams had called her in, and she hadn't planned to stay long. Wasn't that ironic. She was never coming back here.

She yanked open the back door of her car. Plunging Alex into her car seat, Cassie quickly strapped the three-year-old in. By the time she was done and hopping into the front seat, Xavier was on her.

Cassie slipped inside, closed the driver's side door, and shoved down the lock to his protests. She ignored them. She had to get out of here. She couldn't face more attacks on her dignity today. Her quota had been exceeded.

So, of course, her car decided it didn't want to start. She was trapped in her worst nightmare with the man she'd given her heart to on one side boxing her in, and a future that was leading nowhere in front of her. So she did what any sensible woman would do. She put her head down on the steering wheel and cried.

CHAPTER TWO

Xavier stood on the curb looking into the car. He stared so long that his gaze shifted, and instead of the distraught woman crying on the steering wheel, he saw his own dumbfounded reflection in the driver's side window.

The car looked like it had seen better days—a few decades ago. It was the color of rust with a few gray specks sprinkled in for good measure. There was a puddle of some kind of liquid seeping from its underside. Smoke emanated from under the hood. From what he could see on the inside, the interior was threadbare, and a few springs poked out from the fabric.

None of that penetrated more than the sounds of Cassie's cries. He'd seen her shed tears before. Every time he'd have to leave she tried and failed to hold back tears. But she'd never once cried hysterically with her whole body shaking and misery etched on her face.

His gaze went from Cassie crying in the front seat, to the baby girl, Alexandra, crying in the back seat. Through the glass that separated them, Alex held her arms out for him. Her gray eyes implored him to do something to make it stop, to make it better.

Xavier was rarely at a loss for words. This would be the top time of his life that he didn't know what to say. But there was something he could do.

He went to the passenger side of the car. It was unlocked. Xavier pulled the door closed behind him as he climbed inside.

Cassie lifted her face, tears staining her cheeks. Xavier couldn't look at her directly in the eyes. Instead, he reached over her.

She shrank back from him. Pressing her body into the driver's side door. Her hands curling over her chest as though she were protecting her heart.

He tried not to let her reaction get to him, but it did. This was the woman he had loved fiercely four years ago. If he were honest with himself, and he rarely was, he still loved her.

Cassandra Butler was the only woman he'd ever loved. The only one he probably could ever love. And he'd lost her to another man. Wherever that man was, Xavier wanted to punch him in the face for leaving his family in such a state.

For starters, this car was a death trap that shouldn't be allowed on the road. But even before that, Xavier had noticed that Alexandra's sundress was a size too small. Cassie's sweater was as threadbare as the seat cushions, and he could see her collarbones protruding just a tad too much.

But he couldn't think on any of that now. He had a mission to complete. Xavier reached down below the dash and pulled the lever to release the hood of the car. Still not looking at Cassie and trying to mute the sobs of the little girl in the back seat, he got out of the passenger side and lifted the hood.

Carlos stood on the sidewalk watching the entire scene with the curious eyes of a preteen. "What can I do?"

Fran would be proud of his adopted brother at that moment. That was exactly the right response. But Xavier didn't even know what he was supposed to do.

"Go to my truck and get the tools out of the back."

Carlos did as he was told as Xavier tried to solve the only problem he had any details on. The hood of the car blocked his view of Cassie. Pretty soon, the cries died down. But as Xavier looked at the mess of oil and wires under the hood, he still had no clue how to solve a single problem before him.

He'd tried for the last four years to get Cassie off his mind and out of his heart. Every night he failed as he dreamed about her. Every morning he failed as her voice sang in his daydreams. They had been apart for years, but every time he looked up at the night's sky, every time he saw a wildflower, she was never far from his thoughts.

And now here she was, with his child. It had to be his child. Those eyes. The feminization of his name.

Xavier closed the hood of the car and came around to the driver's side. He knocked on the window. He watched as Cassie took a deep breath to calm herself. Then she rolled the window down.

"Did you fix it?" she asked, looking ahead and not at him. The little girl sat on her lap. She turned sleepy eyes to Xavier and smiled. He noted that, along with the gray eyes and black hair, she had the same dimple on the right side of her cheek as he did.

"No. I can't fix it."

Alex held her hands out to Xavier. He lifted a finger and ran it down the side of her face. Her grin spread even wider as she gazed back at him.

"We need to talk," said Xavier.

"No need. I can get it towed back to my place."

There was a twitch in her jaw. Cassie wasn't a liar. At least not the Cassie he knew. The girl he'd known years ago believed lying was a sin. But when there was something she was trying to avoid, her lip would twitch, as though the full story was trying to come out, and she was trying to hold it back.

"Fine," he said. "We can talk while the tow truck comes."

She turned, facing him for the first time since their reunion, and glared at him.

"I think there might be some raised voices during this conversation," Xavier continued. "Maybe Alexandra should play with my friend, Carlos."

"I'm not giving my baby to a stranger."

"He's not a stranger. He's a good kid who lives on my ranch. I'd trust him … with my life."

"I have a little sister," said Carlos, coming up behind Xavier and poking his head in the window. "I know how to entertain little girls."

Cassie looked from Carlos to Xavier, down to Alex, and back around again. Finally, she opened the door and passed Alex to Carlos. As the two went off and sat on a bench a few yards away, Xavier came around to the passenger side. He opened the door, climbed in, and sat down on the worn down seat.

They were quiet for a few moments. Partly because his back was uncomfortable in the seat. The one-year-old scars that covered his back warred with the springs of the seat.

The other part was because his body felt alive again for the first time in four years. He was sitting next to Cassie. But she wasn't in his arms. It felt wrong.

"Alex is what, three and a half?" Xavier asked.

Cassie didn't answer. She crossed her arms over her chest, making her collarbone look even more pronounced and her body emaciated. She'd been small when he'd known her before, but now she was painfully thin.

"She's mine, isn't she?"

Cassie turned and glared. "What? You think I'm the kind of girl to sleep around?"

"Cassie." Xavier held up his hands.

"You think that there were other guys after I promised you my heart and gave you my body?"

"I didn't say that."

"Then what were you trying to say asking if you were the father?"

"I was asking for confirmation."

"You know how the process works. You don't need me to teach you. Man lays with woman. Baby is produced."

Her nostrils were flaring. There was a sheen of sweat across her forehead. But her chin remained high.

Xavier could only stare. Who was this woman? It was not his sweet and gentile Cassie. There were dark lines around her eyes as though she weren't getting enough sleep. The creases of her mouth had frown lines. There was a paleness he didn't like along with the thinness to her. The last four years had been rough on her. Why hadn't she reached out to him? But more importantly, where was her husband? The man she'd married after she'd promised him her heart.

"I don't understand why you're so shocked," she continued. "I'm sure this isn't the first time you've had this conversation with a woman you've had a one-night-stand with."

"One-night-stand? I was going to marry you."

"You can drop the act now. It's been years. Besides, you got what you wanted, and I didn't come after you asking for anything. I'm not asking for anything now. You can go back to your philandering ways and leave me and my daughter alone."

"Our daughter."

"She's been your daughter for fifteen minutes."

"No. She's been my daughter for nearly four years, and you didn't tell me about it."

"You didn't come back for me."

"Yes, I did. I came back, and you were gone. Gone and married to someone else."

It still hurt to even say the words out loud. His Cassie, married to someone else just months after she'd promised to be his forever. But instead of the pain radiating from his heart and spreading through all his limbs, it stalled as he looked down at her.

Cassie was gaping at him as though he was speaking with a forked tongue. As though the words coming out of his mouth made no sense. The pain receded, and for the first time in four years, a spark of hope was kindled deep in his heart.

Maybe he had gotten it wrong? Perhaps he had been misinformed? Dear God, please let him be misled.

CHAPTER THREE

Cassie caught a glimpse of herself in the rearview mirror of her car. There were tears running down her face. Her nose was red. And her lips were trembling.

She was a mess.

She'd sworn never to let another person see her like this. She'd held it together inside the music store as she was being told she'd lost her job. She'd held it together when her parents had sent her packing from the only home she'd ever known. She'd held it together while she'd been in shelters where she wasn't guaranteed a bed every night.

She'd held it together when she'd gone looking for Xavier at the place he'd called his home only to have the people there laugh in her face about her predicament. Nine months after he'd left her, just a few days before she was due to give birth, she made her way to the inner city row homes he'd said he'd lived in but never took her to visit. The neighborhood had been as rough as he'd said, but by that time in her life, Cassie had seen worse as she bounced from group homes and shelters.

The family she'd found inside had no idea who she was, where he was, or what she expected them to do for her. Xavier had been back and was long gone, with plans to never return is what they told her.

489

They also mocked that she wasn't the first girl to come looking for him because he'd promised them something.

It had been the last bastion of hope that she'd held onto. She left with her head high and her hands raw. There was nothing left to hold onto.

She'd cried her eyes out that night and went into labor the next day. She'd stopped looking for anyone to offer her help the moment she'd held Alex in her arms. She knew that no one would have her back but herself. And she'd sworn that if ever she came face to face with Xavier Ramos again, she'd tell him off without a care.

And now she was trapped in her broken down car with him and bawling her eyes out as he questioned the parentage of their child. Just the perfect end to this nightmare of a day.

"You didn't come back for me," she accused.

"Yes, I did," Xavier insisted, but Cassie wasn't truly listening to him.

Xavier had always been able to spin tall tales and tell fanciful stories to get her to smile. It was how he'd wormed his way into her heart and other places. She wouldn't fall for it again. She just needed to get him out of her car so that she could get home and cry. Though she wouldn't have long to cry in her tiny studio apartment. Rent was due in a couple of weeks. Even if she got another job, she wouldn't get paid in time.

"I came back, and you were gone."

More lies. She'd been there day he'd told her he was coming back. She'd gone first to the airport and waited for arrivals the entire day. Thinking she might have somehow missed him, she turned up at his family's house later that night.

It was all just more lies. She wasn't the naive girl he'd seduced all those years ago. She had been toughened up by the real world, and it took more than a charming grin and pretty words to get close to her these days. In fact, she hadn't gotten close to anyone since that one and only night with Xavier. She just couldn't bring herself to trust another man.

"Gone and married to someone else."

That caught her attention. Married? To someone else? Exactly what did he think of her?

She felt her chest tighten as she glared at him. She wanted to shout at him, but her jaw was stiff. Her belly roiled with contempt.

Even after all he'd promised her, after everything she'd given to him, how could he believe that she would make vows to another man?

"I got a few days early leave after five months, and I came looking for you, to surprise you. Your parents told me you were gone. That you'd gotten married, moved away, and was expecting your first child."

Cassie could believe that. She knew her parents had concocted a story about her leaving the parish just as she'd begun to show. None of that was true. But she didn't want to get into any of the truth of the last four hellish years of her life with the man who had consigned her to her fate.

"Where's your husband?" asked Xavier.

Cassie glared at him. When she'd told her parents that she and Xavier had been married under God, they asked her the same question. Over and again for three months until they couldn't hide her sin any longer. When they could no longer hide her shame, they sent her away.

"You're not wearing a ring," said Xavier.

Cassie balled her left hand into a fist. She shoved the lack of evidence down into the seat cushion. Her hand met with the metal of the worn fabric of her old car.

"Either he's gone," said Xavier. "Or he never was there to begin with."

"You got that right," Cassie muttered, her gaze narrowed, pointing all accusations at the man before her.

"Why didn't you wait for me, Cassie?"

"I couldn't."

"Why not? Was it your parents?"

A vein throbbed in her forehead, threatening to burst and spill all the thoughts she was trying to keep to herself. She pressed her lips together, but they trembled. She bit her lower lip, but it still opened and her every pain and sorrow gushed out like the waters of a broken dam.

"I can't," she said. "I just can't do this right now. Can you just stop, please? I just need this day to stop. My car is dead. I lost my job. I can't make next month's rent. And now here you are. They say God doesn't give you more than you can handle, but my plate is full. So, can you just stop?"

He did. Xavier turned away from her and faced front. They sat in the car in silence for five glorious minutes.

They both looked out of the passenger side window at Carlos playing with Alexandra. The little girl was grinning up at him as though he were her new favorite toy. Soon, Alex's eyes were dropping. Carlos lifted her, brought her into the cradle of his arm, and began to rock her. Pretty soon the toddler was asleep.

Cassie wished she could hire the kid as a babysitter. Alex didn't take to too many people. But she'd immediately taken to this Carlos and her father.

"Is he your kid?" Cassie asked.

"No. He's one of my brothers' kids."

"I thought you were an only child."

"I am. I mean one of my Army brothers."

He sat erect, keeping his back off the cushions of the passenger seat. Cassie had never had occasion to sit in that seat, but she'd seen the inner metalwork peeking out anytime she sat groceries there. A part of her got a bit of satisfaction knowing he was in some discomfort.

But that satisfaction soon gave way. Cassie was gazing up at him. Xavier was looking down at her. His gray gaze was so full of concern. She remembered him looking at her with what she had believed was love in his eyes.

Her traitor heart flipped, and she turned away. The sudden move had the metalwork of the driver's seat pressing into her spine. Good, she needed that jolt of pain to remind her of what might happen to her if she let down the guarded wall she'd built around her heart.

"I have to go," she said.

"Where?"

She didn't answer.

"You're coming home with me."

Cassie shook her head and reached for the door handle. "The last time I went anywhere with you I wound up pregnant and alone. I'm not going down that road again."

"Cassie." He didn't raise his voice. But the command in it made her stop. "You're going to tell me where you live. We're getting your things. And then you and my daughter are coming home with me."

Cassie opened her mouth to argue. But nothing came out. The truth was, she had no clue as to what she was going to do next. She had no money, no transportation, and the roof over her head was about to be pulled away. She couldn't go back to another shelter.

She turned to face Xavier. His features were set into a stern look that broked no argument. Cassie didn't have the energy to argue. She didn't know which way to turn. For one moment, it would be nice if someone else took charge of her disaster of a life.

Xavier owed her this much. It would just be for a moment. Then she'd figure out what to do on her own because she certainly couldn't trust him to keep his word.

CHAPTER FOUR

Xavier pulled up behind the tow truck lugging Cassie's car. The truck stopped at the address that Cassie had given. She tugged at the door handle from the back seat of his truck, but it was locked. Xavier had half a mind to keep it that way.

He thought he'd grown up in a rough neighborhood. This place made his old stomping ground look like an oasis. There were boards in many of the windows in the apartment complex. Graffiti covered the brick. And he was sure he just saw a drug deal go down between two adolescents.

He unlocked his door, then went around to Cassie's side. Before he could hand her out, she already had a sleeping Alex in her arms and was stepping onto the sidewalk. Everything in him urged Xavier to march in front of the two to protect them both. But he had to deal with the tow truck driver first.

The driver lowered Cassie's car to the street. Behind Cassie's back, Xavier paid the guy to come back tonight and tow the heap to the junkyard. There was no way either Cassie or Alex would ever get in that death trap again.

They also wouldn't be coming back to this dilapidated structure that someone was trying to pass off as living quarters. Once inside the building, his nightmares got worse as roaches reigned free. The stench burned his nostrils. The sounds made a seasoned soldier like him jerk and jump.

Inside her apartment was no better. His stomach hurt and the scars at his back tugged to think that they'd been living in this filth. The apartment was mostly bare. Other than a few toys littered around the room, there was only a mattress laid atop a box spring on the floor. Clothes were spilling out of a worn suitcase. A small square television sat on a metal chair, bunny ears protruding from the top at odd angles.

"Gather up everything," Xavier instructed Carlos.

Xavier tried to keep his face nonjudgmental, but he was judging. She'd rather live like this than reach out to him? He turned to Cassie. She was rocking Alex who was wavering between waking up and falling back to sleep.

"Do your parents know you live here?" he asked.

"I don't know where my parents are." Her gaze never left the child whose eyes finally decided to close instead of remain open. Alex settled back in the crook of her mother's neck and began breathing evenly and softly. "We haven't spoken since Alex was born. Last I heard, they left town out of shame for their unwed daughter who got knocked up by a forked-tongue sinner."

Her head was high in defiance, but her shoulders looked like they would break if just one more piece of straw landed on them. Xavier decided not to fight her perceptions of him. He'd have them too if he'd had to live like this.

He had had to live in his own version of hell these past four years. War had taken a pound of flesh from him. It was a pain he deserved. Cassie hadn't been the only casualty of his ability to persuade people.

That last night with Cassie hadn't been about persuasion. He truly would've waited for her, as long as she wanted. He didn't need to remind her that she was the one who'd pressed for more.

In the war, he hadn't had time to wait to get what he wanted. Xavier had been trained in strategic communications in the army. His persuasive abilities had gotten him bits of information that was necessary for his unit to function and the army's mission to progress.

In his last deployment, he'd gained the trust of an informant and got information that was crucial to finding and taking down targets. But there was always collateral damage. That collateral damage showed up the next day as a child suicide bomber took out his unit and the community they'd been building.

Lives were lost that day. Luckily, no one from his unit was buried that day. Still, scars were formed that never truly healed.

The skin on his back pulled as he hefted Cassie's suitcase down the stairs. Xavier had gotten used to his scars. But he still walked around in hell every day. And now his angel was back, standing before him, and he couldn't reach out to her.

Four years ago, when he'd accumulated a couple days leave during his training, he leaped at the chance to get back to Cassie. His thought had been to surprise her, but also just to be near her. To hold the woman he considered his wife in his arms. To hear her melodic voice sing to him, speak to him. Instead, he was left sucker punched in his heart, and his throat seized.

He'd always known he wasn't good enough for Cassie. His every thought, his every action since the day he'd met her had been to make himself worthy of her. The only way he knew to be respectful was to serve.

But that wasn't good enough for her parents. They'd turned their noses up at him the one time Cassie had introduced him. They'd sneered when he'd turned up on their doorstep in uniform. He was certain they took some satisfaction in delivering the news that Cassie was married and expecting.

But it was a lie. It was all a lie. There was no husband. But there was a baby. His baby.

With all of their worldly possessions packed in a suitcase and trash bags, he packed them in the truck, fastening a sleeping Alex securely in her car seat. Cassie hopped in the back beside their daughter while Carlos took the front seat. The drive back to the ranch was in silence as everyone eventually fell asleep.

The quiet was welcome as it gave Xavier time to think. The one thing he knew for certain was that now that he had Cassie back, he was never letting her out of his sight again. He knew just the way to make sure she'd be with him until the end of time. He just had to convince her to say yes again.

He looked at Cassie and Alex asleep in the back of his truck.

He may not be the man she deserved to have, but he was the one she had, and he would not let her down. Not ever again.

If she took his hand, in earnest this time, he could offer them a home, security. Maybe even one day she might come to love him again because he had never stopped loving her.

CHAPTER FIVE

In her dreams was the only time Cassie found peace. That and watching Alex sleep. But whenever Alex closed her eyes, Cassie was always right behind her, and then the dream would start.

It was a simple dream. She wasn't flying. She wasn't rich from winning the lottery. She didn't have magical powers and could become invisible.

No, there was nothing magical about the dream. In it, she just wasn't alone anymore. She didn't have all the constant weight and pressure on her shoulders.

Still, Cassie hated the dream. The reason why? Xavier was there.

In the dream, he had one arm around her shoulder tucking her into the nook between his chest and chin. He held Cassie's cheek in the other hand, tilting her face up for a feather-light kiss. He looked at her with love in his eyes and spoke words of adoration.

"There's no rush." Those were the only words he ever said to her. That and the three little words that made her heart skip beats even while she was asleep.

After the kisses and the sweet words, they would turn and observe their surroundings. They had a small house, nothing fancy. A small yard. Two bedrooms, one for them and one for Alex. The rooms were all furnished with nice furniture, no hand me downs or worn furnishings. And in each bedroom was a four-poster bed up off the floor where bugs couldn't join them.

Cassie was happy in the dream. She had no worries. She was cared for. She could sing, and her heart wouldn't be heavy. She hadn't sung a happy song in so long. But she did in her dreams.

Oh, how she hated the dream. Because every morning she'd wake up. And then it was back to her bleak reality.

She was being jostled awake now. Her eyes jerked open. Her first thought was Alex. She reached over to the car seat to find it empty. Panic slammed into her chest.

"She's fine," said a calming voice. "She's right over there."

Cassie sat up and followed the trajectory of the finger pointing out the window. She saw Alex waddling along with Carlos who held her small hand in his. A young girl with the same dark hair as Carlos had her arms open wide as she bent down to Alex. To Cassie's surprise, Alex went right into the girl's embrace without a fuss. Her little was never this familiar with strangers.

Where was she? Who were these people? What was this place?

Cassie turned back to face Xavier. He was standing over her. He was so close she could smell his cologne. It was the same brand he'd worn years ago. She hated the comfort that washed over her. She wanted to curl into his chest and bury her face into his chest. Instead, she strong-armed him away from her.

"Where are we? Where did you bring us?"

She stepped out of the truck and into a slice of heaven. There was green as far as the eye could see. Where the green pastures ended, the mountains began. In the distance, she saw men riding horses at a trot. Goats mulled around a fenced in enclosure. A burst of color beyond that hinted at a flower garden. When she turned to look behind her, she saw that she stood in the driveway of a row of quaint cabins all gathered in a semi-circle.

"Welcome to Purple Heart Ranch," said Xavier. "It's a rehabilitation ranch for wounded vets."

"You were wounded?" Her hand rose, as though reaching out to comfort him. As soon as the words came out of her mouth, she wished she could shove them away. She didn't care that he was wounded. She shoved her hand in her pocket and looked away from him.

Xavier nodded but didn't elaborate. "This is my home."

He waved his hand in front of a small one story home. It could've come out of Cassie's dreams. There was a small patch of yard. A rocking chair sat on the porch. A small flower bed lay off to the side of the house.

With her suitcase in hand, Xavier climbed the few steps and opened the front door. Cassie noted that the door was unlocked, something she hadn't done in the last four years. She stepped inside the open door and had to pick her jaw up off the floor.

She had to be dreaming. Because this was the home she'd been dreaming of for the last four years. Down to the flowery lace on the couch cushions.

There was a sofa, with not only couch cushions, but a crocheted throw. A coffee table sat in front of the sofa along with two plush chairs. Tucked in the corner was a record player. Over top of the old fashioned stereo was a library of records. Cassie itched to thumb through them, certain she'd find many of her favorite modern gospel records and old spiritual recordings.

When they'd first began seeing each other, she'd turned Xavier onto gospel. They spent many evenings sitting in his car and listening to music. Sometimes, she'd sing to him. Other times, she simply sat in his embrace while the speakers crooned to them. By the end of their year together, he'd amassed quite a hall. She was sure all those records were there, with many more added.

"There's two bedrooms. You and Alex can have this one."

Cassie followed as Xavier led her down a short hall. Two doors faced one another. Before going into the room he indicated, she stole a glance into the opposite room—his room. There was a large king-sized bed with a dark comforter. The headboard was made of intricate woodwork. Another record player sat on a nightstand on one side of the bed. The album cover leaning on the record player was by one of her favorite singers, a singer she'd introduced him to.

She turned from his room and looked into the room he indicated would be hers. The bedroom was bigger than the studio apartment she'd just vacated. The bed was on a four-poster frame with clean sheets and a bright comforter. There was a dresser and a closet big enough to house everything she came with and room for more.

It was perfect. Just like a dream. "What's the catch?"

Cassie rounded on Xavier as he put her luggage into the room. He scratched at the back of his neck, not quite meeting her gaze for a moment. When he did, she saw that there was something hidden in his gaze.

"I've learned over the last four years that nothing in this world is free," she said. "What do you want? What do I have to give you for staying here?"

Gray eyes gazed down upon her. Cassie had once thought she could read Xavier. She knew when he was exaggerating and when he was telling her the honest truth. She knew when he was trying to hide his sadness or shame and when he was truly happy.

Shame and vulnerability mixed with resolve in his gray gaze now. Whatever he was about to say, she knew she didn't want to hear it. She knew she wouldn't like it.

"The ranch is zoned for families," he began. "You and Alex can stay as long as you want. Forever, in fact."

She waited, certain the proverbial bomb had yet to drop. Xavier licked his lips, holding onto his bottom lip with his teeth a second before letting it go and detonating this fantasy world he'd brought her into.

"You'll just have to marry me," he said.

"Marry you?"

Her stomach dropped into her toes. In all her imaginings about coming face to face with Xavier Ramos again, she never imagined this scenario.

CHAPTER SIX

"Marry you? Because of zoning?"

Xavier hesitated. The zoning issue was a convenient excuse. But the truth was he'd been ready to pack his bags and leave the ranch at the end of the week when his time was up. He'd never planned to marry anyone else because, in his heart, he was already married. And then, he'd been blessed with another glimpse of his wife.

"Oh," Cassie sighed. Those navy blue eyes darkened with a cold cynicism. "I get it. This isn't about me. It's about you. In order for you to stay here, you have to get married, and I'm just convenient."

"Cassie, no—" But he faltered.

Though the blue of her eyes was on the darker spectrum, Xavier had always regarded them as sapphire gems. They'd always reflected light back at him. Never once since he'd known her had Cassie's eyes been filled with distrust and contempt.

He wanted to tell her that he still loved her. That he'd never stopped. But the dark shade of her gaze told him that she wouldn't hear him.

"I'll do it," she said. "I'll marry you. I'll move in."

Reeling wasn't exactly the right word to describe the twist and turn of his emotions. His heart pounded in his chest. But the cold that he felt in his fingertips and toes let him know it was not a happy occasion.

"But this is just a marriage of convenience," she continued. "My convenience. I'm no longer that fool girl who believed a man would sweep her off her feet. This will be a purely business arrangement. Not even platonic, because we're not friends. This will be the last time you use me, do you understand?"

There was no triumph in his gaze as he regarded her. All he felt was shame. What had happened to the joyous creature he'd left all those years ago? Whatever it was, it was his fault.

"Do we have a deal?" she said.

Cassie held out her hand to him. Xavier stared at her slim fingers. It was the same hand he'd held in his. The same hand he'd planted chaste kisses on. The same hand he'd clutched to his heart when she'd agreed to marry him the first time.

Shaking it now he felt dirty. But it was a means to an end. Xavier had talked people into and out of many things. He'd gotten people to divulge information without them realizing it. He'd droned on, planting seeds, until someone thought that his idea was theirs. When he turned on the charm, he always got what he wanted.

Xavier wanted to be in Cassie's life. But not in the way she'd just outlined. His hand felt clammy after clasping with hers to seal the deal she'd outlined.

But what other choice did he have? He couldn't let Cassie and his daughter go back to the squalor he'd taken them from. And now that he'd seen her again and knew that she was available, he'd do anything to get her back into his life. And then there was Alex.

"It's lunchtime," said Cassie. "I need to go get Alex. She's not very good with strangers."

They looked out the bedroom window. The view gave them a clear sight into Fran's front yard. Across the yard, Alex was the center of attention of the small crowd gathered. She had a huge grin on her face as she petted Maggie's dog.

Star, a pug with a face only a mother could love, laid her head in

Alex's lap to the child's absolute delight. Alex ran her chubby hands up down the patchy skin on Star's back. Maggie had told them that Star had had a skin disease that caused hair loss. Alopecia, she'd called it. Xavier had felt a special kinship to the dog as their backs looked alike, with skin missing in spots.

"It looks like she's fine," said Xavier. "Would you like to come out and meet everyone?"

Cassie stepped back from the window. She crossed her arms over herself, as though she were protecting her heart, and shook her head. Xavier couldn't help but notice the dark circles under her eyes. Despite her fire a moment ago, she looked exhausted.

"Tell you what," he said. "Why don't I watch Alex for a while, and you can settle in here?"

She eyed him skeptically.

"You've been doing this on your own for four years. I can take the afternoon shift. Why don't you take a minute and get settled? There's food in the fridge. You can take a nap. When you're ready, I'll introduce you to everyone."

Cassie swallowed. Xavier watched her throat as the lump passed through. Her shoulders relaxed slightly. One arm released its hold.

"She's allergic to dairy," Cassie said finally. "She doesn't like meat."

Xavier frowned at that. He was a carnivore down to his bones.

"It's a textural thing. Alex is special needs. She's nonverbal. And she's small for her age."

"There are doctors on the ranch," said Xavier. "They can see her and give us some help with any issues she has."

"I didn't do anything wrong," said Cassie. Her hands were balled into tight fists at her sides. That chin went sky high again.

"I didn't say you did. I'm sure you did the best you could under the circumstances."

Circumstances he'd left her in. But if he'd known, he would've left the army entirely. He would've gone AWOL to be with his family. He would've been at her side every step of the way.

He wished he could reach out to her now. Take her in his arms and hold her and let her know that everything would be okay from this moment on. But he knew she wouldn't let him.

Cassie had never been a prideful person. But there was a hardness to her now. A toughness that didn't suit her soft features.

Cassie crossed her arms over her chest and turned on her heel to go into the kitchen. Xavier had the urge to go to her and make her a plate, but he knew that wouldn't be appreciated either. He didn't have her trust.

But he had another little woman to make up time for. Xavier opened the front door and headed next door to Fran's. When he entered the yard, Eva and Maggie were both cooing over his little girl. When Alex saw Xavier, she made a beeline for him, arms outstretched, smile wide.

Xavier bent down and scooped the little girl up in his arms. He'd thought nothing could top his love for Cassie. But this little bundle of joy made his heart feel like it would burst.

Alex wrapped her arms tightly around him, as though she knew exactly who he was. That she was a part of him and now they were back together and whole.

"I always knew one day a woman would show up with a bundle of joy with your name on it."

He turned to face Dylan, the leader of his squad. The man regarded Xavier and his daughter with interest.

His daughter. He had a child. He was a father. He should be feeling overwhelmed. But all he felt was grateful, blessed, thankful that he'd found them when he did.

"I just never expected you to take in the mom as well."

"It's Cassie," said Xavier.

Dylan's brows rose. "The Cassie?" He whistled. "And that's clearly your kid."

Xavier rounded on his friend and leader. "Of course it's my kid. What are you saying about Cassie?"

Dylan held up his hands in defense. "You said she'd married someone else."

"Turns out it was a lie. Her parents told me that. They just wanted me out of her life. If I'd known …"

He pulled Alex in, resting his nose in the soft curls of her hair. She smiled up at him and placed a kiss on his cheek. Xavier's heart squeezed.

"I see you've moved her in," said Dylan. "So, it looks like you're staying? You're not taking on any contractor work any time soon?"

Xavier had applied for several overseas military contract jobs. His communication skills were a prized commodity, and he knew he wouldn't find any trouble getting work. He just hadn't cared to look while he was in residence on the ranch.

The money he received from the Army was enough for his bachelor life. But now that there were three mouths to feed, he'd have to consider other options. Perhaps some contract work in the states. But he didn't care to think about any of that now with Alex toying with his nose.

"I suppose there will be a wedding this weekend?" said Dylan.

"Yeah." Xavier sighed.

"Why aren't you happy about it?"

"She thinks I used her. She thinks I don't care about her."

"Is that all?" Dylan clapped him on his shoulder cap, careful to avoid his scarred back. "You've got a lifetime to prove her wrong."

That was true. When he'd said those vows the first time, he'd meant every one of them. This time he'd make it legal, and no one and nothing would tear them apart. He'd talked her into loving him once. He could do it again.

CHAPTER SEVEN

From the living room window, Cassie watched Xavier with his friends. The women smiled up at him, but not in a flirty way. In a friendly, we care about you way. The guys laughed with him and bumped shoulders with him. Five small dogs ran about his feet. The two children looked up at him as though he hung the moon. And then there was Alex.

Alex was cradled in his arms. She grinned up at him. She touched his face. She kissed his cheek. And all the while, Xavier held her to his chest like she was precious.

Cassie ached to be in her daughter's position. She ached to have Xavier look down at her with adoration. She ached to be surrounded by people who cared about her and her wellbeing. Even as Alex squirmed and jostled about in his arms, Cassie knew Xavier would never let their little girl fall. And if somehow Alex got loose, there was a small army of people surrounding him as back up.

Cassie turned away from the window with a sob in her throat and an ache in her heart.

Her community in the church had shunned her when she'd started seeing Xavier. Her parents had cast her out when they'd found out she was pregnant. The friends she thought she had hadn't come to her aide when she'd escaped the home her parents packed her off to. She'd been left alone.

Cassie wasn't sure she could ever put her trust in another person ever again. Looking in the fully stocked fridge, her stomach grumbled. For the past four years, she could never afford to fully stock one shelf of a refrigerator. Looking in at all the fare, she didn't think she could eat a thing. Her stomach was in too many knots.

She looked away from the kitchen and back down the hall to her bedroom. That soft mattress and clean comforter called to her. But she knew she definitely couldn't sleep. She was far too anxious about the deal she'd just struck with Xavier.

Marriage? A real one this time. Not a doomed promise under a starry sky.

Cassie turned from the comfort of her new home and slipped out the back door. She slunk around the side of the house so as not to be seen by anyone. Once certain no one had seen her, she walked a path, entirely directionless. The ranch was beautiful. It was the place she'd always dreamed of raising a family.

She came to a railing where horses roamed free. She leaned against the railing. She couldn't remember the last time it had been this silent. Nights in the shelters were filled with cries, groans, and snores. Nights in her apartment were filled with shouts, moans, and gunshots. The silence and tranquility of this place unnerved her. With no one around, she opened her mouth and sang a song.

She sang softly, quietly, not wanting to be heard by anyone but herself. But her voice rose an octave as she came to the crescendo of the song. As she let the final note trill from her tongue, the silence settled around her again. But it wasn't so daunting anymore.

"That was simply lovely, my dear."

Cassie turned to find an old man smiling at her. His features called from a foreign land, India most likely.

"I'm sorry," she said. "I didn't mean to disturb you."

"You brightened my day. I would say that God gave you a gift with that voice, but clearly, it was a present to Himself so that he could hear you sing."

A smile tugged at Cassie's lips. She was typically suspicious of anyone, having been burnt so many times in the last four years with people meaning her well and then abandoning her. But something about this man, and the way he kept his distance set her at ease.

"They say when we sing, we are giving God his breath back." He tilted his head up to the sun and smiled brighter. "Unfortunately, God decided to fill me with my own breath. I can't carry a tune, I'm afraid."

A small tinkle of laughter reached her ears. Cassie was surprised to find it was her own laughter. How long had it been since she'd laughed with someone other than Alex?

"I've heard that song before," he said. "I can't remember where."

"It's a very old gospel song. I like old hymns."

"I know a young man who loves old hymns as well. I catch him singing them often while he's working the fields. He prefers an audience of one, like you."

Cassie assumed he was talking about Xavier. There weren't many young men who preferred old secular music these days. In her recent neighborhood, all she ever heard was the grinding sound of electronically synthesized beats and shouting.

"I used to sing at my father's church." She had no idea why she said that.

Cassie opened her mouth, but then closed it. She'd been about to tell him more of her story. She didn't tell her problems to anyone anymore. Not even God. But she felt the urge to bare her soul to this quiet, old man.

"Your eyes lit up just then," he said, wagging a finger at her. "You clearly loved it. But I get the feeling you don't sing there anymore?"

"I moved away from home a long time ago."

"If you're in town, I would be honored if you would visit my church and add your voice to our choir."

It had been years since Cassie had been to church. She'd gone while she was pregnant, and a few times after Alex was born. She soon grew tired of the questions about where her husband was and the looks of disapproval. Something about this man told her she would get no such looks from him or his congregation.

"Are you local?" he asked.

"I am now. I just moved here. On to the ranch."

"On to the ranch?" His brows rose. "Are you by any chance a friend of Xavier Ramos?"

Cassie grimaced. She wouldn't call Xavier a friend. But he was about to be her husband.

The man chuckled. "Say no more, my dear. You must be Cassandra?"

"How did you know my name?" She advanced on him, coming to stand in front of him.

He extended his hand. "My name is Dr. Patel. I'm also Xavier's pastor."

"His Pastor? Xavier never went to church."

"Maybe not the man you knew."

"And you know about me because he … talked about me?"

Again the man smiled. "You know I can't reveal those details."

But in a way he already had. It was the only way Pastor Patel would know her name. What had Xavier said about her?

It didn't matter. Even if he'd told other people about her, it was probably to confess his sins toward her. She would still guard her heart against him.

"What I can say is that I am very glad you're here," said Pastor Patel. "For his sake as well as yours. Now each of your healing can truly begin."

CHAPTER EIGHT

Xavier stood in the bedroom door staring down at his daughter. She was so peaceful in her sleep, much like her mother had been when she'd fallen asleep in his car. When they'd dated, he'd driven them out to the countryside on long drives. Cassie would always fall asleep in the passenger seat. He'd gotten into the habit of pulling over and just staring at her.

She'd always awaken, embarrassed. He'd simply kiss away any mortification she might have felt at being watched. On the drive home, she'd fall asleep again, and they'd repeat the process.

And then there was the night they spent together where she'd slept in his arms. He hadn't slept a wink that night, so enraptured was he of the woman who had given her heart, her body, and her soul to him. And this is what that night had produced; Alex.

Xavier had a plan to get himself and Cassandra back on a long and winding path where she'd trust him enough to fall asleep in his arms. He'd rehearsed the words in his head. He knew the moves he was going to make. He was just waiting for Cassie to return.

The sun had started to set thirty minutes ago. Sean had told him he'd seen Cassie walking near the pond an hour ago. Xavier had decided to let her have as much time to herself as she needed. But he was getting anxious.

He tried to tell himself he'd gone years without seeing her. But the last two hours without her were pure torture. Even though he knew she was on the grounds, he ached to be near her.

Finally, the front door opened and closed. Xavier held himself still. Even though everything in his being told him to go to her, he didn't. He let her come to him.

Cassie's soft footsteps got nearer to him. His heart kicked at his chest, reverberating on down to his ribs. Cassie came up to his back, though he knew it was Alex she was coming for.

Xavier felt Cassie's heat at his back. Instead of the pulls and tugs of the scarred skin there, he felt a soothing warmth. Xavier didn't like for anyone to touch his back, but if Cassie had chosen to place her hand there, he'd be in heaven. Of course, she didn't.

"She's asleep?"

"Yeah," he said, making space for Cassie in the doorway to the bedroom she would share with their daughter.

Cassie didn't go inside. She leaned against the opposite post and stared down at their little angel. Xavier wished the frame was smaller so that he could accidentally brush against her forearm. But Cassie had turned sideways, so there was no way an accidental touch would happen. He truly had his work cut out for him.

"She had potatoes and broccoli," said Xavier. "The broccoli made me doubt that she was my child."

His chuckle died when he looked over to find Cassie glaring up at him. Too soon for jokes. Got it.

"And she ate her weight in blueberries. There's a bush out back, and she picked them herself with Carlos and Rosalee's help. Those are the kids next door. They're already in love with her. And Eva and Maggie said they'll babysit whenever you need."

Cassie turned and walked away from him mid-sentence. She walked back into the living room, to the mantelpiece where photos of him sat. She ran her fingers over the picture frames. They were mostly pictures of him in the service with his squad. Curiously, she picked up a picture of him and Dr. Patel.

"You told your pastor about me?"

"I told everyone about you," he said. "About the songbird with the sweetest voice I'd ever heard."

She placed the picture frame down and moved onto his records. She fingered his cardboard coverings of the vinyl. Still sitting in the storage bag was the album he'd picked up today. That particular album, he'd searched years for.

"I'm the one that found this when the order came into the store," she said. "I should've known then."

The record was the one they'd listened most to on their drives, including the night they shared together. She shoved the album back inside the paper bag until the artwork was covered.

"So, this is where you've been the last few years?" she asked.

"The last year, yes."

She nodded, as she continued perusing various items in the room. Xavier kept a close watch on her features. The lines on her face told him she wasn't happy. He figured she thought he'd been living in the lap of luxury while she'd been struggling in something worse than poverty. But it hadn't been that way at all.

"Before that, I was in a hospital," he said, "recovering from my injuries. Before that, I did back to back tours in Afghanistan. I only came home the one time."

She glanced up at him. But only briefly, before she turned her back on him.

"The one time when I was looking for you." Then he asked the question he dreaded, but he needed to know. "Where were you?"

"My parents sent me to a home for sinful little girls who fornicated outside of wedlock and got pregnant." She grinned, but there was no humor in her voice. "When I got away from that horrible place, I went to your family. They said you'd come and gone. They laughed at me. Said I wasn't the only woman who'd come looking for you."

"They lied. Well, they misled you." There had been other women before her. None that had gotten pregnant, he'd been careful. He'd only lost his mind when he'd had her in his arms. "I came for you, Cassie."

"Well, you came too late. Or too early. Or whatever. The fact is you weren't there when I needed you. And now I don't need you."

She lifted that defiant chin. He would've believed her, if not for the tired lines around her eyes and the sag of her shoulders. She needed him. She needed him bad, and he would do everything in his power to convince her of that.

"It's not too late for us," he said, taking a step toward her.

Cassie held out her hands like a crossing guard halting traffic. "Don't you dare. Don't you come near me."

"You know I would never hurt you."

Her hands dropped, and she laughed at that, a full belly laugh that hurt Xavier's ears. "You couldn't do anything else to hurt me."

Xavier kept his distance, studying the movements of this target. Because she was the sole mark he was aiming for. With her square in his bullseye, he came to a realization. Like a hunter reading the signs left behind by his prey, Xavier saw all the hallmarks.

The anxiety, the mistrust. The sleep deprivation. The aim for emotional detachment. The hostility and the need for social isolation. Those were the hallmarks of PTSD.

As a soldier, he was trained to recognize the signs and to deal with them in his fellow comrades. He knew better than to convince her to feel a different way. To just stop feeling hurt and betrayal. To tell her that things were about to change for the better. Even though all of that was true. But that couldn't be his approach. He'd have to do this by the book.

"What happened to you was not your fault," he said. "You didn't deserve it. I admire you so much for how you've managed to handle what was put on you."

Cassie looked at him. The bitter humor drained from her eyes. There was so much pain in her eyes it broke his heart.

He took a tentative step toward her. "I am proud that my daughter has a mother with so much courage and strength."

Her breath caught as she inhaled. Her lip trembled as she took in the breath. She turned away from him. But she couldn't hide. He saw the tremble skitter across her shoulders.

Xavier didn't want to make her cry again, but if that was the way to pierce her armor, he'd do it. He had to get through to her. He had to convince her that he was a safe place to land.

"I'm sorry they hurt you. I'm sorry I hurt you. You are a good person, Cassie."

A sob broke through. So quiet, he almost could've imagined it. But he was close enough to taste the salt of her tears in the air between them.

"I just need you to know that I'm here for you, Cassie."

He reached out his hand to her. His index finger was just millimeters away from her shoulder. He almost had her in his grasp when she turned and smacked his hand away.

"I said don't touch me. I don't want your pity."

"It's not pity."

"I don't want any of your smooth talk either. That's what brought me here."

Standing before the woman he loved, the woman he'd lay his life down for, Xavier felt that another explosion had gone off around him. But this time it was right in front of his face. And if he wasn't careful, he'd lose more than another pound of flesh. He'd lose not only his heart but the heart of the woman he loved. Cassie wouldn't die a physical death. But her spirit was on its last breath. He'd need to tread carefully and lightly if he was going to save her soul.

CHAPTER NINE

"You look so lovely."

The four women around Cassie all nodded in agreement as they gazed at her reflection in the full-length mirror. Cassie ran her palms down the length of the white dress she wore. It was a simple sundress with a modest bodice that hinted at her cleavage, a ruched waist, and a flaring skirt that ended just below her knees.

Sarai, the former model of the bunch, had given it to her. She was down on her knees with needle and thread making the final alterations so that the dress fit Cassie like a glove. Eva, the scholar of the group, had done Cassie's hair up in a loose bun with wisps hanging to frame her face. Ruhi, the nurse, and Maggie, the vet, had been on the floor playing with Alex, but now joined everyone in the mirror.

"Don't you think your mother looks so pretty?" said Ruhi. She had Alex on her hip. Alex lifted her hand and waved at her mother.

Cassie wiggled her fingers back at her daughter. She still marveled that her daughter was comfortable with every single person on this ranch. For the three years of her life, Alex had not wanted to be held by anyone but Cassie, making daycare an issue. But she happily went into the arms of every resident here at the Purple Heart Ranch, including the brawny soldiers whom Xavier called his true brothers.

"Can you say pretty?" Ruhi sing-songed to Alex. Alex simply grinned at the soon-to-be mother. It was evident that Ruhi was practicing for her own child, but this was a milestone that Alex might not ever be ready for.

"She doesn't respond," said Cassie.

"No," smiled Ruhi, entirely undaunted. "But she understands. She'll talk when she's ready. Won't you, Alex?"

Alex bobbed her head as though she did understand. But her focus was on Ruhi's bright and colorful jewelry.

"And when she does start talking," said Eva, "you'll wish she'd be quiet again."

Eva looked over to her little sister who sat quietly in the corner. Rosalee was playing with Cassie's bouquet, arranging and rearranging the wildflowers in the gathered bunch. The young girl looked up and frowned at her older sister. The women gathered all giggled, but not Cassie.

Cassie didn't appreciate the joke. These women didn't know what it was like to have a special needs child. To wonder if the fault in the child was a result of something that happened in the pregnancy or something that didn't happen. Cassie lay awake many a night looking down at her daughter wondering what she'd done wrong to leave Alex ill-equipped to face the world.

"Rosalee was a preemie," said Eva coming to stand beside Cassie. "She had to stay in the hospital a few weeks before they let our parents bring her home. But look at her now."

Cassie did. She looked at the healthy, bright, spirited little girl. She would've never been able to tell that the child had a rough start in life.

Eva gave Cassie a squeeze. "Alex is beautiful and perfect. I'm so excited that she's a part of our family now. And you as well."

Cassie tried not to stiffen in the woman's embrace, but it was a losing battle. She'd gone without any affection for so long she couldn't remember the simple mechanics of a hug. Cassie was sure Eva caught her discomfort with the display of affection, but she didn't mention it. She simply released Cassie and gave her back her personal space.

Cassie let out a sigh of relief. But at the tail end of the sigh was a breath of remorse. Cassie had always wanted close friendships. Her parents had only allowed her to socialize within the church, and when they'd cut ties with her, not a single one of the friends she thought she had even reached out to her. She didn't want a repeat of that pain. It would be best if she maintained her distance from these women.

"Alex wasn't a preemie," Cassie said. "They think she has Autism, but a highly functional form of the disorder. We won't know for sure until she's older."

"The medical field still doesn't know what causes Autism," said Ruhi. "It could be genetics. It could be environmental."

"So either something in my DNA or something in the place I was living?" Cassie couldn't help it. Her hackles rose. She held out her hands for Alex.

Ruhi passed the child back to her mother. Her face was a mask of compassion as she regarded Cassie. "There's so much we don't under-stand about the miracle of life. This wasn't your fault, Cassie. I was still drinking wine and alcohol a month before I knew I was pregnant."

Ruhi put her hands over her belly, caressing her hump as though she were rubbing her child's back. Cassie had done neither of those things ever. But she remembered being pregnant and alone and out on the streets.

Alex wiggled until her mother set her down. The little girl made her way back over to Ruhi and climbed onto her lap. Children didn't know how to cast blame or hold grudges. It was a lesson Cassie needed to learn.

Cassie wanted to apologize for her outburst, but she couldn't make her mouth form the words. These women had shown her nothing but kindness in the two days she'd been on the ranch. But Cassie couldn't help her fear that the kindness would be yanked away from her at any moment.

At that moment, a door was yanked open. A tall man with dark skin stood in the doorway blocking out the sun.

"Shut the door, Sean," said Maggie. "Xavier can't see her before the wedding. It's bad luck."

If only they knew how much bad luck was between Cassie and Xavier. The open doorway was the least of their problems.

Sean came in and closed the door behind him. He made a beeline for Ruhi and planted a kiss on the bridge of her nose. Alex, who was still on Ruhi's lap, reached up and touched the jagged scar on his cheek.

"I'm so sorry," said Cassie.

Sean glanced over at her and smiled. When he did, the scar seemed to melt away. What was left was a very handsome man.

"I don't mind," he said. "I'm just happy she got your looks instead of her father's."

A smile jerked the edge of Cassie's lips.

She tugged her lower lip into her mouth to tuck the smile away. Sean straightened from his wife and made his way over to Cassie. "Xavier wanted me to give you this."

Cassie took the box from the man's hand. She opened the lid and gasped. Inside was an exact replica of the ring Xavier had given her four years ago.

Despite her sense of betrayal, Cassie had held onto the ring for the first two years. She'd worn it on her left hand throughout her pregnancy. But by the second year, she'd realized Xavier was never coming for her, and she put the ring away. It had been stolen at some point during her days moving from shelter to shelter.

"You're exactly as I pictured you," Sean said.

Cassie felt an irrational urge to run and hide under his gaze. What had Xavier said about her to his fellow soldiers?

"You're far more beautiful a woman than I thought he could ever get. And you're way too good for him. Just give me a signal if you want to make a run for it."

Cassie couldn't hide the second grin he'd elicited from her. She read sincerity in his hazel eyes. A man with such a brutal scar would've known adversity. He might understand what she'd been through. Perhaps she could have one friendship on this ranch after all? But the other women shooed Sean out of the room.

"These men," said Maggie. "I'm so glad you're here, Cassie. We finally outnumber them."

"Now we can enact our master plan," said Sarai.

"Which is?" asked Cassie, genuinely curious.

"To turn the barn into a she-shed," said Eva. "Arts and crafts everywhere."

"And we'll watch romantic comedies on movie night," said Maggie.

The women giggled at their dastardly plan. Cassie looked around. Despite herself, the grin that Sean had born spread a bit more across her face at the sisterhood she found herself surrounded by.

"My dad says you have a beautiful voice," said Ruhi. "I hope you'll join the church choir."

"Oh, that would be amazing," said Eva. "That is if you decide you like our church."

"Of course she will," said Maggie. "And she'll be just in time for the church picnic tomorrow."

Cassie hadn't been a part of a church community in years. She hadn't felt welcome in the Lord's House with a baby in her arms but no ring on her finger. Could she really go back to church now, after all these years? She might find a welcoming community there if she came with a ring on her finger.

"That is if you feel up to after your wedding night?" Maggie was saying.

Maggie waggled her eyebrows eliciting another round of giggles from the women gathered. Alex clapped her hands at the joyous laughter spreading around the room. Rosalee rolled her eyes and made her final arrangements to Cassie's bouquet before handing it to her.

Cassie felt heat on her cheeks. Her wedding night would be nothing like these women's first night with their husbands. She'd demanded a purely platonic arrangement. She didn't even want to be Xavier's friend in this relationship. Didn't she?

"Oh, this brings back memories of my wedding," said Ruhi.

"It should," said Maggie. "You only got married two weeks ago."

Cassie couldn't help but do a double take at the woman's belly bump. Two weeks ago? Ruhi had to be a couple months pregnant if she was showing.

Ruhi caught her stare and laughed. "Oh yeah, it was a shotgun wedding. Even more scandalous …" She leaned forward and stage-whispered. "It's not Sean's baby."

"And … he knows?" said Cassie.

"Of course," Ruhi chuckled. "He suggested we get married after my boyfriend dumped me. Michael, that's my ex, he's not ready to be a father. But Sean wanted both me and my baby."

"So that he could stay on the ranch because of the zoning?" asked Cassie.

"Don't believe the zoning line that these guys feed you," said Sarai. "None of these men do anything they don't want to do. And that includes Xavier."

"Since I've known him," said Maggie, "he's said he would never get married. He never said why though. You're back in his life for a couple of hours before he proposes …"

She let the sentence linger.

"He could've moved down the street," said Eva. "He could've driven here every day. I don't think it's about the ranch. He's marrying you because he wants to."

The women sighed at the thought. What they didn't understand was the possibility of Xavier choosing her was even scarier than him being obligated to marry her. Love was fickle. Just because it came to town one day didn't mean it would stay forever.

CHAPTER TEN

Xavier walked up to the gazebo. Just two months ago they'd decorated it for Dylan and Maggie's wedding. The decorations hadn't come down because Fran and Eva had used this spot next for their vows. Followed by Reed and Sarai. The decorations had gotten an Indian-Southern Baptist makeover when Sean and Ruhi had taken center stage a couple of weeks ago.

The only addition Xavier made for his nuptials with Cassie was to add a record player and speakers at the back of the gazebo.

"Never thought I'd see you standing here," said Dylan.

"Never thought I'd get her back," he said.

But he had gotten her back. Physically, if not spiritually. Xavier knew Cassie still didn't trust him. But after they said their vows, he'd have a lifetime to prove to her that he would never leave her again. He'd make her see that he'd meant every one of the vows he'd promised her four years ago. And now he had new ones to tack on that he'd hold fast to every day of their lives.

In the distance, he saw the girls begin their promenade toward them. He made out Cassie immediately. Not simply because she was dressed in white. Because she was a beacon. He'd always find her.

As his gaze focused in on her, he was transported back to that moment five years ago when he'd seen her walking down the street. The sun had lighted on her shoulders, surrounding her with an angelic glow that warmed him from afar. He'd followed her then. She was coming to him now.

Back then, she'd turned to him with a small smile on her face. Now, she gazed up at him with a blank expression. Her features were set not in joy but in duty.

He knew that the main reason she'd agreed to this arrangement was for Alex. Her sense of duty to their child overruled her lack of feelings for him. Her distrust of him because she still believed that he'd abandoned her, misled her, and never came back for her.

Xavier cursed himself for not looking harder for her. For simply taking the word of her parents and not pressing to find out for himself if she had married someone else. To at least seek her out and have a conversation with her to ensure that he wasn't her choice.

He would never doubt again. He would never have to. In just a few minutes, she would be his forever.

Fran placed the needle on the record, and the crooning sounds of Evangeline Taylor filled the early afternoon air. It was the song playing on their many drives through the countryside. The song playing the night he'd promised her forever. It was a gamble to play it now, but the words the singer crooned were as true today as they were all those years ago. The love he had for Cassie was eternal.

From the distance, Xavier saw the light of recognition in Cassie's eyes. Cassie's steps faltered. Luckily, the other women were there by her side. Maggie put a hand to Cassie's back. Eva put one to her shoulder.

Cassie nodded at them. She took a breath and continued down the aisle by herself. She was walking not only toward him, but she was also walking into the family on this ranch. Every one of these people would have her back from this day forward. No one would ever turn her away or turn away from her.

Rosalee held Alex's hands as they walked down the aisle ahead of Cassie. The girls distributed flowers they'd picked from the gardens on the ground as they went. Halfway down the aisle, Alex gave up the flowers and made a beeline for her dad.

Xavier held out his arms and scooped up his little girl. He'd only known her for two days, but he couldn't imagine his life without her. He gave Alex a kiss and then they both turned to her mom.

Cassie's steps were slow and unsteady at first. But she put her shoulders back and kept going. He watched her chest heave as she took deep breaths. He wanted to go to her, but even more, he needed her to come to him. And pretty soon, she was standing before him.

"We are gathered here today to join this man and this woman," Dr. Patel began.

Xavier was already joined with Cassie. Even though they'd been apart for years, the connection to her had never left him. He felt the bond down deep in his spirit. Today, that link would become official.

"The heart is an exceptional organ," Dr. Patel continued. "It can fill to the brim with love. Just when you think it cannot fill anymore, it floods with more love. But just as it can overflow with love, it can break open with hurt and sorrow. A broken heart heals and is almost immediately ready to allow more love in. Until it breaks again. What it takes most people a lifetime to learn is that after each break the task is not to close up the heart, but to leave it open and never let it close again."

Xavier could see Cassie's shoulders tremble as the older man spoke. She hadn't met his gaze. Her eyes were glued downward. She was focusing on the ring on her finger, the exact replica of the one he'd given her four years ago.

He ached to reach out to her and let her know that she would never have to take that ring off again. That he would have her back from this day on. But he knew she wouldn't yet accept his touch. Not yet.

"Xavier has prepared his own vows. Will you join hands to receive them?"

With Alex in one arm, Xavier reached out for Cassie with his free hand. He saw her fingers clench and unclench, only to clench again.

But then she moved her bouquet to one hand and gave him her free one.

Had her hands always been that small? He knew her fingertips hadn't been this rough when they were younger. He added to his vows that she would never have to lift another finger if she didn't want to. He would give her all his sustenance, his support, his strength from this day forward.

"Cassie," Xavier began. "You were my guide to love. I heard your voice, and it opened my heart. It was your light that led me and kept me steady when I was in the darkness. You are my rose garden in a junkyard. You grew inside my heart in a place where love was never meant to exist. You took root and made something beautiful. I promise to tend to you and nourish you and sing to you. That is what I know helps flowers grow, and you are the most beautiful blossom I've ever witnessed. You've had my undying devotion for years, and now, like a weed, you're not getting rid of me."

There was some giggling and chuckling from the audience. Dr. Patel smiled wide. Alex rested her head beneath his chin and placed her hand on his heart.

Cassie's eyes were near to overflowing with tears. She opened her mouth and then shut it. She shut her eyes tight, but the tears streamed down. She glanced from Xavier to Alex, and then down again. She shook her head and pulled her hand away from his.

"I'm sorry," she said. "I can't."

She turned from him and walked down the aisle from where she'd come.

CHAPTER ELEVEN

Cassie was living in a dream. It was the dream she had every night when she closed her eyes, and Xavier was there. He'd hold her close and tell her everything would be all right.

And then in the morning, she'd wake up. She'd wake up to the loneliness and heartache and stress and disappointment of the real world. She'd curse the dream and dread going back to sleep every night, only to curl up into the dream world again and face the cycle of waking disappointment.

But she was awake now.

She stood there with everyone's eyes on her, and all she could do was wait for that horrible moment when she was wrenched from sleep.

But the sun was shining in her face, and her eyes were wide open.

She was awake, and Xavier was making these promises to her. He was far more poetic in reality than in her dreams. Of course, he was. This was the real Xavier. He'd always had that gift of gab along with that charming personality. It would be so easy to believe the words coming out of his mouth.

But she couldn't.

Even if this was reality, she knew it wouldn't last. It couldn't. She'd been down this road and had the tire marks on her heart to prove it.

Reality had come to a dream world. Her mind couldn't wrap around it. So, she ran away.

The sounds of gasps drowned out the music playing on the record player. A few of the women who'd stood at her side a moment ago rose as she passed by. But just as soon as they stood, they each sat back down.

Of course, they did. She wasn't their family. She'd just rejected her way into their group.

The last person she saw was Sean. But he grimaced and rubbed at his shoulder. Ruhi gave him a whack as she glared at him.

He turned to her. "I swear I didn't give any signal."

It was for the best. If they weren't going to stick by her without Xavier, then they never would have stuck by her in her everyday life. It was just another heartache she'd avoid. She didn't need to be abandoned by anyone else. She'd reached her quota years ago.

And so she ran.

But she hadn't gotten too far. She didn't know where she was going. Cassie stopped running and looked up at the sky. God was only supposed to give you what you could handle. Why was He constantly putting more on her plate then?

Her heart pounded and ached. She just needed a few minutes to herself to settle down and get it under control. She spied salvation at a pier overlooking a small pond.

She walked over the wooden planks, her heels clicking as she avoided the holes between each board. Cassie sat down. She dangled her feet over the edge, making sure not to get her dress dirty. It was a loaner, and she planned to return it to Sarai in the same condition she'd been given it.

She caught her breath. But, still, her heart pounded. So robust, so loud, she was certain it was coming out of her chest.

Cassie was so focused on the pounding of her heart that she hadn't heard the footsteps coming up behind her. Xavier lowered himself down to a sitting position on the pier. His legs were so long that the tips of his shoes tapped the surface of the water causing a ripple to break the smooth lines and disrupt the peaceful water.

He said nothing. He also sat at the farthest part of the pier, not encroaching on her space. When they were younger, he'd press boundaries with her. Always getting a little closer, kissing a little longer. But the man he'd become, this man, hadn't rushed in.

"I can't," she said.

He nodded, looking out across the water. "Okay."

And that was it. No cajoling, no smooth talking. Just simple agreement.

Cassie's heart pounded louder in her ears. Shouldn't she feel relieved? Instead, she felt even more bereft.

"We'll have to move off the ranch in two weeks," he said.

Right. The ranch. That's what this was all about. That was his only concern, not her.

"I had only been looking at one bedroom apartments, but I'm sure I can find a small house to rent in a couple of weeks. It won't be much on what I get monthly from the Army. But it will be better than that place you called home."

"House?"

He turned to face her now. "Yes. A house. For the three of us."

"Us?"

Xavier's gray eyes made a slow trek across the features of her face before returning to gaze directly into her eyes, his own features stern with resolve. "Marriage was an option. Breaking up our family is not. I understand if you don't want to be my wife. But we're life partners, forever. You and Alex are my responsibility. If later, you decide you want to marry someone else … we'll figure it out."

He'd turned from her during that brief pause in his statement. When he spoke of marrying someone else, the stiff posture of his back slumped, caving inward. His carefully blank features darkened with despair when he said *they'd figure it out.*

But Cassie didn't want to marry anyone else. Those vows she'd spoken years ago had imprinted on her heart and closed it off to anyone else. With the words Xavier had spoken today during their brief and ill-fated ceremony, he'd wrenched the doors open.

With her heart open, Cassie saw what could've been if he'd come back in time. Maybe they could've been a family? Maybe they could've been a couple, a true husband and a wife?

But she was also reminded of what did happen when none of those dreams had come true. The pain. The hurt. It was all waiting there, ready to pounce again if she left her heart open. That's why she had to close it. To protect herself.

"I can't change the past," Xavier said. "Neither of us can. We'll drive ourselves crazy thinking what could've been. I can only give you right now and promise the future."

He turned to face her. Cassie tried to block out the earnestness she saw in his eyes. He'd never lied to her when they were together. He made fun, he made things up, he stretched to the truth to get her to laugh. But never a lie.

Every time he'd left and said he would come back, he had. Including the last time. They'd just missed each other.

"I will never leave you again. You will never be alone. You will never be in need."

Inside, Cassie was drained from trying to close the chambers of her heart. A feat that had been easy days ago proved impossible at this moment. Her heart was wide open, and the memories of what love felt like were rising to the surface. She was so full of the memories that tears pooled at the corner of her eye.

Xavier reached out and caught the first teardrop before it could fall. "I promised myself I'd take things slow with you. Give you the room you needed to learn to trust me again. I can still do that. I can wait forever for you. I just need you to know that things have never changed for me, and they never will. You're the only woman I've ever loved. The only woman I want in my life. Since the day I met you, I've done everything in my power to prove myself worthy of you. That's what I'm going to do for the rest of my life."

Cassie looked up at Xavier. The years fell away, and she saw the young man, so full of promise, that she'd fallen in love with. The man who hadn't thought himself worthy of her. The man who'd gone away to better himself so that he could take care of her. In an instant, all the hurt melted away. She felt overwhelmed by the love she felt for him.

She reached up and took Xavier's face in her hands. She wished she could melt his sorrow away just as hers had gone. "You were always worthy of me."

His eyes searched hers. Hope shone in the gray depths, like a ray of sun peeking out after a cloudy day.

"I'm yours," Cassie said.

Xavier's eyes closed as though he were saying a silent prayer of gratitude.

"Now and forever."

And for the second time in their lives, Cassie and Xavier sealed their vows with a kiss.

CHAPTER TWELVE

Xavier didn't let go of Cassie's hand as they walked away from the gazebo to the reception. The barn doors were thrown wide open with the sweet smell of barbecue already mixing with the earthy smell of the hay surrounding the structure. Picnic tables were set up both inside and out of the barn which housed the guy's gaming consoles. Though Xavier noticed there was now a supply cabinet taken over with arts and crafts supplies in the corner that hadn't been there before.

The art supplies couldn't hold his attention. The woman on his arm captured his every waking thought. When Xavier and Cassie had returned from the pier, hand in hand, they'd skipped the rest of the ceremony, having already renewed their vows over the water before the eyes of God. They'd picked up pens and signed the marriage certificate before their friends instead.

Spoken promises were one thing. This time, Xavier was determined to make this deal a legal and binding contract that no man, woman, or parent would put asunder. And he'd done that. Mrs. Cassandra Ramos had his ring, his promise, and his power of attorney. No one and nothing would ever come between them again.

Better yet, this time the occasion had been witnessed by their family. Cassie didn't realize it yet, but she was in a gang that she would never be able to get out of. The residents and workers of the Purple Heart Ranch had a way of collecting people. Once you were in, there was no getting out.

From the speakers inside the barn that they'd faced outwards, the music picked up, but no one danced. Faces screwed at the sounds of the old spirituals that Xavier and his new bride loved. But one by one, everyone began bopping their heads and moving their feet in time to the upbeat gospel music.

Couples twirled on the dance floor. Dogs yipped between feet. Xavier spun Cassie in his arms until the smile that had been so fleeting on her face the past hour spread and then stayed put. She was grinning wide and laughing when he brought her close. Her smile went tentative, like a crack in a fine piece of China where the adhesive glue was still drying.

"You know I used to dream of this," he said, peering down into her navy blue eyes. "Us dancing on our wedding day surrounded by our family and friends."

She tugged at her lower lip before letting it and the words loose. "I dreamed it, too."

She looked away when she spoke the words, as though she didn't want him to see the tinge of sadness at the edge of her eyelids. Xavier placed his index finger under her chin and turned her face back to him.

"It's not a dream anymore," he said. "It's our future."

She let out a small sigh as she took a step deeper into his hold, as though she were about to relay a secret that she only wished him to hear. "I hated waking up from that dream. But I also hated going to sleep and dreaming because I knew it wasn't real."

"It is real. This is real."

"I know."

She took another deep breath. With each breath she took and released, he visibly saw the tension leaving her body. Until finally, Xavier felt Cassie relax in his arms. So, he dipped her.

Cassie gasped as her world turned upside down. When Xavier

righted her, she blinked rapidly, and then she grinned. Her grin stayed as he pressed her to him, into a hold that she never had to leave.

She slid her hand over his shoulder and squeezed. Then her hand slipped down his back and again squeezed. It was a touch of affection, but it hurt. Xavier couldn't hide the wince. It had been a long time since a non-professional had touched his back. But he would endure the pain if it meant his wife's happiness.

His wife. Cassie was finally his wife in name and in deed. He'd pledged to never let her go, but he did allow Reed to cut in. And then Dylan. Followed by Fran, and finally Sean.

Xavier stood back and watched Cassie loosen and lighten as each of his friends, his brothers, swayed with her and twirled her around. When she was finally returned to his arms by Dr. Patel, she resembled the girl he'd fallen for all those years ago.

Her blue gaze was more an opaque topaz than a dark night at sea. Her cheeks were pink. Her smile was wide.

Xavier was eager to have her all to himself as soon as possible. He was thinking up ways to make an exit when the music changed to a Top 40's girl power anthem. Maggie and Sarai made a beeline toward Cassie, sweeping her up into their all-girls conga line. The men stood back, grinning ear to ear, as they watched their wives shimmy and wave their hands to a tune that asserted they didn't need no man. But as soon as the song was over, each woman happily returned to the arms of the man they'd pledged to make their lives with.

That included Cassie. She walked slowly toward him. Her careful hairdo now undone. The bright makeup fading from her face under the sun's rays and with the exertion from the nonstop dancing. She was a vision.

But looking past his wife, Xavier saw his perfect opportunity for escape. Curled up under one of the picnic tables he saw his daughter lying on Star's belly. Spin rested his head on Alex's knee, and Soldier kept watch.

When Cassie came into his arms, he pointed. "We should probably put her to bed."

Cassie turned to where he pointed. Her *ahhh* caused the other women to turn and *ahhh* as well. Xavier crawled under the table and retrieved his sleeping daughter, but not before everyone whipped out their cellphone cameras to take pictures of the little angel and her fierce protectors. Finally, with his daughter in one arm and his wife on the other, he made his way back to their little cabin on the ranch.

At the threshold, Xavier looked from the sleeping toddler to his wife whom he was supposed to carry over the threshold.

"You wanna take her so I can carry you both over the threshold?"

"Don't be silly." Cassie pushed the door open and entered. "We haven't done anything traditional so far. Why start now?"

They laid Alex on the bed in the room she'd shared with Cassie the other night. The sun was starting to set and cast a soft glow over the interior of the room. In the lighting, Alex truly did resemble a sleeping angel.

"She's so beautiful," Cassie sighed.

"Just like her mother."

"You got your ring on my finger, you don't have to flatter me anymore."

"Yes, I did. I got my ring on your finger. Again. It'll stay there this time."

Looking down at Cassie, Xavier felt breathless. His hands tingled, and he knew the only thing that would stop the sensation was reaching out and bringing his wife into his hold. He reached for her, and she came to him.

Xavier leaned down and pressed his lips to hers. They'd skipped this part at the ceremony, but they made up for it now. He pulled her close telling her with his body that he would never let her go. He deepened the kiss trying to wipe away four years of hurt and anguish. But even as his body was ready to give her more, he pulled back.

"We can wait," he said.

Cassie opened her eyes and blinked at him as though she were waking from a dream. One side of her mouth lifted into a shy grin. "I don't see the need. You just promised yourself to me forever. In the eyes of God, we're married."

Xavier sent up a silent prayer of gratitude. That was exactly the answer he was hoping for. He pulled Cassie back into his embrace, determined that nothing would keep them apart.

"Eggs."

His lips hovered over hers. Just a breath between them when she made her request.

"Eggs?" Xavier asked. "You want eggs?"

"I didn't say that," said Cassie.

They both turned to the bed. Alex sat up, wiping the sleep from her eyes. She looked at them brightly as though she'd slept the night away and was ready for a new day.

"Oh, my gosh!" Cassie shot out of Xavier's arms and rushed over to the bed. "That's her first word. You're hungry, baby? You want eggs?"

"Eggs," Alex said, holding up her arms for Xavier.

"Eggs? You mean Xavier?"

"No, darling," said Xavier, coming over to lean over his little girl. "I'm Daddy."

"Eggs," Alex repeated, frowning this time, opening and closing her hands in the universal language of a toddler that said pick me up.

Xavier chuckled as he picked his daughter up. "All right. Eggs, it is."

CHAPTER THIRTEEN

Cassie was surrounded by warmth. Not heat from a fire or a furnace. It was the type of warmth that came from being snuggled up under covers on a winter's night. It was the type of warmth that came from a cup of tea with just the right amount of honey. It was the type of warmth that came after a kiss was left on the lips.

She had been kissed recently. It had been a brief touch of the lips, but the feeling lingered on into her dream. She knew she was dreaming. She knew she was dreaming of Xavier. But there was no dread in her heart.

Her heart was open in the dream. Open and ready to receive love. His love.

It was Xavier's arms around her. It was Xavier's kiss at her temple. It was Xavier giving off that warmth. For the first time in years, she hadn't held her breath in the dream. Neither had she dreaded waking up.

She turned her head and looked up at him. He smiled down at her with love in his eyes. He leaned closer and pressed his lips to hers.

Warmth tingled in her fingertips where she grazed the fine hairs of his temple. She felt the stubble of his new day's growth on her chin.

She tasted the slight tang of the barbecue they'd had at their reception.

Wow, this was the most vivid, sensory dream she'd ever had.

Then she realized. "I'm not dreaming."

"No. Not unless you're inside my head as well as my heart." Xavier closed his eyes and winced. "Wow, marriage has made me cheesy."

"I liked what you said. It was perfect. Everything is perfect."

She brushed her hand over the stubble on his chin. The dark hair growing there made him look slightly dangerous, and that thrilled her. She'd always known in her heart of hearts that Xavier wasn't a bad guy. He was good to his core, even though he liked to play the bad boy.

Xavier slid his thumb over her cheek. A trail of heat traced his movements. "Everything's good right now, but just wait. I'm going to make it perfect. I promise you will never have to worry about a thing again."

She pressed her forehead against his, hoping that he would hear the truth of her words. "I don't need anything else. I have everything I ever wanted."

She had a home that she would never be kicked out of. She had the man of her dreams holding her in his warm embrace. The only thing remaining that she wanted was to consummate this legal marriage as they'd done their spiritual one.

"Eggs?"

But that would have to wait until they trained their daughter to sleep in her own bed, in her own room.

Cassie looked between her chest and Xavier's. Alex was curled up between them, eyes open and shining bright. That was another thing Cassie was thankful for. She had her daughter who was speaking now.

Alex rubbed the sleep from her eyes. She sat up from her space in between both of her parents. She grinned at her mother, then she held out her arms for her father.

"Eggs."

"It's Daddy," said Xavier, taking his little girl into his arms. "Try it, angel. Dad. Dada."

Alex ignored him and snuggled into his chest. She looked up to her mother and held one arm out to Cassie. Cassie scooted closer so that she was included in the cocoon.

Cassie rested her head on the other side of Xavier's chest and smiled over at her daughter. Alex looked content. Xavier gave a sigh of contentment. Cassie felt their happiness echo in the boundless chambers of her heart.

"Of course you're the one to get her talking," said Cassie, looking up accusingly at her husband. "You always had a way with women."

"There's only one woman I want to have my way with." He waggled his eyebrows.

Cassie blushed. She'd forgotten that side of him, the side that liked to tease and taunt her. In retaliation, she gave him a whack on the back.

Xavier winced. His back bowed as he cradled Alex to his heart.

Cassie sat up in alarm. "Xavier?"

"It's fine." He sat Alex on the floor. The little girl walked away from them and began exploring her father's room. Xavier stood. He tried to smile, but the wince was still there.

"It's not fine," said Cassie. "I'm not that strong. Are you hurt?"

He sighed. "There's something you should know, something I need to show you."

So many things went through Cassie's mind. What she did not expect was for Xavier to unbutton the dress shirt he'd worn on their wedding day. They'd all fallen asleep in their wedding clothes. Cassie was a rumpled mess of white fabric. But she couldn't focus on her state of dress, she was far too taken by her husband's increasing state of undress.

Cassie looked from Xavier's bared chest and the rippling muscles of his abdomen, to her daughter on the floor playing with his shoes, and back to Xavier's finely honed flesh.

"Xavier, now is not the time for that."

He gave her a smile that didn't reach his eyes. He balled the shirt up and tossed it on the bed. "I told you I was injured while in the service."

"Yes."

Slowly, he turned. Cassie couldn't hide her gasp. His back was a ruin of dark, angry skin.

"It was a suicide bomber," he said. "In retaliation for information I was able to gain from an informant. People always told me that my mouth would get me in trouble one day. They were right."

Cassie took tentative steps toward him. "Does it hurt?"

"I'm not in constant pain anymore, but it can be uncomfortable in some situations."

Like the discomfort from being slapped on the back. "I'm so sorry. I didn't know."

Cassie folded her hands over her chest. Xavier turned to her. He unballed her fists, putting her fingers on his chest.

"When I thought you had moved on," he said, "I didn't have a care in the world. I took a lot of chances because I didn't think I had anything to live for."

Cassie lowered her head from all the sorrow she felt in her heart. Xavier tilted her head back up, and the tears fell. He wiped them away one by one until she saw him clearly.

"When I was lying there thinking I was going to die," he said, "I heard you sing to me. It was all I could think about; that one day I might hear you sing again. That's what got me to hold on for another day and then another. In the hospital, someone had an Evangeline Taylor CD. I'd listen to it on repeat. It got lost along the way until I found the album in the music shop, and there I found you."

Cassie wrapped her arms around his neck, careful to avoid his back.

"I'm not going to break, Cassie."

"I just don't want to cause you any more pain."

"Having the two of you in my life, I doubt I'll ever feel any pain again." He put his nose into her hair and breathed deeply.

"Ohh, that one was a little on the cheesy-side."

"Wow, I've really turned into a complete cheeseball."

CHAPTER FOURTEEN

Xavier felt on top of the world as he handed his wife out of his truck. Cassie stayed close to him as he lifted Alex from her car seat and kept her in his arms. He had his daughter in one arm and the woman he loved in the other. Life couldn't get any better than this.

He'd parked his old truck between a shiny new Lexus and a fully loaded minivan in the church parking lot. Looking back at the three cars, Xavier wondered if he should invest in a new car, something more fitting for a family man. He was a little tight on funds at the moment.

That was another thing he needed to look into, getting a job. He hadn't needed much living on his own at the ranch. But now that he had a wife and child, they'd both need new clothes. Alex would need toys. And he wanted to cover Cassie in jewelry and new appliances and music and whatever else he could think of.

She'd gone without for far too long. Yesterday was the last day of her living in poverty. He'd put her into the lap of luxury. He just needed to earn a few more coins to do it.

"Hey, Xavier," grinned a woman in a low cut dress that definitely wasn't church picnic appropriate.

"Good morning …" Xavier couldn't remember her name. He never remembered women's names. They'd always been a momentary distraction for him to help him try to forget, for just a few seconds, what he'd lost in his past.

"Melanie and I saved a seat for you on our blanket."

Melanie was standing beside her unnamed friend in a skirt that was raised high enough to send up its own prayers.

"Thanks," said Xavier, as he draped his arm around Cassie. "But I'll be sharing a blanket with my family."

The two women turned to Cassie. "Oh, is this your sister?"

"No," said Xavier. "This is my wife."

"Wife?" said Melanie. Her mouth fell open, and her gaze went wide. "You're his wife?"

Cassie shrank back. She'd never been one for confrontations. She never liked being out in public where women would gawk at the two of them as though they didn't belong together.

"And the little girl?" said the other woman. "Is she your daughter?"

"Yes, this is my daughter, Alex."

It was the first time Xavier had seen Alex frown. On the ranch, she offered smiles and giggles to every single person. But in the face of these two women, she looked close to tears.

"Oh," said Melanie. "I see."

Xavier knew what the two were thinking. That he'd only married Cassie because he'd knocked her up. Xavier pulled Cassie closer to him and placed a kiss on her temple.

"This is Cassie Ramos, my first and only love. I fell in love with her four years ago, but we were torn apart. I haven't been the same man since. I finally found her again just a few days ago, and I put a ring on her finger as soon as I could. No, she'll never get away from me again."

And with that, he moved his family forward and left the two women gaping after them.

"You didn't have to say all those things," said Cassie.

He looked down at her. Her navy blue eyes were as clear as a sparkling gem as she regarded him. There was a small hint of something that looked like pride at the corners of her eyes. The sight made Xavier feel ten times taller.

"Why not?" He pressed a kiss to her forehead. "It's true. You are the love of my life."

She grinned as she nuzzled into the space beneath his chin. "But you don't have to put on a show every time one of your exes comes over."

"I don't have any exes," he said. "Not since you."

They stopped in a clearing. To their right, Dylan and Maggie had already set up their blanket, and the dogs were all sitting obediently waiting for Maggie to deliver treats. Alex shot out of her father's arms and made a beeline for the dogs. When the dogs saw Alex, they forgot their obedience, stood and wagged their tails as the little girl came in their midst.

Xavier turned back to Cassie. He noted she stared at him with an unreadable expression on her face. He pulled out their blanket and spread it wide, before taking her hand and tugging her down with him.

"Cassie, there's been no one in my life since the day I met you. I flirt a lot, yes. I seek out attention, but that's where it ends. I haven't even kissed another woman in the last four years. It just didn't feel right. No one was you."

She took in a slow, deep breath before she met his gaze. "Me, neither."

"And now you're all mine again. Now and forever."

Xavier leaned down and kissed his wife, his one and only love. He'd only meant for the kiss to be a pressed promise to her lips. But the moment he tasted her sweetness, he lost himself and deepened the kiss, searching for more of the taste he'd lost and now found.

"Get a room, you two."

If they hadn't been on holy ground, surrounded by families and children, Xavier would've given Reed a lewd gesture. Instead, he made a face at his brother who'd set up a blanket on the other side of them.

Xavier sat back on the blanket and watched Alex run circles

around Maggie's dogs. A few other children came over and tentatively approached the dogs. Xavier looked at the kids in their fine clothes while Alex's clothes were rough around the edges. He'd need to take his daughter shopping soon. She would have the best of everything.

He ran his hand up and down Cassie's shirtsleeve. A thread came loose. He'd have to do the same for his wife.

"What's that look on your face?" Cassie asked.

"Just plotting how I'm going to give you the world."

"You and Alex are my world."

He grinned back at her as his heart swelled. How had he lived the last four years without her smile? The memory of it was a pale comparison to the real thing.

He leaned in and pressed another kiss to the corner of her lip. He held his breath this time. Otherwise, he'd surely spend the entire picnic making a meal of his wife.

The sounds of music filled the air. Cassie turned to the makeshift stage, that was really just a patch of concrete at the back of the church. The choir began a rendition of an old gospel song that was on their favorite Evangeline Taylor album. Cassie closed her eyes and swayed her head to the music.

"Sing it for me," said Xavier.

She opened her eyes. She tugged at her bottom lip, hesitating for only a second. Then, looking at only him, she began to sing.

This was the voice that had called him out of the agony of the bomb on that fateful day. This was the voice that pushed him to open his eyes and greet a new day every morning. This was the voice that he kept in his heart and held tight. Now, it was out of its cage and singing loudly for everyone to hear.

As Cassie hit the higher notes, Xavier realized the music had stopped. So had the singing choir. The only thing that could be heard was Cassie's voice.

Cassie's gaze was still on him. She didn't see that everyone in the entire congregation had stopped what they were doing. They were all now staring at her in delight and amazement.

When she hit the final note, she smiled at him. But a second later she realized the deafening silence. Her smile fell, and she turned and saw. Embarrassment covered her cheeks.

"Cassie, that was beautiful," said Ruhi, coming forward from the ranks of the choir. "Please, come and sing with us."

"I …" Cassie began, looking between Ruhi, the crowd, and back to Xavier.

Before Cassie could demur, Xavier rose. He brought his wife to stand alongside him. He guided her to the front of the crowd, onto the concrete stage with the other singers. He placed her front and center in between Ruhi and Maggie and then stepped back.

Cassie's eyes pleaded with him. But Maggie took one of her hands, Ruhi took the other. She turned to the women who smiled encouragingly at her.

The choir began another familiar tune. Cassie took a deep breath. After a second, she joined her voice with theirs. Cassie's voice trilled overtop of every other singer, like an angel flitting by over the tops of the heads of mere mortals. No one in the congregation spoke, no one moved. All eyes were rapt on Cassie as her voice rose stronger.

When the song came to an end, there was silence. Then, a beat later, the backyard of the church was filled with thunderous applause. Maggie and Ruhi embraced a pink-cheeked Cassie.

Another tune began. This time a call and response song that had all of the congregation joining in. Xavier opened his mouth to join in when someone tapped him on the shoulder.

"Specialist Ramos?"

Xavier turned and faced a man who was just as big and broad as he was. The man sported a cropped haircut favored by those in the military, but he wore no uniform. Likely ex-military. And then recognition dawned.

"Mason Jones? Of Strategic Maneuvers Contractors?"

Mr. Jones stuck out his hand, and Xavier took it.

"Are you a member of this church?" asked Xavier.

"I do some work with Dr. Patel," said Mr. Jones. "He's a great man, does a lot for the soldiers returning to civilian life."

On that, Xavier had to agree. He would not have adjusted well to everyday life without his sessions with Dr. Patel.

"I was going to call you next week," said Mr. Jones, "but it's good that I saw you here. There's a spot that's opened up with my company. We need a communications expert in Yemen."

Xavier looked down at Alex who ran around his legs followed by Star and the rest of the dog pack.

Mr. Jones stepped out of the way of the ragtag bunch, a smile on his face as he did so. He faced Xavier before continuing on with the details of the job. "It's out of the combat zone, which should work now that I see you have a family. But it is a three-month contract."

It was a sweet deal. Three months was hardly any time when deployment could last half a year or longer. And he'd be safe, out of combat.

Xavier had already seen the pay scale for this type of contract work. He'd be able to give Cassie and Alex more, the clothes they needed, a speech therapist for Alex, all the toys she could ever dream of, maybe an addition to the house for more children because he knew he wanted more children with Cassie and soon.

"Think about it," said Mr. Jones, "and let me know."

<h1 style="text-align:center">CHAPTER FIFTEEN</h1>

"You have to join the choir," said Ruhi.

"Oh, yes, you must," Maggie piped, reciting the same tune. "We'd love to have you."

All around the two girls, Cassie saw other choir members bob their heads as though they were harmonizing a new chorus. Out in the gathered crowd, many people had risen from their picnic blankets and were still applauding the performance. Cassie waited for the urge to duck her head at the praise to come over her.

It didn't.

She'd always been modest about her singing talents. But the appreciation she felt from this crowd made warmth spread all throughout her chest. For the first time in a long time, Cassie wanted to join in and not shy away from the crowd.

"Sarai can't hold a tune," Ruhi continued. "And Eva has study group a lot right now since she's getting close to midterms."

"Plus your voice is out of this world," said Maggie Her brown eyes sparkled brightly with excitement. She even panted a bit like one of her dogs. "We need you."

It had been so long since Cassie had joined her voice to others in praise. It had been a long time since she'd lifted her voice in praise to the Lord. She and the Savior hadn't been on speaking terms for a while.

But now, for the first time in years, Cassie sent up a prayer of gratitude. She had so much to be thankful for. In just a couple of days, her life had changed drastically.

She'd lost her job and gained the position she'd always wanted for herself; that of homemaker. She'd lost her housing and found the home of her dreams. But most importantly, she'd found the love of her life and opened her heart again.

God was smiling at her. He probably always had been. It had been Cassie who had closed her heart and turned away from His light.

Now that her heart was once again open, she looked up to see herself surrounded by a community eager to embrace her. She had a home, security, and something she never thought she'd ever had back in her life again. Love was back in her life.

The chambers of her heart opened even wider until Cassie was certain she'd burst. It was scary to be this open. She felt vulnerable, as though something unwanted could slip inside. But even though she was wide open and exposed, she felt protected.

"I think she should be a soloist," Maggie was saying.

Dylan came up from behind and gave Cassie a nudge with his shoulder. "Don't let these two talk you into something you don't want to do."

"Says the man who talked me into marrying him less than an hour after meeting him," said Maggie.

Dylan wrapped his wife up in his arms and planted a kiss on her forehead. "Smartest thing I ever did."

"Just give me the signal, and I'll get you out of here," Sean stage-whispered in Maggie's ear.

Ruhi waggled a finger at the man. "Don't get me started on you, buddy."

Sean caught his wife's finger and proceeded to plant a kiss in the palm of her hand.

Cassie smiled at the two couples. She didn't give any signals. She didn't want to push these women away. She didn't want to push anyone away. She felt warm and welcomed, and she wanted to keep herself fully immersed in the feeling.

Cassie saw Alex running around Reed and Sarai's picnic blanket. Alex had the hugest grin on her face as she chased the dogs and was chased by the dogs. The only thing missing from the picture was her husband. And then she saw him.

Xavier's back was to her. The fabric stretched smooth across the planes of his back. No one would be able to tell that there were scars there. They were scars that only she saw, only she touched.

He'd promised to take care of her, to have her back. And she would do the same for him. This was the first day of the rest of their lives.

She'd spent so long being apart from him that the short distance seemed like a vast desert. She wanted to be by his side, standing before him, standing behind him every second of the day. Cassie excused herself from her new family of friends, with promises to come to the next choir practice, and made her way over to her husband.

As Cassie got closer, she noticed Xavier was talking to a man. He wore no uniform, but something about his stature read that he'd spent time in the military.

"We need a communications expert in Yemen."

From the back, Cassie saw Xavier nod his head as though in agreement. She knew that that was Xavier's job in the military. She supposed this man was looking for recommendations for an expert overseas.

"It's out of the combat zone, which should work now that I see you have a family. But it is a three-month contract."

Wait? His family? Three months?

But surely they weren't talking about Xavier going overseas. He'd just promised Cassie he'd never leave her again. She had to have missed a part of the conversation. So why was Xavier shaking the man's hand as though he was sealing a deal?

"Think about it, and let me know. The job pays well, better than an army salary. You're our first pick."

"Thank you for considering me. I'll give you a call in a couple of days."

Cassie heard a crashing sound. It filled up her ears until they were ringing. It punched at her heart until she was certain a hole was in her chest. She felt the chambers of her heart clench as they shook.

Xavier whirled around, eyes wide as though he sensed danger. His gaze met hers. There was concern etched on his face as he looked down at her. Off in the distance, Cassie heard an animal cry out in pain.

"Cassie? Sweetheart, what's wrong?"

She was in his arms, but her limbs felt numb. That cry had come from her. She could barely make out her own voice as she spoke. "You're leaving?"

Xavier's hold tightened on her. His face was still a muddle of confusion.

"You're leaving me. You're leaving us."

The fog cleared from his gray eyes as comprehension dawned, and he sighed. But more importantly, he didn't deny it. Cassie turned to go, to get away from there. But his arms clamped around her.

CHAPTER SIXTEEN

The sound of Cassie's cry of pain sent Xavier into a panic. The sight of her shoulders caving in and her face contorting and then that godawful sound coming from her hit him in his gut.

He thought the worst day of his life had been when he'd come back to find her gone, married to someone else. That pain was topped by finding her and his daughter living in squalor. Seeing her in pain, because she thought he was abandoning her, gutted him.

When she tried to leave, he caught her in his arms and held. "Cassie, honey, I'm not leaving you."

She shoved at his arm, trying to break free of him. "You're going overseas, back to war."

Xavier grasped both of her shoulders tightly in his hands. "For a job, to get money to provide for us."

But still, she turned to and fro, desperate to get out of his hold. Her head tilted away from him. Her eyes closed as though she couldn't even stand to look at him. Tears pricked the edges of her eyelids.

All around them, people were starting to stare. Xavier was used to being the center of attention. But he knew Cassie hated it. She much preferred to add her unique voice to a chorus than to be singled out.

Too bad for her. She needed to be set straight on this point, and it didn't matter to Xavier if everyone knew this fact.

"Cassie, I want to give you everything you deserve, a better life."

That stopped her flailing. She stilled, opening her eyes and peering at him. She took deep, heaving breaths of air that he worried she might be hyperventilating.

"I never wanted any of that," she hissed. Her next words came out on a sob. "All I ever wanted was you. But you can't stand being with me for long. You keep leaving."

Xavier brought her into his embrace, tucking her head beneath his chin and wrapping his arms around her thin shoulders. God, she was so thin. She'd gone without for so long because of him. He couldn't let that continue. He needed to put food on the table, new clothes on her back, give her a bigger house. This job would provide that. He just needed to make her see.

"It's just a few months," he began.

She shook her head and started backing away again. "You said that the last time."

She was right. He had said that the last time they'd seen each other. But he'd come back. Every time he'd come back for her. This would be no different.

"Cass—" He reached for her, but she jerked away from him. "It's my job to take care of you. This is my only skill."

"No. It's leaving; that's your only skill. I'm not waiting anymore. I should've known better than to let you into my heart again."

She continued backing away from him. Her blue eyes turned cold. Her jawline went hard. With each step she took away from him, Xavier felt shards piercing his heart.

"I'm the one leaving this time," she said. "I'm taking Alex and going."

"Cassie, you are not leaving."

"Why not? You do it all the time. We're not staying so you can leave over and over again. That's worse than being abandoned."

She turned away from him then. Tiny explosions were going off behind his eyes as he watched the love of his life, his reason for staying alive, walk away from him. Was this what she'd felt when she'd thought he'd left her?

It was worse than the peeling of the skin from his burns. He felt his soul was being excised from his body. Xavier felt as though all was lost. And then Cassie whirled around and faced him, and things got worse than he'd ever imagined.

"Where's Alex?"

It took Xavier a second to tear his gaze away from his wife and focus on his daughter. But Alex was not on the blanket. He looked to the neighboring blankets where the other ranch inhabitants had set up. But they had all dispersed, and Alex wasn't on any of those blankets either.

"You were supposed to be watching her," Cassie accused, her voice going shrill.

"Don't worry." Xavier was certain one of his friends had his daughter. "We'll find her."

CHAPTER SEVENTEEN

All eyes were on them as they argued. Well, Cassie argued and shouted at her husband making a spectacle. She'd had gazes on her and whispers around her when her pregnancy began to show. The shame and solitude had cloaked her then. So much so that she had willingly climbed into the backseat of her father's station wagon when he'd wanted to send her away.

Now, she didn't care about the eyes on her. Shame and shunning were the furthest things from her mind. All she cared about was finding her daughter.

"She was playing on the blanket," said Sarai.

"Then she was with the dogs," said Maggie.

They'd found all the members of the ranch and Alex wasn't with any of them. Cassie felt bile rise from the pit of her stomach. She wanted to turn an accusing eye on Xavier, but she couldn't lift her head from the support of his chest. If he hadn't been there to lean on, she'd certainly collapse to the ground.

"She's here," he insisted as he leaned down to her ear. He gave her a squeeze and didn't let go.

The members of the ranch began turning here and there, shouting Alex's name.

"She's nonverbal," Cassie said, but her voice didn't carry far over the shouting. "She won't respond."

It's why Cassie never took her eyes off her daughter. Until these past couple of days. Because she'd let her guard down after the wedding. She'd opened her heart. She'd gotten hurt again. And now her daughter was lost.

"Don't worry," said someone. Maybe Eva? Cassie was too out of her mind with worry to determine. "She couldn't have gotten far. No one in the congregation would let her come to any harm."

But Cassie didn't know these people. They didn't care about her. Except they'd all stopped what they were doing and began searching the grounds for Alex.

"All right, everyone, listen up." Xavier's voice broke through Cassie's fog. His arms tightened around her even more as he spoke. "We're looking for a little girl. Gray eyes, black hair. She was in a blue dress. Her name is Alex, but she won't respond, so we have to look everywhere. We'll break into groups and search."

A calm settled over Cassie as she watched Xavier take charge. Though she was still shaken, she had every confidence that he'd find Alex and bring her back into her arms, safe and sound. When he did find Alex and put her daughter back in her arms, Cassie wanted to go back into Xavier's arms.

She wanted to go back to sitting on a picnic blanket in his loose embrace. She wanted to go back to how she'd woken up this morning lying next to him. She wanted to come right back to this moment of leaning on him for his love and support.

Try as she might, Cassie couldn't get the chambers of her heart to close again. They were wide open and giving gratitude and thanks to the people searching for Alex. But mostly, the chambers would close because it was so filled with love for the man who held her in his arms.

The girls from the ranch were at her back. Their husbands were fanning out leading the search party. The community was looking out. And Xavier was at the helm, leading the search while holding her close.

From the safety of his arms, Cassie knew that no matter how hard she tried, she'd never be able to shut him out. Even through all these years, he'd never left her heart. And she knew she'd never left his. No matter where he went, he'd always be with her. Even if that was to Yemen or anywhere in the world.

He might leave for a time, but he'd always find his way back to her. They'd always find their way back together. Just like they'd find Alex.

"We'll find her," he promised now.

And Cassie believed him. "Last I saw her, she was with the dogs."

"Wait," said Xavier. "Where are the dogs?"

CHAPTER EIGHTEEN

Xavier held Cassie's hand tightly in his. He believed with every fiber in his being that they'd find Alex. Still, his heart pounded each second he didn't know where his little girl was, what she was doing, if she needed him.

How had he considered leaving for months and not seeing his baby girl, not holding Cassie? He felt sucker punched at the thought of it now. Not just because Alex was outside of his reach. He felt gutted because, after all these years, he finally had Cassie back within his arms, and he was not ready to put even a mile of space between them.

It was out of the question. He couldn't leave his family behind. He couldn't take them with him. His only option was to stay.

He'd stay and find another way to give them what they needed. She insisted they had everything she needed, but he couldn't deny his desires to give them more. He'd just find another way to do it.

But he agreed with Cassie. They needed him. They needed each other. Right now, they needed to find Alex.

Xavier gripped his wife's hand even firmer as they followed behind Maggie. The animal lover called out to her dogs. But silence greeted her at every turn. Until they came to the doors of the church.

Spin, the Irish Terrier who was a menace on wheels, poked his little head out of the open church doors. He cocked his head at his owner as though she were disturbing the peace. Then he turned and made his way back inside. Everyone followed the dog inside the church and down the hall.

And there they found her.

In the pulpit, in the makeshift manger that was always present, lay Alex. She was curled up sleeping on the hay. Her head lay against Star's patchy belly. Stevie and Sugar sat in a cocoon around her legs. Soldier sat up on his hind legs, parked in front of them all, as though he stood watch. Spin went over and sat down with his fellow comrade.

Each of the dogs opened one or two eyes and looked up at the humans as though offended at the intrusion. Meanwhile, Alex slept peacefully under their care.

No one stepped forward to disturb the sleeping girl or the dogs protecting her. Xavier tugged Cassie over to the pews, and they sat. The others made their way back out the doors as quietly as they'd come in leaving Xavier and his family alone.

"I'm sorry," he said after a while.

"I took my eye off her, too."

"No. For considering the contract work. It was the only way I could think of to provide for the two of you."

"I told you, all we need is you."

Xavier turned to his wife, the reason his heart beat, the reason he drew breath. "Cassie, I would never abandon you. I promised."

She tore her gaze away from Alex. When she faced her husband, she lifted an eyebrow. "I wasn't going to let you."

Xavier chuckled. The few punches that had landed in his belly earlier dissolved to flutters. His heart felt like it was both full and floating at the same time. That's what love felt like, a heavy lightness.

He leaned down to capture his wife's lips. Cassie met him more than halfway. Their lips brushed for a second before Xavier felt the need to deepen the kiss and claim what had always been and would forever be the very key to his soul.

"Eggs?"

Xavier chuckled as he turned from his wife to his waking daughter. "Hey, beautiful girl."

The dogs parted to make way for him. Xavier lifted Alex into his arms and returned with her to the pews to sit next to her mother.

Alex looked over at her mother and held out her arms. "Love?"

Cassie blinked. "What did you say, baby girl?"

"Love," Alex repeated opening and closing her hands to be picked up by her mother.

"I think that she thinks your name is love," said Xavier.

Now it was Cassie's turned to chuckle as she lifted Alex into her arms. "That would make sense. Since I always tell her *I love you*."

"Love." Alex squeezed her mother and kissed her cheek. "Eggs." She turned to her father and reached up to give him a kiss as well.

"I love you too, baby girl," Xavier said. "I love you both."

"And we love you," said Cassie.

"Love." Alex nodded and snuggled between her parents.

EPILOGUE

"Good morning, my love."

"Morning, Love. Breakfast?"

Cassie grinned down at her sleepy-eyed daughter as she stretched in her bed. In the last few months, Alex had added a few new words to her repertoire. Mom was one, but the little girl still insisted on calling Cassie *Love*. Cassie didn't mind at all. It was what she was surrounded by inside and out these days.

As she pulled the comforter off Alex to aid the kid in her getting-out-of-bed routine, Cassie stepped over Star who lay in front of Alex's night table, ever the guard dog.

"You want pancakes?" Cassie asked as she pulled a never been worn shirt from Alex's chest of drawers.

"Eggs."

Cassie knew Alex didn't want scrambled eggs or an omelet for breakfast. The liquid meat was still a textural issue for Alex.

No. Cassie knew that when Alex called out for eggs that her hubby was in the vicinity. And sure enough, her suspicion was confirmed a second later when his arms swooped Cassie up from behind.

"Xavier, careful."

"What?" he said, planting kissing along her neck. "I can't sweep the most amazing, beautiful, talented woman off her feet when I want to?"

"It's probably not a good idea for the next nine months."

Xavier froze. He carefully placed Cassie back down on her feet. He stepped away from her. Then stepped back, his gaze focused on her belly.

"Are you telling me?"

Cassie nodded.

"Are you sure?

She nodded again.

Xavier swooped her up again. Instead of chiding him, she laughed and relaxed into his embrace.

"Eggs!"

Xavier swooped Alex up to join the threesome. "You're going to be a big sister, kiddo."

Alex nodded as though she knew what her father meant. She probably did. The child was wise beyond her years. She just didn't show it in the conventional way.

"We're going to need a bigger house," said Xavier, looking around the large room as though the walls were closing in on him.

"Don't you start it. We have plenty of space here."

The man looked doubtful. This wasn't a battle Cassie was prepared to fight. She was too busy fighting morning sickness.

"Why are you back early?" she said in an effort to distract him. He usually didn't head back in from morning chores until Cassie and Alex were up and dressed and sitting down to breakfast.

"Ruhi's in labor. They're about to head to the hospital now."

With that message delivered, they filed out of the house and into the shared driveway of Sean and Ruhi's house. The very pregnant woman was waddling down the steps. Sean was at her side, carrying her overnight bag and looking like he wanted to swoop his wife up into his arms as well.

Cassie got in line to give her friend a hug before Ruhi ducked into the car. When Sean shut the passenger door, Cassie leaned in and stage-whispered to him, "Give me the signal if you want to run."

But Sean was as cool as a cucumber as always. He gave Cassie a peck on her cheek, then Alex a buss on the nose.

The group watched as the new parents pulled out of the drive and headed down the long and winding road that would lead them out of the Purple Heart Ranch and into town.

"This time tomorrow, there'll be another kid on the ranch," said Fran.

"This time in six months, there'll be yet another," said Dylan.

All eyes went to Maggie, who nodded, confirming the truth of her husband's words.

"You can add us to that playground," said Reed.

Sarai beamed in feigned annoyance, but the woman positively glowed as she stood inside her husband's embrace.

"Us too," said Xavier, breaking his and Cassie's news.

Fran looked to Eva, but the woman held up her hands.

"Don't even think about it, buddy," Eva said. "We've already got two to keep us busy for now."

"For now," Fran confirmed.

Chores were suspended as the group spent the rest of the day together waiting for news of the first baby of the ranch. As the sun went down, the news came. The girls cheered the loudest as their ranks increased. A new baby girl would come home to the ranch in a couple days.

She would be embraced by everyone who lived and visited here in this place of healing where five soldiers came to rehabilitate their wounds and wound up reviving their spirits by making convenient arrangements that turned into lasting love.

This may be the end of this squad's story, but a new squad is on their way to the ranch.

Follow the continuing story of the Wounded Warriors of the Purple Heart Ranch with
In Over His Head
Book Six in the Brides of Purple Heart Ranch!

ALSO BY SHANAE JOHNSON

Shanae Johnson was raised by Saturday Morning cartoons and After School Specials. She still doesn't understand why there isn't a life lesson that ties the issues of the day together just before bedtime. While she's still waiting for the meaning of it all, she writes stories to try and figure it all out. Her books are wholesome and sweet, but her are heroes are hot and heroines are full of sass!

And by the way, the E elongates the A. So it's pronounced Shan-aaaaaaaa. Perfect for a hero to call out across the moors, or up to a balcony, or to blare outside her window on a boombox. If you hear him calling her name, please send him her way!

You can sign up for Shanae's Reader Group to receive bonus scenes, sales and new release alerts at

https://shanaejohnson.com/ReaderGroup

Also By Shanae Johnson

The Brides of Purple Heart

On His Bended Knee

Hand Over His Heart

Offering His Arm

His Permanent Scar

Having His Back

In Over His Head

Always On His Mind

Every Step He Takes

In His Good Hands

Light Up His Life

His Strength to Stand

His Grace Under Pressure

The Rangers of Purple Heart

The Rancher takes his Convenient Bride

The Rancher takes his Best Friend's Sister

The Rancher takes his Runaway Bride

The Rancher takes his Star Crossed Love

The Rancher takes his Love at First Sight

The Rancher takes his Last Chance at Love

Silver Star Ranch series

His Pledge to Honor

His Pledge to Cherish

His Pledge to Protect

His Pledge to Obey

His Pledge to Have

His Pledge to Hold

Flying Cross Ranch series

His Vow to Love

His Vow to Treasure

His Vow to Adore

His Vow to Trust

His Vow to Respect

His Vow to Defend